PRELUDE TO TERROR

HELEN MACINNES wrote twenty-one distinguished spy thrillers, earning herself a worldwide reputation as the unrivalled queen of international espionage fiction.

Born in Scotland, she studied at Glasgow University, where she met and married Gilbert Highet, a renowned classics scholar. From 1937, when her husband accepted a professorship at the Columbia University, they made their home in New York, becoming US citizens in 1952.

Above Suspicion, her first novel, was published in 1941, and brought her immediate success and an enormous following, which was to support her throughout her long career. Her novels, all bestsellers, have been translated into at least twenty-two languages, and four have been made into films: *Above Suspicion*, *Assignment in Brittany*, *The Venetian Affair* and *The Salzburg Connection*.

HELEN MACINNES died in New York in 1985.

HELEN MACINNES

Prelude to Terror

The characters in this novel, and their actions, are
purely imaginary. Their names and experiences have
no relation to those of actual people,
except by coincidence.

This edition published 1994 by
Diamond Books
77–85 Fulham Palace Road
Hammersmith, London W6 8JB

First published by William Collins Sons & Co. Ltd 1978
First issued in Fontana Paperbacks 1979
Ninth impression February 1990

ISBN 0 261 66438 7

Made and printed in Great Britain

To Gilbert,
my dear companion,
who has gone ahead
on the final journey

1

The sun was edging round and soon would flood the tenth-floor living-room. By the time a July noon came to New York, thought Colin Grant, this place would be turned into a pressure-cooker. Pull down the shades, shutter yourself as if you were in Spain; yes, that was the obvious solution. Except that the light would be dimmed, and the small breeze blocked. There was no air-conditioning to solve these problems: O'Malley (who owned this place and had leased it for a year to old friend Grant) hadn't gone to that expense; or perhaps it was his contribution to energy-saving. O'Malley was seldom here, anyway, jaunting off to Europe for his firm. Some day, Grant decided, I'll get around to asking him what possible business is now keeping him for a year in Geneva. But, as one old Washington hand to another, information was better volunteered than requested.

He spread the photographs over the desk – one of the few relics from Washington, along with a collection of books and records, and his typewriter and files. O'Malley wouldn't object to the coolest corner in the room being turned into a miniature office. 'Just keep the place clean and aired, and scare away the burglars,' he had said. And pay maintenance, Grant thought wryly. Still, it had seemed a bargain last November, when he had seen the sun, welcome in winter, streaming into the living-room. He could work here, if not cheerfully – considering the emotional and mental agonies of these last months – then at least in privacy during the morning hours. For a moment, with his hands on the photographs of still-life paintings, his thoughts veered to Jennifer . . . Jennifer lying on a quiet pavement, her head smashed by a murderer's bullet. And the killer still free, roaming Washington streets . . . Stop remembering, he told himself, let the wound close. Jennifer was gone.

He forced his attention back to the work before him. The article on still-lifes – seventeenth-century Dutch versus contemporary American – was due next week. He began studying the photographs again, picked up his pen. He began writing.

Once started, the sentences ran easily. His idea for dealing with the subject held his interest, kept his mind concentrating. The Dutch tables laden with fish and vegetables, the pheasants and geese hanging in a dark kitchen ready for plucking, the piles of fruit, wine-flasks and spilled goblets, a discarded lute (it was easy to see what seventeenth-century tastes were, either above or below stairs), made a rich contrast with recent American offerings – a soup tin, giant size, in lonely splendour; a huge baseball bat; or a lavatory bowl. He had just written a pungent phrase about that last little item when the doorbell rang. Three sharp little bleeps. Oh God, he thought and paused before his next sentence. Ronnie Brearely. That was the ring she used.

Leave her ringing? A repeat of three bleeps conjured her standing on the doormat outside, ready with some excuse, bearing gifts and smiles. Answer the summons? If he didn't she'd be back again on a new pretext, or there would be phone calls and invitations and all the protective kindness she seemed to think a widower needed. Better face her – this time really administer the last rebuff. I'll choose my own women, he thought, his face tight with annoyance. He dropped his pen, rose,

pulled on his shirt and buttoned it almost to the collar.
The bell was ringing again as he opened the door.

She was wide-eyed and breathless, the usual sweetly
innocent approach that she favoured. Today the bright
smile was a little uncertain. Perhaps she was beginning
to get the message, he thought, hope rising: he had been
trying to send it for the last three months, ever since she
had decided to adopt him. Adopt him? Jerry Phillips,
with whom he played hard tennis three times a week,
had a harsher phrase for it. 'She's got you in her sights.
Look out, man! You're her third husband. It's in her
eyes.' Grant had laughed that off: women were feeling
sorry for him, there was a lot of sisterly affection around,
they weren't all predatory, and how the hell did you
rebuff kindness? 'Your serve,' Jerry had said, and won
that game and the next one too.

Ronnie was talking in her soft half-laughing way, her
words cascading all around him. She broke off. '*Are* you
listening? Really, Colin—'

'Sorry. I'm in the middle of writing an article.'

His cool voice and non-smiling face stopped her short.
Briefly. 'Well, let me put these things in the fridge,' she
said, using the large brown paper bag filled with eatables
to buttress her first step over the threshold. Her sudden
movement caught him one step too late, and she was
into the small hall. She had reached the kitchen with
quick short steps, even before he had finished the
thought that if she had been a man, he would have said,
'Get the hell out.'

'I just happened to be in the neighbourhood,' she told
him brightly as he entered the kitchen. She was empty-
ing the paper bag. 'I won't really disturb your work, go
ahead with it, I'll just get this Brie into the refrigerator
and wash this Bibb lettuce for you.' She looked at the
sink and the counter-top, shook her head in amused
disapproval. Her shoulder-length hair, auburn veering

9

into blonde, had been carefully curled into long thin tendrils, hundreds of them, springing out from a tight band above her forehead – the frizz effect of the with-it girl. Tanned arms were well displayed by the peasant blouse; so was one of her shoulders by the slipping neckline. Tanned legs, too, slightly straddled in the current *Vogue* pose that went with one hand on hip. And below the swinging skirt were twists of thong around slender ankles to anchor elaborate espadrilles that no Basque fisherman had ever dreamed of in his wildest fantasies. 'I'll tidy up around here,' she said, dropping her large canvas handbag on the table beside the food, and turned to the sink. 'Needs it, doesn't it? Where's that cleaning woman I found for you, Colin?'

'I have a cleaning woman.'

'Once a week? Ridiculous.'

'She suits.' Particularly his budget.

'Go right ahead and finish your work.'

He began replacing the Bibb lettuce and Brie and strawberries and French bread in the paper bag. A bottle of Liebfraumilch, chilled and beaded with perspiration, was lurking inside there, too, along with a tin of pâté. A damned waste, he thought angrily, but the last husband – so the talk went – had been generous with his alimony. (The first husband had handed over a Long Island cottage and his apartment in New York City.)

She glanced round, stopped work. 'But you have to eat lunch, darling. Let me fix it. At least you can give me a drink. Hock would be just right for this warm day. There's a bottle inside the—'

'I know. And I'm not having a drink or lunch.'

'Surely,' said the soft voice, soft smile, soft sell, 'surely you can't be playing tennis this afternoon with Jerry – far too hot. You don't have to be at the Gallery until four o'clock. Plenty of time to have a light lunch *and* finish your work. What is it, anyway?' She was out of the

10

kitchen, that beachhead abandoned, heading with her brisk step into the living-room. 'Oh,' she said in dismay, 'this place is going to be impossible in August. Impossible. When does the Gallery close for the summer – mid-July, isn't it?' She studied the reproductions strewn over his desk. 'You work far too much.'

'Not enough.' He placed a book quickly over his manuscript.

'Sorry,' she said. 'No peeking, I promise.' She moved away. 'You were so *comfortable* in Washington. Such an enchanting house, small but perfect. Did you really have to give up all that, and your job too? Believe me, Colin, Jennifer was one of my oldest friends, and she would never, but never, have wanted you to live like this.'

She had known Jennifer at school, that was all. And she had only visited the house in Washington once. He hadn't even been there that week-end: off on a business trip to talk the Philadelphia Museum into an exchange of paintings with Florence.

Ronnie was saying, 'Don't you miss the State Department, Colin?'

'I wasn't State Department,' he said sharply.

'Oh well, your cultural exchange unit was under their wing. They paid for all those exhibitions. At least, they backed them, didn't they?'

'It wasn't my cultural exchange unit. I was a junior assistant to the Director, and I—' He stopped short, caught his rising temper. Why waste breath talking? He'd never get rid of her at this rate. 'Time to leave, Veronica.' She disliked her full name. His use of it now, and the ice in his voice, should be enough to freeze her out of here.

She didn't appear to hear him. 'A big drop in your income,' she observed, all sadness and sympathy. 'That's what worries me, Colin. August, for instance. Where are you going to spend August? All alone here, in *this* place?' She looked around Dwight O'Malley's living-room and shook her head.

'There's nothing wrong with it. Come on, Veronica, time to leave.'

'But I've only been here twenty minutes.' She was half annoyed, half teasing. 'Can't you spare one of your devoted admirers just a few moments?' She picked out a book, which she had been eyeing, from the shelf behind his desk. Now she was serious. 'Really, Colin, I do admire you. This, for instance.' She held up the book. It had been published ten years ago when he was twenty-nine and brash enough to think his ideas would dazzle the art world. A slight little volume, now out of print, but it had helped him get the job in Washington. He took it out of her grasp and replaced it on the shelf.

She was saying, 'You could write so easily in Springs. You'd love the cottage. There's a desk in the guest-room, and it has French windows and a terrace all of its own. Why don't you come there in August? Plenty of swimming – your choice between the Atlantic and the Sound. Tennis, too. And, of course, the kind of people you'd love to meet.' She rattled off the well-known names of three painters, a writer, and two museum directors. 'There are even people around who are rich, but filthy rich. The kind who buy paintings and need advice. So good for the Gallery's business, don't you think?'

He could only stare at her.

'That's part of your job there – advising people on what to buy. Isn't it?'

He turned on his heel. 'That way,' he said.

'Colin—'

He had left the room. She followed slowly. By the time she reached the hall, he was at the front door with her handbag and package in one arm.

'Colin,' she said, 'if you would only *try* August down on Long Island—'

'No.'

'Why not? It's so cool in the evenings, quite unlike New York. And I promise you'll be left alone – I won't disturb you. I promise.'

He opened the front door. 'Goodbye.'

'Goodbye? Just like that.' She mustered a forgiving smile as she took the handbag. She ignored the parcel of food. 'Darling, I'm sorry I arrived at the wrong time. Forgive me?'

So she hadn't got his message. 'You forgot something.' He thrust the paper bag into her arms, urging her over the threshold.

For a moment, soft sweetness vanished. The pretty mouth hardened, widened, with lips now spread in anger. 'You—' She regained part control and quieted her rising voice. 'You can give this to your lousy elevator boy.' She dropped the package at her feet. 'There goes the hock,' she added, smiling normally once again.

He closed the door. She had got two things wrong: there was no elevator boy, lousy or otherwise; and the wine bottle, probably bolstered by a thick cushion of Brie, had given no sound of breaking. It would all have been comic, except for the ugly moment of fury. Medusa. In that brief instant, the mass of red ringlets had changed to snakes.

Depressed and angry, he made his way back to the living-room. He was already feeling a touch of guilt – it was the first time he could remember being actually rude to a woman. He had better keep Medusa in mind.

No more work on the article was possible. The phrases wouldn't come, his train of thought disjointed. He tried cooling off in a shower, resisted the idea of going out for a late lunch – too heavy on the budget. Always that

13

damned budget to think of. He'd have to get a full-time job: free-lance articles bolstering his part-time work at the Schofeld Gallery were barely enough to cover New York expenses. The Gallery carried prestige, of course. Its reputation was high, and his position there as adviser in acquisitions sounded impressive enough. He had been lucky to get it, even if it seemed only a temporary halt in his real career. My God, he thought as he opened a tin of sardines and poured himself some beer – it would be a heavy enough evening ahead at the Gallery with the cocktail party for Dali's illustrations of Dante's *Inferno* beginning at five – do museum directors never die? At present, they all seemed to be well under retirement age, and lusty. As the junior officers in the British Navy used to toast in their wardroom, 'Here's to a bloody war or a sickly season!'

He drank his beer with the first smile he had had on his face that day: partly because of the black humour of the junior officers' toast, partly because of the amount of useless information that was picked up over the years and then suddenly surfaced at appropriate moments. He might be drifting along in his career, but his memory was still working. Even if he might not wish for bloody wars or sickly seasons, he had one firm desire – the one that had been with him for the last ten years. He couldn't paint – he had tried that, and admitted his failure. But he did know something about artists, past and present. And what better job than getting their works, often buried in private collections, out into the public daylight? Not by force or thievery. Getting them out through the power of friendly persuasion. With, of course, strong guarantees for their safety and protection. No private collector was ever going to unlock his sweet treasures unless he could trust their temporary guardians. That's where the cultural boys in the State Department had been useful during his nine years in Washington: their backing had influenced several very hard heads among some of the foreign art-gatherers. But in the last three years there had been a decline in government interest as exhibition costs mounted and inflation soared. Understandable, of course. Social services and defence made art a very poor relation. What was the lecture he had been given by that determined New York Congresswoman when he had faced her on one of the minor but inevitable House committees? Man could live on bread alone if need be, but he'd surely perish on a diet of frills. Her word, frills. So much for fine art and expanded knowledge. New York, New York, you're a helluva town, where the debts pile up and the streets go down.

Now don't get bitter, he warned himself. The Congresswoman was worried – pushed by a hundred thousand voters clamouring for bread alone, which included a TV set, petrol at cheap prices to give them some week-end driving, and all the other inalienable pleasures that accrued automatically at birth. So don't get bitter. Besides, there were some important exhibitions being carefully nursed around the country. The bit museums could still manage that. But it took a splash of a name like Tutankhamen, or the Mona Lisa, or the Venus de Milo, to catch public support. What about the great works of art that were never on view? Unknown, because they were hidden inside a castle, a mansion, a palace, a private collection perpetually closed. Their owners, of course, saw a virtue in this, a nobility of purpose. What was the phrase he had heard so often? 'Preserving art for posterity . . .' Whose posterity? Theirs?

Cut that out, he warned himself for the third time, or else you'll lose any friendly persuasion you once possessed. And it did succeed, sometimes – just often enough to keep alive your belief in human generosity. But even that phrase sounds too sarcastic. Preserve me from becoming the middle-aged grouch with a permanent sneer and jaundiced eye, he thought as he cleared up the kitchen: without beliefs and enthusiasms, our daily bread would turn to a diet of ashes. Now, why didn't I tell that to the Congressperson?

All clear in the kitchen. Desk in the living-room put in order, ready for some more immortal passages of impassioned prose in the morning. Nothing more to be done here, in this empty apartment. Or should he forget about duty, and skip the party? The exhibition had been his idea originally, but Martin Carfield had taken it over, and a cocktail party had been tacked on. Max Seldov, who usually supported Colin, had backed down and decided that a party was in the Dali tradition. Old Schofeld, of course, thought anything that pleased their clients was good for art, as well as for the Gallery.

An empty apartment to match an empty life, he thought as he stood in the bedroom, peeling off his damp shirt, preparing for another shower, his eyes on Jennifer's photograph. It stood on the chest of drawers, always there, always watching his moods with those teasing blue eyes and a smile just breaking on her lips. Her head was tilted slightly, as it used to be when she was listening to something preposterous, her smooth dark hair falling over her brow. In another moment, she would speak, saying something equally preposterous, and they'd both burst into laughter.

He had chosen this particular photograph of Jennifer to keep beside him, and blot out the memory of a face almost unrecognizable, cruelly smashed by a bullet in the side of the head. A late September afternoon, a small quiet street in Washington. A boy speeding on rollerskates. Jennifer walking far ahead. The boy – fifteen perhaps, one of the two witnesses said, maybe sixteen; thin and tall, all arms and legs – steadying himself with

16

his two skates drawn parallel as he drew near Jennifer. 'All too quick,' the nearer of the witnesses had said. 'Only saw dark blue clothes and the hair. I thought he was going to veer around her, scare her; they do that, you know. I didn't even see a gun until I heard the blast.' One shot, and the skater was flying on his way, down to the corner where the busier street began. And was lost. And never found.

Colin Grant touched the photograph. 'You're curing me,' he told it. He could now, objectively, almost coldly, let himself recall the witnesses' accounts. The wound was healing, although the scar was permanent. Then he began dressing. He'd arrive at the Schofeld Gallery ahead of time, even if he walked the six blocks, choosing the shaded side of the street, from here to Madison Avenue. What else was there to do? Besides, Schofeld's had air-conditioning.

As he waited for the elevator, he suddenly remembered, looked back quickly at his front door. The paper bag was gone. Now, who the hell—? The service man had been off duty since noon; the front elevator was automatic; the tenants opposite were away for the summer; the people next door had jobs that kept them absent until six o'clock. Ronnie – surely not. Yet who else? She's telling me something, he thought angrily. She's wiping out all reminders of a temper tantrum, and let's forget today: it didn't happen. My God, did that woman never get the message?

In spite of weather and late-afternoon traffic, he covered the six blocks in six minutes flat. His anger had receded. But he was still unaware of the thin middle-aged man, waiting near his apartment house, who had been hard pressed in keeping up with Grant's stride. The stranger watched him disappear into Schofeld's, made sure he

17

stayed there, and then used the telephone in the bar-and-grill on the opposite side of Madison.

'He's there.'

'Good,' said a woman's voice, clear and decided. 'Keep an eye on the place till five thirty. If he doesn't leave by then, you can take off.'

'That's all?'

'That's all.'

An easy assignment, thought the thin man; it made little sense to him. Few of them did. Why waste money in making certain she'd find her quarry where she expected him to be? There could be no other explanation; and his agency would know nothing beyond his instructions and a good fee. He ordered a beer, took a table at the window, looked out at the street, and kept an eye on both his watch and Schofeld's. Long ago he had given up speculating about women and their motives: one tenth on the surface, nine tenths below. He'd like to see this one, though. The cool decided voice had been concise in giving him phoned instructions that morning. She knew what she wanted, that girl.

By five thirty, the trickle of individual arrivals at Schofeld's had thickened to people in batches. He scanned the latest group converging from their taxis: two portly gentlemen and one tall young man with long waved locks; three women – separate: one old; one around thirty; one early twenties, in gypsy-style dress. He placed his bet on Ms Thirty, chic as all-get-out. It was the turban she wore, all wrapped around her head: couldn't tell what her hair was like, or who she'd be without it concealed. Yes, she was his choice for a cool, determined voice.

Five thirty and two minutes over. Time to knock off. The thin man rose and paid, and vanished from the scene.

2

The Schofeld Gallery stretched far beyond what it seemed from the street. From a single shop-front, fifty years ago, it had expanded – once the Depression and the War were over – to double windows, a solitary picture displayed in each of them against a background of grey velvet. The tone was set before anyone ventured beyond the door: restraint, taste, privacy, and great expense.

Inside was a further study in greys, from silver carpeting to pale oyster walls, a combination that was carried up the wide staircase to each of the three floors above. 'The pictures give the colour,' Maurice Schofeld had said. And modern technology had given excellent lighting and elaborate alarms against fire and burglary. He was a cautious Swiss, highly intelligent in art and skilful in business, and not entirely convinced that the machine age was perfect. So there were guards, one to every floor, trying to look merely part of the background. Today, Colin Grant noted, there were two additional guards inside the entrance. They, at least, seemed as cool as the air-conditioning. Everyone else was at boiling-point.

'Why the frenzy?' he asked Max Seldov, sombre in dark suit and tie, who managed the Gallery along with Martin Carfield. Schofeld himself, pushing eighty, now made only occasional appearances, although his pronouncements still came loud and clear from his hotel suite. Like Jove on Mount Olympus hurling his thunder-bolts. 'The pictures were all in place two days ago, the lighting was arranged yesterday, and—'

'That's what we were worried about.' Seldov looked up the staircase at the second floor where the exhibition had been installed. 'Martin thought that the Dalis should have more general lighting.'

'When I saw them in Venice, they were exhibited in the Doge's Palace – down in the cellars, in a room that was as black at the Night Court itself. Keep the room fairly dark and the lights on the pictures.'

'Pinpoint them?'

'How else? They're meant to scare you.'

'A bit dramatic, don't you think?'

'So is Dante's *Inferno*.'

Seldov was hurrying off, bound for the second floor and some last-moment agonizing. He'd probably leave the lights the way Carfield had changed them. And where was Martin Carfield, smooth of face and manners? There he was, instructing the waiters on the subject of drinks. ('Keep it down to one apiece, we don't want champagne sloshed all over the carpet.') Next, telling Miss Haskins to leave those flowers where they were, and why weren't they white roses as ordered? After that, fussing over the invitation list with the girl (the prettiest one, naturally, with the sincere smile all primed to welcome) whom he was installing at the entrance-desk with two polite young men from the junior staff to make sure invitation cards were produced and collected. I'm the only man in the room, thought Grant, who isn't in dark suit, dark tie. What the hell am I doing here, anyway? He edged away, but not quite in time. Or perhaps Carfield had had him in his sights all along.

'Colin! Good to see you. Glad you decided to come. What do you think of it all?'

'Very impressive.' If it weren't for the pictures in this lower gallery, Raeburn with his pink-cheeked girls, Turner with the Thames on fire, some lesser English School landscapes with billows of green elms and summer skies, the place would look like a funeral parlour.

Carfield paid a long moment's attention to Grant's light grey summer-weight suit, then eyed the pale blue shirt and dark red tie. 'There will be a lot of the media here. The *Times* and the *Post*, a couple of magazines. TV reporters too – some girl for the eleven o'clock news. I think you should handle them.'

'They'll need more than one drink apiece.'

Carfield didn't seem to hear that. 'We'll let Seldov deal with the old ladies. I'll be with Mr Schofeld.'

'Of course,' Grant murmured. Carfield looked at him sharply. 'When is he due?'

'At six. You'll stay until the end?'

That's an order, thought Grant. He smiled, hid a sudden attack of depression, and repeated, 'Of course.'

Carfield nodded his approval, and even extended some of it to the light grey suit. It was of excellent worsted material and well cut. Probably belonged to Grant's more affluent days in Washington. 'Could be worse,' he observed, and looked round at the progress of his preparations. 'But where's Seldov?'

'Upstairs. Judging the lights.'

'In the Dali room?' Carfield's voice rose slightly. 'I want them left exactly as we decided this morning.' He was already half-way to the staircase.

At least, thought Grant, we'll all have some peace down here for the next ten minutes or so. He walked over to the small group of staff members, gathered together in the frozen huddle of waiting. 'Who's for tennis?' he asked, and raised a smile from four of them, polite disapproval from two. (Future Carfields?) That was the trouble around here: everyone so damned polite, all customer-trained. Didn't anyone look at the far end of the gallery and see a Rembrandt, a possible

21

Velazquez, a definite Rubens on the wall outside Maurice Schofeld's most private office, and feel something beyond a price tag and an impressive name? Now come on, he told himself: some of them must, or why spend their lives here? Never underestimate a man because he dresses like an undertaker.

He felt the pull to the Velazquez, unauthenticated or not, and drifted towards the end wall for the rest of the waiting time.

There was a scattering of prompt arrivals, a slight clotting of the stream by half past five. These were the wise ones, able to examine the Dali drawings before the explosion of visitors made viewing impossible. To be seen, however, was perhaps as important as to see. Most of them followed the guard's directions and trooped upstairs. But there were always some who would decide they'd do that when they were good and ready, fortified by a glass of champagne which was to be served on the ground floor. One of Carfield's useless precautions to keep the Dali room unsloshed, thought Grant as he waited glassless (staff rules) for a member of the media to materialize at his elbow with Miss Haskins. Rather than scan the passing strangers like one of the private detectives who were wandering around, he concentrated on the Turner, a partially finished work – a study for a larger canvas – and tantalizing in its unfulfilled dream. Several guests drifted past him. One stopped.

He glanced sideways and saw a woman, beautiful enough to change his glance into a stare. Something stirred in a deep memory, couldn't come to the surface. Perhaps this was just the typical face, with high cheekbones and clearly outlined chin, that he had seen a hundred times on the covers of fashion magazines. If he could only glimpse her hair, he might place her, but her head was entirely covered by a grey-green turban, neat, not bulky, more like an inspiration from the Great Gatsby's twenties than anything from India. Amber earrings emphasized the strange colour of her eyes, almost a golden brown. Her lips smiled. Softly she said as she turned back to admire the painting, 'You don't remember me, Mr Grant?' Softly, and yet with a precise clarity, nothing slurred or flattened.

The voice was the key. Quickly his private computer recalled the facts: Arizona – spring of 1974 – visit to Victor Basset, multi-millionaire – fabulous art collection – lunch on a terrace – a girl with golden hair, a face and figure to match its splendour, large round sunglasses leaving eyes an enigma – girl? Woman, rather, no more than thirty, indispensable apparently, quite efficient, obviously trusted by Basset to keep his correspondence and guests in good order. Trust old man Basset in turn, all six hundred million dollars' worth of him, to make sure his superior secretary had beauty as well as brains. Westerbrook, Lois Westerbrook, that was the name. That was her voice. So he could say, about to shake hands, 'Miss Wester—'

'No! Not that. We don't know each other.' She was pointing at the Turner picture, seemingly absorbed by its flaring colours. His hand, half-raised, dropped back to his side. He felt awkward and stiff, and more than annoyed. 'I'm here in New York as Jane Smith.'

'That's original.'

'On business for – well, you know for whom I am talking. Let's not mention his name. And keep our voices well down. You'll show me some pictures and we'll seem to be discussing them.'

'Why?' he asked bluntly.

'Stop looking at me. Look at the Turner. *Please*,' she added, glancing briefly at him with such an enchanting smile that her commands seemed more like pleading.

23

'We didn't want anyone to know we were contacting you, so I couldn't be sent to your apartment. What I have to tell you couldn't be said over a telephone. It's too long, too involved. Too private. Could you meet me later tonight – my hotel? We can have supper in my room.'

'Aren't you nervous about anyone knowing I am contacting you?' he asked lightly.

'You don't have to advertise your visit.' She left that where it fell. More gently, 'Time for you to move us towards the Constables and show me what to admire in them. Please.' Again, that appeal in her smile.

'I don't get it—' he began, as they left the Turner for greener pastures.

She said, for anyone to hear, 'Now, this isn't by Constable, is it?' She stopped before an eighteenth-century bucolic scene. Her voice dropped once more. 'I'll give you my hotel and room number, if you *are* interested. It's about a job, an assignment that our friend in Arizona thinks you could carry out for him. With discretion and good judgment. That's what he needs. Also with a knowledge of art. Two weeks in Vienna, expenses paid, first-class all the way, and a fee of five thousand dollars.' She walked on to the next picture on view. 'Interested?'

He recovered himself and followed her. 'Just what is this assignment?'

'It's completely legal.'

He wasn't questioning Basset's integrity. 'Five thousand is a hell of a lot of money.'

'To him? You'd charge a stiff fee anyway, wouldn't you? As I said, he needs someone with judgment. And discretion. It's a business deal that has got to be kept quiet meanwhile. Meanwhile,' she repeated.

As he stood in silence beside her, she added, 'It's your

turn to do some talking.' She laughed as though they had been exchanging a small joke.

'When does he want me to leave?'

'At the end of this month. Could you manage that?'

He nodded. The Gallery closed for the summer vacation in mid-July. He was free until after Labour Day. But he still couldn't quite believe this conversation.

She sensed his doubts. 'If you come to see me tonight, we can really talk and you can ask a hundred questions.'

'If I don't turn up?'

'I'll have to make contact with the next art expert on our list. You were the first on it. Our friend's own choice. Flattered? You should be.'

Yes, he was flattered. 'Astonished, too. I didn't even get to first base with him.' Grant's visit to Arizona, pleasant as it was, had been a failure in the art of persuasion. Victor Basset's enormous and first-rate collection of pictures was not for exhibition, kept safely in storage. (Where was storage space for a collection as large as that? The ranch near Prescott was not big enough to house any except a few of Basset's own special favourites.)

'Oh, he agreed with your ideas more than you think. Do you know Basset Hill?'

It was one of the millionaire's houses, only fifteen miles outside Washington, a vast mansion in spreading grounds, seldom used since Basset had settled in Arizona for his health. 'I've seen it.' Who hadn't, if they had been driving around the Virginia border? 'From the outside.' Like everyone else. Even abandoned, except for an army of caretakers, it was an impossible place.

'You should see it from the inside now. All redecorated, reshaped where necessary, heating and humidity just at the right setting for the preservation of pictures.'

'He's taking them out of storage?' Grant was startled, unbelieving.

'And not for himself.'

'For whom?' he asked quickly.

'For the public.'

He couldn't believe it. 'When I met him three years ago he wouldn't even consider—'

'He was considering his own plans.'

'You mean he already had the idea for a museum?'

'And was working on it.'

'Why didn't he mention it?'

'How do you think he made his fortune? By talking about future projects?'

'Why did he agree to see me?'

'He had read your book. He wanted to probe your ideas.'

'I hope they passed muster,' Grant said bitingly. He was annoyed, and showing it.

'*You* did,' she was quick to say. 'Or I wouldn't be here right now.' Something distracted her: she had been keeping an unobtrusive watch. 'I'll explain more tonight. Will you come?' She put out her hand. 'Ten o'clock.' Her handshake was brief, but she left a small card in his palm as she added, clear-voiced once more, 'I mustn't monopolize you. Thank you. Goodbye.' She moved away just as Miss Haskins reached him, with a pretty little morsel in gypsy costume loitering behind her.

Miss Haskins, sibilants hissing, had time to whisper, 'TV girl. Eleven o'clock news. Don't let her sweet blue eyes deceive you.' Then she turned to say, 'Ah, Miss Wenslas, this is Mr Colin Grant, our adviser on exhibitions.' And with that he was left, as he slipped Lois Westerbrook's card into his pocket, to the spiky questions of a bright young woman, socially conscious, who was fascinated by the cost of all this hoop-la. Obviously that was to be her lead-in tonight.

He admitted he didn't know, and (with a shared smile) that he couldn't care less. He branched into a description of other Dali parties, other places, other times. 'In the thirties – before you and I were born—' (that always shocked the young) '—the girls arrived with sausages pinned on to their hair, and watches used as earrings. Dali himself appeared in a diver's suit, with two Afghan hounds straining at their leashes.'

'Oh, come on, now—'

'It happened. In London.'

'Afghan hounds?'

'Perhaps wolfhounds. Never could get them straight.'

'Don't tell me they ate the sausages.'

'Too busy being tangled by leashes and microphone wires. Dali was to give a speech, you see. In French, of course.'

'Did he?' She still was the unbeliever.

'Once he could get his diver's helmet unstuck. It took a strong handyman with a wrench to unscrew it.'

She laughed then, and said, 'You tell a good story, Mr Grant.'

'And true. Read his memoirs.'

'Dali's?' She hadn't heard of them. 'Does he write?'

'Better than he talks. He has a strong Catalan accent.'

She looked at him. 'Well—' she began doubtfully. 'Nice meeting you, anyway.'

'Hope I was of some use.'

She hesitated. 'Were you serious?'

'I'm always serious about artists.'

'Even when they are showmen?'

'Aren't they all, nowadays?'

'I suppose they have to sell.'

'They eat, like other human beings.'

'You know,' she said, brightening, 'that could make a very good lead-in.' She waved a hand and was off, heading straight for Max Seldov. Double-checking? Grant wondered with amusement. Seldov could help in that very nicely: he had been one of Dali's audience on that very hot afternoon in London's Burlington Gallery.

Then there was the *Times* man to see – he at least had read Dali's memoirs and could quote by the yard. Then the *Post*. Then a couple of critics from the magazines – they thought the champagne was an inadequate *brut*, and where was Maurice Schofeld himself? That was their lead, obviously, for next week's articles. By the time the last guest had gone, and Miss Haskins was picking up a few cigarette stubs and counting the burns on the carpet (Carfield had banned ashtrays in the non-smoker's belief that their elimination would bolster the printed signs respectfully requesting abstinence), and the iron gratings were about to clang into place over windows and door, Grant had time to begin thinking of his own plans. It was nine o'clock, the night guards arriving.

Seldov caught him for a moment, out on the pavement. 'Pure hell today, but tomorrow – it will be wonderful. Right? By the way, that young TV girl . . . She's pretty good. She had done her homework.'

'Really?'

'Yes. Knew all about Dali in the Burlington Gallery. Restores your faith in the young, doesn't it?' And Seldov, with three teenagers at the worrisome age waiting for him (or were they?) in Larchmont, gave Grant a clap on the shoulder to send him on his way down Madison, and went off in search of his car.

Grant could at last examine the card in his pocket. Lois Westerbrook's writing was as clear as her voice. The Albany Hotel. Naturally. Expenses first-class, she had said. Five thousand dollars – one third of his yearly retainer at Schofeld's for his part-time appearances there – and two weeks of work. Work? In Vienna? Pure pleasure.

The Albany, on Park avenue, was only eight blocks south. Easy walking distance. He decided on a quick hamburger, and let's cut out the supper idea. If he turned up at Lois Westerbrook's – *if*, he repeated – it would be business all the way. Like her inducement of first-class expenses. Perhaps he was being suspicious. Basset's offer, coming just at this time, was what really astounded him. Nice things like that just didn't happen to him. Not recently, anyway. Or was his luck changing again? Let's face it, that talk about the Basset Hill museum, brief as it had been, had caught his interest.

Dreams, he thought, and put them aside along with his rising hopes.

3

Lois Westerbrook had brushed her hair free from her turban's clamp, exchanged her tucked and frilled dress (the newest rage) for white silk pants and black shirt. High heels had been replaced with flat sandals, amber earrings with demure pearl studs. Beads were no longer worn as a tight neck-band; a simple long gold chain now broke the severity of the shirt. Eye-shadow was reduced in intensity, lipstick lightened and mouth reshaped. She hoped, as she surveyed the transformation, that it would reassure Colin Grant: this was the way he had first seen her, Basset's good right hand, at the Arizona luncheon. It would also emphasize the fact that she had taken considerable trouble this afternoon to stay unidentified in New York. Caution had been, was still necessary; she would give him all the reasons why. If he came . . . Would he? She gave one last glance at her reflection in the mirror. You obviously believe he will turn up, she told herself. But only one half of her mind was on herself and her successful visit to Schofeld's. (Not even the *Times* critic, who had visited Basset for an interview, had recognized her.) The other half was on Gene Marck, now waiting in the sitting-room next door. Or was he still phoning?

He had arrived just before nine, when she was in the shower. A strange man, with moods that varied from hot to cold. Tonight he was in one of his coldest. He hadn't even stayed beside her while she dressed; instead he had dropped two brief kisses that were almost as absent-minded as his excuse for retreating into the sitting-room to wait for a call from Washington. She guessed it was more business discussion with the architect who was reconstructing the Virginia house for Basset's museum. Why hadn't Gene stayed in his own room – at the end of this corridor, an arrangement to keep anyone from connecting the two of them – and received his nine o'clock call there? Once the call was over, he hadn't returned to the bedroom. Calls of his own to make? Of course, he was worried. He always worried about details. Which was no excuse to use her sitting-room as a public phone booth.

Anger had slowed her, kept her late, one way of administering a rebuke. Would he even be aware of it? Annoyance was dying: she could shake her head over her attempt at discipline. Gene was Gene. He had his own ways, and nothing would change them. He could be warm and passionate – she had never known such love. He could be detached and remote. But that, she reminded herself, was nothing to do with her. He had told her so. And he did have immense responsibilities. He was Victor Basset's private accountant for the art collection – he kept score on purchases, values, restoration, insurance, all that heavy but important business, and added enough good advice to make him one of Basset's favourite aides. My very favourite, too, she thought, and decided it was time to enter the sitting-room.

Gene Marck put down the phone and rose to meet her. He was of medium height and careful about his weight, a healthy specimen with skin tanned by Arizona sun. His hair was thick and blond, with grey beginning at the temples. The diplomat's look, Lois Westerbrook called it. (She had always liked men who were older. Gene was forty-eight.) Now he was studying her dress. 'Very suitable,' he said with marked approval. 'Well worth waiting for.'

31

So his mood had improved. She could safely allow her own to sharpen. 'I didn't want to disturb your phone calls.'

'Now, now,' he said warningly, but a quick smile softened his serious face, strong-boned, tight-lipped, transforming him into a warm and amiable man. It dropped away, just as suddenly as it had appeared. Once more he was businesslike and alert.

Worried too, she thought, noticing the furrow that deepened between his eyebrows, always a sign of stress. His clear blue eyes had that distant look as if he were seeing beyond her and this room. 'How did you get on today? Did you meet—'

He took her in his arms, interrupted her with a kiss.

'Careful! My hair and lipstick! You don't want Mr Colin Grant to raise an eyebrow, do you?'

'When is he due?'

'I told him ten o'clock.'

'That doesn't leave us much time.'

'You telephone too much,' she reminded him. 'Why didn't you use the bedroom phone?'

'You'd have been a distraction.'

'Were the Washington calls so important as all that?'

'Just checking on Grant,' he said. She didn't quite believe it. The dossier he had made on Grant, now lying on the desk, was complete enough. His arms had tightened around her again, and he was kissing her on either cheek. 'See,' he said as he released her, 'I didn't disturb your lipstick one bit. How is Mr Grant these days? Much the same, or changed?'

'Changed. More difficult. Perhaps less confident. More hesitant. Wary, I think.'

'Suspicious?'

'That's going too far. Let's say he thinks he is nobody's fool.'

'Good.' He had spoken too emphatically. He saw the

32

slight surprise in her eyes. 'You're nobody's fool, either, my love.'

Except yours, she thought. 'Gene, when do we tell Basset – about us?'

'You want to lose our jobs? We've hidden our feelings for three years. He'd never really trust us again. You know the house rules. No philandering between the inmates. Basset wants our minds kept on his business. Full value for the money?'

'We *do* keep our minds on—'

'As we've been doing in the last ten minutes?'

It was a point. She had to smile. And then sighed.

'I know,' he said softly. 'We'll get married when we have made enough to keep you in the style to which you've grown accustomed. Enough, too, to let you resign from your job. I don't want a part-time wife.'

Just a part-time mistress? The logic escaped her – he hadn't much time for anyone these days. His argument about losing Mr Basset's trust was stronger. It would be a matter of damaged pride: no one could deceive Basset. He was a past master in secrecy himself.

Gene was back to the business on hand. 'I think I'll slip out before Grant gets here, telephone you from my room, and then you can invite me over to meet him.'

'Why not stay?'

'I don't want him to find us too cosy. I'll leave before he does, make an innocent exit.'

'Oh, no!' she said, the words jerked out of her at the thought of another lonely night.

'I'm afraid so.'

'Someone else to see?'

'It isn't a woman, if that is what's troubling you.'

Perhaps it was. In Arizona it was easy to know what women he could meet: all were visitors to Basset Ranch. Here, in New York . . . She tried a small joke. 'Careful, or I'll have you followed.'

His blue eyes turned to ice.

Nervously she added, 'I had Colin Grant followed today. It's very simple.' She forced a laugh. 'It worked. I found him exactly when and where. You see, Gene, you are not the only one who checks and double-checks.'

'Was all that necessary?'

Her own voice hardened. 'Grant never did like large parties. Consult your dossier. Brawls, he used to call them. He might never have appeared. I damned well wasn't going to get dressed up for nothing. So I made sure of him.'

The cold stare left Marck's eyes. The sudden smile was warm and sunny. He tried to mollify her. 'I see I don't have to tell you what to say to him.'

She wasn't placated. She was as capable as Gene, sometimes more so. 'I can write my own script,' she said sharply.

'Yes, sir!'

He didn't salute, but the words gave the same effect, a sergeant replying to a junior officer who was inferior in every way except in rank.

The smile had disappeared.

'Gene—' she began, ready to back down. She stopped as she heard the knock at her door and pointed frantically towards her bedroom. Gene was already on his way there, to take its exit into the corridor once it was safe.

34

4

Grant arrived at the Albany with only a few minutes
to spare. At ten o'clock exactly he was entering Lois
Westerbrook's sitting-room. Subdued colours, flowers, a
choice in couch and chairs, enough space and interior
decoration to justify the excessive expense of this hotel.
The pictures on the wall were nondescript; not one
bookcase was provided. The windows were shaded,
framed in satin, and possibly overlooked Park Avenue.
One door, connecting with another room, was ajar.

Lois Westerbrook noticed it too, and moved swiftly
over to shut it. She waited there for a moment (listening
for the sound of closing from the bedroom's outer door)
and then turned back to Grant. Really, she was thinking,
didn't Gene trust me to handle this interview? Then why
hadn't he stayed here and played overseer? He must
think that we've got Grant firmly hooked. That was
Gene's word. She didn't like it, but it went with the bait:
a free trip to Vienna and a five-thousand-dollar fee. Who
could resist it? Gene had asked her, especially a man
who had taken a big cut in salary when he left Washington. And was available. (The Schofeld Gallery was
closing for the summer in mid-July. Gene's dossier on
Grant was complete, if succinct.) 'Do sit down, Mr
Grant. Any trouble on your way up here?'

He chose one of the firmer chairs, and assured her
that there had been no difficulty at all in reaching her
room without being noticed. In the lobby there had been
a small group of new arrivals, straight off the plane,
with an amazing hodge-podge of luggage for a place like

the Albany – Vuitton combined with cardboard boxes tied by string: ostentatious I-couldn't-care-less, the new fad of the unaccustomed rich, like blue jeans costing eighty dollars a pair.

'And in the elevator?' she asked as she crossed to a tray of drinks. 'Some brandy?'

'Scotch, please.' She had been a little flustered, he thought, but she was coming back to normal even if she was paying too much attention to pouring his drink. He himself hadn't been exactly calm. He had hidden his embarrassment, he hoped, by seeming to take more interest in the room than in her. That black and white outfit suited her, reminded him of the girl in frontier pants and shirt, with an Arizona tan and a Beacon Hill accent. 'I rode up with three of the new arrivals – Hollywood characters – dressed as if they had been hauled off the beach at Santa Monica, and a woman they called "Countess", and a couple of Venezuelans. At least, they spoke Spanish and talked of Caracas. They got off at this floor and I slipped out with them, trying to look like an oil promoter.' He still felt ill at ease. He hadn't liked that approach to her room. It wasn't the Albany that impressed him, with all its expensive restraint and its super-wealthy or titled guests, but this feeling of unreality.

'You were really discreet,' she said. 'Soda or plain water?'

'On the rocks.'

She poured herself a glass of white wine and brought the drinks over, with a folder under one arm, to the table beside him. She sat down opposite, placing the folder on her lap, and raised her glass. 'To you, Mr Grant.'

The formality amused him: he was being briefed on the tone of this meeting. He raised the over-generous glass of Scotch in reply, laid it back on the table untouched – safer to let the ice thin out that triple dosage. There was a marked silence. In another moment, he was thinking, I'll be reduced to looking around and making some trite remarks about imitation Louis XV chairs. There was always the weather, of course. And he laughed.

That broke the tension. Lois Westerbrook relaxed visibly. He wouldn't be so difficult after all. 'I agree,' she said.

'With what?' Now where was she leading him?

'Your opinion about the change in me. This afternoon – at Schofeld's – you found me slightly comic, didn't you?'

'Not that. Decorative. Highly fashionable.'

'But comic,' she insisted.

'You merged right into the scene.'

'Yet, I *was* serious. I meant every word I said. And I'm still serious.'

'Anyway, you're recognizable now.' She really was a beauty, he thought, a self-assured, competent and cool-minded beauty with liquid gold hair and agate eyes. He had liked her better as she opened the door to him, when she had seemed flustered, cheeks pink, lips soft with uncertainty.

'That's just the point, Mr Grant. I *had* to make sure you wouldn't be connected – through me – with Mr Basset. Your Maurice Schofeld has visited the ranch. He has a good memory. Especially for women.'

'Why didn't you just call on me at my apartment? People do, you know.' This girl loves too much mystery, he was thinking: or is it to impress me? Then, as she only smiled and shook her head, he saw a possible explanation. 'You had to make sure, he quoted back, 'that you wouldn't be connected with me. Doormen talk. Right?'

She rose and laid the folder down on the chair. 'I

haven't much to offer in the way of supper. Just sandwiches. I didn't want a waiter barging in.'

'And connecting you with me, or me with you?'

She had reached a service-cart, lifted the silver lid that covered a napkin-wrapped mound. He was the most annoying man, she thought: unsettling. Did he see everything as a joke?

'No thank you,' he told her. 'I've had supper. You go ahead.' He hoped that would stop her being the perfect hostess. In a way, it was touching: a woman putting a guest at ease with food and drink. The normal impulse, of course. Or did she want him to be so much at ease that he wouldn't have one critical faculty left? 'I think we'd better start talking, don't you?'

She replaced the lid on the salver of sandwiches, leaving them untouched. She was still thinking about his apartment, for she said, a touch defensively, 'Your doorman might very well talk, if a certain reporter just stopped for a few moments to chat with him.'

'What reporter?' Now that was carrying things too far.

'A very investigative type. He's writing a book on the way the ten richest men in America use – or misuse – their spending money. Victor Basset is one of the specimens under his microscope. Somehow he was tipped off that I was in town. That roused his natural curiosity, I suppose. Perhaps every lead must be followed.'

'I sit corrected.' Grant smiled and took his first drink.

She returned to her chair, lifting the folder with distaste.

What was in it? he wondered for the third time. 'It looks as if Basset's present project is already blown,' he suggested.

'I don't think so. Or else there would have been some mention of it in the newspapers. No journalist can resist a scoop if he has the facts. At the moment, this one is merely wondering why I should be in New York as

"Jane Smith". However, she'll be leaving early tomorrow for Los Angeles. There she'll disappear, thank heavens. I'll return by stages to Arizona.'

'Did Basset think all this up?' The trouble they've taken . . . Grant's interest was really aroused now. He even forgot to ask himself if this was what she had been aiming for.

'Mr Basset wanted you for this assignment. That's all. The arrangements were left to us.' Her mind flickered briefly to Gene Marck. 'As usual,' she added with a smile.

Us? . . . Grant let that drop meanwhile. 'What is the assignment?'

She studied him quietly. Gene had been wrong about this man: he wouldn't take the job unless he heard the details – not even for a free trip to Vienna and five thousand dollars. She plunged in. 'There is a picture up for auction in Vienna, early in August. Mr Basset wants it. He has wanted it for forty years, but it wasn't for sale. Now suddenly it's available. It would add considerably to his collection of Dutch seventeenth-century paintings: the "Golden Age" period.'

'Who is the artist?'

'Ruysdael. It's one of his river scenes. Diagonal composition. Lots of green. Date – possibly 1642.'

He looked at her with some surprise. She knew something of what she was talking about. Never underestimate a pretty face, he told himself. Nor a millionaire's taste in art; nor his talent for dissimulation. He could see Basset now, although it was three years since they had met: friendly but impassive, quick to listen, slow to speak. And he recalled his suggestion when they were discussing Basset's recent acquisition of a Vermeer. Interesting, Grant had said, to have an exhibition of Vermeer and other interior painters in juxtaposition with the exterior painters of that same period. Basset had

39

merely inclined his head, smiled faintly, made no comment. 'Is he thinking of a seventeenth-century Dutch room for his Basset Hill museum? Exteriors and interiors?'

She nodded. 'That's why this particular Ruysdael is so important to him. He owns some of Ruysdael's earlier winter scenes; also those painted in the later period – trees, and richer detail; and two of the frozen rivers with ice-skaters. But none of the horizontals – they've mostly been snapped up by museums, or are buried deep in some collector's private hoard. As this Ruysdael was for years.'

'So now it's available. You're certain of that?'

'Certain.'

'Basset wants me to buy it for him? Not in his name, I take it. That would intensify the bidding and jack up its price.'

'Considerably. But it isn't the price that worries Mr Basset. It's one of his competitors. Antagonist is a better word. If he thinks Mr Basset wants something, he'll do his best to get it for himself. The art world has its own quota of dirty tricks.'

'Surely Basset has an agent in Vienna who could have handled this discreetly?'

'Yes. But however careful the agent might be, he is still known to be connected with Mr Basset. If there was some likely bidding at the auction, and Mr Basset's agent kept pressing on, that would rouse a lot of speculation. Too much. You see, the man who has put that Ruysdael up for sale wants as much anonymity as Mr Basset. For a different reason. His freedom is at stake: perhaps his life.'

Drama suited her. Her cheeks were pink-tinged again, her eyes wide with excitement and indignation. 'Pretty high stakes,' he said gently, and watched her with increasing interest. Definitely not an act, he decided: she wasn't even aware of the effect she had produced. 'Who is the man?'

'A Hungarian. Once a well-known collector. He lives near Budapest.' She stopped, regained her detachment. 'This has nothing to do with your part of the assignment. I talked too much.'

'I must know as much as possible about the picture's history. Its owner lives in Hungary, and he wants to leave? He needs a nice little bank account all established, somewhere abroad?'

'That's it exactly. He has sent out his Ruysdael ahead of him.'

'Just a moment, there. The Hungarian government took over all the private collections. They are the property of the state.'

'Except,' she said, smiling, 'for those paintings that were hidden – two or three of the smaller pictures that could easily be squirreled away.'

'Hungarian foresight, you might say.' So far, it made sense.

'His Ruysdael isn't a large canvas, you know. You could bring it back to New York quite easily. Carry it on the plane with you, in fact. No customs duty: it's a seventeenth-century work of art. Genuine antique.'

'Hold on. I have to bring it to New York?'

'Why not? It's done every day.'

'Scarcely,' he said dryly.

'Well – it is done. Isn't it?'

He said nothing. It was done; if not every day, certainly every month: the safest way for the big galleries and dealers to transport a valuable painting firmly under the eye and hand of one of their representatives.

'Our Hungarian will be in Vienna by the time you return to New York. There's no problem, then, about Mr Basset meeting you quite openly and taking delivery. We have to play it his way: complete secrecy until the man is safely out of Hungary. You see, Mr Basset is known to be a long-time friend of our Hungarian. In fact, they were in touch just a month ago. How else do you think Mr Basset learned about the Ruysdael?'

'And there's the weak spot,' Grant said. 'The Communists are no fools. Any whisper of that meeting between Basset—'

'I didn't say they met!' she said indignantly. 'I said they were in touch. Secretly.'

'Or what about any whisper of a Ruysdael, whose owner had fooled the Hungarian government for the last twenty years or so? They'd damn soon find out who he was. There are collectors' old catalogues, and long-ago records of sales—'

'But not before Mr Basset's friend is safely out of their reach.'

'Will he ever be?'

'He will change his name, get a completely new identity.' She paused, added, 'This was all his idea in the first place. He's willing to take the risks involved. He doesn't intend to be a penniless refugee.'

'Just a far-sighted one.' Grant went back to his own problem. 'I don't know if I like the idea of bringing the picture—'

'No trouble at all. We'll attend to any Austrian licence that is necessary for export: no bother there, the picture never belonged to them. You'll have papers to prove it is legally your property. So don't—'

'My property?' he broke in. He grinned, adding, 'What if I just walk off with it?'

'Not your style, Mr Grant.' She lifted the file on her lap and opened it, let her eyes fall on the list of facts about the life of Colin Grant. 'We know it.'

'Is that a file on me?' He was outraged. 'Basset's idea?'

'No. We just had to be sure you were the man he

thinks you are.' Had she lost him? 'Don't you see, we *had* to know—'

'Who's "we"?' he demanded.

'Myself, and Mr Basset's financial adviser on his art collection – very important for this Vienna venture. Also for Mr Basset's latest enterprise: the Basset Hill Museum. So, of course, we had to know something about you, Mr Grant. You are one of four now being considered—'

'That's unnecessary,' Grant said roughly.

She branched off at once, away from the Basset Hill Museum and its potential director. 'I hate the dossier idea, frankly. But yours is quite innocuous.'

'You make me sound dull.'

'Hardly that. Now, let's see—' She began skipping down the page in front of her.

Colin Grant, born 9th July 1938. – Father killed Omaha Beach, 1944. – Mother becomes interior decorator, supports children (one son, two daughters). – Grant attends Yale, 1956. – Liberal Arts, 1960. – Question-mark at 1961. – Army, 1962. Stationed Frankfurt, 1963-64. – Fine Arts, Columbia University, 1965. – Guide at Museum of Modern Art, 1966. – Temporary work at Metropolitan Museum of Art, 1966. – Published *Explorations in Art*, 1967. – Washington, in search of a job, 1967. – Advisory Assistant to Director of Cultural Affairs, Division of Art, Department of State, 1968. – Married Jennifer Stone, 1971. – Visits to museums abroad, 1972-74. – Visit to Arizona, 1974. – Wife murdered, Washington, September 1976. – Question-mark at resignation, December 1976. – Moved to New York, January 1977. Present address, occupation, *etc.*, *etc.*. . .

She said softly, 'We were very sorry – about your wife, I mean.' She skipped the question-mark that followed – of course, he couldn't bear it any more. What other reason for resigning? She looked up, caught his eyes watching her.

She really feels for me, he thought, and kept silent.

'There's one question I must ask,' she said. 'About that blank year: 1961.'

'It was a very blank year.'

'Could you fill it in for me?'

He tried to make light of it. 'I thought I was a painter – shook off the family and went to live in Greenwich Village with three other hopeful artists. One large attic. A lot of talk. Great expectations: but not one of us could do more than dab and dribble. I quit when I realized I wasn't a painter – never would be – not in the way I wanted. It takes more than ambition and self-confidence to make a man something he'd like to be. It takes talent, too. Sorry, that's all the explanation I can give.'

'So you joined the army.'

'I needed a job and steady pay. It got my head together. I started looking at museums when I was in Europe. My escape, I suppose, from drill and regulations.'

'Also, you learned German. Yes, that will be useful.'

'Do you have to sound like a schoolma'am?'

'I'm sorry.' She looked it, too.

'A very attractive schoolma'am.' he said more softly. 'Oh well, that takes care of 1961. Doesn't it?'

She nodded. He had been honest with her, and it must have been painful. She could fill in the gaps: 'Shook off the family' – a bid for independence? No more assistance needed from Mother Grant? Pride wouldn't let him take it when he had failed. Instead, he enlisted. 'Drill and regulations.' So he was just an ordinary private. No connection with Intelligence.

Something amused him. 'How do I pay for the Ruysdael? Just sign a cheque on my Citibank account?' All four hundred and thirty-two dollars of it.

'Oh, that's arranged. Mr Basset's firm, Allied Electronics, has an office in Vienna, and—' The telephone rang. She rose to answer it very quickly. With relief, he thought. It was someone whom she knew well. She was saying, 'I have an old friend of yours visiting me. Do drop in. He'd be delighted to see you, I'm sure.'

'Delighted to see whom?' he asked as she returned to her chair.

'Gene Marck. You met him with Mr Basset in Arizona. He's the adviser on our art purchases and insurance and increasing values. That sort of thing.'

All I remember about him, Grant thought, was that he didn't talk much, even less than Basset did. A watch-and-listen type. 'Wasn't he a new member of the staff?'

'Yes. He had only been with us a few months.' She was rushing her words now. 'He was an accountant with one of the big art dealers in Houston, did some business with Mr Basset, and impressed him. Gene knows a great deal about the art field – the money side of it, that is.'

Grant made no comment.

'He will tell you how the Ruysdael payment can be made.'

Yes, thought Grant, like everything else, that would be very nicely arranged.

Eugene Marck made his appearance, refused a drink, stayed for fifteen minutes, excused himself politely (he had just spent the day in Virginia, at Basset Hill, needed some sleep before tomorrow's busy morning), and left for the Pierre, where he was staying. In the short visit, all very friendly, all very welcome-to-the-team-my-boy, he cleared up the remaining points of business.

First: Grant should leave for Vienna on the 26th July. This wouldn't pinpoint his arrival with the auction itself. It would take place in the earlier half of August, in one of the smaller Viennese auction rooms. Date, time, and location would be given him later.

Second: Grant could talk about his forthcoming visit to Vienna: it might cause comment if he didn't. Or if he didn't have a good excuse for it, such as two or three articles to be written about the seventeen Brueghels in the State Museum. (Just a suggestion, Marck had added tactfully.)

Third: Grant would receive plane tickets and hotel reservation within the next few days. Also a letter from Victor Basset authorizing him to select a picture and bid for it at auction. Also a cheque for five thousand dollars. In Vienna, he was to keep a list of his expenses: he would be reimbursed on his return to New York.

Fourth: Marck would be in Vienna too, but he would remain well in the background until the auction was over. Immediately on the acquisition of the Ruysdael, he would meet Grant in the private office of the auctioneer, along with the treasurer of Allied Electronics – who was authorized to write the two necessary cheques, one to the auctioneer (for his fee) and the other to the listed seller of the picture (using the seller's new identity, of course). Grant, as the purchaser, would receive all the necessary documents, along with Marck's telephone number in case of some unexpected difficulty. Emergency use only.

Fifth: Basset wanted the Ruysdael. At any cost. Grant was to remember that, and bid accordingly.

'That's everything, I think,' Marck said, rising from his chair. 'Quite clear?'

Grant had listened in total silence, making sure he missed nothing in the quick flow of words. His memory was good, better still when he used it visually. He'd make a résumé of Marck's instructions as soon as he got home, while they were still fresh in his memory. Once written down and read, he would remember them. But

I'll destroy my notes, he promised silently, studying Marck's alert face. One thing was certain: Marck had added considerable volubility to his watch-and-listen attitude of three years ago. 'Why two cheques?' Grant asked. 'I thought art galleries took charge of the entire payment, deducted their commission, and sent the rest of the money to the seller of the painting.'

'In New York, yes. In Vienna?'

That silences me, thought Grant. I don't know the regular routine in payments abroad. All I know is what usually happens here.

'Mr Basset prefers to pay the auctioneer's fee when the seller is a friend who needs every dollar his picture can bring him. Hence the two cheques.'

'Very thoughtful of Basset.'

'He can afford to be. Anything else?'

'Yes,' Grant said. 'I'd like to examine the Ruysdael before the auction.'

'It is being kept out of sight – you can understand the need for that.'

'I do. But I'd like to make sure it isn't a fake. If I have any doubts, I'll call in an expert. I know him well. He can be trusted. Discretion is part of his job.' He had startled them both, no doubt about it. 'We could use that private office you mentioned – keep the whole thing under wraps.'

Marck said coldly. 'We have already had expert advice on the painting. It is no fake.' His quick smile appeared, warm and engaging. 'Your suggestion was good, but we really do think of all the possibilities.'

You certainly do, thought Grant. They shook hands. 'So,' Marck was saying now, 'you have friends in Vienna? That's nice.'

'One or two – if they are still there. It has been a few years since my last visit.'

Marck nodded, and made his way to the door. 'Good night, Lois,' he said, almost as an afterthought.

'I have to leave, too,' said Grant, rising to his feet. 'Good night, Miss Westerbrook. And why don't you come to Vienna?' She was indeed looking as though she had been left out in the cold.

'Stay for another drink.' She sounded almost urgent.

'Sorry. Some other time, I hope.' He shook hands and was out of the opened door. Marck was drawing ahead of him. Walking fast. I get it, thought Grant: all these security-minded boys with their fixations. Who's to see us in this empty corridor?

He marked time by lighting a cigarette, and let Marck take the first elevator down. The second one came almost immediately and descended without another stop, so that when he reached the ground floor he could see Marck heading for the double glass doors on to Park Avenue. He made his way slowly past a collection of baggage and cardboard boxes cluttering an otherwise elegant lobby, and pushed both doors open for himself – the doorman was too engrossed in conversation with the chauffeurs of three black Cadillacs strung along the curb. The rank was empty of taxis. Grant had to step out into the street to hail a cab. And up there, crossing Park Avenue at 64th Street, was Gene Marck. He looked like a man who knew where he was going. But with his direction, first north, then east, he was certainly not bound for the Pierre on Fifth Avenue. Marck's stride was brisk. His exhaustion from his hard day of travel must have vanished, along with his urgent need of sleep.

Grant opened the cab door, ignoring the doorman's galvanic rush into last-minute assistance, and climbed in. 'I think,' he told the man, 'I have enough strength to close the door myself.' He banged it shut, gave the driver his address. Then he was thinking of Marck again

48

and that well-organized flow of instructions. An intelligent, capable man; slightly devious, too. But it was no concern of his how Marck spent his time off the chain. He had plenty of his own business to complete: a pad of paper on his desk, thorough notes to be made and read with concentration. He'd be lucky if he got to bed before three o'clock. That wasn't a complaint. Now that he was by himself, he could admit to a rising excitement. He laughed out loud.

The cab driver glanced at him in the rear-view mirror, and shook his head. Some guys had all the luck. Good looks and clothes to match, and not one goddamned care in his world. If he had a wife in the hospital and one kid into dope, the other pregnant (my God, what kind of high school was that?), and was hacking at night to make ends meet, shut away like a bloody prisoner in this cab with a protective screen to guard his head and a wrench at his feet ready to use – yeah, just let him feel like a laugh then. The tip was generous, something he hadn't expected after the Albany doorman's brush-off. He grunted his thanks, gave a nod, drove off with a screech of gears and the rattle of tin.

New York, New York . . . Grant went indoors, and to work.

5

Grant left Kennedy at seven o'clock, scarcely believing that he had actually caught the flight for Vienna. All kinds of small details – the must-do's and the have-to's and the don't-forget's – had piled up in the last few days. Who said bachelor life was an easy one? Not when O'Malley's apartment, with a good collection of books and records and elaborate stereo systems, had to be made secure, quite apart from discontinuing the small services that simplified daily life. But the newspapers and magazines had been cancelled (don't leave them gathering outside the door, the superintendent had warned him: invitation to forced entry) and the laundry collections and the milk and twice-weekly food deliveries; and O'Malley's mail (a couple of letters addressed to the apartment instead of his office) forwarded to him in Geneva with a scrawled note that Grant was leaving for a week or two in Vienna. Add to all that, a trip to lower Manhattan to have his camera registered: he had left it too late for the mails to handle, had forgotten, in fact, that his passport was on the point of expiring – he still broke into a mild sweat at the memory of that discovery.

However, he had finished his article for *Perspective*, and shaken himself free from Ronnie Brearely's sweet sympathy. No more offers of a room with a view on Long Island. Three phone calls had come after her Medusa performance outside his front door. The first two he had cut off, didn't reply to her gentle 'Colin?' The third had caught him unawares and he had answered it at once. The usual invitation to a week-end on a cool beach.

'I'll be out of town in August,' he said when Ronnie paused for breath.

'Where?'

'Vienna.' She'd find out anyway. She went to talkative parties.

'All alone, Colin?' She sounded horrified at the dreariness of his situation.

He could see where that was leading, and quickly scotched the snake. 'No. I'll be with the prettiest redhead this side of the Mississippi.'

A long pause. 'Do I know her?'

'I wouldn't think so. She's much younger than you.' Cruel, but necessary. 'Goodbye, Veronica.' Most definite.

She hadn't returned the goodbye. The receiver was banged into place. A quick and final end.

Final? Yes. In his last game of tennis with Jerry Phillips, his old adviser about the Brearely predicament, there was a bit of really good news. Veronica had latched on to Phillips.

'You know what you're getting into?' he had asked Phillips, becoming adviser in turn. Phillips wasn't listening. Any week-end out of New York in August was a good week-end, and Ronnie wouldn't be the only girl on the beach. He had then double-faulted his service, and lost game and set.

Perhaps, thought Grant, I should have reminded him that it didn't take a week-end to have Veronica on your back. All I ever did was to accept an invitation to one of her dinner parties, never held her hand, never even dropped a kiss on her cheek. Ah well, anyone who forgets his own advice as quickly as Jerry Phillips can't be warned. That solves my Brearely problem. What the devil did she see in me, anyway?

He unbuckled his seat-belt and relaxed with a generous double Scotch. The air-hostess had almost as strong a hand as Lois Westerbrook when it came to pouring a drink. A very efficient girl was the beautiful Lois. The reservations for the Hotel Majestic in Vienna had arrived last week by special messenger with his cheque and the plane ticket. Not a return ticket, just one for the eastbound flight. Easily explained: his return home wouldn't take place until Basset could meet him in New York and take possession of the Ruysdael, and Basset couldn't meet him until this Budapest friend was safe in Austria with a new name and new identity. It all hinged on the man's escape.

The painting itself, according to Gene Marck, was already out of Hungary. How else could Marck say that it had been examined by an expert and judged authentic? It must be in Vienna, well hidden. No doubt (Grant was guessing again, but it seemed the logical succession of facts to him) the auction would take place as soon as the man from Hungary had made his successful escape. This would allow Grant to take the next day's flight back to New York. Too bad if it cut a day or so from his two-week stay, but he didn't like the idea of hanging around Vienna along with a Ruysdael . . .

What if the man's escape was delayed? Ended in disaster? Well, Victor Basset would have his painting. And the Hungarian – Grant shook his head. He finished his Scotch, drinking to the man he didn't know and would never see, wishing him a safe journey through forests or swamps, hidden in decrepit barns or deep in the bowels of a Danube river boat. However he travelled, it would be rough.

Not a journey like this one, thought Grant with a sharp touch of guilt as he accepted another Scotch and the smiling intimation that orders for dinner were being taken. Did he wish lamb or chicken or fillet of beef?

Our Hungarian will get out, he told himself at the end of his second drink. Gene Marck had been confident enough. He was a natural planner. The only thing he had been wrong about, in his detailed instructions to Grant, was his talk about the necessity of having a cover story to stave off any suspicions among Grant's friends. Not one of them had asked why he was going to Vienna. Each and every one had thought it a good idea, a natural. Why not take off for a couple of weeks, enjoy yourself? They'd have done the same thing if they weren't tied down by the kids, too expensive a deal nowadays to take them all along – or by the office, a new contract coming up, had to stay within easy reach of New York.

The women had said, 'How wonderful! That's what I've always wanted to do – wake up some morning and decide I'm going to Europe for two weeks. Why not four?'

Why not? If he hadn't to bring back a valuable painting to New York, if he could have handed it to Marck in Vienna, saying, 'It's all yours,' he'd have made it four or six weeks, or even three months. It was seven years since he had been in Austria. Before he met Jennifer . . .

He slept on the plane, waking up as they touched down at Zürich for a short stop and a stretch of the legs in the cold morning air. Then a flight over mountain peaks between heavy towers of cumulus. From below, they'd seem like white eiderdown puffs. Up here, they were giant citadels, solid walls of powerful menace lining the careful path of the plane. 'Bad weather ahead,' said the hostess, removing his breakfast tray, 'but not for us. We'll arrive on schedule, nine forty-five Vienna time. We'll miss the storm.' A comforting thought from a comforting girl. She had red hair, too, beautifully in place in spite of an overnight journey. For the last time he thought of Ronnie Brearely and his blatant lie.

Anyway, she couldn't check up on its truth or untruth, not at this distance. Yes, he knew what his trouble was: he never enjoyed cutting down anyone to knee-level, particularly a woman. One thing he had learned, though, in those recent months: be on guard, don't trust completely. There are deep bogs in them thar meadows.

After the small buses, standing-room only, had brought the new arrivals over the vast stretch of runways to the spread of airport buildings, everything was simple – some long walks down spotless corridors, with a thorough but quick search for concealed weapons at one checkpoint: memories of the terrorist raid on the Vienna offices of OPEC kept the security boys watchful. The luggage roundabout worked efficiently and, within minutes, customs examination was over and Grant was ready to leave for the outer hall in remarkably good humour, considering he'd like a shower and a change of clothes. Fortunately, he had managed a quick shave and washed the sleep out of his eyes somewhere over Salzburg.

The main hall had its quota of people come to welcome the new arrivals. He made his way among them, stopped for a moment to set down his suitcase and adjust his overnight bag, check his watch with the new time on the big clock, and look for the sign directing him to the taxi exit. At that moment, a man stepped in front of him.

'Mr Grant?' The man was young, early thirties perhaps, neat in a light grey suit, fair hair well brushed; a pleasant face and quiet manner. 'I am here to meet you. I have the car parked just to the side of the building – a short walk. Let me.' His English was good. He lifted the suitcase, glancing at its label, and was already two paces away towards the main exit.

'Just a moment.' Grant caught up with him, ready to grab back the suitcase. 'Who sent you to meet me?'

'The Danube Travel Service. Sorry to hurry you, but the police have strict regulations about parking near the airport.'

This could be another example of Gene Marck's (or Lois Westerbrook's?) efficiency. I'll give this man until we reach the street, then I'll hail a cab, Grant decided. 'I can carry my own case,' he said, and felt more reassured as the man released it. 'How did you know who I was?'

'You were the only man who fitted the description that Danube Travel gave me.'

'Who supplied them with that?'

'A telex arrived last night, with description and instructions. You're going to the Majestic? Nice place. You'll be comfortable there.'

'Where did the telex come from?'

The man shrugged. 'I just got an order this morning to meet the nine forty-five flight from Kennedy. My name's Frank. I'm your driver for your stay here.' He turned as they reached the street. 'Just around this corner, Mr Grant. Not too far. If you don't mind, I'll hurry ahead and make sure we aren't getting into trouble with the police.' He had his car keys out, and now he was scanning the road he was about to cross.

A driver for his stay here? Grant shook his head. Lois Westerbrook had promised him first-class travel all the way, but this was really pampering him. Besides, what the devil would he do with a driver? He could manage very well with walking around Vienna, helped out by the odd taxi when he needed one. He followed Frank across the road. He ought to be grateful for the neat black Mercedes, whose doors were now being unlocked: the few cabs around were already taken.

'In here, sir,' Frank was saying, holding open the rear door. 'You'll be more comfortable.' He made that certain by taking the suitcase and dropping it by the driver's seat.

They took the long highway north-west from the airport near Schwechat. Frank was an excellent chauffeur, holding the steady pace of sixty miles an hour with no compulsion to pass every vehicle in sight or to tailgate the car ahead. When they came to the little town itself, he took a left turn, saying easily, 'We'll make a small detour to the south-west and avoid the traffic block on the main road. It was bad earlier this morning – thought I'd never get to the airport.'

'You're the driver,' Grant said. 'What's the trouble with the traffic?' He was remembering the spider-web of highways around Vienna.

'Ever since that Danube bridge collapsed last year we've had one big headache. Besides,' Frank added, 'the route I'll take is much prettier. We'll be in the country most of the way.' He lowered his speed to fifty as they turned on to a narrower road.

And Grant, remembering that the unique thing about Vienna was that hills and woods and vineyards often began on the immediate outskirts of city streets and concrete, found no fault with that. 'How much longer will this detour be?'

'Just over half an hour. I know the short-cuts well. In fact I follow this route most of the time. It's easier on the nerves.'

Anything would be better than the monotony of a long straight highway, thought Grant. 'Your English is excellent. American accent?'

'I was two years in Chicago. But I missed the mountains and forests. Here, a three-hour drive at the weekend and I'm among the big boys – nine thousand, ten thousand feet high.'

So they talked about climbing and skiing as Frank drove through woods and villages. As he had said, the

56

empty roads he was so skilfully following, branching from one to another without any delays or traffic jams, were much prettier.

'Isn't that Baden?' Grant asked, suddenly jolted into vigilance. The country town lay south of Vienna – probably some twelve, even fifteen miles south.

Frank pointed to the cosy houses, nestling between trees and multitudes of flowers. 'Quite recovered. You'd never know what it went through in forty-five.'

'I know,' Grant said curtly. This peaceful place had been the most raped – from young girls to grandmothers – and the most systematically looted town in all of Austria, perhaps in western Europe.

Frank sensed his disquiet. 'We'll take the road to Mayerling – no traffic there, pure country – then swing up to Vienna. No trouble at all. I'll have you at your hotel in good time.' He looked round to add, 'No extra charge. Your drive is paid for.'

Grant just shook his head, restrained a smile. He had to admit that there was no urgency in reaching his hotel: he had no meetings, no business to attend to. For the next few days he was entirely free to do as he pleased. He relaxed, settled back in the comfortable seat of the Mercedes. The airport was a long drive from the city, so why fuss over a few extra miles? He might as well enjoy a taste of scenery before he plunged into city streets: this twisting road, as empty of traffic as Frank had promised, displayed plenty of it.

Frank was looking worriedly at the sky, bright blue only five minutes ago, now darkening with a mass of clouds moving in from the west.

The cumulus clouds have caught up with me, Grant thought. 'Rain?'

'And plenty of it. Glad we're not in the middle of a traffic jam.'

'What about this road?' It was running straight now, along a narrow valley with wooded hills on either side.

'Good surface. No problem, even in a downpour. There's less wind-force here than on an open highway.'

'There's someone who already has a problem,' Grant said, pointing just ahead. A small grey Fiat was drawn up at the side of the road, its hood raised. A man straightened his back from his inspection of the engine and looked at the oncoming Mercedes. A girl, sitting by the opened door, swung her legs out on to the ground, and rose. She had smooth dark hair, cut short to show – even from this distance – the neat silhouette of her well-shaped head.

'Do we stop?' Frank was asking, slowing his speed.

'Sure.' Grant recovered from his initial shock. The girl could have been Jennifer if her hair had been longer. She was the same height, had the same proportions. 'They don't look like terrorists to me.'

Frank didn't smile. But he agreed, for he brought the Mercedes to a halt. He spoke in German. 'Can we help?'

'Nothing can be done. I've checked,' the man replied in German, closing the hood. 'It's the battery. Just faded out on us. Can you give us a lift to the nearest place where I can find a tow-truck?'

'That will be on the outskirts of Vienna itself,' Frank said in English, looking at Grant.

'Better tell them to hop in,' said Grant, opening a door. The first isolated drops of rain, large and heavy, were beginning to plop on the car's roof, promising a sudden deluge. The girl made a dash for the Mercedes, hands over her head, her blue summer dress fluttering round her excellent legs, laughter in her voice as she said, 'Thank you,' and then *'Vielen Dank!'* as she slipped in beside Grant.

'English will do,' he told her.

'Bob!' she called in delight to the man who was now

leaving car keys under the Fiat's visor, 'we found an American!' He ran to join them – a man about Grant's own age, of medium height, with even features and longish brown hair. He was dressed in tweed jacket and flannels. He came round to the other side of the car and climbed in, so that Grant – a little to his surprise – now found he was sitting between the newcomers. Even if his feet had a precarious hold on the raised central section of the floor, he was comfortable enough once he had hoisted his overnight bag into the front seat beside his suitcase.

Apart from the fact that she was slender, the girl didn't take much room: she had pulled herself as far into the corner of the seat as possible, leaving extra space for him. 'No need to do that,' Grant told her, and won a shy smile. She still kept her distance. For a moment, he watched her profile, her face now turned to frown at the heavy rain. No, she wasn't like Jennifer: not close up. This girl's eyes were dark brown, not blue; her features were less perfect, pretty but not startlingly beautiful. Definitely not a replica of Jennifer, not even in manner. Jennifer would have been talking, making amusing comments with her usual vivacity, getting them all to smile and relax. This girl seemed withdrawn, almost cold in her detachment. Or painfully shy? Nervous?

Her companion certainly wasn't. His manner was easy, as if being picked up on a lonely country road were a daily occurrence. 'My name is Renwick, Robert Renwick. This is Miss Avril Hoffman, at your right elbow. Sorry to put you to this trouble. We're grateful for it. We were due at the office ten minutes ago.'

I see, thought Grant in a flight of romantic guessing: business associates (boss and secretary?) returning from a night in the country. Travelling light, too; but Miss Hoffman's outsize shoulder-bag could hold two tooth-brushes quite easily. 'Glad to help out. The name is Grant, by the way, Colin Grant.'

Renwick stared at him. 'Colin Grant?' He was incredulous. 'Well, well, well . . .'

The next thing he'll tell me, Grant was thinking, is that he has read my book – one of the two thousand and sixty-three people who have actually bought it. Or perhaps he borrowed it from a library: that was usually the case. In spite of the lack of royalties, it was soothing to an author's ego even if it didn't help his bank account.

But Renwick said, 'We have a friend in common.'

'Oh?'

'Dwight O'Malley.'

Grant raised an eyebrow. 'O'Malley?' was all he could say.

'Yes. Old Dwight. He was supposed to be here this week-end. He called me last night from Geneva – has to postpone his visit for a few weeks. Mentioned that he'd just had a note from you, and was sorry he'd miss you. Told me to try and track you down at your hotel and hoist one for him.'

Geneva was correct: so was Grant's scrawled note to O'Malley before leaving New York. Grant's attack of disbelief ended. The amusing side of life was its pleasant surprises. Coincidences did happen. 'How long have you known him?'

'Off and on since college. He went into the army along with me. You did your service with him in Germany, didn't you?'

'We trained together, but in Germany I stayed with the poor bloody infantry. O'Malley went into —' Grant stopped short. O'Malley had disappeared into some hush-hush outfit: codes, it was thought. Intelligence? Was he still following along with that? Grant looked with a fresh eye on Robert Renwick. 'Were you posted to Germany too?'

Renwick nodded. 'Up among the potato fields. Never will forget the smell of dung that the farmers scattered around. When I asked a Fräulein what was the awful stench, she giggled and said *"Landluft!* Country air, we call it." Never could eat a potato since then.'

'Are you still in the army?' Grant asked bluntly.

'No. I'm at present attached – temporarily – to our Embassy here.'

'So you're just visiting Vienna?'

'For a couple of months.'

'Where's your home ground? Washington?'

'Actually, it has been Brussels for the last few years.'

NATO? Grant wondered. Tactfully, he said, 'I used to live in Washington. Thought we might have more friends in common.' He looked at the silent girl, who was still fascinated by the torrent of rain sweeping over the car's windows.

Renwick noticed his speculation. 'Avril's a pure Londoner, even if she spent the first three years of her life in New York. I'm helping her lose her accent.'

'Neat duty you've drawn in Vienna,' Grant said with a grin, and refrained from asking more questions. He had reached the end of the allowed quota, he decided. Renwick's frankness – if he were connected with some form of Intelligence – had better not be tested much more. Then Grant asked himself three questions: Why so much frankness? A method of winning trust? Or just natural friendliness? Renwick would be a gregarious type, as much outgoing and forthright as the girl was introspective and silent. 'Avril is a charming name,' he told her profile. 'Were you born in April? Then you should like rain-showers.'

She turned her dark eyes on him. They were her best feature, he thought – large and soft and luminous, reminding him of a Byzantine portrait. She smiled. 'Only if it's warm rain.'

Renwick cut in with, 'What about you? Staying long in Vienna, city of my dreams?'

'Two weeks, I hope.' Perhaps less, damn it.

'Business or pleasure?'

'A little of each. Museums and *Weinstüberl*.'

'Of course, you're the expert on art.'

'Hardly.'

'Don't know much about painting,' Renwick confessed. 'I belong to the I-know-what-I-like school. What's your favourite field? Impressionism, Abstract, Contemporary Realism, or just good old-fashioned Dutch and Flemish?'

Grant's spine stiffened. The girl might have sensed it. 'Isn't this rain appalling?' she asked softly.

'In Brussels, of course,' Renwick went on, very casual, very conversational, 'they still worship the seventeenth-century masters. You see nothing but reproductions of them all around the place.'

'It was a pretty good century for painting,' Grant said evenly.

'Still is, for those who are now investing in it. Ironic, isn't it? The artists got enough to keep them alive, and—'

'Oh, Sir Peter Paul Rubens didn't do too badly.' Let's get off this subject, Grant warned himself, and tried a small diversion. 'He didn't only paint bouncing beauties and collect a fortune: he also was a diplomat, travelled widely, and turned secret agent when necessary. Interesting life, wouldn't you say?'

Renwick wasn't diverted. He went on, 'Today the prices have gone sky-high. In Brussels, even the enthusiasts for—' He leaned across Grant to ask the girl, 'What was the name of the painter who was bought for two hundred thousand dollars a few months ago?'

'Ruysdael,' she said. 'Salomon van Ruysdael.'

'Good old Sal. Two hundred big ones. Enough to have him leaping out of his grave. Even the Bruxellois thought it ridiculous.'

'It's a bit high,' Grant agreed. He was worried. Not only by the mention of Ruysdael, but by the price. God, he thought, do I find myself carrying back to New York a picture that's into six figures?

'What would *you* pay for a Ruysdael?' Renwick asked, all innocence.

'If I had the cash?' Grant mustered a broad smile. 'Well, I don't know. Between fifty and seventy thousand, I suppose – depending on its state, of course.'

'I hear they've been getting a hundred and fifty thousand, recently. But this two hundred thousand sale—' Renwick shook his head. 'I'm in the wrong racket. I'd better take up painting.' There was a brief laugh all around, and then silence. Renwick reached into his pocket for a small notebook and pencil. He wrote: Boltzmanngasse 16, tel. 34-66-11. 'That's our Embassy,' he said. 'Ask for extension 123 and get through to me direct. Okay?' He tore off the page, handed it to Grant. 'Get in touch if you need any help.'

'Help?'

'Some emergency – you never can tell.'

'I'm here to enjoy myself,' Grant told him. 'And I do know Vienna. I'll find my way around.'

'I'm sure you will,' Renwick said soothingly. He leant forward and tapped Frank's shoulder. He spoke in German again. 'That garage looks a likely place. Let us out over there.' He held out his hand to Grant. His grasp was firm. 'We'll meet again, I hope. Many thanks. Come on, Avril – let's get that new battery and find us a taxi.'

'You're going all the way back?' Grant asked.

'May have to – if there's no tow-truck around.'

Avril said, 'At least it has stopped raining.'

Grant watched them go. She isn't as simple as all that, he was thinking. There had been a sudden smile repressed, a moment's laughter in her eyes, when he talked about Rubens. Avril Hoffman and Bob Renwick had only to wait five minutes at the gas station. 'There he is,' Renwick said as their grey Fiat with Prescott Taylor at the wheel made a careful turn to reach the garage. 'Right on the button,' he added, glancing at his watch. 'Hi, Prescott! Did you get your feet wet?'

'Only slightly damp.' The trees at the side of the road, where the Fiat was left abandoned, had been thick enough to shelter Taylor from most of the rain and Grant's quick eyes. 'Did it go well?'

'Hope so.' Renwick helped Avril into the front seat, climbed in after her. 'This will warm you,' he told her, crushing her between him and Taylor. 'Didn't even bring a cardigan, you idiot. What do you think Austria is? The Caribbean?' Then, serious, he turned to Taylor. 'At least we started him thinking. My God – the questions he asked: you'd have thought I was the one being quizzed. He's no slouch. I'll say that for him.'

'Frank – how did he do?'

'He makes a pretty good chauffeur: said nothing, listened to everything.'

'That's what he wanted, wasn't it?'

'That was the deal. Without his information, we'd be fighting this thing blind.'

Avril said, 'He frightens me.'

'Frank? He's on our side, honey. For the time being.' Frank Krimmer had been more co-operative than the usual Israeli agent. Those Mossad guys were tough . . . 'He's friendly. Even if our interests don't always coincide, he's – well—' Renwick searched for the right word, but everything he thought of was too soft in feeling. Frank could be as rigid as a block of granite. 'Well,' Renwick ended lamely, 'he's helping us as much as we help him.'

Avril said, 'He never really jokes – only on the surface, but not deep down.'

'He may not have much to joke about,' Renwick said grimly, and Prescott Taylor nodded his agreement.

'But,' she insisted, 'you joke all the time, both of you.'

'Which means we are two gentle lambs,' Renwick told Taylor.

Avril said stiffly, 'That's carrying it too far. I was only saying—'

'I know, my pet.' Renwick squeezed her shoulder. 'Where's your own sense of humour? Caught a chill on that damned road?'

'I never did see Mayerling,' she said.

'We passed it – one small store waiting in the rain for the tourists.'

'There's the hunting lodge too, where the Archduke and his Vetsera—'

'All for love. Touching. You know, I never thought much of that double-suicide story. What about two murders, made to look like a death-pact? Could have been political. Archduke Rudolf was not behaving like an Emperor's proper son and heir.'

'I still want to see the hunting lodge.'

'You can't. No one is allowed to enter its gates, unless she's a Carmelite nun. And then she stays for good.'

Taylor said, with a touch of impatience, one hand smoothing his thin fair hair back over an incipient bald spot, 'Before we scatter, what's our next move?'

'With Grant? We wait.'

'Not too long,' said Taylor worriedly.

'Not too long.' Renwick turned to Avril. 'Cheer up, old girl. The nuns say a prayer every day for the soul of the Archduke Rudolf. Doesn't that make you feel good all over?'

'What about La Vetsera?' Avril demanded.

'The Archduchess and I never mention that name.'

'Oh, Bob! Really—' But she was laughing.

'We drop you here, Prescott,' said Renwick, 'and you

can taxi in style to the Embassy. You don't want to be seen arriving in a rented car with a low-grade attaché.'

'Certainly not. Especially when he's a newcomer, of very temporary status, who can't be taken seriously.' Taylor was giving his proper-Bostonian imitation. 'Just one of those nuisances that get foisted on us—'

'Like me?' Avril asked. Her dual citizenship had raised an eyebrow for the first week or two. After that, acceptance – especially when her work was only part-time, helping out with a shortage in translators.

'But such a charming nuisance,' said Taylor, 'proficient in six foreign languages.' He drew up the Fiat at the curb, disentangled his long legs, saying, 'Why the hell don't you get a car with room?' as he closed the door behind him.

'Now,' said Renwick as he took the wheel, 'here's what I think we should do in the next few days.' He began detailing the problem, words explicit, sentences concise. The quizzical tone of voice had vanished. Avril listened intently, her face as grave as his.

6

Just who were these people? Grant kept coming back to that question. Speculations had been pouring through his head as he showered and had a closer shave than he had managed on the plane, and then – in the terry robe that the Majestic provided for its guests along with heated bathroom floors – a second, if belated, breakfast of croissants and coffee. Now, still wearing the comfortable robe, he flopped down on the bed (one of two in this giant room, full-size each of them) and might have fallen asleep except that his mind wouldn't let him.

He tried a soothing explanation. Coincidences did happen. This guy Renwick knew Dwight O'Malley, and it was quite natural for O'Malley to drop Grant's name in the middle of a telephone call between the two. Okay, perfectly acceptable: small world, and that kind of thing. But the steering of the conversation on to Ruysdael? The mention of inflated prices – as if Renwick guessed or had a vague suspicion that I was about to acquire a Ruysdael – might have been made with a purpose: to jolt the truth out of me that I was suffering from momentary shock because of this unexpected rise in value. Why? he would have asked: are you a prospective buyer? Right there he'd have known – not guessed, but known – that I was covering for someone. Most definitely. I don't have enough cash to buy a Ruysdael at even a few thousand dollars; or pay for a hundred-dollars-per-day room in a luxury hotel. Dwight O'Malley knows that damned well.

But O'Malley hadn't known (and therefore Renwick

hadn't known either) where I was going to stay. All I mentioned in my note to O'Malley was the fact that I was leaving New York on the 26th for Vienna. That was vague enough. Or was it? Renwick had only to check the passenger list of the overnight flight to Vienna – and he'd have my arrival to the minute. Whereupon I was met by a nice quiet type like Frank, who seemed to be authentic: he knew whom to meet and where to take him. Damn it all, *did* he know about the Majestic – or did he learn that from the label on my suitcase?

Which brings me to Herr Frank himself. He sat there, able to hear everything we said, all along that Mayerling road. Renwick wasn't whispering: his voice had been normal. What's more, Renwick wouldn't have been so forthcoming about himself, about Brussels and NATO (only a fool would have missed drawing that inference), if there were some unknown chauffeur picking up every word he uttered. Renwick knew Frank: they were in this together.

'Hell and damnation,' he said aloud, his muscles tightening. He sprang up from the bed, stood for a moment, rigid with anger. They were pushing him around like a bloody pawn. We'll see about that, but first things first.

He began unpacking his case. His two suits had travelled well, but they looked somewhat lonely in the vast wardrobe. It reminded him to search for the notice, which hotels were obliged to post, giving the cost of the room. He found it discreetly displayed behind the bedroom door that led to his small private hall. One thousand seven hundred schillings a day, not including breakfast. That brought the total over the hundred-dollar mark. Lois Westerbrook, or Gene Marck, had slipped up there. Badly. That was the trouble with these guys who worked for the super-rich, lived with them, became accustomed to wealth: they forgot how other people lived. First-class accommodation Lois had promised him. Sure, he had travelled like that often enough, but this went far beyond first class. This was unadulterated luxury. Have a good cover story ready for your friends, Marck had warned him and even suggested a couple of articles on the Brueghels in the State Museum. Blast his eyes, did he think you could write two short articles on seventeen intricate masterpieces? One thing he had done: he had made up Grant's mind not to go near the Brueghels, not this trip. Damn me, Grant thought, if I'll take any hand-me-down idea from a man who estimates art in terms of money: this painting is depreciating in dollar value, so sell; this one is rising, so buy. You'll double your investment in three years: a greater future than pork bellies on any commodity market.

He cooled down while he finished unpacking the overnight bag. Jennifer's photograph, now covered for safe travel by transparent plastic instead of glass, went on the dressing-table. He could see her dancing around this room, thin negligee flowing loose, her laughter rising as she dropped on the chaise-longue in a Récamier pose. Jennifer . . . And there was a flash of memory, to the man who called himself Frank, talking pleasantly of skiing and mountain-climbing. In the winter, Jennifer and he had gone skiing; in the summer, they had climbed mountains. Did Frank know as much as all that about him? A carefully dropped allusion to make Frank quickly acceptable? Just one of us, good old Frank.

All right, Grant decided, his lips tight, I'll check up on Frank. He finished dressing, then searched in the telephone book for the Danube Travel Service, half expecting no entry to be found. But it was there. He rehearsed a few sentences in German and made the call.

After the eighth ring, a woman answered. She sounded efficient, even if dilatory. Yes, this was Danube Travel, could we be of assistance, sir?

'Is Frank there?'

'Which Frank?'

'The one who met me at the airport this morning.'

'We met several people. On which flight were you?'

'Arriving from New York at nine forty-five.'

'Oh yes. Just a moment.' After some brief consultation, she said, 'I am sorry, but Frank is not here at the moment. Is there a complaint?'

'No, no. Excellent driver. But I don't need any car for my visit to Vienna. Has he cancelled that arrangement?'

She rustled a page. 'I don't see any further bookings.'

'Good. How much do I owe you for this morning?'

'It is paid.'

'Who paid it?'

'The party who ordered the car.'

'Who was that? I have to thank him. You understand?'

'Oh.' She was uncertain. 'I understand, *gnädiger Herr*. But I don't see any name.'

'Impossible,' he said, deciding to sound short-tempered. 'You must have some record of the payment.'

'It was charged to one of our regular clients.' And that, said her tone of voice, was all she was going to tell him.

'Did the telex come from New York? You must know. Or from Geneva?' From New York, it was possibly Lois Westerbrook. From Geneva – Dwight O'Malley.

'There was no telex. The order was telephoned this morning.'

Quickly, he asked, 'Is Frank one of your regular drivers?'

That nearly caught her unawares. Her voice was vague as she replied at last, 'Now and then. When we are busy—'

'—you need extra help. Of course.' Grant was most understanding. 'Well, I guess I can't write that letter of thanks.' He rang off.

No telex. Frank's explanation at the airport had been a lie. Or, as Frank might see it, a necessary diversion from the truth to get Grant safely into the Mercedes. And the detour via Baden to the Mayerling road? Another manoeuvre. One thing was certain, Robert Renwick had taken considerable care to keep his meeting with Grant as secret as possible. But why?

The question would have no answer until he met Renwick again. I'll call him, Grant decided, arrange to see him, demand some explanation. Was that what Renwick really wanted – another encounter, with a fair exchange of information? I've got to know what's behind all this mystery – or as much as he can tell me. Would he tell me? Could I believe him? Is he as much a fake as Frank? Well, I can check on him too.

Grant found his travel address book with its page for names of friends and business acquaintances who lived abroad. A slip of paper fell out, with the Schofeld Gallery's imprint at its head: that was Max Seldov being helpful – a brother-in-law here in Vienna, who owned the Two Crowns Hotel. 'A fine man, you'll like him,' Seldov had said. 'Married my youngest sister, may she rest in peace.' For a moment, Grant's mind was side-tracked by the Two Crowns. Later, he told himself, later. Now, he'd telephone Geneva. He might catch Dwight O'Malley in his office before he left for lunch. If not, he'd leave a message: urgent – call back at six o'clock. Damned if I'm going to spend my first afternoon in Vienna hanging around a telephone.

The hotel operator put him quickly through to Geneva. O'Malley was there, just out of a meeting and about to leave for a luncheon engagement. He was exceedingly friendly, though. Covering a slight nervousness? 'I'll keep it short,' Grant told him. 'I met a friend of yours today.'

'Oh?'

'The one you told I was coming to Vienna.'

'Oh yes. Thought you'd like him. Did you?'

'That's why I'm calling you. How much should I like him?'

'He's completely dependable, if that's what is worrying you.'

'It is.'

'What did he tell you about himself?'

'He's on some official business here. Connected with NATO, I guessed. Right or wrong?'

'Right. Listen to what he says, Colin. He knows his way around – won't give you bad advice.'

'What about some truth as well?'

'That's a two-way street, old boy.'

'I think I'll call him and find out.'

'You have his number?'

'Yes, for emergencies.'

'Surely this isn't one, is it?' O'Malley's voice was perturbed. 'Colin, are you in some kind of jam?'

Grant considered. 'Not in any trouble. Just damned angry and puzzled.'

'Don't call him,' O'Malley urged. 'Better if you let me handle this, straighten it out for you. Just relax and enjoy Vienna until our friend contacts you.'

'Will he?'

'Of course. As soon as possible. Okay? He must have liked you – he doesn't pass out his telephone number to everyone he meets. He's a busy man.'

'I'm flattered,' Grant said mockingly.

'You should be,' O'Malley said. With that touch of censure he ended the call.

Grant went back to his own life. He riffled through his address book. He'd have lunch somewhere outside the hotel, at a café table in the fresh air, perhaps, and then walk around to get his sense of direction working. It had been seven years since his last visit to Vienna. He might even drop in to see Helmut Fischer who ran an art gallery near the Kärntnerstrasse – he was still there, judging from his card last Christmas. Or he might scout out the Two Crowns, see where it was located and what it looked like. 'Two weeks in Vienna?' Max Seldov had said, a delighted grin spreading across his thin face. 'That's where I spent a few years as a child – still have some relatives there, the ones that survived. I took Eunice to visit them ten years ago, when the kids were younger and could travel at half-fare. A different proposition today. Where are you stopping?'

'Not sure yet.'

'Look, if you want a real nice place, try the Two Crowns. First-class, but small. Quiet. The food's good. You'll like it.'

'Is it central?' Grant had asked, searching for a polite refusal.

'Just off the Schotten Ring.'

'I had thought of a hotel nearer the Opern Ring.' The Majestic was close to that district, easy walking distance from all the big museums.

'And that will cost you an arm and a leg. Why don't you look at the Two Crowns? Ask for Bernie, he owns the place – you could drop in to see him, bring him news of me and the family. Here's his name and address.' Seldov had written them down on a small sheet of Schofeld stationery and pressed it into Grant's hand: Bernard Mandel, the Two Crowns, Schotten Allee. 'A fine man, you'll like him.' As an afterthought Seldov added, 'He'll make a special rate for you. I'll tell him.'

Grant had laughed. 'And I'll only lose an arm?'

'Perhaps just your little finger,' Seldov said smiling.

All right, Grant told himself now, let's have a look at the Two Crowns. What about Gene Marck, though, with his news of the date and place of the auction? No problem: Grant had his Vienna telephone number,

73

would notify him at once about any change of address. Marck would be shocked by the idea of the Two Crowns, yet it might be the place an art critic would stay without cracking his budget to pieces. Too bad to give up all this comfort, he thought, as he glanced around the room. He liked luxury as much as the next man. But it just wasn't in keeping with his cover story. He'd have to stay here, of course, until Robert Renwick made contact with him. After that, he could drop out of sight, and – what was the current phrase? – keep a low profile. For there was one thing that worried him most of all, was never far away from his level of consciousness: a man's life could depend on his actions. One false step by Grant could end that man's chances for escape.

It was a challenge, of course: a deed in a treacherous world. It was also a responsibility, growing heavier by the hour. This was not the way he had wanted to visit Vienna, but it was too late to back out. Keep your mind fixed on the challenge, he told himself as he stepped out of the Majestic's impressive lobby into a broad thorough-fare and turned left towards the Opern ring. Around him were handsome buildings of light stone, decorated and expansive in nineteenth-century style, with here and there structures in subdued contemporary, so that they fitted in with their older neighbours as well as filling the gaps made by bombs and shells. Sunshine and flowers and trees, bustling traffic, well-dressed people, a general feeling of optimism – it seemed as though the nightmare of 1945 was buried with the discarded rubble. Perhaps they were putting a good face on it all, like the modern buildings that obliterated the war damage. If I were a Viennese, thought Grant as he crossed the wide square before the Opera House, once gutted by flames and now duplicated in splendour, I'd always be conscious that Czechoslovakia's barbed wire and Hungary's armed watchtowers were less than thirty miles away. So what would I do? Enjoy today, and concentrate on tomorrow's neutrality, that comforting if fragile word. Eat, drink – appropriately, he was approaching the Kärntnerstrasse, heading for one of its restaurants – and give a damned good imitation of being merry.

The Kärntnerstrasse had changed, miraculously. Its once crowded and noisy traffic had been banned. Only pedestrians allowed, and flower stalls, and café tables under bright umbrellas. This was where he'd lunch, even if it was only a sandwich and beer. He wouldn't have to give that imitation of being merry. His depression had dropped away and was replaced by a sense of intense pleasure that he hadn't known for ten months.

His euphoria would have been short-lived if he had been aware of the stranger who, loitering near the Majestic's entrance, had picked up his trail, had seen him settle down at a café table. Only then did the man leave, straight for the nearest phone, and return – keeping a safe distance and careful watch until relieved of duty. It was almost two o'clock. She'd be here, any moment.

7

'May I join you?' she asked. 'All the other tables are so crowded.' Avril Hoffman sat down across from him, signalled to a waitress, and ordered strudel and coffee. 'The working girl's lunch,' she told Grant. In an undertone she added, 'Don't recognize me.' She glanced around her at the people having a late and leisurely meal under bright-coloured umbrellas.

He recovered from his surprise. 'That was quick,' he said, thinking of his phone call to O'Malley. He remembered to lower his voice. 'You got my—'

'Yes. It seemed urgent.' Now, it was the large pots of petunias that seemed to catch her attention.

'How did you know where to find me?'

'Let's talk of something else. Meanwhile. And not too much of that, either.' She made herself comfortable, hitching the strap of her handbag over the back of her chair, smoothing the skirt of her blue dress, picking up a paper napkin.

'Just two strangers sharing a table,' he suggested, and politely moved his glass of beer to give her more space.

She nodded. 'With an occasional remark, and lots of silence in between.'

Anyway, she could talk: this morning he had doubted it. 'We can always discuss your favourite subject.'

She looked at him quickly, smooth dark head tilted, eyes large and wondering.

'The weather,' he said with a grin.

She laughed, and pretended it was over the slice of strudel that came with its dollop of whipped cream. '*Was für Kalorien!*' she told the waitress, who obviously paid little attention to calorie-counting. Avril pushed aside the cream with a fork, and began eating. 'Slow up, there!' she warned him. He had almost finished his sandwich. 'I should leave first.'

'And I follow you?' At least she knows where she's going, which is more than can be said for me.

She tested her coffee, frowned, and added some sugar. 'At a distance, of course.' She ate some more mouthfuls of strudel before she spoke again. 'Kapuziner-kirche, Neuer Markt. Meet me there in ten minutes. I'll be driving a white Volkswagen, German plates. Get in quickly. Make sure you aren't followed.' She called the waitress and paid the small bill, explaining that the apple strudel was excellent but one had to suffer to keep one's weight down, *nicht?* The waitress understood, shook her head in smiling sympathy as Avril left.

Did the gentleman want another beer? 'This will be enough,' he told her, but she might as well give him his bill now and save herself another journey back to this table. He was ready to leave three minutes after Avril's departure. The Neuer Markt was only a block away, but he'd better approach it indirectly.

This time, he was paying attention to anyone who moved when he moved, halted when he halted. Frankly, he felt ridiculous, yet her eyes had held a real warning, even anxiety. For him? Beautiful eyes, he thought, dark brown, soft and expressive – the *occhi parlanti*, speaking eyes, that Italians praised. He was reasonably sure that no one was following him; to make certain, he walked further up the crowded Kärntnerstrasse than necessary before he branched off, first by one, then by another of the several old streets that complicated this district. He circled around, chose another little street, and entered the long stretch of the New Market, where, at the far corner, stood the Capuchin Church.

He had barely reached it when he saw the white Volkswagen approaching. For the few moments that were needed, he became engrossed in the church's baroque architecture. The car slowed down, its door opening, and he was inside.

'Quick enough?' he asked.

She nodded, but her eyes were on the traffic and the one-way directions of the narrow streets. 'No one followed?'

'If anyone tried it – well, I made it as difficult for him as possible.' Seven minutes of weaving through crowds and winding his way along packed streets. 'Who would be tailing me, anyway?'

'People who don't want you to talk with us.' As he shook his head in amused disbelief, she added, 'Didn't you know you were followed today, right from your hotel to your table? If we could track you, then others can, too.'

Followed, and duly reported? So that was how she had reached him quickly and surely. 'I'll remember that,' he said, the smile wiped from his face, his voice showing his annoyance. 'You had a man parked near my hotel? Or in the lobby?'

'He was there as a matter of protection.'

'I don't need or want any protection, thank you.'

The silence lasted until she brought the car into the Ring, where driving was less tortuous along the wide and extensive boulevard of various names, but whose course was constant, encircling the heart of the city. 'Do you like roses?' she asked suddenly. 'There's a park just up this way – it's a quiet place to talk.'

'Talk is certainly needed.' He was more relaxed now, could even laugh at the idea of protection. 'But will Renwick allow it?'

She didn't answer. She was thinking of Bob Renwick's last injunctions. *Be as frank as possible. Tell him what he*

*needs to know. Get his co-operation. It's up to you, Avril.
You'll handle it well.* 'Oh dear,' she said, and sighed.

Grant studied her. 'You're his messenger-girl, aren't you?' he asked gently. There had been something pathetic in that sigh.

'Such as I am.'

'How did you get into this work?'

Here come the questions, she thought. Bob had warned her to expect plenty. 'Languages. French and German at school, and some Hungarian at home. My mother was brought up in Budapest – a diplomat's daughter. Then on a summer holiday I visited Florence, and fell madly in love. And so, of course, I had to learn Italian. I knew it quite well before I found he had a wife and two children living in Perugia. So goodbye to nineteen-year-old dreams. But I kept on learning Italian. You see, languages do help you to travel. That became my next ambition – living abroad, seeing new places. Restless? Yes. But romantic, too.'

'You definitely got into adventure when you teamed up with Renwick. When did that happen?'

'A few years ago. I was working in my father's office in London – he imports and exports. And Bob walked in one day on business, and heard me trying to pronounce Russian.'

'So that was your next language. Any more?'

'Some Flemish. For a time, I lived in Brussels.'

'And now you're in Vienna, speaking most beautiful Austrian. You'd pass as a *Wienerin* any day. Where are you working?'

'At the American Embassy. There's a shortage of translators at the moment. I fitted in – temporarily, of course.'

'But you're British, aren't you? How did our Embassy—'

'Dual citizenship. My parents lived in New York for

almost six years. I was born there.' They had turned off the Ring into a space for cars before a large park. 'We weren't followed,' she said as she switched off the engine and pocketed the keys. 'Shall we walk?'

This corner of the park was all garden, Grant saw, enormous acreage, and with nothing but roses. Trees and bushes, laden with clusters of velvet petals, every hue, every size and shape and variety, flanked the long paths or circled into beds of vivid colour. He stood quite still for a few moments, and then he looked at Avril and raised an eyebrow. She smiled in delight at his approval. 'My favourite place in Vienna,' she said.

They began their stroll between the lines of roses. There were other people around, but the garden was so extensive that there was plenty of choice in solitary paths. It seemed as though the tourists, like Grant himself, had never heard about this section of the park: either that, or there was too much else to visit in their short stay here.

She wasted no time. 'We hear you have some questions.'

'I have. Who is Robert Renwick? Who is Frank? You, I know about: a translator working for Renwick at the Embassy.'

'No, I work mostly for Prescott Taylor. Bob calls on my services occasionally – just as he does with the other girls in the secretarial pool. Bob and Prescott avoid each other as much as possible. Publicly, that is.'

'You're their link?' A neat arrangement.

She nodded. 'Frank, however, belongs to another – another organization. He isn't an American. That's all I can say.' Not a word about Israeli Intelligence, she thought, until we can clear it with Frank, and that I doubt.

'But he's working along with you?'

'Our interests coincide.'

'And what are they? Can you tell me?'

'Well—' She considered for a moment. 'Completely confidential, you understand?'

'Completely.'

Her eyes searched his. Hesitation vanished. 'It might be best for me to describe our fields of interest. That could give you an idea of our joint effort here.'

So they were three men – a diplomat, an Intelligence-officer, and a non-American – who shared a common problem in Vienna. 'I'm listening.'

'Prescott Taylor is an attaché, and one of his jobs is dealing with defectors. He sorts them out, as it were, and if he thinks they are the real thing, not just KGB-trained infiltrators, he will steer them into the right department in Washington, where – after examination and further testing – their information can be put to use.'

Grant waited. She had paused, perhaps for breath, more probably for a careful selection of her next words.

'Frank,' she went on, 'deals with refugees. Vienna is a gathering-place for them these days – just look at a map and see how it's situated. He helps them after they get across the frontiers; sometimes before that, too.'

'Is he an Israeli?' The Jewish refugees from Russia made Vienna their first stop.

She side-stepped a direct answer, said tactfully, 'Several countries are interested in the refugees. After all, some of them are fakes trying to take up residence in the free world.'

'Time-bombs?'

'If they slipped past – yes.'

'So we have a man who deals with defectors, and another with refugees. Pretty similar interests. Where does Renwick fit in?'

'There's quite a difference in interests,' she corrected

him, postponing the subject of Renwick himself. 'Defectors slip into an embassy or consulate and ask for asylum and secrecy. A matter of safety: they've been Communists, often in important or sensitive posts. They bring hard information as a guarantee that they are authentic. But refugees are quite another problem. Usually they are anti-Communist, private people, not connected with their government. All they have to bring is their possessions – usually only a suitcase. However, there are others, too, who have managed to hide their valuables and want to smuggle them out. It's too dangerous to risk carrying them. So they are sent by other ways – by a friendly foreigner, for instance, with special diplomatic privileges, or by some businessman who travels regularly – before their owners cross the frontier.'

'A pleasanter arrival than most.'

She glanced at him sharply.

'No, no. They've got my sympathy. But these refugees have money to live on. In that case, they don't need help from Frank. Do they?'

'Not if they can travel openly, with all their papers in order. There are some who aren't so fortunate: they have no exit permits; they must make secret border-crossings. These are the desperate ones. Yes, I'd say that men like Frank are much needed.'

Another world, he thought as he stared at a mass of *Tropicana* roses blazing red in the afternoon sun. 'And Renwick?' he persisted. 'What's his particular field?'

'Terrorists.'

'Good God.' Terrorists. How did they connect with refugees or defectors? 'Are you expecting another attack like that on the OPEC offices?' Two years ago, five oil ministers who were meeting in Vienna had been kidnapped, and one of their staff murdered.

'We don't deal with the Middle East,' she said, a touch on the defensive.

'Renwick concentrates on Europe?'

'From a particular angle.'

He waited, resisting another question. He'd learn more, and more quickly too, if he kept his mouth shut.

'Bob is stationed mainly in Brussels with a counter-terrorism unit. *Not*,' she added, as she noticed the speculative look on Grant's face, 'an action squad. The West relies, so far, on police or regular army to deal with any confrontation. But NATO was worried enough by the spread of terrorism to establish this unit. Its operation depends on brains, not brawn. Bob's particular assignment is the money angle. Who is subsidizing the terrorists, and how?'

'I can think of several governments who'd enjoy seeing the West plagued by terrorists, home-grown or imported. Yet – subsidies to all these groups?' Hundreds and hundreds of them around the world. The Russians' General Accounting Office would have a permanent headache. Besides, the Soviets didn't like spending their own money, or, for that matter, their own men.

'Not to all of them. Many are small, disjointed, irrational. They flare up, make their protests with hijackings or scattered bombings; and then they disintegrate – or get arrested. There are others, however – the real menace. Their aim? Dissension, terror, havoc, and always against the West. They have been well trained. Now, they are well directed. In some cases, they have been linked together. The threat is there. And increasing. Because of the money behind them.'

Yes, that could be one hell of a problem. But subsidies?

'Look,' she said, as if she sensed his scepticism, 'they earn no regular pay-cheques, they have no careers except violence. Yet they can afford rent and food and cars and lawyers. They don't wear rags either, nowadays. They have the right clothes to let them circulate among us, arouse no suspicions about their actual missions. They have been taught how to attack and kill; they have the weapons and supplies to do the job. And they travel by air, sometimes thousands of miles. That's expensive. Why, I couldn't afford on my salary to take a return trip to Hanoi, or North Korea; or Japan or Latin America; or Africa. But they do. So where is the money coming from?'

'They've robbed and stolen, both guns and money.'

'And have the police on their trail. The ones who concern Bob are those who can get large sums of money without the danger of being arrested for a criminal act.'

'Surely,' he insisted, 'subsidies like that can be traced to their origin.'

'Eventually, yes. That is why the Communist countries now find it more discreet to use indirect means.'

'Laundering the cash?' he suggested.

'It's more complicated, and much deadlier than that – for the victims.'

'I don't follow you.' He was perturbed.

'Bob can give you more details—'

'Damn him. What about you, right here and now? Don't you think I need to know?' he asked, his worry flaring into anger.

She hesitated, then nodded agreement. 'In the last three years, there have been several refugees from Communist countries who sent out their valuables ahead of them. These were sold privately if the buyers were the type to ask no questions. If a prospective buyer was an honest man who'd balk at secret deals, the valuable property was put up for auction. Everything open and legal.'

Grant looked at her sharply.

'Whatever money was paid, here in Vienna, whether by private transaction or through public auction, went into a bank account in Geneva. We've had reliable information on that. But we have still to find out the name of the man who owns that bank account.'

'The auctioneer would certainly know who got paid—'

'He doesn't see the purchase cheque. His fee is paid separately by special arrangement, it seems. As for the property he has sold – he has been told that discretion is necessary: for the original owner's safety, he should keep silent. He thinks he understands; he has sympathy for those who live behind barbed-wire frontiers, he doesn't want to endanger any refugee's escape. That's his story. Or perhaps he is just another smart operator. He is certainly not completely unaware of what's going on. Not like the man who bid at the auction last year, and got some magnificent jewellery – a million-dollar price for a complete *parure* of diamonds and emeralds, smuggled into Vienna from Prague. Original owner? Disappeared in transit.' She paused, drew a long slow breath. 'The new owner, of course, knew nothing at all about that disappearance. He was totally innocent. Like several others, whose payments all ended in Geneva. Of course, we didn't know about the Geneva bank account then. It was only six weeks ago that we got the first hint of it.'

'This man you say was innocent – he signed a cheque. To whom was it made out? He could have told you that.'

'Yes – if he had attended the auction himself and signed a cheque. He didn't. He couldn't be in Vienna – probably lives abroad. So he engaged a reputable agent to bid for him, supplied him with an open letter of credit – that's the usual procedure, including the fact that the agent wouldn't divulge the identity of his employer.'

'Why the secrecy? Some problem with his tax collector?' Trust the multi-millionaires to know all the dodges, Grant thought with amusement.

'Either that, or he wanted to avoid publicity. It isn't

safe to draw attention to great wealth nowadays. Fear of robberies, kidnapping—' She shook her head.

'Well,' Grant tried, 'if you don't know his identity, why don't you approach the Geneva bank? Put on some official pressure. Surely a documented report from NATO must carry some weight.'

'We can do that when we know the name of the bank. That's what we are searching for.'

He could see the difficulties. At present, Renwick would have to persuade *all* the banks in Geneva to divulge their private records for certain possible dates. Would they? He, too, shook his head and then made another try. 'Couldn't you persuade the agent to give you the name of his employer?'

'Possibly – if the agent were still alive. He had a fatal heart attack.' Just a few days, she reminded herself, after our Hungarian defector started talking. About auctions in Vienna. About a Geneva bank account.

'How many auctions dealing with refugees' smuggled-out property?'

'We know of fourteen. The buyers were absent.'

'There could be other agents, then. Fourteen?'

'No. There were three agents, all told, qualified to handle everything.'

'Three? That leaves two—'

'They have also died.' All three of them within one week, she thought.

He was aghast. 'Two more heart attacks?'

'No. Two accidents: one in Munich, the other in Zürich.'

'Well,' he said, 'well—' He tried to find a reason for three sudden deaths. 'Are you sure,' he asked slowly, 'that they knew nothing about the real purpose of these auctions?'

'Nothing. As little as the man who is about to bid for

a painting.' In fact, much less – now that I've dropped this warning she thought as she watched Grant's face.

Tight-lipped, he asked, 'Do you have proof of this conspiracy?' For conspiracy it was, an ugly word to cover an ugly deed.

'Proof, six weeks ago, from a defector who was in the KGB, and drew our attention to Geneva as one of the places where funds for terrorists were available. Proof, from Frank, who has lost several refugees – all men and women with valuables sent ahead of them. Proof, from our defector, of their secret arrests – his list of names coincided with our record of missing refugees. Proof, from Frank's source in Budapest, of the execution last month of a one-time art collector.' She hesitated, glanced at Grant, saw he was more than half-way to the truth. 'The man who owned the painting that Mr Victor Basset wants – Ferenc Ady.'

'Dead?' He was incredulous, but she had meant what she said, every word of it. Dead . . . executed last month . . . 'In June?'

'June twenty-ninth, to be exact.'

Eight, nine days before Lois Westerbook had met him. His mind went numb.

Avril said gently, 'Frank can tell you where and how. He has an eye-witness account.'

There was a long silence. 'Does Basset know?' he asked at last.

'Not yet. We are trying to contact him – judiciously: persuade him to keep the information to himself for the time being. He could be just the type to lose his temper and confront the people who got him into this mess. And there would go our investigation, months of preliminary work in Brussels, six weeks here in Vienna, and all to begin over again.'

'What about the Ruysdael?'

'Oh, Basset will get it. You'll be attending the auction on Friday.'

'*This* Friday?'

'It's early,' she agreed, misinterpreting his astonishment. 'This auction is way ahead of the usual season – that begins in September. But the Klars have been holding pre-season auctions for the last three years – to accommodate their foreign clients, they say.'

'Hold on, hold on! The Klars?'

'Klar's Auction Rooms is where the auction is. This Friday. Eleven o'clock. Didn't you know?'

'Not yet. They said they'd let me hear as soon as the auction was scheduled.'

'It has been arranged for the last three weeks – on July eighth, actually.' And that, she thought, was the day after he had met Lois Westerbrook and Gene Marck. She didn't press the point: superfluous, judging from his face.

The series of shocks subsided. His voice became matter-of-fact, almost cold. 'Are either Westerbrook or Marck, or both of them, connected with this plot to divert money to Geneva?'

Avril hesitated. 'We've no evidence of that. We do know that last December, and again in March, Lois Westerbrook came to Vienna and bought two Impressionists for Basset's collection: a Monet and a Degas. There was nothing complicated about those auctions. She appeared, quite openly, as Basset's representative. He wasn't a friend of the owners of those paintings, so he didn't insist on secrecy to protect their safety.'

'How were the payments made?'

'By cheque. Through his Vienna firm. The man there, who was authorized to sign the cheques, is close-lipped. He doesn't disclose any of his boss's financial business. Admirable, of course. But – for us – infuriating. We enlisted a less stalwart employee, who tried to find the cancelled cheques. They weren't on file. Destroyed, perhaps.' She sighed, smiled ruefully. 'Tantalizing, really. Basset is the sole buyer at those auctions whose name we actually know, yet we couldn't risk approaching him with mere suspicions and deductions. That might have blown our investigation before it was completed. Rob Renwick is thinking of an indirect way to reach Basset, make him listen, but only when the timing is right. You see?'

'Not altogether,' he admitted. He'd see better if she'd tell him more. 'What about Gene Marck – Basset's adviser on purchases?'

'He visits Europe half a dozen times a year. Partly on business for Basset, partly for his own pleasure. He's a convivial type – lots of acquaintances in Vienna.'

Convivial was not exactly the way Grant would have described Marck. Of course, he told himself, he had only seen Marck twice: the first time, silent and respectful; the second time, capable and brusque. There were men who kicked up their heels when they went abroad, the old who's-to-see-me syndrome – a release, perhaps, from too tight a routine at home. Disciplined would be his word for Marck. And Lois Westerbrook? 'I can't see Westerbrook betraying Basset's trust. She is just another innocent who—'

'Are you sure?'

That brought him up short. 'I'm not sure of anything,' he admitted unhappily. But he did remember her face when she had told him about a man who was trying to reach freedom. 'Ady . . . Was that his name?'

'Ferenc Ady.'

Was all this really true? Uncertain, baffled, his anxiety increased. So did his distrust. He watched her face, so frank and innocent, wondering if eyes that were so deeply warm and sympathetic could be deceivers. 'Why did you tell me so much?' he asked bluntly.

'Because you needed to know. Because we have a need to know, too.'

'I've a feeling you already have most of my story.'

'We guessed it, and then verified what we could.'

'Don't you want a play-by-play description?' he asked bitterly.

'Not necessary.' She smiled. 'You aren't under suspicion, Mr Grant.'

So I'm in the clear, he thought with a surge of relief. 'What do you want from me?'

'The name of the man who owns the bank account in Geneva.'

'And how do I get that?' Fantastic, he thought, totally impossible.

'The treasurer of Allied Electronics—'

'The guy with the closed lips?'

She almost smiled. 'He will write the cheque when you take possession of Ruysdael's *View of Utrecht*. Notice the name on the cheque. That's all.'

'That's all?' It seemed simple enough.

'But please be careful. Don't draw attention to the fact that you are interested. Please!'

There were a lot of pleases around there, he thought. Was she worried about his safety, or the success of this little mission?

'Something is still puzzling you,' she said.

'You left one thing out.'

Her eyes widened.

'How did Renwick become interested in me in the first place?' Did I blow it? Yet I followed Marck's instructions. I believed in them, damn it. Secrecy, security, no contact with Basset, complete discretion. All to save a man's life, a man who was already dead.

'Through Lois Westerbrook. She's been under surveillance ever since she bought those pictures in Vienna. It made us curious when she turned up in New York as

Jane Smith and hired a detective to have you followed. That was on the day of the Dali exhibition. She was making sure that she'd meet you at the Schofeld Gallery. Unobtrusively.' Avril was smiling.

He said stiffly. 'There were reasons for that.' Shock upon shock, he thought: followed, by God . . . 'Don't tell me you own a detective agency in New York.'

'Of course not. The man who runs it was curious about Miss Jane Smith, who paid his fee in cash by special messenger – all two hundred and fifty dollars of it. Obviously, her bank account was in some other name. He made a few enquiries, and—' She shrugged her shoulders. 'Well – you know how enquiries spread.'

'No, but I can make a guess. Your next step was to check me out?'

'We were interested in her contacts,' she admitted.

'Just making sure I hadn't been attending auctions in Vienna for the last three years.' He had to smile. In a way, this was comic. 'I visited Basset in Arizona. Didn't that seem suspicious?'

She shook her head. 'Victor Basset and you were just—' She stopped short, searching for a kinder word than 'used'.

'A couple of ignorant fools?' How do you like that, Basset? And it's the goddamned truth.

She said quickly, 'You are neither ignorant nor a fool. If you were, Bob would never have bothered about you. And would I have told you so much? But how else can we protect you?'

There was that word again: the second time protection had been mentioned. 'I'm in no danger.'

She was silent. Then she rose from the bench where they had been sitting. 'Aren't you?' she asked quietly as they began walking towards the distant gate. 'Can I give you a lift? Drop you not too far from your hotel?'

'Thanks, no. I'll stay here for a while.' And get my thoughts in better order.

'Then I'll leave you now. Call Bob as soon as you've got the name on that cheque.'

He remembered the Ruysdael. 'I won't have time to telephone anyone until I get that damned painting stowed away safely. I'm responsible for it.' Of course, he reconsidered, the waiting time in Vienna was no longer needed. His instructions would be altered. 'With Ferenc Ady dead, I might be leaving on Saturday's flight to New York.' And goodbye, he thought, to those two promised weeks in Vienna.

She had halted. 'They may not tell you he's dead, not until they want you to leave Vienna.' Perhaps not even then, she thought.

'Why on earth—' he began.

'I don't know; it's just a possibility. In any case, you'll have to play along with them. Forget you know about Ady, or his name.'

'Play dumb,' he said angrily.

'Play it smart – as usual.' There was a brief pause. She added, 'About getting in touch with Bob – you had a good point there. The picture could slow you down. I think one of us will have to meet you near the auction room. We'll let you know.'

Which reminded him. 'I may be changing my hotel.' Or perhaps it wasn't necessary now. He'd be leaving soon, it was hardly worth while.

'*That*,' she said with emphasis, 'might be a very good idea.' He looked at her quickly, but she went on, her voice calm and casual, 'What's the new address?'

'Nothing definite yet. Could be a small place called the Two Crowns, on the Schotten Allee. It was recommended by a friend who works at Schofeld's.'

'Who?'

'Max Seldov. His brother-in-law owns it – Mandel is his name.'

'We'll check.'

Was that really necessary? She was serious. His smile vanished. It was a strange goodbye: no parting word, no touch of a hand. Nothing, except that last long glance between them. And then she was walking away from him.

Light footsteps, blue skirt swinging, slender waist and straight shoulders, smooth head held high. She seemed so carefree – a pretty girl with no thoughts except those of love and romance in a world of roses. Incredulous, he watched her leave.

No one had paid any attention to her going, except Grant. The life of the garden went on: droves of women coming out for an afternoon stroll in the fresh air with clusters of children; old people sitting in pairs, or alone; wandering sweethearts, arms entwined; nature-admirers halting in wonder every ten paces; gardeners, working over the soil, weeding, pruning, and – near the gate – shaping the rose-trees in a bed labelled *Peace*. No one paid any attention to Grant either, as he left.

He was reasonably sure that neither Avril nor he had been followed. (Watch it, he warned himself: don't get paranoiac about that.) Patiently he waited for a taxi, and then settled for the next bus. He had meant to explore the Schotten Ring area – he was half-way to that district, anyway – and search out the Two Crowns Hotel, see what it looked like, perhaps have a drink in the bar. Suddenly he admitted he was exhausted. Blame the long flight from New York, or the crush of today's events, or the thoughts that were crowding his mind. He'd do better to get back to the Majestic, and allow himself to collapse in luxury for this night at least.

8

Because of the time-lag between Vienna and Washington Gene Marck was able to reach Lois Westerbrook with the news of Grant's arrival before she even had breakfast in her suite at the Shoreham. Victor Basset and his entourage, including her own secretary, his valet who was also his chauffeur, had been established there for the last week, allowing him to make easy trips to Basset Hill and inspect its structural alterations.

Gene Marck went straight to his problem. 'Did you order a car to meet Grant at the airport this morning?'

'Of course not.' She was annoyed. Did Gene really think she had been so foolish as to engage some travel service to supply a car? 'I wouldn't think of spreading the news of his arrival.'

'Someone knew he was coming.'

'He was met?'

'Yes.'

'By whom?'

'That's what we must find out.'

'But if there was someone who saw him being met—'

'There was. He tried to follow – but lost them somewhere on the highway into Vienna.'

So Grant's car must have taken a cut-off. 'One of your men?'

'No.'

One of Jack's then. She avoided saying the name. 'One of our friends?' she asked quietly.

'Yes. But he's so damned mad he is blaming us for not having a car ready to follow Grant's Mercedes. His man was stationed at the airport as a porter, wasn't supposed to leave unless there was an emergency.'

'We can't be blamed – who'd have expected it?' Obviously Jack had not, or else he'd have had a back-up man waiting in a car outside. Jack always seemed to have several helpers available.

'That doesn't make him any less angry.' Marck sounded morose, worried.

Grant's arrival was to have been standard, no big deal. A taxi was all that was needed. 'Did Grant arrange this Mercedes?'

'I've tried to phone him at his hotel. Twice. His line was busy each time. Then he was out – a late lunch at the Kärntnerstrasse. He arrived alone, left alone. He evaded—'

'Evaded? He may only have gone into a shop, browsed around. Didn't the man you had tailing him think of that?'

'Too many shops in that district.'

'Open at that time?'

Marck said angrily, 'Some were.' He softened his voice. 'You'd better visit Vienna and have a talk with Grant.'

'Why not you?'

'I'm leaving for Graz right now.'

'Darling, I've a lot to do here! The old man has already decided on two more alterations, and I've got to soothe the architect and the electrical expert and the —'

'When can you get away?'

'But I wasn't supposed to be in Vienna. My third trip within eight months – too much exposure.'

'You can handle that. *And* Grant. Can you be here by Friday?'

In forty-eight hours . . . 'You'll be seeing him on Friday, at the auction,' she objected. Much ado about nothing, she told herself.

'Only briefly. You'll spend more time on him, keep him in Vienna for another week.'

'How?'

'Tell him there has been a delay in that departure from Budapest.'

'Trouble?'

'Plenty – if we don't use that week to find out more about Grant's connections: has he been in contact with the opposition?'

'Ridiculous – he has only old acquaintances in Vienna.'

'That's for you to find out.' There was a small laugh as he added, 'Orders, my sweet. I'm following them – as you will.'

Jack's orders? She was startled. She had never met Jack, only knew him as the man who could give Gene advance notice of especially valuable pictures that might be coming on to the Vienna market.

Gene was saying, 'Or else, my pet, we'll lose all future advantages. Understand?'

She understood. 'I'll try to be in Vienna on Friday morning.'

'Be here,' he insisted. 'See Grant that afternoon, after the auction. Meet me that evening.'

She thought of Gene's abortive attempts to phone Grant after his arrival. 'How did you let him know about the time and place of the auction?'

'I haven't. I won't until tomorrow evening.'

Just the night before? She frowned. 'That's cutting things fine. He won't like it.'

'I'd like it even less if he knew in advance. Not until we are surer about him.'

'You are adding too many worries to—'

'Better start sharing them,' he told her, and ended the call.

She had no appetite for breakfast. She drank some coffee, black and bitter, and began preparing her excuses for Victor Basset. Part truth, part falsehood always made a reasonable explanation. It would have to be a good story – Basset would soon detect any flaw and would think she was asking permission for a pleasure jaunt just at the time he might need her in Washington. What would she tell him?

Gene Marck had phoned her from Vienna. He needed her there to make sure everything went smoothly at Friday's auction. He himself was unable to attend – he was in the middle of urgent and intricate negotiations with his Prague source about the sale of a Renoir in the near future – a sound investment – a real acquisition for the French Impressionist room at Basset Hill. So could she leave tomorrow evening from New York?

Yes, she thought as she showered quickly, it was perfectly plausible. Except, Basset might point out that if there was any delay in her arrival at Vienna, she would be too late for the auction. (He'd ask its time; of that she could be sure.) Then why shouldn't she leave Kennedy this evening? Arrive Thursday morning? Basset couldn't find fault with that. It would be better, every way: she could see Grant ahead of the auction. If there was anything disquieting to be found out – well, Gene would be all the more pleased to have advance warning of it.

She made up her face carefully, dressed with all speed. Basset was always up and around at an early hour; she'd catch him before he left for this morning's appointments. As for her own schedule here in Washington, she would see the architect at eleven thirty, and the lighting expert at two o'clock. Her secretary could easily handle the engagements already made for Basset. He was moving soon to New York, anyway: a few days in a three-room suite at the Regency – he had never liked the Albany's air-conditioning system – to await the arrival of his precious Ruysdael. He'd fume over any delay in Grant's arrival, but that was for Gene Marck to explain – if it happened.

She picked up the phone and asked for Mr Basset's suite. She found, to her surprise, that she was just in time: William, now acting as valet, told her Mr Basset was leaving in ten minutes for an appointment. What appointment? she wondered. She was responsible for all of them, and the first was at ten o'clock. It was now just after nine.

Basset didn't say what the appointment was either, and she had more sense that to question him. He listened to her explanation of why she was needed in Vienna – she emphasized the importance of making sure that the Ruysdael was acquired. Gene Marck had heard – in spite of all precautions – that an art dealer from Amsterdam, a very keen businessman, had learnt of the auction and would be there. The price might be forced up. Quite high, in fact.

Basset had only nodded. He seemed preoccupied, even a little distracted. This she attributed to yesterday's decisions at Basset Hill: he had disliked the lighting in the main gallery, found fault with the ice-cold temperature, and objected to the dividing walls in two of the rooms.

She went on explaining. His sharp blue eyes studied her as she talked, but a mask had slipped over his face – she had seen that before, when he was listening to someone who might be a competitor – and she could read nothing from those closed lips and frowning brows. A really bad mood, she thought; that dinner party with old State Department friends last night must have been a dismal bore. She felt a growing sense of failure: he will tell me to stay here and take charge of Basset Hill's final changes; Vienna is out.

But as she ended her little speech, he only said, 'When do you leave?'

'On the seven o'clock flight from Kennedy. There's nothing direct from Washington to Vienna. If, of course, you agree . . . Miss McCullough can deal with your engagements – I've got them all arranged. I'll talk with the architect and the lighting expert, and make them understand precisely what you want. There is really nothing else. The Regency expects you on Saturday, I should be able to join you there, Mr Basset. My trip to Vienna will be short.'

'When does Grant get to New York?'

She glanced at William, impressing on Basset the reason for her discretion, as she answered, 'As soon as there's a safe arrival in Vienna.'

'When is that?'

'Any day now.' She smiled and added, 'In fact, it could be any hour.'

He glanced at his watch and said to William, now about to turn chauffeur, 'Have the car at the door in five minutes.' To Lois Westerbrook, he nodded. And went into his bedroom.

She left with William. In the corridor, she said, 'He's in a difficult mood today. What's wrong? Didn't he enjoy the party last night?'

'It went on too long. You know how he is about late nights.'

'Where are you taking him now? To have his hair cut?' she asked, to lighten her first question.

'State Department,' William corrected her, enjoying the reflected importance of that visit.

She stared at him. Why all the secrecy? Basset could have told her. She forced a smile. 'Well, just remind him he has an appointment at the Mellon. Ten o'clock.'

'That's been cancelled,' William said, and took the service elevator. Miss Beautiful doesn't know everything, he thought with a grin as he adjusted his chauffeur's cap. Nor did he, for that matter, but that never troubled him.

Lois Westerbrook walked slowly back to her suite. It's

nothing, she was thinking, nothing at all. But the State Department? At last, in her search for an explanation, she found one possibility that satisfied her. Could Basset be thinking of an ambassadorship? Was he seeing his friends in the State Department to drop them a hint of his next interest? Last night he had got nowhere. But this morning? Trust Basset to keep charging on. He had never accepted a reverse. For him, defeat was an impossible word.

Reassured, she went into her sitting-room and telephoned Trans World Airlines. As for her hotel in Vienna – the city was crowded with tourists, but she'd try pulling some weight with the Sacher. That was where Basset alway stayed. Big name, big deal: Allied Electronics had everyone tugging a forelock and saying '*Servus!*' Gene was there, too: his room would be waiting for his return from Graz. How convenient, she thought, her cool and beautiful face coming to life as she laughed at the prospect of at least one night together: no one will have the smallest suspicion except the maids, and we'll tip them well. Besides, all Vienna loves a lover.

Her laughter died away. She was divided between the desire to meet Gene again and an instinctive fear. The truth was, she didn't really want to be seen around Vienna. Not at this time. But orders were orders. She began packing. She must be ready to pick up and leave, once her chores were completed, first with an architect whose idea for a room for masterpieces was to clutter the sight-lines with dividers, and then with that glorified electrician who called himself a consultant. She'd have to draw some loose cash out of the bank too: fortunately she always kept two thousand dollars in travellers' cheques available for any emergency. And her regular passport, of course: no need for fake identity on this brief trip.

How easy it had all been: Basset making not one

objection, too concerned with his own plans to make any comment about hers. She had expected some questions, a complaint perhaps, even a blank refusal. Now, for the next hour, she had only to deal with Miss McCullough, who liked to call herself assistant secretary to Victor Basset, and not (as she was hired to be) secretary to his assistant. She would tell Miss McCullough how to cope, spell out everything, make sure no mistake would be made. The girl, a moon-faced calf, was competent enough – and eager. A little too eager? The responsibilities of the next few days might boost her dreams of promotion. When I get back, Lois Westerbook thought, I'll keep an eye on McCullough. Good secretaries come and go. If necessary, McCullough will be one of those who came and went.

Small problems, however. In Vienna, they might be larger. Gene would never had telephoned her unless he feared some crisis. Where had he called from? Certainly not from the Sacher. And it wasn't from a public phone, not to reach across the Atlantic. From some safe address, recommended by Jack. Jack . . . The one-name man. Or could it be Jacques? (Sometimes Gene softened the first consonant as if it were French.) It didn't matter: Jack or Jacques was a background figure, extremely useful, but distant. He never intruded. Not until today, she suddenly thought.

Frowning, she locked the suitcase, and checked her carry-all for cosmetics and jewellery. Colin Grant – could he really be such a problem? She still doubted that. He'd keep his word, turn up at the auction, and bid to win. He'd never take money and then renege. Not his type. In any case, as Gene had said, she could handle Colin Grant.

She was smiling again as she picked up her book of Basset's engagements and conferences and luncheons and dinners, and telephoned for her secretary.

9

On Thursday morning, the first surprise of the day came with an early call from Zurich.

Grant had awakened before six, completely rested, thoroughly and annoyingly alert. Breakfast wasn't served until seven thirty. Well, so what? As he showered and shaved, he would begin sorting out his thoughts, his brain cleared by his long deep sleep; last night, they had been a jumbled mess by the time he had finished dinner and slumped into bed. He was still baffled – the man who had stepped into the middle of a conspiracy that had begun three years ago and was now flourishing under deep cover. A conspiracy, too, that intended to continue its past successes: they were much too profitable. Therefore, he deduced, it had been, was, and would be ruthless in eliminating any threat. Me, for instance? he wondered. He tried to laugh that off, but hunger had set a sharp edge to his question.

He was dressed and more than ready for breakfast when it was wheeled in, punctual to the minute. And then, just as he had poured out that wonderful first cup of coffee, the phone rang. Replacing the metal cover over the bacon and eggs, he swore under his breath and took his coffee with him to the telephone at his bedside. 'Yes?' he demanded.

'You sound angry. Did I wake you?'

It was Lois Westerbrook, her voice clear and decided, unmistakable. 'No.' But you damn well are cooling a good breakfast. He drank some coffee. At least he had that.

'I'm in transit,' she told him. 'I'll arrive at the same time you did yesterday.'

So she was in the Zürich airport, bound for Vienna. 'I thought you were staying at home.'

'I have something to tell you – impossible to discuss it by cable or telephone. What about seeing me this evening?'

'Why not lunch?'

'I need some sleep – didn't get any on the plane.'

'Where shall we meet? At the Franziskaner?' That should be elegant and expensive enough for the Duchess of Westerbrook.

'No, not there. Some place nearer. Let's say the Hofburgkeller on Augustinerstrasse. You know it?'

He was astounded. 'Hardly your style, is it?' It was a large and rambling place with several rooms, part restaurant, part wine-cellar, part beer-hall; crowded with students, artists, visitors to the Hofburg museums, people from the Spanish Riding School, and ordinary show-me-the-local-colour tourists. 'It will be packed full,' he warned her. 'Noisy.'

'That's why I chose it,' she said with a laugh. 'I know a quiet spot, and we'll go early. We'd better meet at five thirty, just inside the main entrance so you won't have to search for me. As soon as I see you, I'll lead off.'

And I'll follow, he thought. Like some faithful old hound-dog. He drank more coffee.

'Have to go,' she said in sudden haste.

'Run out of coins?'

She laughed. 'I'm in a small shop – planked down ten dollars to cover all costs. Try that, some time. Meet me at five thirty.' The call was over.

The toast slices, stacked in a silver rack, were cold; the bacon and eggs eatable, but scarcely enjoyable. As consolation, the orange-juice was set in ice, and the Thermos coffee-pot had kept its heat.

He finished breakfast, lit a cigarette, glanced through the Viennese newspaper, which the hotel provided with its compliments, and kept brooding over Lois Westerbrook. 'That's why I chose it,' she had said. Anonymity in crowds? And her 'quiet spot' could mean a corner for two instead of the long tables where a dozen strangers were packed together. Of course, the Hofburgkeller's situation might have been her main reason for choosing it: some place within easy walking distance of her hotel. She could slip out, slip back, without being noticed. Taxis and doormen drew attention to departures and arrivals. What hotel? – The Sacher was his first choice: only choice, in fact. She liked her comforts; and its easy access to Augustinerstrasse fitted in with her refusal of the Franziskaner. 'Some place nearer.'

As for the Hofburgkeller, he himself had no objections: he liked local colour and the mix of people; and the beer was good. But Lois Westerbrook? Incredible. (Like ten dollars planked down in some boutique, to make sure of a quick call to Vienna.) Don't forget it ensured privacy too, he reminded himself. Of one thing he was certain. She wouldn't turn up at the Hofburgkeller in the elegant costume she had worn for the Schofeld appearance. Quite a girl was Westerbrook . . . What was so urgent that had brought her flying across the Atlantic?

Again the telephone rang, interrupting his guessing-game. 'Yes?' he asked patiently.

'Herr Grant? Here is Mayerling – at the Mahlerstrasse Bookstore.' The man was speaking English with an Austrian accent.

Identification was easy, however: Renwick. He had lingered over Mayerling with just enough emphasis to remind Grant of a rain-swept road and a disabled Fiat. 'Ah yes. Herr Mayerling.'

'Yesterday you have enquired about the book on Scottish portraits.'

Another small emphasis, this time on Scottish. Schotten, in German. Schotten Allee, and the Two Crowns Hotel? Grant asked, 'Have you found it?'

'Yes. It is in good condition. But old. Would that suit?'

'Possibly.'

'Then we expect you to make a call here. Examine it for yourself. Fortunate that we are near your hotel, so we do not disturb your plans for this morning.'

'One moment – let me find my engagement book.' Quickly, Grant reached his jacket in the wardrobe and extracted a small map of the city from a pocket. Mahlerstrasse – somewhere near the Majestic. Yes, there it was, just off Kärntnerstrasse, a couple of blocks away. 'I could drop in, as you suggest.' This morning, he had been told.

'I have the book put aside for you in my office. It awaits your pleasure.'

'Thank you.'

'At your service, Herr Grant.'

Grant replaced the receiver, smiling over Renwick's imitation of Viennese politeness. A bit of a joker, he thought as he knotted his tie and pulled on his jacket. Perhaps a sense of humour was needed for Renwick's kind of work – kept him in balance, eased the tensions, put dangers into proper proportion; helpful, too, when dealing with amateurs like Grant, who felt they were being edged into deepening waters where the currents were uncertain, strong, and dangerous.

Mahlerstrasse was reached quite easily, after a ten-minute stop at the big bookstore on Kärntnerstrasse, where Grant searched for a guide to the city and bought one small enough to slip into his pocket. He might even find it useful, with its information on bus and trolley-car routes and its thorough index of street names and locations. Having established credentials as a bookshop browser for anyone who might be interested in his movements, he strolled up Kärntnerstrasse and took the first street to his right. And there it was, a window filled with non-fiction books of every kind, both new and second-hand: art, essays and poetry, history, biography, architecture, cookery and flower-arranging, landscape gardening. Quite a feast, and some of it digestible. Here one really could spend a wet afternoon very pleasantly. Over the doorway and window stretched the word, in faded Gothic script, *Buchhandlung*. No proprietor's name, only the word *Bookdealing* – if you translated literally. *Bookstore* to us less pedantic Americans, thought Grant as he stepped over the threshold into a room that was smothered in hardcovers and paperbacks.

They surrounded him, mounting the walls in narrow tiers until they brushed the high ceiling: they covered the tables that formed the cross-aisles in mounds and pyramids. The place was no larger than half a tennis court; its light was dim, blocked – like the view from the street – by the display of titles in the window. The smell was a mixture of dust, crumbling leather, and cigar-smoke, with a surprise touch of pine-needles from a well-polished little desk cowering in a corner beside the entrance.

There were two customers, each in his own aisle engrossed in the volume he was reading even if he was ruining his eyesight; one clerk, precarious on a ladder, searching for a book on the top shelf; a man in a sedate dark suit who was now moving towards the back of the room. No one else. No Avril. No Renwick.

Grant followed the dark suit. The man was perhaps the owner, certainly a senior clerk, with impressive white hair and a scholarly stoop. 'I wonder if I could look at that book on Scottish portrait painters?' Grant asked, as the man turned to peer at him over heavy reading-glasses.

The man pushed his glasses up over his brow, studied Grant intently.

'I was enquiring about it yesterday. I believe you found a second-hand copy.' God, I've come to the wrong bookstore, Grant thought: How do I get out of this?

The man looked around the room – the customers were hidden among the books, the clerk was still searching – and inclined his head towards a narrow door in the rear wall. 'You can consult it there. More comfortable.' He wandered away, glasses once more in place as he picked out a heavy volume from the nearest shelf.

Quickly Grant opened the door, quietly closed it, and found himself in a passageway leading to the back entrance. Midway along this narrow hall was another door. It was open, inviting him to enter. Inside, no one. Only more books, a strong smell of cigars, and two desks, one covered with papers and ledgers, the other quite bare except for a telephone standing mid-centre, all by its lonely self. It was then he really understood Renwick's quaint phrasing – not just Austrian grappling with English, but a suggestion: *we expect you to make a call here*.

He bolted the door before he moved over to the telephone, dialled Renwick's number and extension.

Renwick answered at once. 'Hi there,' he replied to Grant's greeting. 'Sorry about all this, but hotel operators have long ears. Anyway, this is easier than having you find a public phone and standing for ten minutes of talk. Now let me run it through; after that, you can make your objections. Okay? All right, here goes. Memorize. Don't take notes.

'First, the Klar Auction Rooms. They're in the old quarter of the Inner City – near St Stephen's Cathedral.

On Schulerstrasse, 15A. The auction is definitely tomorrow at eleven o'clock. You'll have a chance to preview the pictures and objets d'art that are being offered for sale. They'll be on display in the exhibition room just beyond a cloakroom at the main entrance, where you leave umbrellas and coats and briefcases – compulsory. One interesting point. We managed to get an advance listing of the items being auctioned, and the Ruysdael is not mentioned. They are keeping it as a last-minute offering – but they'll have to show it in the viewing room. So you'll get a chance to examine it.

'The auction itself may be conducted by Kurt Klar – age forty-nine, fat and bald, glasses. His father, Werner Klar, supervises from the background. Kurt's wife, Gudrun, much younger than he, a blonde, well-stacked, is usually bookkeeping in the accounting office near the storage and shipping departments. These lie at the rear of the building – it stretches far back, to Cathedral Lane, where there's the delivery entrance.

'After the auction you'll be taken to the Klars' private office – it's adjacent to Gudrun's counting-house. Herr Doktor Mittendorf will sign the cheque – he's treasurer at Allied Electronics – always takes charge of Basset's expenditures in Vienna. You can expect Gene Marck to be standing by, introducing you to the others, everything duly authenticated.

'Got all that? I'm giving you the general layout, so you'll know where you are. As for the rest of the staff, don't worry about them. They're okay. It's the top boys who have to be the question-marks – the ones who'll gather in the private office for the final transactions. Note who takes the cheque from Mittendorf, ostensibly to forward it to the previous owner. Above all, note the name on that cheque. Then relax: the Ruysdael will be all yours.

'You could ask for it to be carefully wrapped between

cardboard sheets by the packing department. Of course you'll accompany it, won't leave it out of your sight. The foreman there is a reliable character. He'll wait near you while the packing is completed, and he will have the delivery entrance open too. You'll slip out into Cathedral Lane, where I don't think they'll be expecting you – so no tail, I hope. But we'll be there – the same car as yesterday afternoon. It should be a smooth getaway. All understood?'

'I think so.' Front entrance, cloakroom, exhibition room, auction hall, two adjacent offices, and then the packing department and rear exit. 'Except for the smooth getaway. Why?'

'Necessary. Believe me. Frank can explain. He is ready to pick you up as soon as you leave the bookstore. Nice to disappoint the man outside, who has been waiting patiently across the street. Guess he's shy about coming in, doesn't want to be noticed by you. Frank's driving a rented Fiat, by the way – dark blue this time. He wants to talk with you about the Two Crowns Hotel. He knows it well. Anything else?'

'You forgot to remind me about one thing.'

'What's that?' asked Renwick, his voice sharpening.

'Not to take a coat, umbrella or briefcase to Klar's Auction Rooms.'

Renwick laughed. 'Let's hope it doesn't rain. Good luck.'

Renwick put down the phone thoughtfully, didn't speak for a few moments. Then he said to Avril Hoffman, who had been sitting quietly all through his briefing of Grant, 'I begin to think he'll do. Actually, he may do very well.'

Avril refrained from saying, 'Didn't I tell you so?' Instead, she studied her hands. 'One thing disturbs me.'

'Out with it.'

'He doesn't know what he is really getting into.'

'He was already in it – before we even made contact with him. In fact, Avril, our intervention may damn well save his life.'

'I know.' She was remembering the strange series of three apparently innocent deaths. And all because, six weeks ago, a man named Gyorgy Korda had walked into Prescott Taylor's office and asked for asylum. The defector's credentials were high. Trained by the KGB, he worked in Budapest for the Operations Executive Section of the Hungarian secret police. And the information he had brought with him was startling: lists of valuable items smuggled out of Czechoslovakia and Hungary, of owners arrested, of quiet sales in Vienna, to buyers who had been carefully selected. Avid collectors of great wealth in far-off places, who would employ agents and letters of credit; no cheques easily traced. If the Vienna venture was a success, there were plans for extending the operation to Berlin and Paris, where hidden treasures from Poland and East Germany would appear for sale. Yes, six weeks ago was when the alarm must have been sounded: Gyorgy Korda had defected and knew too much; he would talk, and he couldn't be silenced. But others could be – those who were the agents, the direct lead to their employers who would surely know the name of a bank account in Geneva. When you paid out a vast sum, you were hardly likely to forget. 'Bob – do you really believe that the deaths were calculated?'

'One, no. But three? All close together?'

'There's one cheque-signer, and he's still alive – Herr Pompous Closed-Lips Mittendorf. Oh, I know he doesn't need to go through all the rigmarole of letters of credit. He can pay out money direct from Basset's Allied Electronics. Still – it's odd. Isn't it. Why hasn't he been silenced? Or is he one of theirs? Ultra-correct, super-respectable Herr Doktor Mittendorf?'

'Either that, or he can be blackmailed into total silence. Doctor of what, anyway?'

'Mathematics, I suppose,' Avril suggested with a smile. 'A graduate in juggling of accounts?'

'That could blackmail him nicely. Seal up Old Closed-Lips permanently.' At least, thought Renwick, I've stopped her worrying about Colin Grant.

But he hadn't. She was saying, 'Colin, of course, won't be writing the cheque for the Ruysdael. Still, he's there when the cheque is signed, and we've asked him to find out the name on it. Comes to almost the same thing, doesn't it?' She rose, moved restlessly around the small and simple office. 'I'm really unhappy about this, Bob. Truly. Surely there is some other way.'

'Which could take weeks – months – of investigation. We need the information *now*. Ferenc Ady won't be the last victim unless we smash this conspiracy.'

'Will we? Geneva isn't the only place where they bank. Didn't Korda say that London is probably the depository for the Berlin and Paris auctions?'

'If the Geneva operation becomes a total loss, they'll write it off. An experiment that failed. And became a danger, too: we are learning the pattern – we'll know what to look for in London, or Paris or Berlin. Will they risk another failure? Exposure? Publicized in a NATO report? I think not.'

She seemed persuaded, but something was still troubling her.

He said, 'If it's Grant you are bothered about, then forget it. We'll have him protected all the way.'

'We haven't much to protect him with.' You and me, and two agents who may be good at surveillance but don't even carry a revolver.

'Don't forget Frank. I've asked him for help.'

She brightened visibly. 'Then we're not alone.' Frank Krimmer must control a network of Israeli agents: the information he could supply was phenomenal. There were hints, too, that some of his men could terrorize even the terrorists. 'How did you manage to convince him?' Intelligence agencies did not usually share their secrets, even with friends.

'No convincing needed. He has as big an interest as we have in this investigation. Certainly more personal: he knew three of the refugees who've gone missing.'

'Frank is with Colin now?'

'They should be driving up to the Schotten Ring district by this time.' Smiling, he added, 'What's with all this Colin business? A bit soon for Miss Hoffman of London, isn't it?' Damn it all, she took three weeks before she dropped Mr Renwick for Bob.

She covered her embarrassment with a small laugh. 'I had better get down to Prescott's office. He needs help with some translation. Korda has started talking again, and Prescott has the tapes. Perhaps there is something in them for us.'

'I hope Prescott managed to fill out that strange gap in Korda's information.' The man had been trying to impress Taylor and Renwick, had let slip one single name and then clammed up abruptly. All they had been able to learn was that the name, a pseudonym of course, was of the highest importance in this current operation of sell-and-buy. But you couldn't blame Korda: he didn't feel secure, detained here in Vienna.

'Korda's trump card, perhaps,' Avril said.

'I can hear him right now: Get me to America, give me a new identity. Then I will feel safe enough to tell you about Jack.' And who the hell was this Jack? Korda knew and wouldn't expand on it. Not yet. 'Yes,' Renwick said, 'he will stall until he's certain of a passport to the United States. Tell Prescott to dangle one in front of his eyes. We need the info *here* – not next month in Washington.'

'I'll tell him,' Avril said, and left. Bob, she was

thinking, might have placed too much emphasis on the defector's sudden silence. Perhaps Korda only knew a name that was of the highest importance and that was all.

Renwick took a folder out of the safe (with a desk and three hard chairs, that was all the furniture in his cubicle-size office) and opened it. Inside, there were two sheets of flimsy paper with the details that had been gathered about the life and interests of Herr Doktor Heinrich Mittendorf, trusted treasurer of Allied Electronics. He began reading them, spurred on by Avril's comment about the only man who had written a cheque, and hadn't met with an accident, either. Bright girl, Avril, bless her big brown eyes.

Yes, here was something strange . . . Ridiculous, perhaps. But worth some thought. Worth a hell of a lot, in fact, and some searching, too. Where did he start? With the biggest bookstores in town, and work down to the second-hand places. Mittendorf a poet when he was nineteen? Incredible. But forty-three years ago he had been published in Paris, and praised by the lesser Communist press for his 'revolutionary ardour'. His pen-name, under which two of his poems had been issued, was Jacques.

Renwick cancelled his idea about sifting through the bookstores. He would leave that until he had talked with the researcher who had uncovered this little item about Mittendorf's youth. If it had come to light, there must be a copy of the book available somewhere. And the researcher – Ella Jameson, he saw by the initials at the foot of her neat notes – must know where to find it. She had actually read the poems, judging by her comments.

In ten minutes, Mrs Jameson had left her cataloguing in the reference library and was entering his room.

He greeted her with so much enthusiasm that her natural reserve melted away. So few people ever gave her any credit for her meticulous research: she often wondered, in fact, if her painstaking notes were even read with any attention. She began answering Mr Renwick's questions. They veered around several of her little discoveries about Mittendorf – she couldn't be sure which of the points Mr Renwick raised was of most interest to him. Yes, she spent most Saturdays in small second-hand bookstores – her hobby, as it were. She had now quite a collection of curiosities, volumes long out of print. The name Mittendorf had caught her eye as she was examining a shelf of *belles-lettres*. It had been misplaced, of course: years ago, judging by the heavy coating of dust on that row of neglected books. Naturally she had bought it: wasn't she working on the subject of Mittendorf? It was a first edition – the only edition, actually – published in 1934. Three hundred and fifty copies had been printed. It really was a rare find: she had checked the catalogues of several libraries, and they didn't even mention it. She got a bargain for the three schillings it had cost her.

'Indeed you did.' Less than nineteen cents for, perhaps, the last extant copy of Mittendorf's youthful poems. 'I'd like to have a look at it some time.' If he had gauged her correctly, it would be lying on his desk tomorrow. 'Whereabouts did you find it?'

Mrs Jameson's smile widened in her delight. 'In the most unlikely place – a small street just off the Mariahilferstrasse. I was searching for Haydn's birthplace and—' She stopped. 'Sorry. I'm afraid my enthusiasm runs away with me.'

'Well,' he said as he rose to his feet, ending their little talk, 'it doesn't seem to interfere with your work. It's first rate, Mrs Jameson,' and he opened the door for her. 'We'll keep this strictly between ourselves. Later – well, I'll mention your efficiency and dedication in my report.' He would too, but scarcely in such high-falutin' words.

That pleased her, sent her back happily to her reference library. People like Jameson don't get credit enough, he thought.

He hadn't brought up the name Jacques. It would only have emphasized his interest in Mittendorf. If Mrs Jameson had recorded it, then it did exist. Tomorrow morning he'd see it, anyway.

Remember, he warned himself, like Mrs Jameson and her enthusiasm his imagination could run away with him, take off at a flying gallop. 'So control it!' he said aloud. 'You may have nothing here at all.' Nothing but an interesting footnote on a lost poet.

He closed the folder and locked it safely away.

10

It had been easy. Grant had stepped out of the bookstore's doorway, avoided looking either across or along
Mahlerstrasse, and halted at the window as if its display
had again caught his attention. Behind him, a car
stopped. He turned, saw a dark blue Fiat with its door
already opened. Four steps and he was inside, and
Frank was driving off. Within moments, they were
swerving down the nearest side street and heading for
the Ring. From Frank, there was no explanation as to
where they were travelling. He merely nodded as Grant
closed the car door and settled beside him. No comment,
no talk whatsoever; this was a different kind of Frank,
in both manner and dress. Yesterday morning, he had
been the neatly tailored chauffeur of a Mercedes-Benz:
now he was dressed in a leather jacket and open-necked
shirt, his hair no longer brushed neatly back, his features
now firmer and more pronounced. The jaw was set, the
nose aggressive, the lips uncompromising.

Either, thought Grant, he didn't want this job, or he
had just left a sharp argument, which he seems to have
lost. Grant broke the silence with an innocuous, 'Where
are we heading? Or are we driving around?'

'We'll do that first.'

'After that?'

Frank's lips tightened. 'It depends.'

'Have we been followed?'

'No.'

'Was there actually somebody waiting to tail me?'
Grant asked, his irritation showing.

'Didn't you see him?' If not, I've got a fool on my hands, Frank's eyes seemed to say as they glanced at the American.

'Didn't risk looking curious.' Damn it, thought Grant, does he think I'm an idiot? 'What did you want to see me about?'

'We're driving in its direction now.'

'That's certainly clear enough.' Grant's sarcasm wasn't wasted. There was another sharp glance pointed his way. A short silence.

Then Frank said, 'First, tell me the background of Max Seldov who recommended the Two Crowns. Oh, I know the obvious details: came to Vienna with his parents from Odessa, emigrated with them to New York; public school; CCNY graduate; now co-director of Schofeld's on Madison Avenue; lives in Larchmont; with Eunice, and three teenage daughters.'

'You've forgotten his war record,' Grant said with obvious annoyance. It had been good.

'No, I didn't. He ended here, with the Allied Occupation Forces in Vienna. Was that when he met Bernard Mandel?'

'I wouldn't know. What's this all about, anyway?'

Frank didn't answer that. 'Does Seldov ever talk politics?' he asked.

'Politics? He's a Democrat, and votes. Apart from that, he reads the *New York Times* editorials, and then turns to its art section.'

'So he is not political?'

'Not the way you make it sound.'

'What made him recommend the Two Crowns?'

'Just trying to help me find a hotel.'

'You didn't ask him?'

'No. What the hell have you got against Max Seldov?'

'His brother-in-law,' Frank said. 'What did you hear about him from Seldov?'

117

'He married Max's sister.'

'That all?'

'He's a good chap – won the hearts of Seldov and his family when they stayed at the Two Crowns – ten years ago, Max said.'

'And that was all?'

'He said I'd like Bernie.'

'Does Bernard Mandel know that you are in Vienna?'

'Possibly. Max was going to write to him.'

'Why?'

'For God's sake—' Grant burst out.

'Why?'

'Just wanted his brother-in-law to find me a room if I needed one. Asked me to have a look at the place and give his regards to Bernie.'

'You didn't say you were booked at the Majestic?'

'I thought that would be tactless. It would certainly have roused too much speculation. Max knows damn well that my budget doesn't stretch that far.' Grant paused, then added, 'Look – I'm finding this bloody unpleasant.'

'But necessary.'

Now it's my turn to shoot out a blunt question, Grant decided. 'Why?' he asked, as aggressive as Frank had been.

'Because Bernard Mandel is a son of a bitch.'

Grant recovered and said slowly, 'Well, that's really telling them.'

'It's no exaggeration.'

'In your opinion.'

'Not mine alone.'

'Well, it certainly isn't Max Seldov's.' His face had beamed with pleasure when he recalled his brother-in-law. He wasn't faking it either.

'How often has he met Mandel?' Frank asked. 'I'm talking of the last twenty years or so.'

Probably only once, on the Seldovs' visit to Vienna, Grant realized. 'Max hasn't done much travelling abroad since the three girls toned down his life-style.'

'A family man? So he brought them on a trip to Vienna and Bernie couldn't do too much for them. He's just a good-hearted generous guy who runs a comfortable little hotel. Yes, that's his public image. There is another, though.'

'He seems to have made his wife happy enough when she was alive.'

'Easy. She shared his politics.'

Politics . . . back to that again. 'Are you going to tell me what you are hinting around, or are you just leaving me dangling?' Grant demanded. He was beginning to sound truculent. He made an effort to control his rising temper.

'I thought I had given you enough hints.' Frank half-smiled. 'Unless you really are as politically ignorant as most Americans.'

'You sure know how to make friends and influence people.'

'Now, now – no need to get mad. Can't you take fair criticism?' Frank asked, his voice mild, his smile spreading.

That was always unanswerable. 'Why don't you let me out right here?' They had turned away from the Ring, and were now taking a route through crowded commercial streets.

'I might have done that if your answers had been different.'

That stopped Grant, who had his hand on the door-release, ready to make a quick exit at the next blocked intersection. He turned his head towards Frank, attempted to read the man's expression. He's been goading me, Grant thought, trying to catch me off

119

balance. He said, his voice tight with anger, 'Nice to know that one's trusted.'

'Not at the beginning. Why should I have taken you on faith? I don't know your friend O'Malley whose word counts with Renwick. But think how you appeared to me, Grant. Did you come to Vienna to do an honest job, or were you specially sent here to uncover who we were and how much we had found out? In other words, were you with us or against us?'

They came to a halt in a jam of traffic. Grant didn't open the door. He released his grip on the handle, slowly, almost unwillingly, but definitely. 'I get your point.' His anger had left him, but his ego was still bruised.

'What did Avril tell you yesterday?' Frank asked.

'Briefed me on the financing of terrorists.'

'You believed her?'

'At first, no,' Grant admitted. 'Later, when I thought more closely into it – yes.'

'You could back out right now. Fake illness. Why don't you?'

'She didn't leave me much choice.'

That startled Frank. He had to swerve to avoid rear-ending the car in front of them, and cursed himself under his breath. 'Are you telling me sweet Avril twisted your arm?'

'No, just told me the facts.'

'And made a request,' prompted Frank.

But Grant wasn't talking.

Frank nodded his approval. 'I'm as interested in that cheque as Renwick is,' he said very quietly. 'You know what you're getting into, of course? These guys we are up against play rough – for keeps.'

'Trying to scare me off? You're doing a good job.'

Better now than later, thought Frank, when he could

mess up weeks of work. I told Bob Renwick that he was taking a risk with Grant.

Grant was saying, 'Well, if you can't tell me what the danger might be, I'll have to keep on making a guess or two.'

'Such as?' Frank asked quickly.

'The Ruysdael painting could be sold for a high price to swell the Geneva bank account, and then snatched. After all, the Hungarian government considers it the property of the state. And if Victor Basset complains about its loss – too bad. They'll say he was trying to steal it. I'll be implicated somehow. End of career. Could be?'

'Could be.' Perhaps worse, thought Frank. 'So how do you safeguard the painting?'

'I'm thinking about that. I'll begin with Bob Renwick's suggestion, and make a smooth getaway from Klar's Auction Rooms. I asked him why. He told me that you'd explain.'

'Do I need to?'

'I think you've already answered it. These guys play rough – for keeps. You meant that.'

'I meant it.' Frank's voice was harsh, his eyes grim. 'You are still with us?'

'Still hanging in.' Grant tried to sound more cheerful than he felt. 'Say, haven't we been down this street before?'

'Just marking time. Wanted to be sure you were in the right mood before you brought greetings from Max to dear old likeable Bernie. There's a garage not far from here. You can leave me there. I'll point you in the right direction – you'll find the Two Crowns easily, it's only a couple of blocks away.'

'The hell with Bernie. I've got problems enough without adding to them.' Another thought struck Grant. 'Or is he involved in the campaign to help our needy terrorists?'

'No, not directly. But indirectly? He can always be called on for support.' Frank hesitated, and then plunged in. 'He's an old-time Communist, joined the party secretly in 1935 when he was twenty, headed for Moscow as soon as Hitler's troops appeared in Vienna, stayed in Russia during the war. We have proof of that – from others who were there at the time. He was back in Vienna by 1945, saying he had been in Maidanek, the camp that got rid of most of its prisoners as the Soviet army was approaching – shot them and threw them into mass graves in a final frenzy of killing off all evidence. Out of thousands and thousands, a few escaped. He claimed he was one of them. It makes a good story, and unverifiable. The camp records were destroyed.'

Listening to the hard, controlled voice, Grant began to understand something of this man: he lived in three dimensions; the bitter past, with dates and facts permanently engraved on his memory; the realistic present, filled with alarms and dangers; the unpredictable future with its hopes and fears and determined dreams.

They were reaching the garage. It was a quiet place on a narrow street, unpretentious, with a small office near its entrance where a man sat in shirt-sleeves behind a stretch of glass windows. He looked up as Frank negotiated the entrance, returned his brief hand-wave, and went on telephoning. Deeper inside, there were the usual oil-stained cement floor, solid walls of dingy white brick, cold lighting from naked bulbs suspended from the rafters and a mechanic, in grease-stained overalls, too busy checking a carburettor to give them a second glance. There were about ten cars around the sides of the garage, leaving the back wall for a jumble of equipment, tools, tyres, and spare parts. One parking space was free. Frank took it neatly, and the Fiat came to a rest.

He switched off the engine and sat staring down at

the wheel. Suddenly he broke his silence. 'I can manage – if I try hard enough *and* put aside my own beliefs – to find the reasons why our enemies want our destruction. But for one of our own people to join our oldest enemy in destroying us—' He didn't finish. He drew a long deep breath, and said, 'It's almost noon. You'll catch Mandel just before he starts lunch, may he choke on his goulash.'

'Must I see this guy?'

'He will be expecting you.'

'Perhaps Max forgot to write to him,' Grant tried.

'You think so?'

No, the ever-dutiful Max would have written. Grant said, 'I'm damn well not taking a room there.'

'Too bad. I've always wanted someone nicely installed in that hotel.'

'Haven't you?' Grant was disbelieving.

'Nothing that lasted. Mandel was too well-informed. But you, now – he will welcome you like a long-lost brother-in-law. For a good reason: he could have been instructed to find – if he got the chance to meet you – just who has contacted you. Look out for that. You might have some fun with it.'

'Do I come back here?' An idiotic question. 'No, of course not. Mandel may have me followed.'

'You're learning.'

'One thing more – I hadn't time to tell Renwick about Lois Westerbook. She arrived in Vienna this morning. She wants to see me at five thirty this evening.'

'Didn't know she was coming to Vienna,' Frank said. He thought over that, but he made no comment. 'Where do you meet?'

'At the Hofburgkeller – her choice. Probably her idea of undercover work.'

Frank was not amused.

'You'll let Renwick know about La Belle Westerbrook?'

Grant opened the car door. 'And before you ask me, I'll be spending the afternoon with an old friend, Helmut Fischer. He's an art dealer on Singerstrasse, just off Kärntner. Now what direction do I take?'

'Turn left. At the first cross-street turn left again, walk a block and you'll hit the Schotten Allee. Look for a gold sign over a doorway, red geraniums at the front steps. And look out for yourself!'

Frank Krimmer watched Grant leave the garage. Then he moved too, heading for the doorway in the rear wall. He passed the lavatory, reached the phone in the small room beyond. His call was answered at once by the man who had been installed, for the last few weeks, on the top floor of the house opposite the Two Crowns. 'Much traffic?' Krimmer asked. Just the regular hotel guests, he was told, and one visitor earlier this morning. 'You had the camera working?' Yes, it was all fixed, in good order again, the photographs were now being developed. 'Let me know when another visitor arrives – that should be in about five minutes. He's in his late thirties, black hair, tall, wearing a grey tweed jacket and dark flannels.'

If he arrives, Krimmer thought. He still had some doubts. He waited impatiently. Four minutes later the call came: the subject in question was just entering the hotel.

So he *is* hanging in, thought Krimmer. Maybe, just maybe, he will do better than expected. 'No photographs necessary. Save the film,' he said, and cut the connection.

He put in several calls, one to Renwick included. 'Changed my opinion about him?' he asked indignantly, replying to Bob's first question. 'Never had one. He's your boy. Not a bad type, on the whole. I've met worse. He makes guesses, did you know? Wait till I tell you his idea about a snatch. It could happen, too. We might start thinking along those lines.' Then he added the news about Lois Westerbrook, referring to her only by the name which Renwick used: Sugarpuss. And, of course, Grant's afternoon with Helmut Fischer. 'And that covers all the recent details,' Krimmer stated, ready to end the call.

But Renwick said, 'We have a piece of news – from Washington. They managed to get hold of Mount Rushmore yesterday and discuss the situation with him. He's listening. Has his own ideas. Might be useful. Meet me in Pete's office and we'll go over them. Usual time. Okay?'

Translate Pete into Prescott Taylor. Usual time meant one o'clock, when most people in the Embassy were out to lunch. And, of course, Mount Rushmore was Renwick's name for Victor Basset. 'He's listening, is he?' Frank was in surprise. 'If it isn't too late,' he added.

'Always the cheerful optimist,' Renwick told him with a laugh. 'See you.' And their cryptic conversation was over.

So Mount Rushmore had ideas of his own, thought Frank. We could expect that. They'll probably turn out to be just another complication: the successful millionaire taking charge, asserting himself, once the shock (and the hurt to his self-esteem, don't forget that) had subsided. It must have been quite a day at the State Department, Mount Rushmore changing into Krakatoa. But after the blow-up, Victor Basset had listened. At least that was to his credit.

Krimmer opened a closet where he stored a few clothes, and exchanged the leather jacket for a well-tailored tweed. He added a tie, and was ready to face any Embassy at one o'clock. This time, the car he selected was a Porsche of undistinguished brown.

He nodded to the entrance-watcher in his glass-enclosed office and swung the Porsche out into the street. He'd reach United States territory, some distance away from the old city, in nice time even with a convoluted approach. Then he gave a broad smile as he remembered Renwick's definition of the successful spook: a man who never journeys from one point to another in a straight line. Not even for a box of matches.

11

Over the door hung a gilded sign embossed with a double-headed bird, which might – with some effort of the imagination – be interpreted as an eagle. On either side of the entrance, a tub (plastic moulded to imitate carved stone) was filled with red geraniums. A wooden plaque, painted to look like bronze, announced that here was the Two Crowns Hotel, proprietor Bernard Mandel, founded 1856. At least the geraniums were real, Grant thought as he mounted two shallow steps. But he had to admit that the building, from the outside certainly, was prepossessing: it was one of the nineteenth-century houses that had invaded a medieval quarter, got their foothold, and defied further change.

Inside? He found himself in a medium-sized lobby made small, dominated by its furnishings. Heavy velvet curtains blocked out the sun and the street. Lighting was provided by pink wall-fixtures of Venetian glass; chairs and couches, heavily upholstered, had bulging arms; low tables – blond wood with a hard glossy surface – had thick tubular legs; shining blond wood again for the massive reception desk; a staircase covered by the angular design of blue and red Turkish carpeting; highly polished parquetry on the floor, with electric-blue rugs; everything in order, everything spotless, a bourgeois heaven.

And empty at this hour, except for a small woman who was almost hidden by the desk. She turned from arranging some envelopes in their pigeon-holes and smiled at him enquiringly. He took a bold step on a treacherous rug, felt it threaten his balance, and halted, reminding himself to walk gingerly. She decided he was shy, tried to make him feel at home with another friendly smile, and asked if the gentleman would like a room.

'No,' he assured her. 'I am looking for Mr Mandel. Is he here? I am from New York. My name is Grant.'

It meant nothing to her. She picked up the telephone, still smiling at him – a sweet-faced woman with neat grey hair and a matronly figure, dressed modestly in a most unbecoming blouse. Her manner changed; she became nervous, frowning slightly, as she conveyed his message. 'I'm sorry, Herr Mandel,' she said, suddenly contrite. 'Of course, Herr Mandel.' She put down the receiver. She sighed. 'I am new here, only three days. Herr Mandel did not want to be disturbed.'

With relief, Grant said, 'Then I'll leave a note.' He was forming it in his mind as he took a careful step towards the desk: *Sorry to have missed you. Your brother-in-law asked me to call and bring his greetings from New York.* And that, thought Grant, might get me out of this without too much skin off my elbow.

'No, no!' she protested. 'Herr Mandel will see you. As soon as I said your name, he was pleased. One moment and he will be here.' She glanced at a door that lay below the steep rise of the staircase, and returned to her problem with the mail. Grant studied the wallpaper. Surely this place must have been redecorated since Max Seldov had seen it. It was quiet, as Max had said; but comfortable? Not to the eyes, certainly.

The door under the staircase opened and closed, and a man appeared with his head bent as if he were searching for something on the polished floor. Offending dust, perhaps? He had a green apron tied round his waist, black trousers, a silver-buttoned green waistcoat, and a snow-white shirt. He paused at a table to straighten an ashtray that was already squared, and looked briefly at Grant. Then he moved to the staircase, his head turned to let him survey the street through the open door, and began climbing. His head was still turned away from Grant, as though he found the screaming blue wallpaper with its splotches of yellow flowers completely absorbing.

He was halted on the third step by the woman at the desk. 'Rupprecht!' she called worriedly, '*What* is this name? Fleisher or Fletcher?'

Rupprecht did not look back at her. He let out two sharp sentences about her stupidity, about the postmark – couldn't she use her eyes, had she to be told everything? And went on upstairs.

The woman bit her lip. She was close to tears, but she managed a shaky smile for Grant before she began studying the stamp on the envelope. 'American – then it's Fleisher!' she told herself. 'Fletcher is from Australia.' She looked up, caught Grant's sympathetic glance. 'It *is* difficult at first.'

Yes, he thought, it was difficult for a middle-aged woman who needed the job and was nervous about losing it. 'You'll soon learn,' he told her.

'I hope so. This is a very good hotel, such nice people. Rupprecht is not usually so cross. Oh, Herr Mandel – this is—' She stopped in confusion over forgetting Grant's name, and turned to sorting the mail. So here was Bernard Mandel, founded 1856.

'Herr Grant?' Bernard Mandel came forward from the same door that Rupprecht had used. 'It gives me pleasure to see you.' His English was pronounced carefully, almost without accent. 'Max wrote me. He told you would come here.' He seized Grant's hand, shook it twice in a hearty grip, and then released it as suddenly as he had taken it. He was a massive figure, rounded and broad-shouldered, handsomely dressed in a grey flannel jacket with green facings. Greying hair receded

129

from an extensive brow. Sharp grey eyes encompassed Grant at one glance. Soft red lips were now spread in a wide smile. His skin was indoors white, and gleaming with exuberance. Or, thought Grant, his jacket is too thick and his shirt-collar too tight. His welcome was certainly warm.

'Anna,' Mandel ordered, 'go and have your lunch. Tell Hans to bring us a glass of wine. Go, go! I shall guard the desk.'

'No wine, thank you,' Grant said. 'I have only a few minutes—'

'No wine, Anna,' Mandel called after the woman as she was about to leave. And not, Grant noted, by the door that Mandel and Rupprecht had used. Mandel's own private office? If so, Grant was not being invited inside. He sat on the edge of an armchair. Mandel sank into the couch. 'And how is Max? Doing well?'

'Very well,' Grant said.

'But that job of his – buying pictures, selling them.' Mandel shook his head, pursed his lips. 'Max, I told him, you do better to run a hotel. Oh, it is hard work, I know, but you have good food, a good bed, and good people around you. Of course, you have no moments of your own, but life is rich, interesting, so many different persons from so many different countries.' This developed into a monologue, kindly and yet slightly condescending, about the Two Crowns and its world-wide clientele. 'As you see, Mr Grant,' he waved an arm around the room, 'we make our hotel like home.' He paused, waiting for confirmation.

'Very homey,' said Grant.

'One thing I am sincerely sorry over. Believe me, Mr Grant. We have no bedroom that is free. Everything occupied.' He looked around him again. 'Of course, our guests are out at this moment, visiting the city. You should come here in the evening, when all are returned.

130

Then you would see how busy this place is. You would enjoy—'

'I'm sure I would. There really is no need to apologize. I didn't come here looking for a room. Max asked me to bring you his best wishes, that's all. He would have been disappointed if I hadn't seen you. So—' Grant was on his feet, ready to say goodbye. Frank, he was thinking, may have been exaggerating – some deep antipathy, perhaps; some personal hurt that had turned to hatred. But Mandel dangerous? Sinister? The worst this type could do was to talk you to death.

'Such a short visit!' Mandel hefted his bulk out of the enveloping cushions and sighed with regret. 'You are quite comfortable in your present hotel?'

'Very comfortable.'

'Good. Which is it?'

'The Majestic.'

Mandel raised his eyebrows. 'Very nice, very nice. But expensive, no?'

Now, what will he write to Max? Grant wondered, and countered with, 'Not for me. My expense account takes care of the bill.'

'Ah, you have business in Vienna?'

'I write articles for magazines.' Grant couldn't resist adding, 'About art.'

'Then people in your business can make some money?' Mandel nodded his head, asked sadly. 'Why does Max not write articles?'

'Max is doing all right, I assure you.'

'But he doesn't travel like you. How long will you stay in Vienna?'

'Two weeks, I hope.' Suddenly, Grant was on guard.

'Two weeks? Some night you must come to dinner here, and meet my guests.'

'That's very kind of you, but—'

'You are too busy with your own friends,' Mandel

131

finished Grant's sentence for him. 'Of course, of course. You have many friends here?'

'A few. I spent some time in Vienna several years ago.' Grant began walking towards the entrance. Mandel accompanied him with a pace so slow that Grant's progress became a step-halt-step-halt agony.

'They must be happy to see you. Been keeping you busy since you arrived? There is so much to do in Vienna. What have you visited?'

'Actually, I haven't seen any of my friends yet. I arrived only yesterday.'

Mandel threw up his hands. His face beamed. 'You came to visit me so soon? I am flattered, Mr Grant.'

'Well, I was up in the University district, and you were only a short distance away. It seemed a good idea – I might not be near the Schotten Allee again.'

'You know Vienna, I see.'

'I like to walk around. And this helps.' Grant drew the small Vienna guide-book from his pocket. The complete tourist.

Mandel waved it aside. 'Yes, yes. I know it. I advise my guests to buy it.'

They were at the front door. 'Well,' Grant said, 'I'll tell Max that you are—'

'A moment, please!' Mandel said, halting abruptly. 'A present – something to send to Max and the family. But I have nothing ready.' He was desolate. Then his face lit up as he thought of something. 'Mr Grant, may I ask of you a favour? I buy a gift for Max, and you take it to New York. No need to declare it at the Customs – you say it is your own property. Will you do that for me? Duty is heavy if I send it by mail – and so long to arrive.'

'Well, if it isn't something that's breakable—' Grant began.

'It will be no trouble for you. I'll choose something easy to carry, something you can slip into your suitcase.'

'You'd better let me know what it is. Its value, too. It will be questioned and probably examined, by the Customs officer.'

'Ah – you do not like playing a little smuggling game?' Mandel was astounded.

'Frankly, no. I don't like complications. Just mark the contents and the value on your package and we'll keep everything simple.'

'Of course, of course. I'll have it sent to your hotel before you leave. What is your room number?'

'307.'

'I am in your debt, Mr Grant. On your next visit, I shall have a room for you here – if you have no expense account at the Majestic.' A hearty laugh, a hearty handshake. '*Auf Wiedersehen!*' He stood at the top of the steps to give a genial wave.

Well, what do you make of all that? Grant asked himself as he openly consulted his guide-book and took the direction for the nearest trolley-car. Apologies to Frank: he could have been right, after all. If it hadn't been for his warning, Grant might have paid little heed to a few odd details. Probably he would have thought they were unimportant, just as he might have seen Mandel as a well-meaning and total bore. Now, however, the details seemed more than odd. They were definitely peculiar.

Such as: Anna offering him accommodation and Mandel maintaining there was no space available; Mandel's delay in coming to meet him – or was he occupied with more important business? Mandel not letting him stray from that decorator's nightmare of a room, instead of inviting him – more naturally – into the privacy of his office. (And wouldn't Mandel, as the proud hotel-keeper, have tried to show Grant some of the other rooms? Thank God he hadn't.) Or Mandel being so quick to accept Grant's refusal of a drink, as though he wanted the visit to be brief. Yet not too brief. Once Grant started to leave, he slowed down the departure until he had his questions answered . . . Then there was the man Rupprecht: he would know Grant again, but did he hope Grant wouldn't know him? That could explain his angry outburst: an excuse, in fact, not to come back downstairs and show his face. (Thin, dark-browed, sharp-nosed, was Grant's memory of that one glimpse.)

Of course, it was possible that Anna understood little about the hotel's reservations; nervous as she was in her new job, over-eager to please, she was simply trying to be efficient. Possible, too, that Mandel's questions were prompted by a surfeit of curiosity, well-intended; a friendly man who was embarrassed by an inconvenient visit. Yet one fact still remained: Mandel had wanted Grant to clear out, and stay out. Comic, thought Grant: the opposite of what he had expected. Yes, comic. And definitely peculiar.

He paused at the corner, and – just in case he was still being watched from the steps of the Two Crowns – consulted the guide-book once more. Half-way to the trolley-car's stopping-place, he saw a taxi and hailed it with relief. Soon he'd have a leisurely lunch in the Kärntnerstrasse, get the taste of the Two Crowns out of his mouth. After that, a pleasant stroll to Helmut Fischer's shop. It would be open by three o'clock.

12

Three o'clock meant ten minutes after the hour. Perhaps more. Grant ought to have remembered that Helmut Fischer was never punctual: he had equal disregard for time and money, an easy attitude to adopt if you were born into a thriving family business. He had inherited it at the heady age of twenty-two, and then astonished the more light-minded among his friends by leaving Vienna when the Nazis moved in. He could have stayed, even made it profitable: some of the old-school German officers, unlike Gentleman Goering, actually paid for the pictures they coveted. But Helmut Fischer was his own master – both parents dead, his sister married to an American – and he meant to keep it that way. First, he retreated into his beloved mountains; and then, when his small village was invaded by a detachment of the master race, made the long and dangerous escape to England. Detention, red tape, poverty, inaction: years he never talked about. Eventually, he persuaded the Free French to use his talents in mountain-climbing and skiing, and was dropped into Bavaria – as the snows were melting and the war was ending. Fischer's anecdotes always finished with a wry touch of humour, usually against himself. And in spite of the discipline of those war years – perhaps because of it? – he still couldn't open his shop on time.

Grant decided not to loiter around its window. Instead, he would continue on his after-lunch stroll, and find out if the man across the street was really interested in him.

Grant had first noticed him – quietly dressed in a dark blue suit – as they almost collided at the corner of Singerstrasse, and thought nothing of it – just someone waiting for a friend at a crowded intersection. But the man had stopped waiting: he walked barely ten yards behind Grant until Fischer's shop was reached, then sauntered across the narrow street as if some window over there had caught his eye. No one could have followed me from the Schotten Ring, Grant worried; no one . . . The taxi hadn't been waiting for him – it was a matter of sheer chance to hail it, a matter of luck to have it stop for him, even if it was driven by a grinning maniac who had whisked him at incredible speed through impossible streets. Nor had he observed anyone concentrating on him when he sat over a long lunch at a café table. Not until Singerstrasse itself was there any hint that he was being followed. Hint? The man was practically bludgeoning him with the fact. Either he takes me for a damned idiot, Grant thought angrily, or he's more of a fool that I am.

Suddenly, the first drops of rain fell, a typical shower, unexpected and heavy. The pavements emptied as people ducked into the nearest doorways or sheltered against a wall. Dodging into a shop entrance, Grant had barely time to turn around before a newcomer jostled him to one side. 'Excuse me,' said the man in the blue suit. 'Cramped, here. But it won't last long.' He stared at the rain, pulled out a cigarette, and settled to wait. 'Have you a match, please?' he asked. He was young, perhaps twenty-six or -seven, as blond as Frank, but heavier across the shoulders.

One of Frank's men? Grant offered his lighter in silence. Frank was the only one who knew about his visit this afternoon to Helmut Fischer – unless, of course, Frank had passed that information to Renwick. 'A bit obvious, weren't you?'

The man bowed as he returned the lighter, and looked away from Grant. In English, carefully correct, he said, 'That was the idea. How else could I draw your attention? Now that you know who I am, you will not be worried.' His lips had scarcely moved, his eyes were on the rain.

I don't know who you are, and I *am* worried, thought Grant. The notion of having someone, even a reliable watchdog, following him around was not much to his taste. 'There is no need—'

'Excuse me. There is need. To notice who might be interested in you.'

'So I'm serving a useful purpose?' Grant's annoyance wasn't disguised.

The young man smiled. 'You may see me again. But not so obvious next time.' He looked up at the sky. 'Clearing,' he said in German, and winked at Grant as he added his thanks for the lighter. A small polite bow, and he was the stranger on his way, stepping into a faint drizzle of light rain as the shower tapered off. Others too were beginning to leave their doorways. Grant avoided watching the younger man's direction, waited for another minute, and left.

As in most Viennese streets, old or rebuilt, the buildings formed a continuous row with only an occasional small difference in height, a matter of one storey more or less. Yet there wasn't any sense of uniformity: walls and windows were varied in design and decoration. No skyscrapers to dwarf smaller neighbours or tower above domes and spires. Where there had been bomb and fire damage – and around this old quarter surrounding the Cathedral it had been heavy – there were replacements, lighter in colour yet not offensively new. Helmut Fischer's shop was one of these reconstructions.

It was much much smaller, in size and prestige, than

137

the old Fischer *Kunstgalerie* had been over in the New Market; if he regretted that loss, he never mentioned it. A new beginning was necessary after his return from exile; and he had made a success of it, resisting expansion into larger quarters or any increase in staff as he gradually re-established himself. He had resisted, too, any heavy investments in art: he hadn't the capital for that. Instead, he offered lesser-known painters, some carefully-selected contemporary pictures, and a vast collection of old masters in excellent Viennese reproductions. Who could afford the real ones? Museums and millionaires. Better a perfect fourteen-colour reproduction of a masterpiece than a wall left blank or filled with second-rate originals. It was partly because of this collection of reproductions, and partly because Fischer had gathered one of the best reference libraries on art, that Grant was now entering the Fischer gallery. But mostly because, he added to that, Helmut Fischer was a man he liked and trusted.

Fischer was at the far end of the long narrow room, deep in conversation with a likely prospect. He looked, as always, ten years younger than his age, and could easily pass for fifty-four. His fair hair seemed whiter although his face appeared to be as tanned and healthy as ever, his figure trim; there was little sign, at this distance, of his keen features showing any dewlap or double chin. Judging from the rapt attention of his client, an elderly *grande dame* complete with extraordinary hat and white gloves, his capacity to charm had not diminished.

Watching him now, Grant was reminded of the first time he had stepped into this shop, a young GI on leave in Vienna, in search of new directions for his life. That was in 1963. Many more visits on his next leave, and a deepening friendship – a mentor-pupil relationship – which quickened again on Grant's third visit to

Vienna in 1970. Then a gap of seven years, bridged by sporadic letters and greetings on Christmas cards. At least, thought Grant, this room hasn't changed except for the pictures: the same white walls and dark blue carpet; the same neat black leather armchairs, the same central table with books and magazines. He moved away from the door, over to a large display of abstract water-colours.

Fischer was quite aware that someone had entered, but true to form he didn't look round or interrupt the lady's plaintive questions. With tact, he began to lead her towards the entrance. 'No,' he was saying, 'I really do advise you not to buy one more picture until you have some space for it on your walls. You must select, Baroness, select. How? Keep your favourites, give the others to your friends; or send them into the attic, or to auction. Space is what you need, not more paintings.' He settled her indecision by a bow over the extended white glove, a light kiss above its wrist, a final goodbye. The door was closed; Fischer could turn to the newcomer who had been concentrating on the abstracts. 'Interesting, aren't they? Much less aggressive than in oils.'

Grant faced him with a wide smile. 'You could have sold her a couple of them. You're too honest to be in business, Helmut.'

'Colin!' Fischer halted in astonishment, then came forward with hands outheld. 'Did you just drop in from New York?' There was a warm hand-clasp, an enthusiastic clap on Grant's shoulder. 'How long are you staying this time? Any why not with me? I still have that guest-room upstairs.'

'I thought it might be occupied,' Grant said delicately. On his last visit there had been a ravishing redhead well established in Fischer's apartment. 'Frankly, I'm not sure how long I'll be in Vienna, or how much free time I'll have. This trip has been a little unexpected. I arrived yesterday. I'm staying at the Majestic.'

'Well, if you get tired of it, you always have a room here. Or why don't you come and visit Grünau again? There's a new road since you were there – cuts driving time in half, down to two hours.'

'At a steady seventy, ascents and hairpin bends included?' Grant suggested. They were now entering, at the far end of the long room, a brightly lit corridor lined with Fischer's reference books. From there, Grant remembered, they'd reach the room with the reproductions carefully filed, and then Fischer's office.

'Come this week-end – oh, the devil take it!' Fischer was dismayed. 'I'm off to Salzburg for three days of Mozart – the Festival. All arranged last January. I am sorry, Colin. Really, I meant that invitation. Why don't *you* spend the week-end in Grünau? All cities are desolate on Sundays: everyone rushing off to the country in little white cars.' As they passed along the stacks of reference books, he noticed Grant lingering near the volumes dealing with the Dutch school, but made no comment. 'Prosperity, prosperity,' he went on, 'everyone employed, everyone with money in his pocket. Delightful. But crowded on the highways. Thank heavens, Grünau is still remote – until the new road is discovered. I give us one more year before we are pushed to the mountain-tops.'

'I really don't know my plans,' Grant began, and then, feeling this sounded like an evasive refusal, added warmly, 'If I can get away, Helmut, I'll take you up on that invitation.'

'Good. The key is in the usual place, food is in the larder. Now let's catch up on our news.' At the door to his office, he halted again and faced Grant. His eyes, bright blue against the tanned skin, were suddenly

140

grave, sympathetic. 'I was sorry, so very sorry, to hear about your wife.'

'I received your note. Thank you for—'

'Three lines – what can they say? What could three hundred say? I never was any good at sad letters.' No more mention would be made of Jennifer: illness and death were two topics that Fischer avoided. In a way, thought Grant, it was a relief to be spared well-intended questions – no details necessary, no painful recapitulation.

'Leni,' Fischer was saying to the young woman at work inside his office, 'please take charge of the gallery. If the Baroness comes back, don't call me. Just ease her out. Gently, now!'

Leni, another redhead (but with glasses and snub nose, and – to judge from the ledger over which she had been sprawling – more adept with figures than with feminine graces), left a sheaf of accounts. 'She won't stay long if she finds only me,' Leni predicted, and with a bob of a greeting to Grant, bounced her way like a young filly along the corridor.

Fischer laughed at the expression on Grant's face. 'Leni is inclined to be abrupt. The Baroness never buys anything, and has nothing to sell. It just passes the time for her, poor old thing: everything in the past; nothing in the future. Now, what about ourselves? Do you like working with Schofeld?' He gestured to a comfortable armchair, sat down facing Grant and stretched his legs.

Time slipped away. With a start, Grant remembered to look at his watch. It was almost half past four. 'I've an appointment at five thirty,' he said.

'Then there is no rush.'

'Except that I've some research to do. May I use your reference library?'

'By all means, my dear fellow.' Fischer concealed his

141

surprise, and led the way into the corridor. 'I didn't know you were specializing in the Dutch painters,' he said as he pointed with a smile to the shelf of books that had caught Grant's attention.

'Oh – just for an article or two,' Grant said vaguely. 'Thought I might find some material here, and save myself a trip to—'

'Of course, of course.' That brushed aside Grant's fumble for an adequate explanation. 'What period?'

'The early sixteen-hundreds.'

'This volume, then. Any particular painters?'

Grant took refuge in one of his old ideas. 'Vermeer and Ruysdael. Interiors versus exteriors, as it were.'

'Interesting juxtaposition,' Fischer conceded. 'Which will you begin with? Ruysdael is less demanding. Once you lose yourself in Vermeer you'd never make a five-thirty appointment.'

'Ruysdael, then, as a starter.'

Fischer had the volume in his hand, opening it to the correct page.

'You know your way around, don't you?' Grant asked, slight astonishment mixed with admiration.

Fischer laughed. 'To be honest, I was reading this section on Ruysdael only three days ago. A man came in here searching for some seventeenth-century reproductions, and the Dutch masters caught his eye, particularly the Ruysdael picture of the Crooked Rhine at Utrecht.'

'Possibly 1642?' Grant was quoting Lois Westerbrook exactly.

'Positively 1642.'

'I was told "possibly", I wonder why?' Westerbrook had done her homework on the information she had dropped at the Albany interview.

'Because,' Fischer explained, 'that view of Utrecht doesn't appear to be signed or dated. You have to look at the back of the painting to see name and date. Strange fellow, Salomon van Ruysdael. He never dated any of his early paintings – not until 1627, in fact.'

'Careless or modest?'

'Probably both. Perhaps he didn't think they were important enough.'

'If he put the date of a 1642 painting out of sight, it seems he didn't think too much of it, either.'

'That doesn't lessen its value today. Of course, you would have to loosen – at the top right-hand corner – the protective canvas attached to the frame if you wanted to see the date on the back of the picture, and make sure it's authentic. There's little chance of doing that for either or us. The painting is in Budapest.'

'Might I see the reproduction?'

'The man bought it. Paid cash. For both the reproduction and the frame he ordered Joachim to make. Very specific about the frame's design and colour.'

'Joachim?'

'Oh, he does all our framing work. His shop is in the alley just behind us. This was a rush job; fortunately the frame was simple. Just a rim of narrow wood, weathered grey. Looked very natural, though, around the Ruysdael.'

'Do you think I could see it?'

'It was collected this morning, I'm afraid – with the antiquing Joachim had used scarcely dry.' Fischer shook his head in amusement.

'You have no other copy of the reproduction?'

'I've ordered a replacement. However, that takes a little time. It's a very fine example of Viennese colour-printing.'

'Quite deceptive,' Grant said thoughtfully. He had bought two of Fischer's reproductions on his last visit. They looked remarkably real to most people, because the printer did not use ordinary paper, but something closely akin to a painter's canvas. Slant-lighting had

143

been employed in the initial process to catch the artist's brush strokes, and with the final touch of light varnish, skilfully applied, the finished product seemed almost authentic. Almost, that was, to the expert. To others completely. 'An art in itself,' he added, trying to conceal his growing worry. 'I'd have liked to see that reproduction. I suppose it followed every detail, including the date on the back?'

'That was omitted. It's a reproduction; not a fake. Unnecessary, anyway: people don't usually ask about it – they take the experts' opinion on the date.'

'What about the man who bought the reproduction? Didn't he notice the omission?'

'No. I didn't bother explaining it to him – wasn't given the opportunity, in fact: he was in too great a hurry to order a suitable frame.' Fischer turned over several pages of the reference book and found what he wanted. 'Here is an exact description of the picture, and a small photograph. Gives you an idea, anyway, of Ruysdael's composition. No date visible, as you see.'

'Thank you,' and Grant meant it. 'What was your customer's name?'

Fischer stared slightly. 'He avoided that. A very abrupt type, everything strictly business. However, he had to leave his name with Joachim so that the picture could be safely collected by messenger.' A faint smile spread over Fischer's lips. 'He gave the name of Smith, John Smith.'

'American or British?'

Fischer looked at Grant with an appraising eye. 'This man worries you, I think,' he said very gently. 'He spoke German quite well – with an accent.' Fischer paused and considered, then added, 'He was older than you – perhaps in his late forties, blue eyes, fair hair – grey at the temples, really quite handsome, but very serious. Oh yes, and medium height.'

There was a small silence. Grant stared down at the book in his hand.

'You know him?' Fischer asked.

'I've met him.' The description fitted Gene Marck.

'You don't sound enthusiastic. A competitor, I presume? At least, I don't imagine you have much in common. He wears the most disastrous bow-ties. Now, why don't you take the book into my office and make some notes at my desk? Just push all the ledgers aside. I'll go and see what Leni is arguing about.' For her voice, abrupt and authoritative, was now carrying clearly into the corridor. With visible annoyance, Fischer hurried away.

Lost in his own thoughts, Grant closed the reference book. As he replaced the volume on the shelf, his mind flashed back to the Albany Hotel in New York – Lois Westerbrook – Gene Marck. Wearing a bow-tie? Grant couldn't recall. If one was worn that night, it had been unobtrusive: Marck's clothes had been discreet to the point of dullness. Then the memory vanished, as a voice he knew snapped his attention to the front room. Yet it seemed so much louder, clearer than he had heard it yesterday in a rose garden.

Quickly he moved to the door. Yes, it was Avril Hoffman. Her eyes met his. She seemed to relax as she saw him – as if she had been watching for him to appear – a brief moment before she returned all her attention to Fischer who was explaining, with considerable pleasure and utmost patience, that it was unfortunate he could show her nothing by Tanguy. Perhaps some Dali drawings? Or a reproduction of Magritte? Now, if she were interested in Klee—

Grant interrupted, addressing Avril directly. 'If you are trying to track down a Tanguy, there's an excellent reference library here. Helmut, would you mind?'

145

Avril was quick to take her cue. 'May I?' she asked Fischer.

'Down this way,' Grant said, standing politely aside to let her enter the corridor. Fischer looked bewildered – the first time Grant had ever seen him completely astounded – although he recovered enough poise to follow. Grant stopped him with a broad smile. 'Let me handle this, will you?' he asked very quietly.

Fischer looked at him, incredulous. Then he smiled too. 'Of course, of course.' He left the corridor door open as he moved back into the main room, partly to pacify a ruffled Leni, partly to deal with a possible client who had just arrived on the scene.

Half-way down the book stacks, Avril said, 'It was absolutely frustrating. I knew definitely you were here – Frank passed the word to Bob – but I didn't know how to reach you. I had to raise my voice. Awful, wasn't it? We have to be quick, so here's the message. You pack tonight, and be ready to leave the Majestic in the morning. Tell the hotel desk that you are spending the week-end at Dürnstein. We'll have a taxi at the main door – ten o'clock exactly. It will drop you near Klar's Auction Rooms, and the driver will take your luggage to your new room. All clear?'

'All clear. But what new—'

'Just do it, Colin. Please.'

'Okay, okay.' The Majestic wouldn't question his departure: his room was paid in advance for two weeks. 'Ten o'clock sharp.'

She pretended to look at a book on the shelf beside her, glanced back along the corridor through the opened door at the room. She frowned slightly.

What had caught her attention? Grant didn't ask. 'Avril,' he said (she had called him Colin, hadn't she); 'would you get Bob to check up on Gene Marck?'

'We have already done that.' She looked along the

146

corridor again. 'We shouldn't spend too much time together. I must go.'

'He came here three days ago. Bought a reproduction of the Ruysdael.'

That halted her. 'Are you sure it was Marck?'

'Almost sure. I'll give you the details tomorrow. You'll be waiting in the car outside the auction rooms?'

'I'll be there. We'll have something to tell you, too. Good news. You may not have to worry much longer about the Ruysdael.' Once more, she glanced towards the room, where Fischer was talking with the man who had followed her into the shop. 'I wish there was another way out of here.'

'There is – by the service entrance. Might seem odd, though.'

She didn't share his amusement. 'I'm afraid so.' She began walking back along the corridor. 'What shall we tell your nice friend?'

'The particular Tanguy painting that interested you is in New York. The one called *Awakening* – will that do?'

'*S Eveiller?*' Her eyes laughed as he raised an eyebrow at her use of the original title. 'Is it really in New York?'

'Yes. Friends of mine own it.'

'So we're on safe ground.'

'Solid.'

They were about to enter the room. 'Leave me,' she said softly, and touched his arm in goodbye.

'And shock Helmut?' Grant shook his head. 'We'll enter together.'

'As strangers,' she reminded him.

The only thing strange about this girl, he thought, is the fact that she isn't a stranger although it's scarcely two days since we met. He followed her in silence into the room.

Fischer hurried to take charge. He was delighted that Grant didn't insist on walking with this charming girl to the door. That was his prerogative as master of these premises, and a successful one: an invitation to return whenever she wanted to pass a pleasant hour among pictures; a shy acceptance – and what an enchanting smile this girl had. Quite won over by these last minutes, Fischer closed the door behind her with one final approving look at her cream-coloured wool suit, beautifully fitted, the skirt just the right length to show a pair of excellent legs. Then he turned to the man who had been studying the watercolours. He too was about to leave, without even a civil good-day as he hurried into the street. Just someone who had drifted into the shop as several did, with only the intent to look, never to buy. Fortunate, thought Fischer, that I don't have to depend on that type to maintain my style of living. His important clients were serious collectors, relying on his taste and judgment. His usual good mood quite restored, he reached Grant, who had been talking with Leni and was now bidding her goodbye. 'Must you go?'

'Afraid so. I'm late.' It was almost five fifteen by Grant's watch. 'I hope you don't mind, but I had Leni call for a cab while I waited for your farewells to end. You do spin them out, Helmut. The prettier the girl, the longer they take.'

Fischer laughed. 'She was most attractive,' he agreed. 'Strange – did she think I was hard of hearing? I don't look that old, surely.'

'Foreigners often raise their voices when they are coping with a strange language,' Grant suggested.

That was accepted. But Fischer had another question, which – as usual – he put indirectly. 'Strange, too, that at first she seemed so vague about Tanguy; yet, as she was leaving, quite knowledgeable.' He shot a quick glance at Grant, his eyes expressionless.

'Your reference library—'

'Of course.' Fischer's voice was suddenly cool. 'Did

you plan to meet her here?' If so, he was thinking, you could have told me: I do not like being used. A romantic assignation – that I understand. A deception? No. Not from a friend.

'I came to see you, Helmut. Nothing else was planned.'

Fischer's smile returned. 'Not even your questions about Ruysdael?'

'Those were,' Grant admitted. 'But where could I find better information?'

'The taxi is here,' Leni announced.

With relief, Grant moved quickly to the door. Fischer's questions were only beginning, and might be unanswerable. Their leave-taking was warm, even if hurried, with an invitation to dinner on Monday (Fischer); perhaps, if possible (Grant); telephone number in Salzburg (Fischer): a promise to get in touch (Grant).

'My thanks,' Grant remembered to call back, raising his voice as he dashed towards the taxi. 'Many many thanks.'

Fischer closed the door. Why so many thanks? Just the exuberance of a young man? Suddenly he felt a twinge of age. 'Leni,' he asked, 'would you say I was hard of hearing?'

13

Of course, he was late. Grant reached the Hofburgkeller at twenty-five minutes to six, and Lois Westerbrook had been counting each overdue second. That he could tell, even as he found her waiting near the entrance, and followed her at a discreet distance – not upstairs to the restaurants and white tablecloths, but down the steps into the basement level where the vaulted beer-hall and adjacent taprooms were to be found. Annoyance was in her step as she marched to a vacant table sheltering near a stone arch, a grey-clad figure in a demure suit guaranteed to attract little attention. Her golden hair was entirely hidden, this time with a plain brown scarf twisted around her head. Her face seemed whiter, its Arizona tan covered with heavy make-up. Eyebrows were scarcely noticeable, lips were pale. Except for the excellent profile that nothing could disguise, the transformation was complete. She didn't even need the tortoise-shell-rimmed glasses that hid her eyes.

As for Grant, nearing her table slowly, his feelings were as indefinite as his movements. Of one thing he was certain: this was going to be a difficult meeting; too bad he had made it worse by being late. Remember, he warned himself, you are supposed to know nothing at all – neither the date of the auction, nor Ferenc Ady's name, nor his death. Blot all that out of your mind: no slip of the tongue. You know as little as you did three weeks ago, when you last met Westerbrook. A difficult meeting? The most difficult he ever had to face, he admitted. And sat down opposite her. 'Sorry I kept you waiting. Traffic . . .'

Now that they were safely together, Lois Westerbrook relaxed. She had taken the chair that faced the wall, her back turned to the giant room. She glanced over her shoulder, right, then left, for a last casual survey of the other tables. She seemed satisfied. She removed her glasses. Her smile was warm. 'At least, we got here before the mob scene starts. I'll have a glass of wine.'

He ordered a carafe – everything came out of barrels in the Hofburgkeller – along with a tankard of beer. I'll let her make the pace, he decided.

'You are very silent today,' she said lightly.

'Just waiting for your news. Bad or good?'

'Abrupt, aren't you?'

'Well, this meeting was your idea,' he countered. 'You had something to tell me.' Which couldn't be cabled or telephoned, he remembered.

'Just a message from Mr Basset. That can wait. First, what about you? Are you comfortable at the Majestic?'

'Who wouldn't be?'

'Then what's troubling you?'

'I haven't seen or heard from Gene Marck.'

'Oh – about the auction? Surely there's no need to worry about its date. It *is* scheduled, you know.'

'When?'

She dropped her voice almost to a whisper. 'As soon as our refugee is safe. Gene will let you know about that. He isn't in Vienna at the moment. Urgent business out of town.'

'When do you expect him back?'

'Soon.' The small hope she had built up – Gene possibly returning tonight, in good time for tomorrow's auction – had been completely dashed by the Sacher's reply to her discreet enquiry: Herr Marck was out of the city; he was not expected back until morning. Gene is cutting it very fine, she thought, her lips tightening. 'Why are you so impatient, Colin?'

He waited until their drinks were served, and took a long draught of beer. 'Not impatient – just at loose ends. Can't make any definite arrangements until I know what is scheduled. For instance, I'd like to spend this week-end in the country: leave tomorrow morning, return Monday.'

She hadn't expected that. 'A week-end where?'

'At Dürnstein.'

'What's wrong with Vienna? I thought your friends would be keeping you well entertained.'

'Not at the week-ends. Vienna empties then.'

She said quickly, 'I'd advise you to stay – Gene may be in touch with you tomorrow.'

'I'll leave the Dürnstein address. He could phone there.'

'No,' she said, her voice sharpening. 'He wants you here.'

'But Dürnstein isn't so far away.'

'Why don't you keep to our initial arrangements?'

'Two weeks in Vienna?'

That caught her off balance again. She cupped the small tumbler of wine in her hands, didn't lift it from the table. She stared down at it, seeing and not seeing. Gene put me in this predicament, she was thinking, summoned me here to do his talking for him. How much do I tell Grant? More than Gene advised? It may be the only way to get him out of this difficult mood. 'You'll certainly be here for another week,' she said at last.

He half smiled, shook his head. 'Is that keeping to our initial arrangements?' So it was one more week, and why even that delay? He made a guess at one possible explanation: they were making damn sure that the cheque for the Ruysdael would be safely deposited in Geneva before he left Vienna.

'One week,' she said firmly. 'That's the message I'm bringing from Mr Basset. He had news about his friend in Budapest.' Very softly, she added, 'There has been a slight delay in his arrival in Vienna.'

'The escape is postponed?'

'No, no. Just a small delay.'

'Once he is here, the auction takes place?' He was openly sceptical. 'Oh, come on, Lois. You know you can't schedule an auction at a day's notice. It looks as if I'll be kept waiting here for several weeks. That is *not* in our initial arrangements. I have plans of my own, you know.'

For a long moment she was silent, her face expressionless. 'You are right. Of course the auction was scheduled in advance.' Would that hold him? she wondered, raising her eyes to meet his. No, she decided, he had to be told a little more, just enough to keep him believing her. *You can handle him,* Gene had said. But only in her own way; not in Gene's. 'You see,' she began, 'we thought Mr Basset's friend would be safe in Vienna by this week-end, so the auction was arranged for tomorrow. You will attend it, even if our refugee arrives later than expected.'

'When and where tomorrow?' How far can I push her into telling the truth? Grant speculated. Extraordinary amber eyes she has when she softens their expression as she is doing right now. Melting is the word for it. And all for me? He repressed a smile.

'Gene will be in touch with you about that. There may be a message waiting for you at the Majestic right now. When did you leave your hotel today?'

'This morning.'

'You haven't been back? Good heavens, you really must have been busy. I suppose you met your friends and time vanished. Now I see why you were late. I forgive you. Look – I thought I might give a small party

153

in my room tomorrow evening – just to celebrate. Why don't you ask your friends to join us? Of course, we won't talk about the Ruysdael. It's still Mr Basset's secret. We all keep quiet about it until you deliver it to him in New York.'

'And that won't be until his refugee is safe in Vienna?'

'Exactly. That's why you've got to spend a few more days here, once the auction is over.'

It all sounded sweetly reasonable, until you started thinking hard into the elaborate stratagem these people – Marck, Lois, and who else? – had worked out so carefully. A few days more in Vienna after the auction, perhaps a week . . . Perhaps nothing. Once the cheque was safe in that Geneva bank account, would the Ruysdael be allowed to leave Vienna? Or would a reproduction take its place?

She was saying, 'The Ruysdael will be fully insured, of course. You can put it in the hotel's storage vault, or even keep it in your own room, or leave it with the auctioneer, or whatever. In any case, just forget about it and enjoy your remaining days in Vienna. I'm sorry, really I'm sorry, that you didn't get your full two weeks. Mr Basset will make up for that, somehow. I know he will.'

The hell with Basset, he thought, and the hell with you too, Miss Amber Eyes. Just forget about the Ruysdael and enjoy myself? At any rate, it sounds as though nothing unpleasant has been planned for me. Or – he suddenly stared at her as she lifted the glass of wine and took her first sip – is that what I am meant to believe? I'm just to relax, have a good time, and stay unsuspecting?

'No comment?' she asked lightly. 'Is this your day for silence? If you see any problem – tell me.'

'There's one thing that does puzzle me. Why doesn't Gene Marck take charge of the picture as soon as I've bought it? I could hand it to him in the auction room after it was paid for, say "It's all yours, pal" – let *him* hang around Vienna with it, until he gets the signal to climb on that plane.'

'There must be *no* connection of anyone of Mr Basset's staff with—'

'Oh, come on, Lois. I could hand it to him in the room where the cheque is signed. Who'll see us there, except people he can trust?'

'But,' she said, 'Gene is leaving Vienna as soon as the Ruysdael transaction is completed. Tomorrow afternoon he will be in Switzerland. Then there's Berlin after that. He's a very busy man, Colin.' She looked at him reproachfully.

He nodded. She could find a reason for anything, this girl. 'Remarkable eyes you have,' he said. 'Doesn't Gene tell you that? Or is he too busy to notice?'

She laughed and said, 'Oh, we are only professional associates. We keep it that way.'

'But you do choose his ties?' Perhaps not as subtle as Sherlock Holmes in probing for a lead, but it might do.

'Oh, that's part of my job. It's best to restrain his taste. Mr Basset likes quiet colours.'

'And Gene's taste is wild?' He finished his beer, looked around for the waitress to order another tankard. It was thirsty work juggling with Westerbrook. Sharply, he looked again – not at the waitress, but at a man and girl who had walked into the room arm in arm. Now they were taking one of the last vacant tables, only thirty feet away. The girl was a buxom brunette. The man was Gene Marck. He wasn't wearing any tie; a polo sweater was tight around his neck. Grant's smile broadened. So much for your Sherlock Holmes effort, he told himself.

'Not really,' Lois Westerbrook was saying. 'His taste is usually good. But he has no colour sense.' She looked severely at Grant. 'Tell me – why did you advertise your arrival by hiring a Mercedes-Benz?'

Grant's smile vanished. They had put him under surveillance even at the airport, had they? Suddenly all the fuss and bother that Bob Renwick and Frank and sweet Avril, too, had taken, no longer seemed unnecessary or ludicrous. 'You said first-class all the way,' he counter-attacked. 'What did you expect me to do? Take a bus, arrive at the Majestic on foot?'

'There were taxis—'

'Find them! And if you are worried about my mistakes, what about yours? Booking me into the Majestic! That's not on my budget, and all my friends know it. If anyone advertised my arrival here, it was you. What excuse do I give them for my sudden affluence, I ask you?'

'Your friends have been questioning you?'

So she was back to that subject again. 'No. They're too polite, although they must be raising an eyebrow about the Majestic. You goofed, Lois. Admit it. Or was it Gene?'

'Really, Colin, you are impossible.'

'Well, not as impossible as to be in two places at once. Like dear Gene.' Grant was smiling again. 'He's just to the right of you, across the room, thirty feet away. You can look. He wouldn't notice. He may not have much taste in bow-ties, but he knows his women.' Grant decided he had said enough. Lois Westerbrook's eyes opened wide in angry disbelief. She glanced over her shoulder to her right, and went rigid.

She looked back at Grant. 'When did he come in?'

'Five minutes ago. A fast worker. He's been nuzzling that bouncing brunette ever since.' Grant had been deliberately frank – one way of working out his own anger against Marck, perhaps. But he hadn't expected Lois Westerbrook to crumble. She had a second look at Marck, his hands entwined with the girl's, his lips at her

156

ear and then at her neck before he drew apart with a laugh. She turned her eyes away and sat in silence, one elbow on the table, her hand covering her face, her head bowed.

At last she said, 'Get me out of here.'

'Past his table?'

'No. Through that door behind me.'

He called the waitress and paid. Lois Westerbrook stared again at Gene Marck. With his back to the room, he seemed to be feeling quite safe from anyone's scrutiny. Perhaps the crowd of strangers around him, or the medley of voices and laughter, or his green jacket and mustard-yellow sweater, gave him a feeling of complete anonymity. Or he just hadn't expected anyone who knew him to be there. Yes, thought Grant as he walked beside Lois Westerbrook, shielding her from Marck's table, we all make a mistake at times. This one, judging from Westerbrook's arm, tense under his guiding hand, was enormous.

She refused a cab, walked away, without one more question about the friends Grant had met in Vienna.

He dined at the Majestic, and then went upstairs to begin packing.

It was approaching midnight when his telephone rang. Grant was in bed but not asleep. He rolled over and reached for the receiver, cursing it silently. 'Hello,' he said roughly.

'Colin?' It was Lois Westerbrook. 'Colin – are you there?'

He sat up, became fully alert. She must be calling from some café – there was the distant sound of *Schrammel* music in the background. Her voice sounded blurred, no longer clear and decided. 'Yes, I'm here. Better speak up – it's difficult to hear you.'

'Wait a moment.' There was the sound of a door closing, and the music was cut off. 'Colin—'

'Yes, yes. What is it?'

'I just wanted to tell you—' She paused.

Her voice was still blurred, indecisive. Was she drunk? 'Have you had something to eat?'

She wasn't listening. She went on, 'To tell you – I'm sorry. I'm sorry I brought you here.' Her voice quickened. 'But I'll fix him. I'll fix him for good. You know what I did? I got into his room.' Her laugh was brief, strange, unnatural.

'Lois—' he began.

She rushed on. 'No danger, no danger at all. He won't be back there till tomorrow morning. Too busy now with that pie-faced bitch of a floozy. I trusted him, Colin, I really trusted that man.' She was almost crying now. 'Trusted him. I helped him with his job, I showed him how to please old Basset, I – Oh, Colin, I'm sorry I got you into this.' She stopped weeping, her voice rose a little. 'You know what I found in his room? He thinks he is the brains, I'm just his fool. He thinks I couldn't guess where he hides things.' That started her laughing again. 'Who's the fool? I found a tin of talcum powder, a hairbrush, a pen.'

She isn't drunk, she's crazy, Grant thought in alarm.

'Don't you understand, Colin?'

'No.'

'They all come to pieces. Little hiding-places inside. Tricks of the trade, Colin. A code-book, a tiny roll of film, and a—' She broke off in sudden panic. 'Time is up. I've no more coins. Call me back. Quick—' and she rattled off her telephone number just before her call was ended.

Tricks of the trade . . . He hesitated. Then he dialled the number.

She must have snatched up the phone even as it began its ring. She was saying excitedly, 'There was a small list of addresses, some initials. These were in the hairbrush.

Its back slides apart when you press and twist.' Another small laugh, abruptly checked. Her voice changed. 'Oh, Colin – I'm afraid.'

'Did you take these things?' Grant was horrified. She's in danger, real danger, he thought.

'Yes. But he won't know it was me. I fitted all his gadgets together again. When he finds them empty, he will blame your friends.'

Friends . . . Grant's concern vanished. Was this another of her clever little stratagems to force information out of him? 'Then why are you afraid?' he asked.

'I'm afraid of what he's into. Much deeper than I thought. Much worse. Colin – please take me to meet your friends. I'll give them all I've discovered.'

Yes, he thought, it's all a beautiful come-on. 'How deep were *you* into all this?'

There was a brief silence. 'Only the money angle – a percentage. Don't you see, Colin, we had to have something to get married on?' The pathetic question ended in a sob.

You bloody fool, he told himself, you nearly believed her again.

She said, 'Colin – please call your friends. One of them could meet me here. At the Three Guitars. Tonight.'

'You're mistaken about my friends. How could any of them help you?'

'Just tell them. That's all. I'll be waiting.'

'You're crazy, Lois.'

'Then why did you listen to me?'

He had no answer for that.

'Tell them,' she repeated. 'They will find me easily. I don't know who they are, but they'll know me. I'm sure of that. Goodbye, Colin. Take care. Take very great care.'

And that was that.

Grant sat very still. Just another confidence trick, he told himself. Yet . . . He rose, lit a cigarette, walked around the room. It was now twelve-fifteen. In Vienna the night was still young. Should he get in touch with Bob Renwick? Try, at least? He'd better get some clothes on, go downstairs, find a public phone. He dressed in haste. Within ten minutes he was calling the Embassy.

Once through, he asked for Renwick's extension. A voice told him that he could leave his name if his call was urgent. He left it. And smoked two more cigarettes until Renwick phoned. Grant wasted no time. He said, 'We might have a defector on our hands – you can guess who: the one who met me at the Hofburgkeller. It could be for real, it could be a trap – another little game plan to let her meet you. Worth the risk, do you think? If so, she's waiting now, at the Three Guitars. She's sure you'll know her at once.'

'Did she talk much?'

'Too damn much even over a public phone.'

'Worth hearing?'

'If she's telling the truth – yes.'

'Okay. Thanks for letting me know.'

'I wasn't sure whether I should—'

'Be seeing you,' Renwick said.

Grant took the hint and put down the receiver. I'm still not sure whether I did the right thing when I called Bob, he thought. I just hope to God it was.

Upstairs again, he undressed slowly, tried to settle himself with another cigarette, went to bed at last. It took him a full hour before he fell asleep.

14

On Friday morning, at nine o'clock, they were gathered
in Prescott Taylor's office. Taylor himself had been there
since eight thirty. Avril appeared ten minutes later.
Frank slipped in six minutes before the hour. And
Renwick – usually the first on the scene – entered at the
last moment, with a small book in one hand, the file on
Herr Doktor Mittendorf in the other.

'Has Korda arrived?' Renwick asked. He looked as if
he could use several hours' more sleep.

Taylor said, 'He's safe.' Taylor had been against bringing the defector back into the Embassy, even for one
brief visit. But he had to admit it was probably better
security than having the four of them confront Gyorgy
Korda in the apartment where he had been living completely isolated and thoroughly guarded. Too many
visitors, all arriving and leaving around the same time,
could attract attention to Korda's hiding place. Easier,
Renwick had argued, to have him brought here, heavily
disguised, and smuggled up to the attic room where, six
weeks ago, he had spent his first three nights of asylum.
Easier for everyone, too: the auction was taking place at
eleven o'clock in Werner Klar's establishment near St
Stephen's Cathedral, a district difficult to reach from
Korda's apartment in Heilingenstadt.

'Safe and not too uncomfortable?' Frank asked with
mock concern. He was in excellent humour this morning. He looked, thought Renwick, as if he had a nice
little ace tucked up his sleeve. 'Any news about Lois
Westerbrook?'

Renwick shook his head.

'Could have been a trap,' Frank suggested.

'We'll talk about that later,' said Renwick. 'Let's concentrate on Korda. You want to begin, Frank?'

'I'll wait.'

'Okay. Prescott, what about you?'

'I saw Korda yesterday. Talked with him at length. He isn't giving us anything more on Jack. I thought it better not to ask whether the name was Jack or Jacques, until we all meet him today. We may have to bluff him into believing we know more about Jack – or Jacques – than we actually do.' Taylor smoothed back his thin blond hair over his bald spot, adjusted his glasses. 'We really haven't too much, have we?' he asked unhappily.

Avril said, 'I've been over that tape where Jacques was mentioned. Several times. I think it *is* Jacques.'

'He could have been pronouncing Jack badly,' Taylor reminded her. 'His accent is far from impeccable.'

'Jacques,' Avril said stubbornly.

'I hope it is,' Renwick said with a smile. 'Because all I've got to add to this discussion is a hunch. Jacques does exist. Here are his poems. Here's the file dealing with them.' He laid them both on Taylor's desk. 'A quick glance will do. I've sidelined the report where it deals with Jacques.'

'May I?' Avril asked, and picked up Mrs Jameson's report once Taylor had finished with it. 'Frank, you'd better read this too.'

Renwick said, 'Frank and I talked about it yesterday. He thought it was a hunch we could use.'

As she read, Avril's eyes widened in astonishment. 'Heinrich Mittendorf?' She put the sheet of paper back into its folder, and lifted the book of verse. 'Old Closed-Lips wrote poetry?'

'Incredible,' Taylor agreed.

'Not bad, either,' said Renwick. 'I read a couple of his verses before I came up here.'

'Incredible,' repeated Taylor. 'Still, we haven't enough to convince Korda that we may be a jump ahead of him and if he doesn't start talking, he won't have anything to bargain with. In fact, his Jacques – the VIP Communist – and your Jacques – the young poet – may have no connection at all. That would only make Korda very very amused, certainly not talkative.'

'Except that,' Renwick pointed out, 'Jacques, the poet is now the treasurer of Allied Electronics, who has already signed two hefty cheques, deposited in Geneva, for a Degas and a Monet whose original owners are now missing or dead.'

'And,' said Avril, 'he's still alive. He's the only cheque-signer who hasn't met with an accident or died of an unexpected heart attack in the six weeks since Korda's defection.'

'Not conclusive,' Taylor said. 'Of course, we could risk using it to persuade Korda we may know more than we actually do. It might work. You see, he *wants* to tell us; he is simply waiting until he is safe in – What's so funny, Frank?'

For Frank had given a raucous laugh. 'Wants to tell us? He doesn't give a damn about any of us. The only one he will help is himself. When we show him we've got the proof on Jacques, he'd choke himself to death in his rush to get his information out. If you'd stop being so goddamned understanding about him, Taylor, you'd tell him that unless he adds to the facts we already possess, he won't get that passport to America.'

'But that,' Taylor pointed out, 'wouldn't be the case. He is definitely leaving here next week.'

'Does he know?' Renwick asked quickly.

'Not yet.'

'Then let's keep it that way meanwhile.'

Taylor wasn't finished with Frank. 'What facts do we already possess?' he challenged, but mildly, so that Frank wouldn't take offence. 'Nothing, really, except deductions and inferences.'

'I've got more than that.' Frank drew a batch of photographs from inside his leather jacket. (Like the two other men, he was dressed for the part they'd play this morning. Frank was driving a delivery truck; Renwick, in a casual sports jacket, was to wait in Cathedral Lane in the white Volkswagen; Taylor was the impeccably dressed diplomat, who enjoyed attending auctions.) 'First of all,' Frank said, 'I'd better tell you how we got these.' He dropped the photographs on the desk. He placed his hand over them, anchoring them securely, and began his explanation.

For the last few months Frank had been keeping a close watch on Bernard Mandel. He had installed two agents, with a camera and some other devices, in the front room of a house opposite the Two Crowns. There had been several interesting visitors coming to see Mandel, always in the morning when the hotel was empty – its guests out on trips or sightseeing. Mandel's friends used the front door quite openly. That wasn't so stupid, either: they were suitably dressed for a front-entrance visit. If they had used the back door, dressed in work-clothes, they would have been noticed by the kitchen staff – always some of them around. Herr Mandel did not receive workmen in his private office.

Yesterday morning – before Colin Grant had arrived at the Two Crowns – there was just such a visitor. He was still there when Grant appeared: he stayed out of sight and left when the all-clear was given – five minutes after Grant's departure.

Frank released the photographs, spread them over the desk, and picked up two of them. 'First, here is the visitor arriving. On foot. Back view of a man beginning

164

to mount the steps. Next, view of same man about to enter the Two Crowns. Height, under six feet – notice his head barely reached the level of the hotel's nameplate. Heavy build, dark suit, feet slightly splayed.

'Third photograph: view of man entering, taking hat off – hair looks dark – and about to shake hands. With Mandel, of course, who is always there to guide his visitors past the reception clerk – chosen for her stupidity, we think.

'Fourth: view of man leaving the hotel. Hat off, held partly to block his lower face. Hair is dark, but white at temples. Large brow, skin looks pale.

'Fifth: view of man descending steps. Carefully. Not young; sixty or so. Puts on hat and we can glimpse his face.

'Sixth: a moment's view of the man's face.

'Seventh: blow-up of that sixth view; and there we have him. Mittendorf.

'Finally, the eighth photograph: view of Mittendorf reaching the street. Hat on, head bent, hands clasped behind his back.'

'Good God,' Renwick said, and took a long deep breath. 'I knew you had an ace up your sleeve, Frank, but I didn't know you had all four of them. That's Mittendorf, all right – the tight mouth is unmistakable, the hands clasped behind his back, the careful way he places his feet.'

Taylor said, 'Congratulations, Frank. Pity you hadn't one of those long-range bugs that could pick up his conversation with Mandel.'

Frank's grin was broad. 'Oh, we have a nice little gadget that can reach as far as seventy yards. Any talk in the hotel lobby is easy to record – straight line of communication. Mandel's office is trickier: first there's a door under the shelter of a suitcase, then a corridor, then the office itself; an inner room, no windows. We've never got much but yawks and growls from that location. Would you like a playback of the few sentences they spoke in the lobby before Mittendorf left? Useful for voice identification.'

'Later,' Renwick said, glancing at his watch. 'Better start moving upstairs.'

Taylor ruffled his hair, smoothed it back into place. 'I really hate throwing ice-water all around. But listen, you fellows – we've got very little to back up our story and loosen Korda's tongue. All we've got is the fact that Mittendorf visited Mandel yesterday morning. He could have been reserving a room for his niece, any damned thing.'

'Prescott,' Renwick said, 'we aren't presenting our case against Mittendorf in a court of law. Not yet, anyway. We're going up to an attic room, where Korda is wondering why the hell he was brought back here. Let me handle him, will you? I'll bluff him out of his skin. Frank – you do your photo act. It was damned good – had me sweating. Avril, bring your tape-recorder. And you, old boy,' he added, clapping Taylor's shoulder, 'will back me up all the way, and – when the interview is over – you can even hand Korda his lollipop. Tell him that, goody goody for him, he will be off to Washington within a week to meet all these nice nice people. New name, new face, new everything. He can even stop having nightmares about the KGB. Okay, everyone?'

Avril left first. Then Prescott Taylor, two minutes later. Another couple of minutes, and Frank, as the visitor was escorted upstairs by Renwick. 'What,' Renwick wanted to know, 'did you actually pick up from the Two Crowns lobby?'

'They didn't talk much,' Frank said. 'Too intelligent for that: they had discussed all their business in the office. Mittendorf said two sentences. 'Yes, remote control would be best. Can you handle it?' Mandel replied, 'I know someone who can.' And that was all.

'Remote control?' Renwick frowned. Remote control for what? 'Was nothing said when Mittendorf first arrived?'

'Platitudes from Mandel, and instructions to the receptionist not to disturb him in his office. Of course, we picked up Grant's interview too.'

'How did he do?'

'Not bad, not bad at all.'

'Feeling better about him?'

'We could have done worse. We could have drawn someone like Prescott Taylor's twin brother.'

'Come on, Frank. Taylor's a pretty good man.'

'Yeah, if he sees everything written down twice and has legal advice to back it.'

'I'll tell you one thing. This morning we would get nowhere with Korda, nowhere at all, if Taylor wasn't up there with us.'

Frank shook his head. These Americans amused him. 'Just give me Korda alone for ten minutes and I'll get somewhere fast.'

Gyorgy Korda was well-fed, well-dressed, well-slept, but bored with inaction. Yes, he agreed, he had no complaints about his security – only about this long delay in his journey to America: it was urgent he should get there soon, he had specific information for the Defence Department.

'But Jacques is of no interest to them,' Renwick pointed out. 'He *is* of interest to us. Jacques, not Jack. We know a lot about him.'

'It is not always possible to remember—'

'Try'.

'Later – in Washington – details may . . .'

167

'We want the details now. As a proof of your good faith.'

'I have already proved that.'

Which was true enough. 'Prove it completely,' Renwick said.

Korda looked at Taylor. 'You know I've demonstrated—'

'Yes,' agreed Taylor. 'This is the final test, Gyorgy. If you don't pass it, how can we recommend you to Washington? Don't you see?'

Korda saw. But he was still hesitant.

'Let's jog your memory,' Renwick suggested, glancing at his watch. 'We'll begin with this.' He produced the book of poems.

Korda's eyebrows, dark under the blond wig he had worn for this morning's journey, rose slightly as he saw the name Mittendorf. But the verses by Jacques were something that merely amused him. 'Never heard of them,' he said with a laugh.

'And the name of Mittendorf?'

The eyebrows now frowned in concentration, his face looked strained. There was no comment.

'We know Mittendorf has been with Allied Electronics for the last eleven years. Excellent cover. Isn't that so? You've met him, Gyorgy. He visited Budapest on several occasions. He wasn't just sightseeing. He met you, didn't he?'

Again, that look of concentration, as if Korda was trying hard to remember the man.

Taylor said to Frank. 'Better show him the photograph of Mittendorf. That may help.' He smiled for Korda. 'Wouldn't it?'

Korda took the photograph showing Mittendorf's face. He studied it in silence.

Renwick said, 'You know, the sooner you start talking about Jacques, the sooner you'll be out of reach of the

KGB. I can understand your hesitation, but it's no way to get our vote of confidence. No way at all, my friend.'

Taylor urged, 'We'll be able to give you better protection in America. Don't delay our departure from Vienna.'

'Can you guarantee that I leave soon?' Korda asked Taylor.

'You'll leave within three days. I promise you.'

Renwick added to that, 'As soon as we've compared your information with ours. Why not let us start comparing right now? Speed your departure?'

Avril spoke for the first time, and in Hungarian. 'Gyorgy, listen to them. Trust them. They need to know.'

'We mean to know,' Frank broke in harshly, also in Hungarian. In English, for the benefit of the two Americans, he said as he took back the photograph of Mittendorf's face and thrust another into Korda's hand, 'See this?' It was the view of the Two Crowns with its identification, on the plaque at its entrance, clearly legible. 'See?' Frank repeated, tapping the name of Mandel with an angry finger. 'Also known as "Kurt", aka "Ulrich", aka "Alexander Rose". How many face names has his friend Mittendorf?'

'Two that I know of,' Korda said slowly.

Renwick nodded to Avril, and the tape began recording. Once started, Korda needed no prompting. Perhaps, as Taylor had said downstairs in his office, the man really wanted to tell them everything he knew about Jacques, and the prospect of leaving Vienna within three days was the final spur to his memory.

He ended his recital. He looked exhausted, yet relieved. Prescott Taylor stayed with him to talk of the plans for flying him to Washington. As she left, Avril shook his hand. 'Goodbye, Gyorgy. Your journey will be safe;

your arrival, too. Good luck all the way.' That seemed to reassure him their promise would be kept. He could even smile and give her an eloquent goodbye in Hungarian. From Renwick, he got a nod of thanks. From Frank, a last measuring look.

Once outside the door and past the two men in civilian clothes who were standing guard, Frank said, 'He could have told me something, perhaps, about Bernard Mandel. Why the hell didn't you give me another ten minutes with him?'

Renwick held out his wrist, pointed to his watch. 'We're late as it is.' It was ten fifteen. 'How do we reach Grant to warn him?'

'We can't,' said Frank. 'He's already on his way to Klar's. Probably stepping out of the taxi right now.'

Avril said urgently, 'He must be warned before he faces Mittendorf.'

'And scare him into making a mistake?' Frank asked. It was one thing for Grant to talk with the treasurer of Allied Electronics; quite another to know he was meeting Jacques, trained by the KGB, a long-time Soviet agent, now in control of the group that was running the Vienna-Geneva operation. The man, thought Frank bitterly, who had caused the deaths of so many – perhaps had ordered them.

Renwick – a sign of intense worry – was silent. We've got Mittendorf, he was thinking, but meanwhile he has got Colin Grant.

'I'll go to the auction,' Avril said.

Renwick shook his head. 'Taylor will be there. He can pass a word of warning to—'

'Colin doesn't know him. He knows me.'

'Even so,' Renwick objected, 'Grant is totally ignorant about Jacques. You wouldn't have time to explain – too dangerous.'

'All I need to tell Colin is that Mittendorf is poison.'

170

'No,' Renwick decided. 'No more exposure for you. You had enough yesterday at Fischer's gallery.'

'I lost the man who was following me,' Avril insisted. 'I made sure of that.'

'He saw you with Colin. What if he turns up at the auction and sees you with him again?'

'An outside chance.'

'Avril – no! We'll let Taylor handle this.'

Frank said, 'Get me a copy of that tape you've just made. There are some references to people I'm interested in. Will you? Thanks, Bob.' They were reaching the floor where Renwick and Taylor had their far-separated offices. 'It's too crowded here. See you on the job.' He left as Prescott Taylor's secretary came hurrying along the corridor.'

'Mr Renwick?' she called anxiously. 'Mr Renwick,' she said as she reached him, her voice discreetly lowered, 'is it at all possible to reach Mr Taylor now? It's urgent.'

'What is?'

'Mr Taylor has to be downstairs at half past ten. To meet—' She dropped her voice still more. 'To meet the VIP who is arriving this morning from New York.'

Victor Basset? Renwick cursed silently.

'Mr Taylor *must* be here. Special request. He is to give all the information possible on something that is important to the VIP.'

'Better let Mr Taylor know.' That's Basset all right, thought Renwick as the secretary hurried off. He arrives from New York, wants all the details available – as though he hadn't been told enough in Washington – stays one night as the guest of the Ambassador, and flies off tomorrow with his precious Ruysdael safe in his hands. But what about us? What about Grant?

Avril said, 'That decides it, Bob. I'll warn Colin.'

'Don't hang around Klar's place. Once you've tipped off Grant, get the hell out. Don't come around to

171

Cathedral Lane, either – you can't risk leading anyone to the delivery entrance. Go home. Stay put for the next few days.'

'But I wanted to be in the Volkswagen – oh, just to see him make a safe exit,' she ended as Renwick gave her a sharp look. 'I really wouldn't lead anyone to the car. I'll have plenty of time to dodge—'

'No. Get home. Stay there. When Grant arrives, keep him there. I want the two of you out of sight until we neutralize Mittendorf.'

Avril nodded. 'Don't worry. I'll be careful.' She started towards the staircase. That was quicker than the elevator.

'Take a taxi,' he called after her. It would save time and difficulties in parking near the auction rooms.

She nodded, gave a wave and a smile, and began running downstairs. *Don't worry. I'll be careful.* Yes, Renwick thought, Avril would be all of that. Yet sometimes, no matter how careful – He cut off a sudden depression. He ought to be bursting with optimism. In his hand, he was carrying not only Jacques's verses and Mittendorf's file, but also a tape that had given him facts beyond anything he had expected. Korda's information, all twenty minutes of it, contained specific dates, places, names. There would have to be a thorough check, of course; and other units alerted – American and British Intelligence would be highly interested in Mittendorf's visits to New York and London— perhaps Interpol too; and certainly Vienna's security forces, if not its police. My God, thought Renwick, we hoped to trap a fox and we've stumbled into a den of wolves.

But, he told himself, all that will take days and weeks, and that is a job for others to handle. Ours is to track down the owner of the bank account in Geneva. Then we'll get NATO to move – an approach to the Swiss authorities on the highest level. No Geneva banker is going to withstand that kind of official pressure, especially when it's backed with evidence of criminal activity and intent. The bank records of this dubious account will be available to us, and we'll discover not only the deposits made, but also – and here's our target – the withdrawals of money: how much, and when, and to whom paid? To whom? That's the answer to all our search. Find that, and we'll uncover the happy band of terrorists who have been worth subsidizing.

Everything depended on Grant, Renwick thought. Too much? His brief elation vanished. Grim-faced, he locked the precious tape of Korda's deposition into his safe. It was fireproof, and – unless the equivalent of a ton of dynamite was dropped on it – shatterproof. The one disappointment in Korda's statement was that the defector knew no more about the Geneva account than what he conveyed to Taylor six weeks ago. It existed: that was all Korda could tell. If only he had known the name of the owner of the bank account, then Avril could have been telling Grant – right now – to forget the payee's name on that damned cheque: just concentrate on the Ruysdael and forget everything else. But there was always an 'if only'. That was what depressed him this morning.

At the Three Guitars last night, for instance . . . If only he could have reached there in time. If only Frank had been able to alert his informant who worked there as a waiter, to watch Lois Westerbrook until Renwick arrived. He did arrive, too, after hauling himself out of Irma's soft bed and dressing in frantic haste. (That ended his affair with Irma, no doubt about that. She had thrown everything she could reach – slippers, ashtray, even a telephone – as he hurried with vague excuses to the door.) But there was no sign of Westerbrook in the Three Guitars.

A trap? That was what Grant had half thought: that

173

was Frank's opinion. And Renwick? He couldn't decide. All he could discover last night, from a discreet talk with the waiter – the man had just received Frank's message as Renwick arrived on the scene – was that a woman – an American, dressed in grey, young, beautiful – had sat at a table by herself. Yes, she had left the table after she had asked for a telephone and been directed to the ladies' room. Yes, she had returned to her table and ordered more wine. A young man, handsome, and well-dressed, had joined her about twenty minutes later; they sat talking in English – perhaps for five minutes, no more – and then they left.

No, the waiter had insisted, she didn't look as though she was being forced to leave. No, he couldn't quit his duties and follow them into the street to see if any other persons were waiting for her there. Yes, the young man seemed to be an American. The waiter had thought, from the way the man joined her at the table, that he was expected and very welcome.

Expecting one of us? wondered Renwick. Or, if a trap, expecting a friend to escort her out of the Three Guitars once her part was played, duty done for the night? Leaving, of course, another of her friends to watch who would come enquiring for Miss Westerbrook.

Well, he hadn't been too obvious. The waiter was a help, steering Renwick to one of his tables, hovering around while he ordered a late supper and asked questions under the pretence of selecting from the menu. He had to eat most of that chicken paprika, too, and spend the next hour as if he were enjoying that godawful sweet white wine. No one paid him any notice when he left, the *Schrammel* music buzz-sawing into his ears, or when he walked five lonely streets before he could find a taxi. He had managed to get three and a half hours of sleep – one hell of a way to begin the day of the auction.

He still had some time before he'd be sitting in a

Volkswagen as near as possible to Klar's delivery entrance. So he called for his favourite girl in the secretary pool. 'Joan,' he asked her, 'could you rustle me up some breakfast?'

She was a straightforward blonde with blue eyes and a willing disposition. 'I brought in some *Gugelhupf*. Would that do? It's cake, but very plain. The Austrians often have it at breakfast,' she added reassuringly. 'Or I could ask Marge for some of her *Linzertorte*?'

'*Gugelhupf* be it. Also the biggest pot of coffee you can brew. And, Joan, make it black as midnight. No cream, no sugar.'

Here I am, Renwick thought, talking of cream and sugar, while the day before me could be pure vinegar, even vitriol.

15

If Colin Grant had thought – after a disturbing night – he would be allowed to sleep until eight o'clock, his telephone decided otherwise. At seven, it rang and kept ringing until he swung himself out of bed. That blasted bloody phone, he'd rip it out of the wall. Instead, he picked up the receiver and heard the voice of Gene Marck. 'Klar's Auction Rooms, Schulerstrasse 15A, at eleven this morning. Auction begins then. Promptly.'

'This morning?' Sleep made Grant sound stupefied enough.

'At eleven. I'll repeat the address.' Marck did that. 'Know where that is?'

'I'll look it up in my guide-book.'

'It's near St Steven's Cathedral. I'll see you, once you've completed bidding.'

'Just a moment—' Grant said sharply. 'Don't I see the picture before the auction?'

'Is that necessary?'

'It's customary. Is there a viewing room?'

'Yes. Open at ten, I believe.'

'You might have given me more warning.' Grant jabbed down the telephone. At least, he thought, I had the last word in that little exchange.

He ordered breakfast in a better frame of mind.

From then on everything went smoothly. Well before ten o'clock he was ready to move out, even remembering to detach the labels from his suitcase and overnight bag. The room, he decided, looked too abandoned, so he left a couple of books by his bedside, three magazines on the desk, along with a scrawl on the memo-pad: Tuesday, lunch 1:00 – *Donauturm Restaurant – Fischer*. Downstairs, the concierge's desk was busy. Grant dropped his key on the counter, didn't even have to make any explanation that he was off for the week-end. The three men on duty were fully occupied: one with a plane reservation that had gone wrong, another explaining the porter's charges on a bill that was being bitterly questioned, the third dealing with a long complaint about theatre tickets. Grant left.

Ten o'clock to the minute, he was in the street, and entering the cab that moved forward as soon as he appeared. The right cab, too: its driver was the young man who had shared a doorway with him yesterday afternoon, while they sheltered from the rain. Within moments his luggage was stowed away, and they were off. 'You know where I'm going?' he asked, noticing they had taken the wrong direction.

'Relax, Herr Grant. Just a small detour.'

'What's your name?'

'Just call me Walter.' A friendly grin accompanied that information.

'Well, Walter, make the detour as small as possible.'

'I'll get you to Klar's in fifteen minutes. Okay?'

'Okay.' Grant sat back in his seat, marshalled his thoughts, and tried to stop worrying.

In fifteen minutes he was in front of Klar's Auction Rooms, a sombre building in an old and narrow street. He looked pointedly at his two pieces of luggage. 'Relax, Herr Grant,' he was told again. 'I'll take good care of them. They'll be waiting for you at your new address.' Walter's grin was broader than ever. 'Better get out.' He gave a cheerful salute as Grant closed the cab's door.

What new address? Grant wondered, tried to look unperturbed, and stepped into Klar's entrance. Forget everything else, he warned himself: just concentrate on every moment of the next two hours – perhaps even three. The Ruysdael had been added at the last moment to Klar's list of offerings – so Renwick had warned him. That meant it was probably the final auction of the day, with most people already leaving for lunch. Ensuring, thought Grant, greater privacy for the sale, and wasn't that the keynote of all Gene Marck's arrangements?

Certainly Renwick's other information was good. There was the cloakroom, just inside the entrance, with an attendant insisting that every coat and umbrella be left in her care. She was alarmed now, about the over-sized shoulder-bag one woman carried. Grant left them arguing, and passed into the room where the items for auction were on view.

Here there were several attendants, mostly young, dressed in subdued black, watching everyone. The crowd seemed small – only about thirty so far – but that may have been due to the size of the high-ceilinged room, which could have held two hundred visitors. It was an ornate place, with wreaths of fruit and flowers carved on the wooden pillars that supported a balcony, encrusted in its turn with puff-cheeked cherubs blowing trumpets. There were no windows, but the ceiling lighting was brilliant with shimmering crystals. On the whole, godawful, thought Grant. He was relieved to see that the pictures were well spaced around the centre of the floor, each on its easel, keeping a safe distance from the late nineteenth century's conception of baroque. Vases, sculptured heads, goblets, jewelled eggs imitating Fabergés were among the items displayed on two long side tables. A notice requested politely, but in large firm lettering, that Ladies and Gentlemen would Please Refrain from Touching or Handling the Objects on View. In small letters, there was a modest statement that, to the best of their ability, the attendants would welcome any questions.

Grant had one. 'May I have a catalogue?' he asked a grave faced young man with carefully waved hair. A printed list of items for auction was found for him – they weren't being handed out too liberally, he noted – and he could begin circulating. As he walked around, he studied the catalogue. To his amazement, the notice of the Ruysdael, inserted neatly between Items 5 and 6 on the list, was numbered 5A. All the preceding items were frankly trash – the better stuff was kept towards the end of the catalogue. Which meant, if his guess was correct, that the first five on the list could be auctioned quickly, and bidding on the Ruysdael might start well before noon. Had Renwick planned for that?

He began searching among the easels, and found the Ruysdael placed between a fine Corot and the sour-faced portrait of a Flemish banker, school of Memling. Grant stood there, arms folded, studying the *View of Utrecht*. He had seen other Ruysdael paintings of this scene – or almost the same – and this one was less successful. Still, it had the same quiet beauty, far-off spires and roof-tops seen across the distance of a smooth-flowing river and its marshlands. Then he looked closely at the simple frame – perhaps only fifty years old, but decrepit; there was a thin line beginning to split its left side, not too noticeable, but definitely a hairline of a crack. He moved around the easel. The back of the frame was covered with a fine canvas, or heavy muslin. It was yellowed, slightly spotted with mildew, and possibly the same age as the frame itself.

'You find this picture interesting?' a woman's voice said behind him. He turned to see a blonde, pink-cheeked and smiling – about thirty, he guessed, even less – with a remarkable figure filling out her black dress in the right places. An attendant? Then he noticed the thin strand of pearls, the small diamond brooch, and the emerald solitaire almost obliterating her wedding ring.

179

And he remembered Renwick's description of 'well-stacked'. Yes, this could be Gudrun Klar, the daughter-in-law herself. Moving around the room like any other attendant? He'd soon learn who she was: the auction would begin in ten minutes.

He smiled back and said, 'To the best of your ability, what price do you think this painting will fetch?'

'It should bring a very good price. Ruysdael has been much sought after in recent months.'

Another woman's voice interrupted them with, 'Please excuse me, Frau Klar. I was told by your attendant over there—' Avril Hoffman gestured vaguely at the thickening crowd of people – that you could answer my question.'

'And what is that?'

Grant moved around the easel to the front of the picture. Half listening to Avril's query, Frau Klar accompanied him. 'Certainly not,' she told Avril.

Avril followed her, not even glancing at Grant. 'You mean, all those six eggs—'

'They are objets d'art, made of the finest enamel, highly decorated,' Frau Klar corrected her. 'They form one collection. They cannot be sold separately.'

Avril looked downcast. 'I'm afraid I couldn't afford all six of them.' She sighed, looking at the Ruysdael. 'Beautiful. But everything here is so – so costly.' Then she pointed to the picture on the next easel, from which the thin-faced Flemish banker stared out at a hostile world. 'Now, that's something I wouldn't have at any price. Just look at him! Old Closed-Lips.'

Grant pretended to be amused. 'Not a bad description.' He paused, and added, 'Probably suffered from dyspepsia.'

Avril laughed, ignoring Frau Klar's freezing look. 'I wouldn't trust him as far as I could throw him. If I were a policeman, I'd arrest him on sight.'

'By the way will the Ruysdael be auctioned quite early?' Grant asked Frau Klar as Avril moved closer to the portrait. She could hear him, even if she seemed fascinated by the banker's hand gripping his purse of gold coins. 'I see it is listed as No. 5A in your catalogue.'

'Quite early.' Frau Klar was still watching Avril.

'Perhaps even by eleven thirty?' He had succeeded in bringing Klar's attention back to him.

'That's a little early. But if you are interested in bidding, Herr Grant – the sooner the better. *Nicht?*'

Grant covered his surprise, nodded in agreement. She had known his name, had recognized him from a photograph or a description. Their encounter hadn't been accidental. Keeping him under close watch? For contacts? He paid no more attention to Avril, seemed unaware that she was leaving. He said, 'I think it's time for us to move in, Frau Klar. It *is* Frau Klar?'

The blonde nodded, all smiles again, her face as round-cheeked as the carved cherubs on the balcony. She said, very softly, 'We'll meet later, I hope.' She looked around her, her eyes quickly searching the crowd, then glanced up at the balcony. She touched her hair, rearranged a curl.

Thank God, Grant was thinking, Avril left unnoticed. Old Closed-Lips . . . Thoughtfully, he joined the stream of people now beginning to flow into the auction room. There was one thing of which he was certain: Avril would never have arrived here unless she brought a desperate warning. Had she understood his?

She had. Avril went straight to the nearest telephone-booth, and called the Embassy. She reached Renwick's extension as he was pouring his final cup of coffee. 'Auction may be over by eleven thirty,' she reported. 'Add ten minutes for signing cheque, another ten or fifteen for packaging, and he will be—'

'I can add, too,' Renwick cut in. 'Leaving now. And you get the hell out as I told you!'

We just made it, she thought, as she went searching for a taxi. Of course Bob had been trying to juggle parking time (one hour and a half was the limit) with Colin's estimated departure: twelve thirty until two o'clock had seemed a safe calculation. Now Bob would let Frank know, and all should be well. Lord, she thought, on how little so much depends. I very nearly didn't get to Klar's Auction Rooms – damn all traffic jams. And when I did, what did I find? Gudrun Klar blocking every possible approach.

Partly exhausted with tension, partly euphoric with success, but mostly thinking of Colin Grant about to start bidding for the Ruysdael, Avril was almost home before she remembered to see if anyone had followed her out of the Auction Rooms. Aghast, she twisted round to look out of the taxi's rear window. She couldn't tell: the heavy traffic behind her made any guess quite useless. Then she told herself, you weren't followed: you got out of that place so damn quick, no one had a chance to tail you. You *had* to call Bob – even if it did slow you up a little. Five minutes' delay altogether, no more than that.

She persuaded herself it meant very little, no added danger whatsoever. Nothing to what Colin must be going through right now.

As Grant had expected, there was little serious interest in the auction of items numbered one to five. They were sold off quickly, almost nonchalantly, by Kurt Klar, who was today's auctioneer. Old Werner Klar, with flowing white hair and furrowed brow, kept appearing and disappearing like an evanescent ghost. He would greet some old friend, speak a few words, move slowly away. Not a happy man, Grant decided; certainly an ailing one. Son Kurt, on the other hand, was fully capable. He was easily identifiable from Renwick's description – small and paunchy, almost completely bald, quick eyes behind round glasses that gave him an owl-like look, but not wise and old, just ageing and anxious. Gudrun, twenty years his junior, would be enough to keep any husband worried. She wasn't to be seen in the auction room, although the attendants were present, carrying this object here, taking that one there, all very efficient – and almost too fast for Grant's comfort. He had his notebook out, pencilling quick calculations on the exchange of Austrian schillings into American dollars, as a guideline once he started bidding. This morning, a slide on the international money market had brought the dollar's value down to fifteen Austrian schillings and eighty-five groschen. Too unwieldy for instant accuracy; he was no computer. He'd settle for the nearest round figure: sixteen schillings to the dollar. As he worked out a neat table for ready reference, some of the earlier sales became less startling when translated into American terms. Sixteen thousand schillings seemed an alarming figure for a dinner set of Meissen, while one thousand dollars sounded almost reasonable. Grant's own bidding might reach over the million mark in schillings. He braced himself.

There was a few minutes' delay before Number 5A was announced, when a dealer rose to make a brief protest: he had not been aware that a Ruysdael painting was coming up for sale; he requested that its auction be postponed until the end of today's proceedings, so that he would have time to call his client in Rome for instructions. The protest shocked Kurt Klar: quite impossible, he stated. His refusal shocked the dealer; he started to leave, changed his mind, sat down at the back of the room. Old Papa Klar appeared for a distraught moment, only to vanish into the wings. The stir in the audience, now numbering some seventy people, subsided into a slight murmur, and then silence. Now here it comes, thought Grant, as the Ruysdael was carried on to the platform and Kurt Klar went into his brief introduction. It might have been the small size of the auction room with its skylighted ceiling – probably once an interior courtyard, now roofed over with glass – but he began to feel his temperature rising. He loosened his tie, kept the pencil in his hand for his signals to Klar, and no longer let his attention wander.

Klar started the bidding at 900,000 schillings. The recalcitrant dealer decided to top that with another 90,000. So, within a couple of minutes, the Ruysdael had already reached 61,875 American dollars. This was going to be a wild downhill sleigh-ride. Klar suggested the equivalent of 67,500, and looked in Grant's direction. Yes, Grant thought, they have been told who I am. He suppressed a smile and gave a small salute, almost imperceptible. The price kept rising by a steady 90,000 schillings.

The dealer and two others had dropped out of the bidding by the time the picture was up to 1,500,000 schillings – a flat 100,000 dollars, according to Grant's rough estimation. Only one man besides Grant was left in the race. He was small and thin, precise in his manner, neat in a conservative suit of navy blue. By the time the bidding reached 2,400,000 schillings, Grant's suspicions deepened: the man in the navy suit wasn't interested in acquiring the Ruysdael – he was simply there to push the price higher and higher.

To test this suspicion but also to cause a little pain, Grant let the man's last bid stand for almost a minute before signalling his compliance with the next suggested price. Yes, judging by Klar's obvious relief, Grant could be right about the competition being offered him. The man, still confident and calm, increased Grant's bid by another 90,000 schillings. A total of 161,250 dollars. Ridiculous, Grant decided: time to call an end to this charade. Around him, all voices were stilled, and the hot sultry air under the glass roof seemed suffocating. Out of devilment, Grant let the man's last bid stand for several minutes, while Klar's voice sharpened as he advanced the price by another 90,000 schillings. '2,670,000 schillings . . . Do I hear a bid for 2,670,000 schillings?'

The man in the blue suit had lost his aplomb. He looked almost wildly at Grant, perhaps realizing for the first time that he (who possibly made 10,000 dollars a year) could be left holding the Ruysdael at the price of 161,250 dollars. Grant let him sweat for another minute, let Klar's glare sharpen as his voice rose in desperation. At last Grant raised his pencil. The man in the blue suit rose and quickly left.

'Sold!' Klar's voice boomed out as he thumped down on this auctioneer's bell. '2,670,000 schillings . . .' And the Ruysdael was carried off the stage.

Stiffly, Grant got to his feet. I've just bought a Ruysdael for almost 167,000 dollars. Correction, correction: allow for all those little groschen . . . 168,454 dollars? Yes, that was the price.

Anyway, he was thinking as he followed an attendant out of the auction room into a narrow corridor, I made sure the price would rise no higher. It was preposterous as it was. He wiped his brow with his handkerchief, readjusted the knot in his tie, and passed through a door that the attendant held open for him with the utmost respect. Most of the people who worked here were complete innocents, he decided; old Klar himself was oblivious to everything around him. Which left son Kurt and Gudrun as willing tools of this conspiracy.

He found himself in a pleasant office, comfortably furnished with armchairs. The elder Klar was there,

185

studying the Ruysdael, which two porters had propped on an easel. Now, with bows for its new owner, they left for the auction room. Werner Klar shook hands weakly, offered vague congratulations, and, with the furrows deepening in his white face, made his own retreat as the door to an adjacent office opened. Gudrun entered, followed by Gene Marck and an elderly man. None of them looked pleased.

Marck shook hands, saying with heavy geniality, 'So you decided to call a halt to the bidding?'

'I was getting some very bad vibes. There were daggers at the back of my neck.'

All three stared at him.

Grant went on, 'That dealer who sat at the rear of the room – I could feel his curiosity sharpening. Possibly he was wondering who was my backer. The higher the price, the more he'd wonder. He's just the type to track down Basset's name. In any case, I didn't call a halt: the opposition collapsed.'

'I was only joking,' Marck said quickly. 'You did very well. Quite a reasonable price, wouldn't you say?' He watched Grant intently.

Reasonable, hell. Grant said, 'Considering the rising market in paintings, nowadays—' He left it at that, shrugged his shoulders. Nonchalant, totally unsuspecting, that's me – I hope. Do they buy it?

All three relaxed a little. Gudrun even smiled.

'Then let's get down to business,' Marck said. 'Grant, this is Dr Mittendorf – the treasurer of Mr Basset's firm. He will take charge.'

Mittendorf was a dull and proper man, dressed to match his sombre manner. He was somewhere in his early sixties, Grant guessed, not quite six feet in height, and heavy. His hair was thick and dark, strangely white at the temples. An enormous brow, eyes that were watchful, and lips that were tightly compressed. Definitely Avril's 'Old Closed-Lips'. Grant smiled and shook hands. Mittendorf's grasp was strong. So was his voice as he spoke a conventional phrase of greeting.

With no more formalities, Mittendorf crossed over to Werner Klar's desk and sat down. He produced a cheque-book, adjusted the lamp to suit him, and brought out his glasses. Every movement was precise and unhurried. A deliberate man, thought Grant, and moved around the room, pretending a brief interest in Old Klar's treasured mementos.

'Please sit down,' Mittendorf said as he took out his pen and pulled off its cap.

'Here!' Gudrun offered an armchair some distance from the desk. 'Please?'

'I'd rather stand, thank you – had enough sitting in that auction room.'

'Weren't you comfortable?'

'It was hot. Those skylights in the ceiling—' He shook his head and smiled again. Mittendorf's pen was in his hand, his left hand curved around the top of his cheque-book as if to hold it in place. It could also cover the payee's name as soon as he had written it. Grant kept on moving, seemingly at ease, and came round to the right side of the desk as Mittendorf was about to sign his name.

'One moment!' Grant interrupted urgently. 'I forgot this. Must keep everything legal.' Out of his breast-pocket he whipped the letter he had been sent in New York along with his airline ticket, and passed it quickly to Mittendorf.

Instinctively, Mittendorf's left hand was raised from the cheque-book to take Grant's sudden offering. And Grant had one brief glimpse of the name: Henri Bienvenue. He saw, too, the amount being paid to Henri Bienvenue. It was the equivalent of 250,000 dollars.

'Legal?' asked Mittendorf sharply, dropping his pen, using both hands to unfold the sheet of paper, but making sure that his left arm was now resting across the face of the cheque.

'Yes,' Grant said. 'That's my authorization from Mr Victor Basset to represent him at the auction. You need it, don't you, before you sign any cheque?'

'I do not,' said Mittendorf, his lips now so invisible that there was only one long thin line to indicate his mouth. 'This letter should have been given to Frau Klar.' His eyes looked over his glasses with a piercing stare at the astonished American.

'Oh, I'm sorry.' Grant took back Basset's letter, and turned to Gudrun Klar. 'I didn't know,' he excused himself with a smile. 'I'm ignorant about these things.' He presented the letter with a small bow. 'Now everything is in order. And the Ruysdael?'

'Yours, for the next few days,' Gene Marck said, breaking his long silence. His face was taut, fine-drawn; either he hadn't enjoyed last night's sleep or today had brought new tensions. His bow-tie – red with white dots – would normally have passed muster, except that he had chosen to wear it with a brown pin-striped suit and the effect was not good. Disastrous, Fischer would have said. No colour sense, Lois Westerbrook had stated.

'How is Miss Westerbrook?' Grant asked casually, as he turned to look at the Ruysdael. Yes, the frame still had that fine incipient crack down its left side; the muslin was the same, mildew and rusted nails intact. There had been no tampering, so far.

'I thought you could have told me that,' Marck said. 'Wasn't she in touch with you last night?'

Grant froze, went on studying the painting. 'Yes, she telephoned. I thought she was drunk to tell you the truth. Ungallant of me, perhaps.' He looked directly at Marck. 'Does she drink too much?'

Marck's tight face relaxed a little. 'I'm afraid so. It has been quite a problem.'

'Too bad,' said Grant. 'By the way, what about insurance?' He indicated the Ruysdael. 'You'll attend to it?' He was conscious that Mittendorf, his cheque-signing completed, was listening to every word and watching each gesture.

'At once.'

'Then you'd better get on the phone. I don't want an uninsured picture worth more than 168,000 dollars to be left in my charge. How long do I have to stay in Vienna, anyway?'

Mittendorf gathered up his pen and cheque-book, rose from the desk. He made his ponderous way to Gudrun Klar. 'This is for your firm, Frau Klar: your auction fee, plus expenses for storage, et cetera, et cetera. And this—' he presented a second cheque folded neatly, 'is for the previous owner of the painting which your husband auctioned. You will see that he receives it as soon as he arrives in Vienna? Excellent. Good day, Mr Grant. Good day to you, Mr Marck. To you, madame.' He bowed over Gudrun's hand.

'Your hat—' Gudrun Klar began.

'In the other office, I believe.' Mittendorf nodded and left.

As she was about to follow, Grant stopped her. 'Frau Klar, I need something to cover this painting.'

'Of course.' Only half of her mind was on his request. She looked at the cheques and found they were a good excuse to let her follow Mittendorf into the other office. 'First let me lock these safely away. I shall not take long.'

Marck too seemed ready to leave. He was opening the door for Frau Klar; their eyes met and held, his hand touched hers and lingered. Something was said, softly, gently; Frau Klar became Gudrun, aged eighteen and giggling.

189

So that's how he works it, thought Grant: control the woman and she'll cajole her husband, and you'll have a venerable firm right under your thumb.

'I'll attend to the insurance,' Marck called back, as his arm guided Frau Klar's waist towards her office.

'You haven't answered my question,' said Grant. Nor had Mittendorf, with his well-judged departure, neatly timed. 'When do I leave Vienna?'

'I'll let you know.'

'Then warn me well ahead, will you? I barely made it today.'

Marck hesitated. 'I may even let you know tonight. When can I reach you at your hotel? Late, I suppose. Then let's say around midnight.' Without waiting for an answer, he closed the office door.

Like hell I'll be there, thought Grant, but let that be his problem for a change. Now the three of them are discussing me. How did I do? . . . He wasn't sure. But he had the name of Henri Bienvenue, whose account in Geneva would be the richer by 250,000 dollars. Also, he had a few minutes to himself. He studied the Ruysdael – a natural gesture, if he was being observed from next door. Then he tilted the picture from the easel, and looked at its back. Quickly he tried to ease the top right-hand corner of the protective muslin away from the rusted nails, but the material was fragile with age and came off the frame in a series of small rips. And on the back of the painting, just as Helmut Fischer had said, he found what he wanted: the date 1642, and the name S. van Ruysdael.

'Mr Grant!' Frau Klar was closing her office door behind her, shutting out any view or sound of two men still deep in consultation. 'What are you doing?'

'Just checking,' Grant said. 'It's authentic.'

'Did you doubt us?' She was indignant.

190

'Of course not. How long have you worked in the art world?'

'Three years. But I don't see—'

'Scarcely long enough to know all the tricks that can be played, even on such a reputable house as Klar's.'

'We had the picture checked,' she said stiffly. 'We aren't novices, Mr Grant.'

Checked, with old and rusted nails still in exact place, and a frail muslin backing that had been intact, undisturbed? 'Of course not,' he repeated, and seemed to mollify her. He was still wondering whose word they had taken, so completely on trust, that the Ruysdael was genuine. Someone so high in command that they'd never question his judgment? This whole damned thing had been run like a military operation.

Frau Klar was smiling again. 'Would you care for a drink, Mr Grant? To celebrate.' She moved towards a carved wardrobe, opening its door to reveal bottles and glasses.

'I'll celebrate later. What I want now is two pieces of strong cardboard to fit the picture exactly, and also a thin plastic sheet to cover both the frame and the painting, protect its surface. It's vulnerable, you know.'

'We can do better than that, Mr Grant. Please come this way.'

He lifted the Ruysdael – it was just over two feet long, and about sixteen inches in height, not difficult to handle – and followed her out into the corridor. From the auction room behind them, there was the sound of Kurt Klar's voice and the sharp ring of the bell. Henri Bienvenue, Grant was repeating to himself, getting the exact spelling fixed in his mind. It was a most suitable name for a Geneva resident, where French was the language used. They thought of everything, these boys.

Frau Klar was passing the main door to her office. Perhaps to draw his attention away from it, she beamed

191

over her shoulder and pointed straight ahead to another door, at the end of the corridor, huge in size, double-panelled, and closed. Grant's thoughts were still with Mittendorf, that wily old bastard. But why so stupid as to increase the value of the cheque from 168,454 dollars to 250,000? The discrepancy would be easily discovered, once Grant delivered the picture and discussed the auction and price with Victor Basset. He halted abruptly. My God, he thought, perhaps I won't be alive to bear witness to the truth. If any substitution for the Ruysdael is made – and that will be quickly discerned by Basset – what better scapegoat to take the blame than a dead man?

'Here we are,' Frau Klar was saying, opening the double door.

For a moment, Grant stood at the entrance to Klar's warehouse. Then, still shaken, still hesitant, his grip tightened on the Ruysdael, he stepped over its threshold.

16

The room Grant entered, enormous in size, artificially lit, was the working premises of Klar's delivery and storage departments. Its cement floor was partly filled with trestle tables and crates half-unpacked. Writing-desks, pictures, antique mirrors, vases, were being pre-pared for shipment. Here and there, mounds of straw. Four men, he noted, suddenly busy as Frau Klar appeared. The rear wall, adjoining Cathedral Lane and windowless to ensure security, was broken only by an immense entrance whose doors stood wide open, letting the sun and fresh air stream in from a narrow street. My escape route, thought Grant.

He could see no parked Volkswagen out there – only a roughly-dressed man lounging against the wall of the building opposite, who straightened his back and turned round to look along the street the minute he glimpsed Grant. It seemed so natural that Grant's sudden hope diminished: probably not a signal to Renwick, just some workman out for a noontime break.

Grant forced himself to look away from the patch of sunlight, and took stock of the strangers around him, wondering which was the foreman whom Renwick trusted. Frau Klar solved that problem for him by raising her voice in sharp anger. 'Max!' she suddenly called out. 'Max!'

Max made his way around a pile of loose straw. He was a thin middle-aged man, with an imperturbable face and deliberate movements, slowed by a slight limp.

'Who,' demanded Frau Klar, 'opened the delivery

entrance? Who gave the orders for that? It is to be kept closed. At all times.'

Max said quietly, 'Except when a delivery is to be made.'

'Well, where is it?' Her voice was hectoring, her face tight with anger. She pointed to the empty threshold. 'Where's the truck?'

'Late. Could have been the traffic. Should be here around noon.'

'Delivering what? Nothing is scheduled to arrive today.'

'Timber from Heller & Sons,' Max said patiently. 'We've got more packing-cases to make for the Frankfurt shipment.'

Frau Klar's temper subsided. She dismissed Max with a wave of her hand and recovered her winning smile. 'Please excuse us, Mr Grant. We are always so busy – difficult to keep track of everything. Now let me show you what we have ready for you.' She signalled to another man who had just finished wrapping a cushion of styrofoam around a majolica vase at a nearby table. He deposited the vase in a nest of straw, and picked up some other item from his table. 'And what do you think of this?' she asked Grant, as the man came forward, holding a large blue carrying case.

'Splendid,' he said, surprised and pleased. It was of vinyl, both light and strong, with three leather straps and buckles and an easy-to-grip handle. 'Looks as if it's just the right measurements, too.'

'Exactly right. We had it specially made for you – a gesture to Mr Basset, one of our most valued clients. Much better than cardboard, don't you think?' She was much amused. Then to the workmen, 'Sigmund – take this painting and cover it with a thin sheet of plastic before you put it into the carrier.' She eased the Ruysdael out of Grant's hands. 'Don't worry. Sigmund is our most expert packer. Pictures are his speciality.'

Grant risked one brief glance at the street: no one there now – just a light truck arriving, groping its way slowly and carefully into close position beside the delivery entrance. He moved over to the work-table to keep an eye on Sigmund's nimble fingers.

Frau Klar kept following him closely. 'Where will you keep the Ruysdael until you leave? It is a problem, isn't it? Of course, you could have left it with us. We are accustomed to storing very valuable articles. Then we could have sent it to you by special messenger on the morning of your departure.'

The last corner of the plastic wrapping was being taped in place. 'Yes, that was one possibility,' Grant said, his eyes never leaving Sigmund.

'You might reconsider, even now.'

'No. I prefer to take the picture myself.' The Ruysdael was being slowly edged into its packing case.

'See that door over there!' Frau Klar caught his arm as her other hand pointed to one end of the room. 'It leads to our storage vault. Burglar-proof, fire-proof. Nothing could be safer.'

Politely, Grant looked. He disengaged his arm, turned back to watch Sigmund's table. The man had finished his job: the blue carrying case had its three brown leather straps already buckled. Quick work, thought Grant. Too damn quick, perhaps. Something is wrong, he felt. He glanced at Max, standing close by, strangely ignoring the truck's arrival.

'There you are, sir,' said Sigmund, handing over the case.

Grant saw Max's warning stare: first at him; then at the pile of loose straw near the work-table. He took the case from Sigmund, saying, 'A very neat job.'

'Max!' Frau Klar was sharply annoyed again. 'Isn't that the truck with your timber?'

'I need Sigmund to help check the unloading.'

'He's free now. Get on with it, both of you!'

Grant cleared his throat. 'Frau Klar – I *am* sorry. May I delay Sigmund for a moment?' He laid the carrying-case on the table, began unbuckling it. 'This is vinyl – not firm enough. No padding inside? Inadequate for a transatlantic journey. We'll need a slight reinforcement. A sheet of cardboard over the face of the picture.' He slipped his hand inside the case. 'I was right: no protective lining.' He pulled the picture out. The plastic cover was transparent. The painting itself looked like the genuine Ruysdael, but the antique frame had no crack apparent. The muslin backing, beige in colour to imitate age, had not one black mildew spot. Nor was it loose at the top right-hand corner.

For a moment he felt a terrifying paralysis of the mind. What next? Confront them with the facts – no, not that. Play it their way, and perhaps make sure of an exit through the delivery entrance. He said to Sigmund, who stood gaping while a startled Frau Klar seemed transfixed, 'Have you some cardboard we could use?' Quickly he made his way around the table to Sigmund's work area, kicking the discarded sheets of styrofoam lightly aside, then the pile of straw. His toe touched something solid, and his foot halted.

'Not there, sir,' Sigmund was saying, suddenly galvanized into action. 'One moment – I'll find some cardboard.'

Trying to laugh, Frau Klar said, 'Is this really necessary, Mr Grant? Surely you take too much trouble.'

Grant pointed to the delivery entrance. 'Better deal with him, I think.' The truck driver, hands on hips, had taken a definite stance well inside the doorway, and was studying a collection of bric-à-brac waiting to be crated.

Frau Klar looked and saw him. 'Max, Max! Get him out of here! Start unloading! And keep him out – you know the rules – no unauthorized personnel allowed.'

The second she had turned her attention away from him to rivet it on the intruder, Grant reached into the straw where his toe had struck something hard. He pulled out a blue vinyl carrying-case, its buckles still unfastened, and replaced it with the duplicate that Sigmund had given him. There was just time to kick the straw back into place – not a perfect job, but it would do – and swing his discovery neatly on to the table, before Frau Klar had completed her tirade and was ready to deal with him again. She hadn't noticed. Grant drew a long, steadying breath.

And Sigmund? He was now returning across the wide stretch of floor with a sheet of cardboard, which – bless his efficiency and the delay it had caused – was already cut to size. Yes, Sigmund might have noticed that final moment of substitution: he could have had – if he wasn't too occupied in admiring his handiwork – a clear view of Grant setting the original carrying-case on the table. Or perhaps he just didn't believe that an American had enough brains to discover he had been duped. At any rate, he said nothing at all as Grant seized the cardboard from his hand, saying, 'I'll attend to it, thank you.' But he was frowning and not altogether happy when Grant pulled the picture out of the vinyl carrier.

One quick check, Grant had decided: glimpse the date and the signature; make sure. Yes, this was the genuine article. He had the Ruysdael.

Frau Klar was impatient. Again she told him that he was taking too much trouble. He only smiled and concentrated on getting the cardboard to fit into the carrying-case along with the painting. He buckled the three straps, gripped the handle. 'Ready to leave. Now you can go back to the auction, Frau Klar. When do you expect it to be over?'

'Oh, around two o'clock. Today we didn't have too many items to dispose of.'

'Sorry I took up so much of your time.' Keep it all natural and easy, he warned himself. He took her hand and shook it quickly. 'Goodbye. Many thanks.'

'But I'll show you out,' she remonstrated. 'This way, Mr Grant.' She gestured towards the door into the corridor.

'Better not disturb the auction.' He began walking to the delivery entrance. 'This is nearer anyway,' he called back over his shoulder, and saw Sigmund bending down to look at the heap of loose straw beside his table. Easy does it, Grant told himself again, and resisted increasing his pace. There was no shout of alarm from Sigmund: perhaps he had been reassuring himself that a blue vinyl carrying-case was still in place.

Just ahead was the wide open door. The trucker and his mate were unloading long thin planks of cheap pine.

'Mr Grant – one moment, please!' the woman called, and he heard her high heels clacking over the cement floor as she tried to catch up with him. But he was almost at the threshold, about to step into the sunlight and fresh clean air.

'Klaus!' she cried out, pointing frantically at Grant's back. Klaus, the biggest and burliest of the workmen, who was helping Max check the delivery of timber, looked up, got the message, and moved quickly to stop the American. But the truck driver, two long planks balanced on one shoulder, let Grant pass and then swung round just as Klaus was reaching him. The planks caught Klaus flat across the chest.

'Sorry, chum,' said the truck driver. He dropped his load to help Klaus regain his footing. 'Sorry, lady,' he told Frau Klar who had reached the delivery entrance.

'Nearly got your legs, these planks did. Could have broken them.' A pity they hadn't, thought Frank.

Gudrun Klar ignored him. And Frank, for his part, was happy she wasn't paying any attention to him. She was determined to get into the street. Curious about Grant's direction, was she? He nodded to his mate, heavily loaded with the cut timber across his shoulders, to stand just where he was – sideways, at the threshold – and block any other exit for the next minute. Grant was out and away. Frank, glancing briefly along the narrow street, saw a burst of speed that could have won the hundred metres at any Olympics.

Frank began helping his mate to get through the doorway, and bumped up against Gudrun still trying to squeeze past. 'Careful, lady,' he told her. 'You'll get a black eye if you don't look out.' He steadied the swinging planks, and then – Grant must have reached the Volkswagen by this time, judging by the rate he had been travelling at – helped his mate to lower them on to the floor. They slithered and fell. Frau Klar jumped back with a gasp. 'Dangerous, I told you,' Frank said, and handed the invoice to Max. 'Sign here.' Max, who had been trying to look as stupid as possible, scribbled quickly. Frank, stuffing the invoice back into the breast pocket of his leather jacket, averted his face quite naturally from Madame as he began talking with his helper about their next delivery.

She was too engrossed, anyway, by the street. Grant had vanished. There were some parked cars, two girls, three men, a boy on a bicycle. Nothing else.

What is she thinking? Frank wondered. That their agent is waiting at the front entrance to Klar's Auction Rooms, ready to follow Grant?' 'Some wait,' he said as he climbed into the driver's seat and switched on the engine. Slowly, at walking pace, he eased the truck along the narrow street.

She had given up. In his rear-view mirror, he saw her enter the warehouse and its doors begin to close. He increased his speed. Even if she had an afterthought and stepped back for another look, the truck would block her view of the white Volkswagen which was at last pulling away from the curb. 'Did you have much of a view from across the street?' he asked the young man beside him.

'Just enough to let me see Grant and Klar come into the warehouse, and give you the signal. I worried about my timing for that. Too quick?'

'It was just right.' Frank was in a jovial mood. 'You saw no argument? No sign of trouble?'

'No. She was all smiles, then. What changed her?' She had been one worried woman, mouth pulled down, eyebrows knitted.

'She and her friends were caught flat-footed, that's what.' Frank's grin was broad. 'One thing I'll say for that guy—' He paused and laughed.

'Grant?'

'He can sprint.'

Renwick had the Volkswagen door open for him. Grant stumbled in, breathing in heavy gasps, the blue vinyl carrying-case safely clutched to his side. The car didn't move. The motor wasn't even running. Renwick, his eyes fixed on the rear-view mirror, only said, 'Keep low! Stay out of sight.'

In this sardine-tin? But Grant did his best, sliding down in the seat until his knees almost touched his chin. Slowly he regained his breath. My God, he thought, I never ran so hard in my life. Strange what desperation can do . . .

'Just a minute or two,' Renwick said encouragingly. He too had slumped as much as possible without losing his rear view of the street.

'Okay,' he said at last, and switched on the ignition. Behind them Grant heard the beginning growl of the truck's engine. Still watching the mirror, Renwick pulled away from the curb. 'She's back inside the warehouse,' he reported, smiling for the first time. 'And there was no one to follow you. They messed that up, they really did. Congratulations, Colin.' He made a careful turn into a busy street, and glanced back once more to make sure Frank wasn't far behind. 'Congratulations, everyone.'

Grant said nothing.

'Are you all right?'

'Just coming out of shock.' Grant tried to smile. 'It was a near thing.'

'Did you get it?'

'Sure.' Grant patted the vinyl carrying-case. 'Right here. They tried a switch. They had the reproduction in a duplicate case.' He began to laugh, and then, remembering Max's blank stare that had given him warning, he fell silent again. A damned near thing, he thought sombrely.

'Did you get it?' Renwick repeated sharply. 'The name on the cheque?'

'Henri Bienvenue.'

'Spell it.'

Grant did. 'Also, I saw the amount being paid to him. In American money – 250,000 dollars. My winning bid was 168,454 dollars. So figure that out.'

'Have *you*?'

'Yes. I'm a dead man.

'We'll see about that,' said Renwick. 'And so far we've done pretty well. Don't you agree?'

'You expected I might be – eliminated?'

'The possibility crossed our minds.'

'From the beginning?' Grant was aghast.

'Right from the start.'

Grant shook his head as he remembered Avril among the roses, hinting at danger, talking of protection, while he insisted – big man that he was – he could look after himself. Big man indeed. Without Max's help, or without Avril's warning about Old Closed-Lips, where the hell would he have been? 'Avril – where is she?'

'Calm down. She's at home, waiting for you to turn up. She has an apartment near the Embassy – with a guest-room ready for any of our friends who need to stay out of sight. It's our version of what the trade calls a "safe house". How did she cope? She hadn't much time to get down to Klar's and warn you.'

'She was brilliant.'

'No suspicion aroused?'

Grant was slow to reply. He was remembering Gudrun Klar and her eyes on the balcony – emerald ring, big and bright, rearranging her hair. At first he had thought it was a habit of hers. Now that he recalled the gesture, nowhere else, at no time, had she raised a hand to toy with her curls. Not a habit. A signal, perhaps?

'Was there?' Renwick's voice was sharp.

'I saw someone move – up on the balcony – just for a split second – as Avril was leaving. A man, I thought.'

'Could he have seen you and Avril together?'

'Yes. With Frau Klar.'

'With *Klar*? Avril approached you when you were with—'

'Look – I was stuck with Klar. Avril had no choice. I was about to move into the auction room.'

'How did Avril leave? Was she slow?'

'Far from it. No one in that gallery could have got down to the front door in time to follow her.'

Except, Renwick was thinking, Avril had stopped to make a phone call. Yet without that call neither he nor Frank would have been in good position for Grant's

202

early exit. 'I'll get you to her apartment as soon as we visit the Embassy.'

'Why the Embassy?'

'You'll deliver the Ruysdael to Basset. He arrived this morning.'

'Hell – do I have to see him?'

'Unless you'll entrust that picture to a doorman.' I thought not, Renwick decided, as he saw Grant's grip tighten on the carrying-case.

'What about you? Couldn't you deliver—'

'I have messages to send.' The name of Henri Bienvenue, for a starter: the sooner NATO's diplomatic approach to the Swiss could be made, the quicker they'd take action. And then there were typed copies to be made from the Korda tape. And Austrian Security to be informed. And – 'Everything piles on top at once,' Renwick said. 'It's an avalanche. We could have done without Mr Victor Basset complicating everything. He means well, but – apart from getting that blasted picture off our hands – he is one big pain in the butt. He decided he'd arrive *sub rosa*, so he came flying in on his own private plane. He has a couple of brawny types with him, ex-Secret Service men, *and* his lawyer, *and* a new secretary. How *sub rosa* is that, with any enquiring journalist sniffing around the airport? The only goddamned thing he didn't do to stir up interest was that he hadn't the ex-Secret Service men running beside his limousine.'

A new secretary – replacing Lois Westerbrook? 'He moves fast.'

'And the waves he's making could swamp our boat before we haul in our catch. Replacing Westerbrook – a clear signal to Mittendorf, who has a hundred listening ears around this town.'

'Westerbrook – did you meet her last night?'

'No,' Renwick said abruptly.

'Didn't you try?'

'Yes.'

'She wasn't at the Three Guitars?'

'She left before I got there.' Renwick said no more, seemed to be concentrating on his driving, although he had angled the little car expertly enough out of blocked traffic lanes while he was talking about Basset.

'So,' Grant made a guess, 'you think it was a trap. Sorry about that, Bob. Hope I didn't land you in real trouble.'

'Do *you* think it was a trap?'

'I wouldn't have phoned you unless I thought there was some truth in what she told me. For instance – she accused Gene Marck of being a trained secret agent. She had found a list of addresses and a microfilm concealed in a hairbrush and a tin of talcum – tricks of the trade, she called them. She wanted to hand them over to you.'

Renwick slowed down. 'She actually said that?'

'Yes. That's why I thought she might be telling the truth. And yet, she's such a beautiful little liar—'

'Colin – if a trap was being set, she'd never have revealed so much about Marck. No, the phone call was for real. She thought it was a public phone – it is coin-operated, but that's only a device to make the Three Guitars' customers pay. Someone must have heard the call and reported it, and they had her picked up. She thought the guy was me. She walked out with him, smiling.' Renwick cursed softly, his face grim. 'And where is she now?'

'There's no trace?' Marck knew about that phone call: *wasn't she in touch with you last night*? Testing me, was he? Instead, he gave himself away.

'Not so far. Not one rumour, nothing. My God, I *did* get there as fast as I could move. Finished dressing in a taxi, believe it or not.'

For the next few minutes, neither of them spoke. They

were following Währingerstrasse, a long and busy street, dodging the trolley-buses that always had the right of way, even when it meant a sudden veer across the face of following traffic.

'Soon be there,' Renwick said. 'Prepare yourself, my boy, for Basset on the war-path.'

'If he expects me to give a play-by-play account—' began Grant.

'He won't have time. He has summoned quite a gathering of Austrians around him – a cabinet minister who's an old friend, the president of Allied Electronics, and some top State Security guy. A hush-hush luncheon at the Embassy. How hush is that? I give it six hours before the gossip starts being whispered around Vienna.'

'I see your problem. Mittendorf will be across the frontier tonight. Probably Marck and his dear Gudrun too.' Then Grant's eyes widened and he smacked the Ruysdael. 'A clear case of embezzlement! A 250,000 dollar payment for a 168,454 dollar painting, right out of Basset's pocket. You could hold Mittendorf on that, couldn't you?'

Renwick's hope stirred. 'Yes, we could hold him on that.' And later slap him down with all the other charges when we get the evidence together. 'The Austrians could nail him inside three hours. I think I'll have to help you face Basset, after all, and get him to prefer a charge of embezzlement instead of marching into Mittendorf's office and heaving him out by the scruff of his neck.' Renwick's smile broke into laughter. 'That's what the old buzzard wanted to do. But now we'll give him – what did he call it? – a viable alternative. He will be delighted. All he wanted was some action. Why don't you want to see him?'

'Because,' Grant said slowly, 'he has a museum job to offer, and I'm damned if I'll look as though I had come panting after it. In fact, I don't want that blasted job, even if it was offered to me.' Yet a week ago I would have jumped at it, he thought.

'Why?' Renwick eased the Volkswagen away from the heavy traffic and entered the wide curve of a quiet street, edged by eighteenth-century houses and walled gardens.

'Because,' Grant said again, even more slowly, 'every time I walked through that museum at Basset Hill, I'd see three pictures displayed there: a Monet, a Degas – both bought by Westerbrook in Vienna – and this Ruysdael. And I'd wonder where their former owners were. Murdered, like Ferenc Ady? Or shut away in an insane asylum? Or freezing in a labour camp above the Arctic Circle?'

Renwick remained silent as they drove past the Embassy's imposing front steps, complete with an empty sentry-box, then, almost immediately, made a right turn through large iron gates into a wide courtyard surrounded by smaller buildings. 'Rear entrance,' he said. 'Less noticeable. Frank and his truck should be near by, parked down the curve of the street. He'll want to hear what you found out this morning. Look, Colin – I'll make a swap with you. You give Frank the details, and I'll deliver the Ruysdael to Basset. That is,' he added with a grin as they got out of the Volkswagen, 'if you trust me sufficiently.'

'I guess I do,' Grant said, handing over the blue vinyl carrying-case. 'If Basset wonders about the torn muslin at the back of the picture, tell him I was just making sure.'

Renwick's eyebrows lifted. 'I'd like to hear—'

'Later. You have messages to send. Now, what about Avril? What's her address?'

'Frank will take you there.' Renwick nodded to the street outside. 'He's waiting and ready and bursting with curiosity. See you soon, Colin. Take care.' He paused, said very quietly, 'And thanks. Thanks from a lot of people.' Swinging the Ruysdael case in his hand, he hurried away.

'Hey!' Grant called after him. 'Take it easy with that case, will you?' With a wide smile, he went looking for Frank.

17

Three blocks away from her apartment, Avril Hoffman paid off the taxi in busy Währingerstrasse. She still wasn't sure if someone had tried to follow her out of Klar's Auction Rooms. It could be more than likely: Gudrun Klar had eyed her peculiarly, as though trying to identify her face. From some photograph, perhaps? Again a possibility.

But of one thing Avril was certain: Gudrun Klar hadn't understood a word of her message to Colin. And even if someone was ready to follow her, she had made such a quick exit that she was sure – almost sure – he had lost her. Unless, of course, when she stopped to telephone, the man had picked up her trail. By sheer luck. That could happen, too. After all, Avril herself had had two pieces of good fortune today: arriving just in time at Klar's; seeing that imitation Memling portrait. She had no prerogative on luck, she reminded herself. And she had been damned forgetful after her phone call. Still chiding herself for that, she took extra care now.

She had a quick cup of coffee in a small café, choosing a table near its window, where, screened by a flourishing rubber-plant, she could have a safe view of Währingerstrasse. Nothing out there to worry her, she decided. After the café, she visited a flower shop and bought some yellow roses; next a stationer's shop for a newspaper. Still watchful, she made a small detour before she reached her apartment.

It lay on a quiet street, in one of several similar houses, all fairly modern, agreeable, thoroughly reputable and not too expensive. There were other buildings – the University area was just south of it, the medical centre and hospitals to its east – which gave a feeling of solidity and security. Many of her neighbours were professional people, or research students, or even Embassy employees like the two secretaries from whom she had rented the apartment while they were on leave. The Embassy itself was less than ten minutes away, which was the biggest advantage of all.

She entered the brick-tiled hall and stopped at the ground-floor apartment, its door wide open, as usual, in the daytime hours. Here an elderly couple lived rent-free in exchange for their services. Mail and packages were delivered to them, and collected by the tenants. Old Man Berger, with the useful excuse of a bad back, had a rule of carrying nothing: he was a permanent fixture in his small office, listening to the radio or reading the daily newspaper, while he guarded letters and boxes until they were safely picked up. Frau Berger kept the hall and staircase scrubbed and immaculate, eking out her husband's pension by 'obliging' some of the tenants who needed extra help. Avril trusted them: they were decent and honest, and not overly curious. Their lives were placid and self-contained. They did their job, and kept the house in neat order.

'Good morning, Herr Berger,' she called as he lowered his radio. 'Anything for me?'

'Soon be afternoon,' he told her. The aroma of midday dinner cooking in their kitchen was savoury. 'Yes, Fräulein Hoffman, here are two pieces of luggage. A suitcase and a bag, delivered by a taxi driver.'

'I was expecting them. My cousin will be arriving later today. I'll take them upstairs now.'

Frau Berger had heard the voices, and made her appearance, white-haired and smiling, wiping her hands on her large apron.

'Too heavy for you, Fräulein Hoffman. And there are also some groceries.'

Avril tested the suitcase, found it was portable. 'I'll manage.' When Colin Grant arrived, she wanted no delay down here. She laid aside the roses and newspaper along with the box of groceries, and carried the two pieces of luggage up the stairs to her apartment. Then, slightly breathless, she ran down to collect the remaining items. Berger had been eyeing her newspaper, so she left it with him.

'How late will your cousin arrive?' Berger worried about strangers entering his apartment-house. 'How will I know her?'

'He,' Avril said with a smile, 'is tall, dark-haired, with grey eyes. His name is Grant – an American. Just send him right up, will you?'

'If the office isn't locked by that time,' Berger grumbled.

'If the office isn't locked,' Avril agreed. 'Don't worry. He knows I live on the third floor.' She was already starting up the stone staircase. Behind her she heard Frau Berger say, 'Far too heavy. All that carrying. And on such a warm day.' It was the closest to a small reprimand that she would ever give her husband. But he had his rules: break them once, and they'd be broken for ever. The radio was turned up higher, and that was his answer.

Avril reached her apartment, got everything pulled over the threshold. She closed the self-locking door and bolted it as usual. (Bob Renwick, who had inspected her choice of living quarters, had insisted she make everything secure each time she entered until it became an automatic reaction – like turning on the cold tap when you lifted your toothbrush, he had said.) Once the roses were put into a jug of water for a long deep drink and the perishable groceries were in the refrigerator, she kicked off her shoes, peeled off the jacket of her suit, flopped on the couch. Just ten minutes, she thought – Colin wouldn't arrive until one o'clock at the earliest – ten minutes to rid herself of this sudden exhaustion.

She had not been followed, she told herself again. She was over-worrying, a symptom of her anxiety about the success of their mission in Vienna. It was so near completion, and yet – tantalizingly – it still lacked the final piece of information. Colin Grant might just manage to find it . . . Had he? She looked at her watch, checked it with the clock on the wall. Twelve ten, exactly. How slowly time moved when you waited and wondered.

She rose and began preparing. Colin's luggage was deposited on racks in the guest-room. Its bathroom was in order, fresh towels and soap. Its own small refrigerator had soda and beer. Scotch and glasses were on a tray. On the desk there was writing-paper, a pen, pencils, and a bud vase in which she placed one of the roses. This week's news magazines lay beside the armchair. She remembered to change a weak light-bulb in the reading-lamp. Satisfied at last, she crossed through the central living-room to her own section of the apartment. She had ten minutes to wash, and to change the dark blue suit which she had thought suitable for a businesslike session at the Embassy that morning. Not the pale blue dress – he had seen that on their first meeting. Not the white suit: she had worn that yesterday.

Yesterday . . . Was that when a snapshot had been taken of her? When Helmut Fischer was bidding her goodbye? She couldn't avert her face – that would have really offended his sense of good manners. Yes, she had been vulnerable at that moment: the man who had followed her into the art shop had ample time to take a quick photograph of her face as she kept her eyes politely on Fischer. What had he used – a miniature

211

camera disguised as a cigarette-lighter, or as a watch? If so, it explained how Gudrun Klar could have recognized her today. Correlate that snapshot with previous photographs taken surreptitiously of all the Embassy staff, and Klar could even have her name. Until yesterday, when she had been seen meeting Colin in Fischer's shop, Avril Hoffman had been only one of several little secretaries hurrying in and out of the Embassy. Now – Oh, stop this! she warned herself: you are crossing fifty bridges before you even approach the first of them.

She forced herself to concentrate on everyday details. She creamed her face and powdered it, brushed her hair, began selecting a dress. Not the coral print – too warm for today's temperature. She'd wear her light green silk, simple and cool. The mirror agreed with her choice: not bad at all, she thought. If only she had more time to stretch out in a swimsuit on some warm beach and give herself a glowing tan. But this summer she'd have to stay white-skinned. She added a touch of faint rose colour to her cheekbones, a light pencilling of her eyebrows for emphasis (her dark lashes needed no lengthening with mascara) and a deeper pink to her lips. Not bad, she thought again as she took one last long view of her appearance. Why all this fuss? Colin Grant was only another short-term guest. Two weeks ago there had been that rather nice but very silent man whom she had described to the Bergers as her uncle. A month before that, her 'brother' had come to spend two days here. I'm running out of relatives, she thought with a smile.

Quickly she tidied her bedroom. With her women visitors, it was easy to explain their stay here: no need to call them aunts or sisters – just friends. The Bergers accepted that. But a man living here as a friend? It would shock them into talking and tut-tutting. Gossip spread

quickly and aroused too much speculation. In less innocent people than the Bergers it could stir suspicions,
questions. What price security then?

By half past twelve, the last of the groceries were on
their shelves, and the roses arranged in a green vase.
Everything was in order. She tried to read – the latest
copy of *Encounter*, then a thin book of Frost's poems –
and gave up. She chose the new recording of Dvořák's
piano quintet for her record-player, and settled to listen.
Ten minutes later, she found she wasn't really listening,
not the way this heavenly music deserved. She switched
it off. Better play it later, when her mood was right.
Twelve fifty . . . Twelve fifty-five . . . Had something
gone wrong? Had Colin failed, or been discovered? If so
– what then? He would be in extreme danger. That
unholy crew down at Klar's – he hadn't a chance against
them. He'd never emerge from that place. Just disappear. Everyone claiming he had left, all stories neatly
coinciding, and such deep regret.

Oh, why did we put him into such a position? she
asked angrily. Why, why? Yet she knew the answer. He
was the only one who could do this job, quickly,
immediately. Any other approach might take weeks,
and not even succeed. 'Now or never,' Bob Renwick had
said, and quoted Shakespeare. *There is a tide in the affairs
of men, which taken at the flood* . . . Shakespeare, that old
encourager. Her natural optimism surged back. Nothing
had gone wrong, she told herself. Colin had reached the
Embassy by this time, and seen Basset. He would be
here soon. Wouldn't he? As if to reassure her, the
doorbell rang. Thank God, she thought, and ran to
answer it.

Frau Berger was there, her pink-cheeked face set in a
worried frown. Two men in white jackets pulled her
aside. In that split second, one of them was already over
the threshold, gripping Avril's wrist, silencing any

213

scream with a heavy hand clamped tightly over her nose and mouth. Behind him, the other man, holding a small black bag, blocked Frau Berger's view as he began reassuring her.

Avril's attempt to scream was smothered by a sickly odour. She tried to hold her breath, but it was too late. Her legs gave way, her body began to fall. The man caught her as she went limp, thrust the small pad of chloroform into his pocket, and carried her to the couch. 'She has fainted,' he called over his shoulder. 'Doctor – here! Quick!'

The doctor left Frau Berger with the sharp order to stay back. He didn't close the door; let the old woman gape from its threshold. He took out a stethoscope, felt Avril's pulse, looked as though he were a true professional.

'Is it bad?' Frau Berger quavered. 'Why did she not call us downstairs when she felt ill? I would have—'

'She did the right thing,' said the doctor's assistant, coming over to close the door. 'She called the hospital and we came at once. And we brought an ambulance. She will need it.'

'What's wrong?'

'Heart attack.'

'I knew it,' Frau Berger said, 'all that luggage she carried upstairs, and the groceries too. Running she was, hurrying; she wouldn't leave anything for her cousin to bring.'

'Cousin?'

'He's expected later.'

'When?'

'Later,' repeated Frau Berger helplessly. Then her native common sense reasserted itself. 'Why do you ask?'

The doctor said, 'You will have to tell him that Fräulein

214

Hoffman is in hospital. Not to worry; we shall keep him informed.'

'Is she—'

'Fräulein Hoffman will have intensive care. Thomas – we'll need the stretcher up here,' he added as he folded the stethoscope into his bag. 'No more to be done meanwhile.' He laid a gentle hand on Avril's brow, shook his head. But Thomas had ideas of his own. 'Get down to the front door,' he told Frau Berger, 'and signal to the ambulance driver. Give him the apartment number. Quick, quick!'

Frau Berger obeyed, shaking her head, saying, 'She doesn't eat enough, poor soul. These girls today, they don't listen.' Her comments faded along with her foot-steps as her solid girth hurried downstairs as fast as it could.

The man playing doctor was annoyed. 'Why didn't *you* go? She's a slow mover, that old woman.'

'I need a little time up here,' said the man who had been given the name of Thomas. That still amused him. Why pick Thomas out of the air? Does he think I'm a doubter? He's the one who's nervous.

'For what? The sooner we leave, the—'

'I want to see this luggage – find out who her cousin is.' Thomas moved to Avril's bedroom, discovered nothing. He drained the chloroform pad down the toilet bowl in her bathroom. The trouble with that stuff was the smell it could leave around, but a needle in the wrist would not have been so certain or quick – not with the way she had tried to pull her arm free. She might look fragile enough, but she had been an unpleasant surprise in those first few seconds. Nearly got a scream out, too. He crossed the living-room, entered the other side of the apartment, and found what he was looking for. He took out some keys.

From the living-room the other was calling, 'Did you

215

give her enough to put her right out? I think she's coming round.'

'She isn't,' Thomas told him. 'I gave her just enough. We want her up on her feet and walking after we ditch the ambulance.'

'What's that you said?' The doctor had come to the guest-room door.

Angrily – for not even his special key was of any use on the small locks of the suitcase and overnight bag – Thomas repeated his information while he took out his knife.

'What are you doing? Don't break it open, you'll have the police—'

'Shut up. The cousin won't call any police. I'm not breaking anything, just persuading.' The gentle probing with the knife was having no effect. 'It's one of those damned combination locks – set by numbers like a bloody safe.'

'Combination? Then leave it!' For it looked to the doctor, more nervous with each added minute, as if Thomas in his sudden rage would try to slice through the lid of the suitcase. 'Leave it, I tell you.'

'Get back to the girl!'

'You, too. I hear Rupprecht's voice. That old bitch is coming up here again.'

Thomas rose from his knees, took an angry swipe at the rosebud in its slender vase as he passed it, sending them both spilling.

'Now why that? Look at the mess—'

'Blown over by a draught from the window.' Those damned combination locks, Thomas thought again as he followed the doctor into the sitting-room. People usually set them by numbers they'd remember easily: day, month, year of their birth. Except that he didn't know who the cousin was, so how the hell could he know the birthday? We'll find out, he promised himself as they

216

came to stand beside the girl; I'll get that luggage somehow, see what it contains. He had just time to say, 'Don't use Rupprecht's name again. Remember!' before Frau Berger was at the door.

'It was for your ears only,' said the doctor under his breath. Then smiling, he said to the woman, 'That's all, thank you. We'll get Fräulein Hoffman safely downstairs.' He signed to Rupprecht to unfold the stretcher.

Frau Berger didn't leave. 'I'll get a blanket from her room.'

'No need. We have blankets in the ambulance. You can go now.' She didn't seem to hear him. She kept standing there, fascinated, as the three men strapped the girl on to the stretcher.

The doctor led the way downstairs. Thomas and Rupprecht did the carrying. Frau Berger brought up the rear. She was shedding a few tears, wiping them away with her apron. The two stretcher-bearers worried her: clumsy men. If Fräulein Hoffman wasn't so tightly tied in place, they could have tipped her out at the turns on each landing.

In the hall, Herr Berger was at the door of his office, a napkin still tucked under his chin although he had finished his second helping of veal stew with dumplings. 'Your dinner is cold,' he told his wife, but she only wiped away her last tear and followed the men out to the pavement. There were few people around at this time of day – just some parked cars and a light truck that had turned the corner and was lumbering along the street.

'What hospital?' she remembered to call, as the stretcher was loaded into the ambulance.

'Damned bitch makes me nervous,' Thomas muttered. He tapped Rupprecht's shoulder, gestured towards the driver's seat. 'Get on with it,' he told him, and climbed into the ambulance. His friend the doctor was already inside, and feeling safe enough to peel off the white linen jacket which had irked him – too tight over his tweed jacket, too warm in this weather. Thomas closed the doors behind him, locked them securely. There were no side windows in this ambulance. The old woman out there could see nothing at all. He rapped on the panel to let Rupprecht know they were ready. There was a brief wait, while Rupprecht fumbled with the unaccustomed gears, and at last they were off.

'A piece of cake,' said Thomas and he got rid of his own white jacket. The girl was stirring now, moaning slightly, but her eyes were still closed. 'It's all right,' he assured the other men. 'Everything is under control.'

'Avril's place is just five doors down,' Frank was saying as he steered the small truck round a corner into a residential street. 'I'll drop you before we get to that ambulance.' Then he gave a second look. 'It's standing at her apartment-house. That's the caretaker's wife, out there on the pavement.' Three men, two of them wearing white jackets, were carrying a stretcher. At this distance, all Frank could see of the patient was a green dress. No blanket?

'Not very adept,' Grant remarked, as they began hoisting the stretcher into the ambulance. The woman on the pavement was calling to them, but they didn't listen.

'They're in a hurry.' Frank's brows knitted. 'Undermanned. Looks as if they had to recruit the driver to help as a bearer.' And he had never before seen a doctor, black bag and all, trying to steady a stretcher with his free hand. Frank didn't ease the truck to a brief halt some four doors away from Avril's apartment-house, as he had first planned. (Not my territory, he had explained to Grant: you go in by yourself, and I'll drive on.) He continued slowly along the street.

The stretcher was safely inside the ambulance, the doctor too. The other white jacket was beginning to follow. The driver, a tall thin figure in neat grey, started to move round to the front of the vehicle, halted abruptly to look back along the street. The truck's unchanged speed seemed to reassure him, although it was drawing too close for his comfort. He ducked his head, averted his face, and hurried on his way.

Frank heard Grant's sharp intake of breath. 'I've seen that man,' Grant said.

'Where?'

Thin-faced, dark-browed, sharp-nosed. 'I've seen him. But I can't place him.' The ambulance was drawing out from the curb with a protesting screech of gears, avoiding a parked car ahead of it, and increasing its speed. Who the hell is that man? Grant wondered. I've seen so many strangers in these last three days – neat grey suit, where?

Frank drew up at Avril's house, called to the woman who was about to re-enter its door. 'Delivery for Hoffman. Is she home?'

Frau Berger turned and pointed to the ambulance, now almost out of sight. 'She's had a heart attack. They are taking her to the—' She was left with her mouth open and her sentence unfinished, as the truck suddenly roared into power and sped off.

Grant's face was tense, his jaw rigid. Frank kept silent too. We couldn't have got here any quicker, he was thinking. We wasted no time. A truck can't barrel through residential streets without raising a howl of protest. I had to drive normally. Even now we may be stopped any minute for exceeding the speed limit. Yet it's one time I might welcome police interference, provided they believe me enough to take up the chase. Must keep that ambulance in sight, see where they ditch it. That they will do – it's too noticeable. If we don't see the car they take, we've lost them for good.

With quiet desperation Grant searched his memory. A neat dresser, tall, thin-faced, dark-browed . . . Suddenly his mind focused sharply. It was the grey suit that had given him the wrong start, led him to nothing. Strip away the clothes, just remember that sharp-nosed face, that strange ducking of the head, as if the man were nervous about being too clearly noticed. Yes, yes, yes – replace the grey suit with green waistcoat and apron, white shirt, black trousers, and he'd see a man climbing a staircase, his head averted, his face turned to that godawful wallpaper. The name, the name – what was the name? 'Rupprecht,' Grant almost shouted. 'That was Rupprecht.'

'Rupprecht who?' Frank kept his eyes fixed on the busy thoroughfare ahead of him. The fast-moving ambulance was making a left turn now. He could only hope it wasn't into a street that was banned to all commercial traffic. He'd have to chance it, though.

'He works at the Two Crowns. He's—'

'Mandel's Rupprecht, by God! Hold this damned wheel.' Frank removed his right hand as he reached quickly into his jacket for a small transmitter.

Grant grabbed and steadied the wheel, while Frank's left hand gripped tightly and controlled the steering. It was a precarious minute, but Frank managed to make quick radio contact. 'Did Rupprecht the porter leave this morning? When? Okay. Keep an eye out for his return. Who's watching the rear area of the Two Crowns? He may go in that way. Perhaps by car. With others accompanying. Report what you see. Have the camera ready! – What's that? Did he now? – Keep watching. And listening!' Then he laid the transmitter on the seat beside him, and took charge of the wheel once more. 'Yes,' he told Grant, 'Rupprecht, wearing a grey suit, was observed leaving the Two Crowns at twelve-thirty. It isn't his day off, either.' He didn't explain who had given him this information, or how it had been gathered, or where.

Grant, his eyes searching for the ambulance which had suddenly vanished on the street they had just entered, didn't waste time enquiring.

Frank was saying, 'Guess who has just arrived at the Two Crowns? Your friend Jacques.'

'Jacques?'

'Mittendorf,' Frank corrected himself.

'Where's the ambulance?' Grant asked in sudden panic. 'Where is that goddamned ambulance?'

'They've ditched it. Watch for any courtyards with wide doorways.' There were several of them: this was a street of small shops separated, here and there, by delivery entrances.

Well ahead, a white car emerged from a courtyard, making a sharp and dangerous turn, and then increased its speed. 'A Fiat,' Frank said. 'I didn't get its number. Did you? Too bad. Let's make a check.' He stopped the truck at the entrance, saying, 'Hop out and make sure.'

Grant dropped down from the truck, ran into the cobbled yard where a couple of automobiles were parked. Behind the cars, with two curious women and an elderly man staring at it in wonder, was the abandoned ambulance. Swiftly he returned. Frank was transmitting again, this time giving the colour and make of the car that had shot out of the delivery entrance and driven so quickly away.

Grant climbed back into his seat.

'Wish I hadn't sent Joe off,' Frank admitted. 'Could use him right here.' It had seemed best, when he saw Grant approaching from the Embassy, to tell Joe to leave. He had questions for Grant that were beyond Joe's knowledge. Joe had done well at unloading timber – a good man – but he had never heard of a Geneva bank account.

'What now?' demanded Grant. 'They wouldn't be so stupid as to take her to the Two Crowns. Bernie Mandel wouldn't risk that.'

'There's a house next door to the hotel. It's unoccupied except for one old woman as caretaker. We think there may be an entry to it through Mandel's office. Haven't been able to get in to prove it, though.' Perhaps today would be the time for that, Frank thought. The police? Only if their help could be engineered without drawing unwanted questions. A tricky situation.

'Mandel has too much to lose. He wouldn't risk it,' Grant insisted.

'We're in his district. Now wouldn't you say that was convenient?'

'Too near.' Grant's thinking was clear, but the words sounded meaningless. 'I mean—' He gave up. I mean, he thought, that it would be as stupid as hell to abandon the ambulance so close to the Two Crowns. 'Why didn't they get rid of it earlier?'

'That would depend on a safe courtyard, wouldn't it? A place where they could have a white Fiat waiting. With no questions asked, no complaints made.'

When Grant didn't answer, Frank said, 'This was a quickly arranged job. That's for sure. Somehow they tracked Avril down this morning. They had to get men together, steal an ambulance, move fast. Snatched her when most people were indoors having their midday dinner. Apartment-house quiet, street empty. Yes, they moved fast. Which means there are loose ends. Which means, in turn, they'll need a short interval to get their plans better arranged. This was only the first phase of their little operation.'

Little? thought Grant bitterly. Suddenly he became aware of the streets through which they were passing.

Two blocks away was the Schotten Allee. 'You aren't going to the Two Crowns?' he asked in disbelief. I wish to God that Bob Renwick was here, he thought, and not this maniac with his fixation on Mandel's hotel.

Frank corrected him with a shake of the head. 'To my garage. Remember it? Time to get rid of this truck. Your friend Rupprecht must have seen us trying to follow him. So we'll do as they are doing – find a breathing-space, send out messages, make a reassessment, call in more help.' Then Frank turned angry. 'What else, Grant? What else do you suggest?'

Nothing, thought Grant. Unseeing, he stared out at the narrow street.

18

There was a feeling of urgency, a feeling of uselessness. Torn between the two, Grant could only follow Frank into the garage, saying nothing, hoping that the right decisions were being made – and made quickly enough.

The truck had been left a few doors down the street, and Joe, the younger of the garage attendants, had driven it away. Grant thought he recognized Frank's helper with the precarious load of cut wood for Klar's warehouse balanced on his shoulders – he certainly had moved speedily enough on Frank's command. So did the man inside his glass booth at the entrance to the garage: he was now phoning Walter, telling him to take his taxi and pick up the two pieces of luggage from the Hoffman apartment.

'Why waste time on that?' Grant asked sharply, as he hurried through the garage with Frank.

Frank waited until they had reached a door in the rear wall. 'Isn't it obvious?'

'No.' A girl was missing, and time was wasted on two pieces of luggage. Both time and a useful man like Walter.

'Through here.' Frank opened the door and urged him into a lavatory. 'Come on, come on!' They passed into a small room, aired by a ceiling-high window heavily barred. There were a rickety table and chair, a wall-telephone, a stool, two more doors – one opening to show a shallow closet as Frank whipped off his leather jacket and hung it beside some odd pieces of clothing. Frank gestured with his head towards the other door.

'Corridor and back entrance,' he said briefly. 'Sit down. Get your feet up. Relax. You look pooped.' His mood had soured: there was nothing he could do with Grant except bring him into his private den, keep him out of sight. This invasion was something that went against all his rules and practices. What choice had he anyway? He was stuck with Grant until Renwick could take him off his hands. But before he called Renwick, he'd contact his two watchers in the house opposite Mandel's place. That was his first priority. He picked up the telephone and began to dial.

'It isn't obvious,' Grant said. 'Two damned pieces of luggage, when a girl—'

'The luggage could tell who you are. Also—' Frank was through now to his house on Schotten Allee – 'you haven't left the Majestic, remember? Keep Mittendorf thinking that way, or do you want him starting a search for you and—' He broke off to speak on the telephone, checking the time on his watch. It was one twenty, exactly.

Grant sat down at the desk, still arguing it out with himself. If his luggage could have that importance, why hadn't one of the three abductors taken it with him? Too noticeable, perhaps? Yes, that might be the reason: impossible to conceal the theft, caretaker's suspicions aroused. He'd better keep quiet from now on, ask no more idiotic questions. Such as, would Mittendorf really send someone back to Avril's apartment with a good excuse, and filch my suitcase and bag? Yes, he damn well would, just to find out who was visiting Avril and why. Grant relaxed his spine, sat more comfortably, and propped his feet up on the table. He felt drained, mentally and physically. He admitted his exhaustion as he let his body slump.

Over the phone Frank was asking, his voice sharp, 'No car yet? Nothing? Only Mittendorf so far . . . When did he get there?'

'Fifteen minutes ago.'

'At one five? And he's still inside the Two Crowns?'

'Still there.'

'Keep watching for that car.' Did I guess wrong? Frank wondered. His brows down, he glared across the small room at a silent Grant. Suddenly, just as he was about to replace the receiver, an excited voice changed his angry scowl to a wide grin. 'I'm here. Repeat that.'

'A white Fiat approaching. Time is now one twenty-two . . . It's stopping. At the house adjoining the Two Crowns. Caretaker has the door open and ready. Two men and a woman – young – entering. The girl is barely walking – supported between the men. Ill. Or drugged?'

'Drugged. Could you see the men clearly?'

'Yes. Got photographs, too.'

'Is Rupprecht one of them?'

'No.'

Then he must be driving the Fiat, Frank thought.

'The car is moving off. No time wasted. Picking up speed.'

'Get its number!' Frank shouted.

'Plate now visible. W632-546. Car now out of sight.'

To be abandoned where? Frank said, 'Got our hearing-aid beamed in?'

'Yes. The men and girl must be in the front room. Heavy drapes across windows as usual, can't see a thing, but we're getting the voices. Time is one twenty-five. We're recording. Some blurs now and again in the sound – slight blocks – otherwise clear enough . . . Now they've stopped talking, or moved into the back of the house. No, wait, I hear the girl coughing – sick, possibly. There's a fuss. A man is cursing. Sounds of movement – something heavy upset.'

'Keep recording.' Frank glanced at Grant, and almost sighed. 'Look – I can't get over to hear the tape. So give me the conversation up until they stopped talking.'

Quickly, he drew out a notebook and pencil from his shirt pocket.

'I'll differentiate between the voices,' he was advised. 'One was deep, the other higher in tone.'

'Okay.' Frank began jotting down the words: What now? – We wait. – Here? – Here. – How long do you (*unintelligible*)? – Until Rupprecht leaves (*unintelligible*) garage at Kärntnerstrasse and drives back (*unintelligible*). – That could take almost an hour. At least! – Shut up. Stop worrying. He's a good driver. Knows (*unintelligible*).

'Is that the end of their talk?' Frank asked.

'So far.'

'Keep listening. Give me ten minutes before you phone me again. I've another call to make.' Frank hung up and waited for a few seconds before he dialled the American Embassy and asked for Renwick's extension. Mr Renwick was not to be disturbed, a stilted voice informed him. 'Get him! Tell him Wolf is on the phone and waiting. This is an emergency.' Frank's tone was savage. It must have startled the woman at the other end of the line; it certainly startled Grant; and Joe, too, who had just arrived with a large brown paper bag in his hand. With one look at Frank, Joe dropped the bag on the table, said to no one in particular, 'The truck's okay,' and retreated to the garage.

Grant leaned foward and looked inside the bag. Sandwiches, my God. And a bottle of milk.

'Don't look so damned contemptuous,' Frank told him, still gripping the receiver to his ear.

'Not contemptuous. Just don't feel like eating.'

'Eat! Stoke up the boiler! How the hell do you expect to get through this day on an empty belly? That's right, just sit there and brood and let your mind sag with hunger. You'll be useless when the action starts. Hand me a sandwich, will you? Cheese. You take the ham.'

Action was the spur word. Grant rose and passed over a sandwich.

'We've learned something,' Frank told him. 'Not much. But a start.' Then he was listening intently to the telephone. 'Yes,' he answered, 'this *is* an emergency. They've got Sweetheart. Picked her up, one o'clock, at her apartment. We're here at the garage. See you.' He hooked up the receiver, and checked inside the outsize sandwich. Cheese, he verified, and took a large bite through the roll's crisp crust. 'Renwick's on his way. He will be here in ten minutes.'

'Ten?' Grant was disbelieving. Minutes slipping away, he thought. And all we have got is some message I didn't even hear.

'Eat,' Frank said. 'Pass the milk. Soothes the stomach.'

'Sweetheart – is that your name for her?'

'Not mine. Renwick's. It fits, don't you think?'

Grant said nothing. At last he began eating, kept his eye on his watch.

Renwick's arrival was announced by a small buzz on the intercom linked with the garage. Joe brought him into the room, and then vanished. Renwick looked round him quickly, nodded to them both. It was now one fifty, Grant noted.

Frank played it cool. 'As you see, Bob, I am breaking all my rules. Forget you ever stopped in here. You too, Grant.' With that taken care of, Frank gave a quick rundown of the last fifty minutes. 'Here is what my boys overheard,' he ended, and produced his notebook. He tore out the small sheet of paper, placed it on the table for both Renwick and Grant to read.

Renwick spoke his first words. 'When was this recorded?'

'It began at one twenty-five.'

'And Rupprecht is driving down to Kärntnerstrasse,

picking up another car and then driving back. Presumably to take the two men and Avril to another address. The house next door to the Two Crowns is only a temporary stop.'

'That's how I figure it,' Frank agreed. 'Rupprecht is dropping off the Fiat at some garage far away from the Two Crowns. Couldn't risk leaving it in some nearby street: parking regulations are stringent.'

'Two big garages in that area. Which? – Where's your telephone directory?'

'This is quicker.' Frank switched on the intercom, and began speaking with the man in the glass-enclosed office. There was a short pause, and then Frank was being given the names of the garages and their telephone numbers. He scrawled them down quickly, and called the first of them. 'No go,' he told Renwick. 'No white Fiat parked there in the last ten minutes.' He began dialling the second number.

'Rupprecht might have been delayed,' Renwick said worriedly. Again he calculated the timing. If Rupprecht was a good driver, he ought to have reached the Kärntnerstrasse district in fifteen or twenty minutes. But traffic jams did occur in the narrow streets. Then his face cleared, and he exchanged glances with Grant, as they heard Frank asking if his friend had managed to find a suitable car to replace the white Fiat.

'He did?' Frank was saying, his voice as smooth as silk. 'Excellent! What make was it? A Fiat 132/2000, black – yes, just as I ordered. Good! Four-door, of course . . . Its licence number? Thanks. Thank you very much.' The call was over, and Frank turned back to face the room. 'Nice girl there,' he observed. 'The Fiat is the 1977 model with a two-litre engine. Plate number: W531-735.'

'When did Rupprecht leave?' Renwick wanted to know.

'A few minutes before I telephoned, she said. She was

229

sorry I missed him. The Fiat was rented for him soon after one o'clock today. Nice girl, but slightly mixed up. She thought I was the one who had ordered it.'

Renwick almost smiled. 'You gave a damn good imitation of that. Now what do we have? Rupprecht heading back to the Schotten Allee, and my watch says it's now five minutes past two. Think I'll leave, Frank – get in position. What about you?'

'Staying here. I must.' Frank pointed to the telephone. Expecting reports from my boys over on—' He broke off, looked blandly at Grant.

'What car can I borrow? I drove here in an open two-seater – useless for tailing.'

'The Mercedes,' Frank suggested. 'It's—'

'Dangerous,' Grant warned.

They stared at him.

'They had me under surveillance when I arrived at the airport. So I gathered from Lois Westerbrook.'

Frank swore. 'How far did they follow the Mercedes?'

'They lost us. Or else Westerbrook wouldn't have been sent to question me about it.'

'Take my car,' Frank told Renwick. 'You know its gadgets.' He spoke into the intercom once more, arranging for the brown Porsche to be ready to leave.

Renwick looked at Grant. 'You stay here. Your job is over, Colin.'

That's what I thought before Frank's truck turned a corner into a quiet street, and I saw an ambulance. 'Like hell it is. Do you need extra help, or don't you?'

'I could use it.'

'Then come on,' Grant urged. The feeling of uselessness was gone. 'See you around,' he told Frank, and left.

Frank took out his small transceiver, laid it on the table. 'I'll keep that turned on,' he said. 'You remember what button to press in the Porsche?'

'The blue one for sending and receiving.'

'That's right. We'll stay in touch.'

'I'll need your help to alert—'

'Sure. Talk with me about that from the car. Good luck!'

The telephone rang, and Renwick halted at the door, his eyes questioning.

Frank took the brief message, passed it on. 'Mittendorf has left the Two Crowns. On foot, as usual.'

Renwick nodded and hurried to catch up with Grant, who was already in the Porsche. 'Mittendorf is leaving the scene.' Wily character, Mittendorf, timing arrival and departure so that there would seem to be no connection between him and the Fiats.

'Let's go,' Grant urged, as Renwick studied the car's dashboard with its various coloured buttons.

'We'll give Mittendorf time to get clear of Schotten Allee. Anyway, Rupprecht isn't expected for the next ten minutes – maybe fifteen,' Renwick predicted.

'How d'you know?'

'Mittendorf. He intends to be well away before any action begins.' Renwick pressed the blue button. It glowed. 'Frank – can you hear us?'

'I hear you,' came Frank's voice from a small strip of gauze concealing a speaker over the rear-view mirror. 'Hey, Bob – one thing I forgot. What the devil do we do with Grant's luggage?'

Which means, thought Renwick, that Frank doesn't want it dumped here. 'Too hot to handle?' he asked with a laugh. 'Okay. Send it to Prescott Taylor at the Embassy. I've left him in charge of the chores.' Renwick turned on the ignition, and the Porsche moved smoothly into the narrow street. 'A couple of minutes more,' he told Grant, 'and we'll be in position on Schotten Allee. Then—' He paused, restrained himself, said quietly, 'we wait.'

* * *

Their position, Grant had to admit, was excellent. Renwick parked in front of two other cars, a short distance away from the Two Crowns, yet near enough for a clear view of the hotel and its neighbour. Could the black Fiat have arrived and left, wondered Grant, while Renwick had been making his cautious approach? Then he realized that Frank's men would have phoned in the alarm, and Renwick would have been alerted. 'He's well organized.'

'Frank? He has to be. This is his field of operation.'

Frank's voice came over the speaker. 'You can bet on that.'

Renwick gave an amused glance at Grant's startled face. 'Just remember you're on candid radio,' he told him. 'Frank – I press the green button for your no-see magic?'

'That's right. And there's a map and a magnifying-glass in the glove compartment. Binoculars, too. Better check now.'

Quickly Grant did so, and found them all in place. He looked up, as he heard a whirring sound. Renwick had pressed the green button: the sound came from inside windows, moving up into place around the car. 'Storm windows, or bullet-proof?' Grant asked with a smile.

'One-way. Opaque glass, light blue – as if for anti-glare. We can see out. No one can see in. From the street, this car now seems empty.'

'What if someone walked right up to us and tried to peer in at the dashboard?' Grant's smile was back.

'Thank God that hasn't happened so far. But remind me to switch off the green glow before I start driving, or we'll have old ladies fainting on the sidewalk. A car being driven with no one at the wheel – that's enough to start a riot.' Renwick noted Grant's amusement. Much better, he thought: the tension was gone; Grant had even stopped looking at his watch. Keep talking, Renwick told himself: get him out of the glum silence that was smothering him back at the garage. 'I expect you've been wondering why we don't jump them when they bring Avril out of the house.'

'I've thought of it,' Grant admitted. Rupprecht would stay in the car – he wouldn't risk being seen and recognized, certainly not near the hotel where he worked. That left two of them: one was solid, the other a pushover. 'We could take them.'

'A knock-down, drag-out brawl, Hollywood style? Yes, that has its attractions. It would relieve our feelings, for one thing. But we'll pass it up meanwhile.' Renwick was watching Grant's face. 'Can you guess why?' he prodded.

'Because of Mittendorf. If we intercepted that Fiat, he would know about it five minutes later. He'd be out of Austria and across the Czechoslovakian frontier in less than an hour. If he decided on Hungary, just over an hour. But we need him right here in Vienna, sitting at his office desk at four o'clock this afternoon.'

Grant shifted his attention from the street – a few pedestrians, an occasional car – and looked sharply at Renwick.

Renwick said, 'He will be arrested then. On charges of misappropriating company funds. Yes, everything's beginning to move, Colin. Gudrun Klar and her husband will be picked up by the police at the same hour. The charge against them is fraud – attempted substitution of a reproduction for a masterpiece. And Sigmund, the expert packer, will be detained: he'll be scared enough to testify that they ordered the substitution. He doesn't know much else, I think: did as he was told, for money, or promotion to foreman.'

'So four o'clock is your deadline. After that, you'll feel free to tackle Avril's problem,' Grant said bitterly.

'Hey, hold on there! What do you think we are doing right now?' Renwick was angry.

True enough. This was one way of dealing with her abduction. Perhaps the only way, Grant admitted reluctantly. 'Sorry,' he said awkwardly. 'It's one hell of a time for them to stage a kidnapping.'

Renwick checked his watch. 'Rupprecht is late. Must have taken a few detours, played it safe.' He was getting restless. 'Frank,' he tested, 'are you still getting us?'

'Loud and clear.'

'Has something gone wrong, d'you think?'

'Like a head-on collision, and Rupprecht breaking his bloody neck?'

'Too much to hope for.' Renwick was smiling again. 'What about that house – no more conversation heard?'

'Some bickering. And a lot of talk about their own troubles. The one with the thin voice has ulcers; the deep voice has piles, and a mother-in-law who won't move out. They had some difficulty with Avril. Had to drug her again. They've been arguing whether they gave her enough or too much. They want her able to walk.'

Grant and Renwick exchanged glances and said nothing at all.

'Hold on, hold on!' Frank's voice called out. 'There's a message coming through.'

Grant kept watching the narrow street. More people were out there now. Placid and well fed, with no thoughts beyond the opening of their shops and businesses after a long midday dinner. Tomorrow they'd be heading into the country – what had been Helmut Fischer's words? – everyone rushing off in their little white cars. Fischer, he thought, Fischer and Grünau . . . 'We'll need some place safe—' he began, and was cut off by Frank's excited voice.

'Hear this!' Frank was saying. He began repeating the conversation that had just been relayed to him, pausing between the two men's remarks to keep their dialogue clear. 'Get her ready. It's almost time now. – What kept Rupprecht so long? – Just making sure he wasn't followed. – Is he driving us all the way? He won't like that. – He has no choice; he's the only one available who knows the road. Think you could get us there? You'd lose us (*two words blurred*) woods. – I know that area. Used to visit the *Heuriger* (*two words unintelligible*) damned ulcer. – But you don't know the cottage, and Rupprecht (*several unintelligible words*).' Frank ended his quotes. 'Got that?'

'Woods,' Renwick said, 'and the *Heuriger* . . . Yes, they go together.' For Grant's benefit, he expanded it. 'In the Vienna woods the *Heuriger* are the taverns beside the vineyards.'

Where, thought Grant, a green pine-branch is hung over the *Heuriger* door to tell everyone the new wine is being served. He nodded, didn't say, 'I know.'

'Could be Grinzing or Sievering. Or Nussdorf. That's a lot of country.'

Frank's voice said, 'Well, how's this? My file on Bernard Mandel says he once owned a small tavern in the Vienna woods – near Grinzing. Still keeps it as a summer cottage. Is that how Rupprecht knows the road so well?'

'Could be. But Grinzing stretches far. Got the address?'

Grant caught Renwick's arms and pointed. A Fiat, four door, black in colour, W531-735, was passing at a leisurely pace. It didn't slow up, it didn't stop. It continued to the end of the street, turned the corner.

Renwick said, 'He'll be back. He's just scouting.'

'Who?' Frank sounded annoyed.

'Rupprecht. Careful bastard. He'll be difficult to tail. What's that damned address?'

235

'It's on the left of Neustrasse, far up the hill toward Höhenstrasse – no number, just a name: *Waldheim*.'

'Displayed?'

'Are you kidding? Take the third roadway into the woods once you pass a restaurant with a French name.'

'Left of Neustrasse, French name, third road into the woods, *Waldheim*. How far into the woods?'

'One hundred metres or less.'

'That's—' Renwick cut off his calculations. 'Here's Rupprecht again, just passing us. And this time he's stopping. Frank – get hold of Prescott Taylor. Tell him to contact Braun and Slevak for me: he knows where. We'll need support.'

'You'll get it. Look in the compartment under the seat. You may need that too.'

Grant's eyes were on the house before which the Fiat had halted. The men must have been ready to leave. The minute the car stopped, they were already through the door, with a woman supported between them. She was huddled into a shapeless grey cape, a scarf around her head. She could have been anyone: they had disguised her efficiently. They looked neither right not left. One of them had his arm around her shoulders, the other had a grip of her wrist as they hurried her down the steps to the pavement. Then two boys came running towards them. Avril drew her free hand out from the cape, pulled the scarf around her head. She stumbled with the effort it had cost her. But the boys, perhaps ten or eleven years old, only stopped for a few moments to stare at the girl, and ran on. If questioned, they might remember a girl with dark hair, who nearly fell, and two angry men.

'She tried,' Renwick said softly. 'And look at those people across the street – did they even notice?'

'The boys have stopped again,' Grant said. They had

236

turned to look back at the car. Avril had been half-pushed, half-lifted inside. The taller and heavier of the two men faced the boys, like a bull about to charge. His lips moved – swearing at them, no doubt – and they ran on. 'They'll remember him.'

'A mistake,' Renwick agreed. 'Never antagonize any eleven-year-old boy.' He was watching the Fiat. It was beginning to move. The Two Crowns had no one at its entrance. The house next door looked totally unoccupied once more.

Grant opened the glove compartment, and drew out the map. It had several sections, and he chose the one that dealt with Vienna and its surrounding countryside. Carefully he folded it to show the area around Grinzing. 'Remember that green button,' he told Renwick, who had slipped the gear into drive.

'And you duck out of sight, until we've passed the hotel.' Gently he eased the Porsche out into the street. But at the Two Crowns there was no face at the window, not one tremor of a curtain. The Porsche picked up speed, and they were safely out of Schotten Allee.

19

It was, as Renwick had predicted, a difficult job to keep track of the black Fiat. It had headed north as soon as it left the inner city, and followed the long stretch of busy thoroughfares, one threading into another, stitching old-time villages and country outskirts into the spread of Vienna. Early afternoon traffic was heavy, often blotting the Fiat momentarily from sight. Renwick wasn't chancing any close tail – Rupprecht had already proved himself to be a wary type who'd be keeping constant watch for everything that followed too persistently. One small consolation, thought Renwick: the amount of cars, buses, trucks on this route was an advantage as well as a drawback; he could conceal the Porsche very nicely from Rupprecht's watchful eye. It was a strain, though: he had to admit that, as the Fiat well ahead of him dropped again out of sight, stayed unseen for three nervous minutes, and then reappeared.

'At least,' Grant said, 'he's travelling in the right direction for Grinzing.'

'So far.'

'Have you doubts about the address Frank gave us?'

'No. His files are usually accurate, and he's been working on Bernard Mandel's case for months. If he says Mandel has a cottage in the country, then Mandel has a cottage in the country. But we don't know if Avril is being taken there. It's a good possibility, that's all. So – we'll keep following that Fiat. By guess and by God,' Renwick added as the Fiat disappeared from view.

'These damned buses,' he said, gritting his teeth. Another anxious minute, and the Fiat was again in sight.

Now they were driving through Heiligenstadt. Later, thought Renwick, if we get through this day, I'll remember to laugh. For the Fiat was passing the little house where Gyorgy Korda, defector, had been hidden for the last six weeks. Briefly, he had the impulse to tell Grant, brighten this part of the journey for him. Later, he told himself again – once Korda is on that plane for America. His own spirits lifted.

'I know this place,' Grant was saying. 'I came out here seven years ago to visit the house where Beethoven wrote the "Pastoral" Symphony. I found a small tavern. Had a garden at the side, though. Sort of eased the blow. Everything changes, I suppose. Nothing stays the same.'

Suddenly, he thought of Jennifer. Not even grief stayed the same. In these last few days, so much had filled his mind, so much had kept him moving, that no time had been left for bitter memories, or – let's face it, he told himself – for self-pity. Was that really what intense preoccupation with private sorrow could degenerate into? Grief for the past that overwhelmed the present, cut off the future? Perhaps that imbalance could only end as a perversion of honest emotion. There were some who began to mourn more for their own loss than for those who had been snatched away from them.

'These roads change too damn much, that's for sure,' said Renwick. They had been passing along a suburban street lined with gardens and trees that shielded wide-eaved houses from the traffic's noise and dust. No longer was there a flat broad thoroughfare with a steady stream of cars and buses, but roads that branched, or twisted, or climbed a gentle curve. The problem of tailing the Fiat had changed too; now it was an unexpected crossway, or the turn of the street around a cluster of heavy trees,

239

that made surveillance at a discreet distance almost impossible. 'We'll chance this one,' he decided as they reached a division of Grinzingerstrasse and took the right fork. The Fiat was out of sight, could have chosen either of the two roads.

Grant scanned the map. 'They both lead to Grinzing, anyway – keep apart until they meet west of the village. When they join up again, that's the start of Neustrasse. We're there, Bob!'

And a long way to go, Renwick thought, but he smiled and nodded. One mistake even now – for it was barely three thirty – and Rupprecht would alert Mittendorf. They were bound to be keeping in touch with each other. If so, that wily old buzzard wouldn't be found in his office at four o'clock. He might not make a dash for the frontier, not until something stronger than a suspicion of danger was verified, but he'd take himself to some safe address until the final report came through from Rupprecht. Even if the alert was cancelled, there would be no return to his office. For by that time he would have been warned by one of his trusted employees at Allied Electronics that the police had come visiting at four o'clock. Yes, a mistake even now, thought Renwick – and almost made one.

They had come through the quaint street of vintners' houses, squeezed past the parked cars around the old church on the village square, taken the cut towards Neustrasse. Suddenly, there – just ahead of them where the two roads through Grinzing came together again – was the Fiat. Renwick swung the Porsche behind a stationary bus, almost rear-ended it. He stopped less than two feet from its broad back.

'Good brakes,' said Grant. Good split-second reaction, too.

'God,' Renwick said, and drew a long breath, 'I was

about to pass the bus. We'd have run full tilt into them. What took them so long, anyway?'

'Must have been some hold-up on their route.' There were several cars closely following the Fiat out of that road, an angry bunching together which was the usual sign of a traffic delay. 'Rupprecht didn't see us, Bob. The bus blocked a clear view. Those cars behind him were what he was worrying about.'

Could be true, thought Renwick. He backed off slightly from the bus, but held his position behind it. 'You big beautiful monster,' he told it.

'You were cussing them out only half an hour ago,' Grant reminded him.

'I'm converted. I'll love them for ever and ever.'

'How long do we wait here?' Other cars were passing; one honked derisively at the timorous driver who wouldn't risk flanking a stationary bus. 'Rupprecht must be half-way up Neustrasse.'

'Suits me.' Renwick was still a little shaken. 'Just three more seconds, and he would have seen us. If he remembered the brown Porsche parked on the Schotten Allee—' He tightened his lips, glanced at his watch. Three thirty-three. Twenty-seven minutes to go.

Still thinking of that four o'clock deadline. 'Let's look at the good news,' Grant suggested. 'They have entered Neustrasse. Mandel's cottage could be their destination. Frank may have been right after all.'

'So you thought he could be wrong?' Renwick was amused.

'Didn't you?'

'Let's put it this way: he is often right, but when he's wrong – he can equal the worst of our mistakes.' Then Renwick looked at the blue button faintly glowing on the dashboard, and laughed. 'Still there, Frank?' No answer came. 'He's off rounding up some support. I hope.' Renwick reversed the car until it could sweep easily around the bus, and started up Neustrasse.

It was lined with more vintners' cottages, their window-boxes laden with bright petunias. Each had its walled courtyard, whose wide entrance doors stood partly open to show barrels and tables and more flowers. All of them had their own individual vineyards, long and narrow, stretching like a spread of stiff fingers up the sloping fields. Everything was precisely measured: mine and yours clearly marked off; no doubt about who owned what. As the neat houses thinned out and the vineyards were drawn further apart, Renwick could risk more speed. Grant exchanged the map for the binoculars. 'Just preparing for the bad news,' he told Renwick.

'Ah yes. There's always that. Let's have it.'

'Frank could have over-guessed – he's dead set on nailing Mandel. But what if the Fiat kept on going, never stopped at Mandel's place?' We wouldn't have a chance of tracing them if they continued on Neustrasse until it reached Höhenstrasse. Not far off, either. That long highway wandered around the crest of the adjacent hills, plunging deeper into the Viennese woods. How many hidden cottages and chalets could be scattered through there? Grant's lips tightened angrily. He tested the binoculars. 'Damn it, they won't be any use,' he said as he found that the trees, beginning to replace the fields and vineyards, were even now, sparse as they were, blocking any view of the road above.

You won't be any use either, thought Renwick, if you let bad news begin to look like disaster. He said, 'We'll have a quick look at the Höhenstrasse.' The Porsche went into high speed.

'Special souped-up job?' Grant's brief attack of astonishment gave way to approval. 'Trust Frank to have the best.'

Frank's voice broke in, faint but definitely pugnacious. 'You're damn right.'

'Where are you?' Renwick asked.

'Like you said, rounding up support. And next time, buddy boy, have a little more faith in me. You'll find the Fiat at Mandel's. Want to bet?'

'Next time,' Grant told him, 'I'll remember big uncle is listening.'

'Bob, have you a transceiver – once you leave the car?' Frank asked quickly.

'Yes. But if you're further off than five miles or so, I won't reach you.'

'Then one of you stays with the car and keeps in touch. See you!'

'Hey – one moment! When do we expect you?'

'Working on that problem right now. Five o'clock?' Frank settled any objections by switching off, temporarily at least.

Five o'clock . . . 'We're not waiting until then,' Grant said. 'Or are we?' he asked angrily.

Renwick didn't answer. 'There's that French name,' he said as they passed a restaurant whose outside terrace was smothered with flowers. 'Begin counting the side roads on our left. Duck before we pass the third. They know you by sight, don't they?'

Rupprecht certainly did. And he might be wary enough to have someone watching the entry to Mandel's place. 'There's the second road,' Grant said and slid low, head averted.

'Okay,' Renwick told him within a minute.

Grant sat up in time to see a fourth road, narrow and curving, like the other three, back into the woods. He had a glimpse of a small roof, a chalet set among beeches and pines some distance from the highway. 'Secluded area,' he observed. 'And all so peaceful and innocent. What size is Mandel's cottage – could you see it?'

'Not visible. He hasn't cut down any trees for a view of the valley below. He's blocked in, completely.'

'Did you notice anyone at all?'

'Couldn't see a thing except a green jungle. It's secluded, all right. Well – here we are.' They had climbed to the end of Neustrasse, and reached its junction with the roads along the heights. The woods had thickened, too.

Grant took one look, and shook his head. Useless, he thought, as he set the binoculars down. We'll have to depend on Frank's judgment. Our only other choice would have been to follow the Fiat so closely that we could have seen where it turned off. And be seen. 'Okay,' he said as if to reassure himself, 'we know what surrounds Mandel's place.'

'That was the idea.' Renwick had already reversed the car and was heading downhill. The powerful growl of the engine became a low and gentle purr.

So this had been just a reconnaissance trip, Grant thought. Or was he humouring me? Am I so damned difficult to handle? . . . Perhaps I've been too much on edge. Calm down, calm down . . . You don't have the answers to everything. At least Renwick has made sure that no one saw us loitering near the entrance to *Wald-heim*. Probably the few minutes spent on this manoeuvre weren't wasted after all. '*Waldheim*,' Grant repeated with a smile. 'Bernie's little home in the woods. Trust him to choose a name like that. But where do we leave the car? Down at the restaurant, climb back through the trees?'

Not bad, thought Renwick, not bad at all: he has got his brains together again. 'We'll try some place nearer, first. Like here.' He slowed down as they approached the side road that lay above Mandel's, made a quick turn into it, followed it for a short distance until he found a small clearing between the trees. He edged over the grass, halted the Porsche close to a thick curtain of leaves. He looked around him. The chalet was still out of sight; even its roof was now lost to view. And the highway behind them was hidden by a surge of bushes. Satisfied, he switched off the engine. 'Now we think up a good excuse if someone comes asking what we are doing among his beech trees.' Simultaneously they glanced at their watches. It was three fifty-five.

'Well?' asked Grant as they got out of the car.

Renwick gestured at a batch of fir trees. '*Waldheim* should be just south of there. I made a rough check of the distance between its side road and this one. It's no more than two hundred yards, if that. Then, according to Frank, it is about a hundred yards from Neustrasse itself. So that pin-points it. I'll scout around.'

'I'm coming with you.'

'Someone stays here for Frank's next message. That's you, Colin.' Renwick's glance took in Grant's well-cut grey suit, light blue shirt, dark blue tie, all carefully selected for this morning's appearance at Klar's Auction Rooms. 'You don't look much like a hiker lost in the woods.'

'We city folks get lost too.' Beyond that, Grant didn't argue. He had to admit that Renwick's old tweed jacket, open-necked shirt and scuffed shoes blended better with the country scene. He didn't like it, but he stayed by the car and watched Renwick disappear behind the cluster of trees. At another time he would have enjoyed the bland sunshine, the crisp air, the dappled shadows cast on the grass by the gentle stir of leaves overhead. There was the rustle of water from a small stream near by, a sense of protection from the surrounding hills. Today, the peace flowing around him only intensified his restlessness.

Renwick, however calm and contained, must have been just as worried as Grant. He hadn't taken the binoculars – in too much of a hurry. Nor had he examined Frank's special compartment under the driver's seat. Grant stepped back into the car and began searching. He found the compartment. Locked, of course. He tried the car key; it fitted. As he turned it carefully, a drawer slid out. It contained a loaded .22 automatic, two clips of extra ammunition, a silencer, a knuckle-duster, and – good God, thought Grant as he stared down at a hand-grenade.

Gingerly, he closed the drawer. Next, he examined the glove-compartment more thoroughly to see what other surprises it might contain. They were harmless enough: a small first-aid kit, a thick slab of chocolate, a compass, a flask containing brandy, another road-map – not just for the Vienna area this time, but for Austria and its surrounding frontiers. Frank, the well-prepared traveller . . . Where the devil was he now? or Bob Renwick?

Five minutes passed. Three more. Grant's frustration deepened. And then Frank's excited voice boomed into the car. Grant lowered the volume of sound, said, 'Repeat that!'

'All sewed up at this end. Four less to worry about. Taken quietly. One in his office, three in the warehouse.'

'What about the American?'

'No sign of him or his bow-tie.'

So Gene Marck was still free. 'Could an alarm have been sent out?'

'Don't think they had time. Everything was quick, efficient.'

'There could still have been someone around to warn him. What happens to Sweetheart, then?'

Frank didn't answer that. 'Are you alone there?'

'Yes. Our friend went ahead.'

'Damn fool. We'll be at the place by five fifteen. Sorry

246

– that's the best time we can make. We'll approach from the south. What's your position?'

'To the north – on a side road above the one you described.'

'Tell your friend his two boys will join you – where you're parked.'

'Tell them I'm leaving,' Grant said. 'Right now.'

'Secure everything.'

'I'll take most of it with me.'

Frank laughed. 'Okay, buddy boy. You're a fast learner.'

Silence came back to the car. Grant switched off the blue button. Quickly he pulled open the drawer and began packing Frank's little arsenal. To make it easier, he stepped out of the car. The small automatic he slipped into his belt after checking the safety-catch; the extra ammunition went into one jacket pocket, the other bulged with the grenade; knuckle-duster and silencer were stowed in trouser pockets. He lifted the binoculars – these would have to be carried in his hand – and began locking the doors. All secure, he thought, and tucked the car keys safely into his breast pocket. Behind him, a thin high voice said, 'Hands up! Or you're dead.'

Grant turned slowly. A small boy, wooden gun pointed, stared at him intently. Grant raised his hands and said, with equal seriousness, 'You've got me, partner.'

The boy began to smile. He lowered the gun. 'You talk funny,' he said.

'Not as funny as I look,' Grant told him, and dropped his hands. The boy – if sizes were the same here as in America – could be ten years old.

'What have you got in your pockets?'

'The crown jewels.'

'Where are you going?'

Grant held out the binoculars. 'Bird-watching.'

247

Another boy, older, perhaps twelve or thirteen, came out from behind a tree. A third, no more than nine, followed. Brothers obviously, with the same blue eyes and the same fair hair cut short, all three wearing grey lederhosen and checked shirts made from the same cloth. They stood there, thinking up their next questions. Grant jumped in ahead of them with some of his own. 'Is that your house?' He pointed in the direction of the chalet. It seemed a safe beginning to the answers he needed. Boys roaming these woods kept their eyes open.

'No,' said the oldest boy. 'We live down there.' He pointed vaguely to the south.

'Oh, at *Waldheim*?'

There was a chorus of 'No,' and a laugh.

'Who lives there?'

They looked at each other. The oldest boy said, 'Old Gruber and his dog. They live there.'

'Don't you like old Gruber?'

'Oh, he's all right. He doesn't shoot us with his rifle, or set the dog on us. Just gets angry and shouts.'

'And chases us,' the smallest boy piped up. Again there was the shared laugh, covering their own secrets. He stared at the car. 'What is that?'

'A Porsche, silly,' his oldest brother said. He scrutinized it critically. 'Doesn't look much.' He walked over to the window, tried to see the dashboard. 'How many kilometres?'

'Thousands and thousands – it's old,' Grant said. 'Next time I'm going to get a Fiat, a nice new Fiat. Black.'

'Like the one we saw?' the youngest boy asked.

'Where did you see it? At *Waldheim*?' Grant kept his voice easy. 'When old Gruber chased you?' he added with a smile.

'It wasn't at *Waldheim*,' the oldest boy corrected Grant. 'It was over at the little house.'

248

'*Not* a house,' said the boy with the wooden pistol, taking aim at a tree. 'A barn.'

'It's a house!'

'It isn't!'

'People live in a house. Not a barn, stupid!'

Grant decided on one last probe. 'And it belongs to *Waldheim*? Is it near the big house?'

The boy nodded. Questions bored him unless he did the asking. 'Fritz!' he called to his younger brother who was heading for the woods further north, his gun banging away at some invisible quarry.

'How near?' Grant persisted.

'On the hill behind it. In the trees.' The blue eyes were studying him closely. 'Why do you ask? What are you doing here?'

'Looking for a house to rent for August.'

The answer was acceptable. Curiosity died. The boy's attention switched to the hunter, who was now out of sight. 'Fritz!' he yelled. 'Wait!' He grabbed his youngest brother by the hand and followed at a fast run. Soon they had vanished from sight.

One long deep breath of relief, and Grant was heading in the opposite direction. He paused to look back as he reached the clump of firs that Renwick had selected as his starting-point. The brown Porsche, its colour blending with the tree trunks, its body sheltered by the spread of boughs, was unobtrusive. Nothing stirred. The voices had faded into silence. Reassured, he stepped into the trees.

20

The small group of fir trees led Grant into the wood itself. Branches were thick, heavily leaved. There was no regular trail, only a natural path where maples and beeches receded enough to give space to move. Renwick must have followed this, he decided, and started down the gentle slope. Underfoot the earth was soft and moist, giving little grip for smooth-soled shoes. Twice Grant skidded. His pace eased, but not his anxiety. He pulled off his tie, jammed it into a pocket, opened his shirt, let his skin breathe. Too damned eager, he told himself: Renwick may have taken another trail back to the car – he could be reaching it right now. He halted, wondering if he should return to wait by the Porsche. And lose more time? Or be accosted by someone from the chalet, who'd be more curious than the boys? Just at that moment of mounting worry, he saw Renwick walking slowly uphill towards him. 'What kept you, damn it?'

Renwick's face was taut, his words clipped. 'It's no go.'

Grant stared at him blankly.

'No Fiat. Only a jeep parked at the side of the house. One man sitting at a table under a tree, reading a newspaper. A dog, sleeping at his feet. That's *Waldheim*,' Renwick ended in disgust.

'He was in front of the house? How about the back?'

'All windows shuttered tight, except for two – his room and the kitchen, probably. No one is there. Nothing stirring. Not a sound.'

'What lies *behind* the house?'

'A meadow.'

'No hill?'

'Beyond the meadow, yes. A small hill. Mostly wooded.'

'Come on, come on.' Grant urged. 'We'll talk as we go. Plenty to tell you. Frank came through at four fifteen. Here, help me unload some of this arsenal. Take these.' He handed over the automatic and its extra clips; the silencer, too. 'I'll keep the knuckle-duster. And this.' Briefly, he showed the grenade.

That shook Renwick out of his mood. 'Where the—'

'You were sitting on it.' Grant was already starting down the slope.

'Okay, okay,' said Renwick as he caught up with Grant, 'I'll let you see for yourself.' The sooner this was over, the better. 'This way.' He changed their direction. 'We head to the west, or else we'll strike the *Waldheim* road – it's down there, south of us. There's no one guarding it. I checked. Crossed over, in fact, to get to the wood on its other side and see the house from that angle. Better lower our voices. We'll be there in three minutes.' Their voices had been low enough. Now Renwick's approached a murmur. 'You had plenty to tell me?'

'About that hill beyond the meadow. How far is it from *Waldheim* itself?'

'Not too far. Scarcely a hundred yards.'

'Any road across the meadow?'

'The road stops at the house.'

'No sign of a trail? Or tracks of car wheels on grass?'

'What are you getting at?'

'There's a small house, or barn, somewhere on that hill. The Fiat is there.'

Renwick's quick stride came to an abrupt halt. 'Did Frank tell—'

'No. I have my own sources.' Grant's smile was brief. 'Now let's keep moving.' He set an even faster pace.

'What sources?' Renwick was not amused.

'Three kids, car-struck. I got them off the subject of the Porsche on to a nice new black Fiat.'

'The three that were wandering through the woods? I heard them, didn't know what to expect, jumped for cover.' Renwick pointed to his right trouser-leg smeared with drying mud. 'A bad moment, actually. We were just above *Waldheim*, and the man down there heard them. I thought he was about to rise, come searching. Then the kid with the gun yelled. "Bang! I got you!" and they ran off.'

'So that's the game they play. No peace for old Gruber.'

'Gruber? Your sources are excellent. Or imaginative?'

'Their argument was real enough. The mighty hunter called this place in the woods a barn. Older brother said it was a house – because people were there.'

People were there . . . 'The kids *did* see the Fiat?'

'They saw it. How do we get this news to Frank? He's aiming for *Waldheim* at five fifteen, approaching from the south. Your two men will reach the Porsche just about that time too, but what good is that to us?'

Renwick tapped the transceiver he carried in his breast pocket. 'No problem with them.' With Frank? That could be more difficult. 'What about Mittendorf?'

'Arrested on schedule. So were the two Klars, and Sigmund. Neat job, expert. No fuss.'

'No alarm sent out?' Renwick asked sharply.

'Frank didn't think so. There wasn't time, he said. And yet—' Grant hesitated.

'Yes,' Renwick agreed, 'there could be some joker in Mittendorf's office—' He didn't finish. 'What about Gene Marck?'

'He hasn't been found so far.' Grant almost smiled as

252

he added, 'Perhaps he'll show up at the Majestic tonight.'

'Why should he do that?'

'He wants to get in touch with me. He arranged it – even set the time to suit me. Around midnight.'

At first, Renwick had been amused; then thoughtful. But he made no comment, cut off any further remark from Grant by placing a warning hand on his arm. They slowed their footsteps, came to a halt. Renwick drew Grant to the side of a large tree and knelt, gesturing to him to keep low as he pointed down the steep bank in front of them to a patch of partially-cleared ground. Grant had a clear view of a large wooden house in Austrian country style. Broad eaves, two rows of balconies that stretched the full length of the walls, carved shutters that were tightly closed over a multitude of small windows. *Waldheim* . . . Grant took a more detailed look with the binoculars. The place was deserted, except for the man sitting under one of the remaining trees with a large German shepherd dog at his feet.

Suddenly the dog was alert. Uneasy. It rose, faced the wood, seemed to look directly at Grant. He saw its hackles rise, heard the distant growl. Old Gruber (old? – he was middle-aged, heavily built) spoke to it sharply. On command, the dog sat. Another command, and it lay down, its ears still pointing, its eyes on the trees above. Gruber's lips moved. (Those damned boys again – was that what he was saying under his breath?) For a long moment, he glared up at the wood. Then he picked up his newspaper and began reading.

Carefully, Grant and Renwick got to their feet, slowly backed away to move swiftly along the top of the bank, keeping a safe screen of trees between them and the house. Again Renwick pointed. Down there, Grant saw, was the meadow – a green carpet sprinkled with wild flowers, stretched between *Waldheim* and a wooded hill.

Not really a hill, more like a gentle slope that began flush with the meadow, and rose very gradually for the first hundred yards or so. Only then did it begin to push up, swell into a rounded crest. But the important thing was that its lower stretch of trees curved round to meet the wood in which Renwick and he now stood. He raised Frank's excellent binoculars.

The difference was astonishing. To the naked eye the meadow had seemed virgin pure. With the field-glasses picking out texture and shades of colour, there showed faint but definite tracks where the fine short grass had been pressed down. Pressed down in one direction: parallel lines, a car's width apart. They began where the *Waldheim* road ended, crossed the meadow obliquely, and disappeared into the trees that edged this side of the wooded slope. The near side to us, thought Grant. His excitement grew as his eyes found the gap between the trees, wide enough to let a car pass through them. And the small house, or barn? Surely it must be in that clearing almost at the edge of the wood, just beyond the car's entrance. 'Damn this elevation,' he said softly: it wasn't good, the bank on which he stood was only eight feet high at this point, impossible to look down into the clearing. As his eyes searched desperately, he thought he saw the corner of an eave, a sharp jut of something more solid than the leaves that screened it.

'Yes; that could be it.' He passed the binoculars to Renwick.

Renwick adjusted them. He began with the meadow, traced the parallel lines to the edge of the trees. There he paused, looked intently. He nodded. 'A house. Definitely. Well hidden.' The car must be there too: only one set of tracks over the meadow, and recent tracks at that – the flowers in the path of the tyres were crushed but still fresh, unwilted. He lowered the field-glasses, handed them back to Grant. He glanced at his watch, lips tight, eyes worried. Do we wait, or do we move in?

'Shouldn't be too difficult to reach,' Grant was saying. 'Come on, Bob, let's have a closer look.'

'Frank won't be here for another twenty-three minutes.'

'And headed for the wrong house. No way of warning him?'

'If he hears Rupprecht get off a shot or two, he'll catch on. So will Gruber.' The element of surprise would be lost, and that was what Frank had been aiming for.

Another problem: Frank and his men would park their car and come in through those woods south of *Waldheim*. They'd be on foot. Like us, Renwick thought. And where will we be if an alarm is given and the Fiat starts racing for the highway?

'Will he catch on in time?' asked Grant. 'All it will take is one warning shot from Gruber, and Rupprecht—'

'I know, I know!' They wouldn't leave Avril behind, either. She had too much valuable information to give. Had they started questioning her? Or was she still half drugged? 'We can't wait for Frank. Let's move.'

Their path through the trees began to descend. They approached the wooded slope. Voice very low, Renwick said, 'We'll have to scout around the house before we can plan an assault.'

Grant nodded. Plan? We are crazy, he thought, but his hopes were rising.

'We know they have three men. There could be more,' Renwick warned. 'They'll be armed.' And with something heavier than a .22 automatic.

'First we'll concentrate on that Fiat.'

Renwick repressed a laugh, shook his head. 'Colin, I think you're in the wrong profession.' They began dodging from tree to tree, keeping total silence.

* * *

255

It wasn't much of a place. The boys had both been right: half-farmhouse, half-barn. Old and decrepit. It was two-storied, with its three small upper-floor windows all closed. Their shutters, in bad repair, hung drunkenly on their hinges. Downstairs, the shutters were less neglected; they had been swung open. So were the windows, there. The house, even if it stood within a large clearing, was cosied by the heavy woods on the hillside. The air was still: not even the breath of a small breeze stirred the leaves.

Grant exchanged glances with Renwick. They nodded, and began to move around the trees that encircled the cleared ground. No one was on guard, at least on this side of the house. Careless, thought Grant. Or too confident that they couldn't be traced to this hideaway? For a few moments he gave grudging credit to that wily bird, Bernie Mandel: the main house was not to be used – had that been his stipulation to Mittendorf? If anything went wrong and *Waldheim* was searched, neither police nor State Security would find one shred of evidence that it had been occupied – not even a cigarette-stub, or a bed disarranged, or food in the kitchen except for Gruber's own small supply. Should the house in the woods be discovered, good old Bernie would play the injured innocent: some intruders must have invaded his property, arrived when the caretaker was out buying his newspaper and groceries, you just couldn't trust anyone these days. An excuse for everything, and explanations galore – that was Mandel. No wonder Frank was so intent on nailing him.

They reached the trees at the back of the house. The door there was boarded over, but the shutters were open; so were two windows. In the breathless air, sound carried clearly. Voices . . . Renwick and Grant halted, stood motionless behind a spread of low branches. Two men's voices: one pitched high and complaining; the other harsh and domineering. The complainer sounded familiar. Even his phrases seemed to be an echo of that earlier conversation which Frank's men had taped on the Schotten Allee: how long had they to wait, when would the others arrive? That, thought Grant, is the one with ulcers. The other? No, not the big fellow . . . His memory flashed back to the Two Crowns, a man mounting a staircase, a harsh voice raised in contempt for the nervous woman at the reception desk.

Renwick's expression showed he had identified the complainer, but he shook his head when the second voice cut the other down with 'Acht, shut up! You've been yapping for ten minutes by my watch. Our replacements *will* be coming. Jacques is arranging it. Do you question *him*?'

Grant moved closer to Renwick. 'Rupprecht,' he whispered.

Renwick nodded, kept listening, but the compulsive talker had been silenced. Where's the third man? he wondered. He raised two fingers, and shrugged a silent query as he held up one finger alone. Grant got the message. He pointed to the second floor above them. Except, he was thinking, it had no windows in the rear, and only three at the front, all of them closed. If the big man was up there, guarding Avril, he would be finding it suffocatingly hot. They might see him out here, any moment, taking a quick breather.

Renwick had just the same idea. He pulled out the automatic and silencer, fitted them quickly together. Frank's pop-pistol: only good for close range, but almost soundless. Then he beckoned towards the other side of the house where the barn stood, and they edged carefully through the trees. Grant fitted the brass knuckle-duster over his right hand, tried to force the binoculars into the empty pocket, found them too big, and held

257

them out to Renwick. Renwick half smiled, dropped them under the nearest maple.

There was no one at the side of the barn, but Renwick's caution continued. It was doubly necessary: the cool damp woods encircling the clearing had retreated far back at this point, leaving a wide naked space that was frankly disconcerting. From here, however, they could see the rough trail sweeping up towards them from the meadow. We'll have to get across this open ground, Grant thought, to reach the corner of the barn.

Once we're round it, we should find its entrance. And the Fiat? It must be there. It was nowhere else in sight.

Grant eyed the distance in front of him. So did Renwick. They nodded. Lightly, they sprinted over that open space, soft grass deadening their footsteps. They reached the front corner of the barn, began to edge round it. Suddenly, they were face to face with the third man.

For a breathless second, they stood staring at him. He was equally frozen. Then, as he reached for his gun, Grant drove his right fist into the heavy jaw. The man's head jerked back. As he staggered, his eyes wide with astonishment, Renwick crashed the automatic down on the back of his head. His legs buckled, his eyes closed as he fell and lay motionless. Renwick picked up the man's revolver. 'Out for the duration,' he said as he stepped over the inert body, and headed for the barn's entrance. It was open, perhaps for a speedy exit if necessary. The Fiat was there.

'All yours,' murmured Renwick and moved quietly towards the front door of the house. Grant slipped off the knuckle-duster, exchanged it for the grenade. Do I remember, and will it work? I can only try, he thought, made sure that Renwick had reached the side of the house door, pulled the pin and released the spoon. He began to count, gave up. He tossed the grenade lightly in front of the car's radiator, watched it begin to roll underneath. Then he ran.

The explosion was shattering. Bigger than I remember, thought Grant. Distantly, he heard a rifle-shot, the bark of a dog – a far-away background to the leap of flames snatching at the barn roof.

Pressed close to the house wall, Renwick nodded his welcome to Grant. 'That should fetch them.'

As he spoke, two men burst out of the doorway obviously unsure of what had happened. Rupprecht, revolver in hand, was cursing wildly; the other, silent for once, was struggling to pull out his gun. Renwick shot them both: Rupprecht in the knee and shoulder; the other in the right shoulder alone. Grant, shoving them aside, was into the house.

He raged through three small rooms. No one there. Up the narrow wooden stairs, treads shaking as he ran, and into a small corridor. Two rooms. The first one, wide open; the second with its door closed. He crashed against it splintering the lock. Inside an airless room, lying on a bare mattress with hands and feet tied, was Avril.

There was no time to free her. The fire was spreading from the barn; the sound of furious crackling intensified. He snatched the grey cape from the floor, wrapped it around her, and carried her into the corridor. A mass of smoke at the far end was pierced by a yellow-red tongue of fire. Grant's frantic pace increased as he started down the stairs. Half-way, he heard a surge of searching flame roar along the corridor above him. By the time he reached ground level, the entire upper floor was ablaze.

Grant carried Avril through the trees to the edge of the meadow, laid her down on the grass. Renwick was beside him, helping him unknot the ropes that bound her. Her eyes were wide open, staring up at the sky.

She said, 'Now I don't have to pretend . . .' Her voice died away, and she sighed. 'Pretend that I am still drugged.' She laughed weakly, and as the ropes were untied she tried to sit up.

'Lie still!' Renwick told her. 'Keep her covered with that cape, Colin. She'll get chilled in this air.' He took out his transceiver and made contact with his two agents, who had been waiting beside the Porsche for the last ten minutes. 'Yes, yes,' he said impatiently. 'Hadn't time to switch on. Sorry about that. We were pretty busy. We need you right now. Fast! Take the side road below where you are parked. Keep on going beyond the house. Move!' He stuck the transceiver into his pocket, watching Grant rub the circulation back into Avril's wrists and ankles, and picked up the two pieces of rope. From across the meadow came the roar of a car leaving *Waldheim*.

Grant jerked round to see Gruber's jeep being driven rapidly towards them.

'Frank. And Walter,' Renwick identified its two occupants. 'Colin, can I borrow your tie? I have three men to hand-truss, and—' He held up two pieces of rope.

Grant drew the tie out of his pocket – his favourite, at that – and passed it over. Renwick began running towards the flaming house. As yet, the trees, green and moist, were resisting the intense heat. No wind, thank God, not even a touch of breeze. The pillar of fire reaching for the sky, hadn't spread: the luckiest thing that has happened to us this day, thought Renwick. Except Avril's rescue, he added.

'How's that?' Grant was asking Avril. 'Too rough?'

She shook her head. Her wrists had lost their numbness. 'They begin to feel part of me again.' Indeed they did: the cigarette burn began to sear her right hand once more. She tried to smile and stop her sudden tears. 'Oh, Colin—'

'It's all right,' he said gently.

'I was so scared, so horribly—'

'I know.' He smoothed the damp hair away from her brow, touched her cheek.

She closed her eyes. The tight cramp that twisted her leg muscles began to ease its grip. I'm safe, she kept thinking. I'm safe. And they learned nothing, they hadn't time to learn what we knew about Jacques and a Geneva bank account. 'Another hour, perhaps less,' she was saying. 'If you hadn't come—'

'But we did.'

'I just couldn't lie there for ever, pretending—'

'It's over, Avril, all over.'

'Yes,' she said softly. 'It's over.' Even the spasms of sickness she had fought back, as she lay seemingly unconscious on that mattress, had gone. 'I'm thirsty,' she said.

'Soon,' Grant said. 'As soon as Frank is here, we'll find some water.' These woods trickled with streams: the mud on his wet shoes testified to that. He sat down close beside her and faced the meadow as the jeep braked violently in front of him.

Frank was in a raging temper. 'Well,' he said, 'a nice fire you set. We'll have all the neighbourhood here in another five minutes.'

Grant, who had thought until now that he hadn't done such a bad job with the Fiat, stared back. 'You'll find Renwick tying up the three men.'

'You have them?' Frank's anger lessened visibly.

'Two wounded, one unconscious. How do we get them out?'

'I've sent for my camper.' Frank pointed back to *Waldheim*, around which a minibus had just skirted to head across the meadow. Behind it, a car zoomed in from the road in fast pursuit. 'Renwick's men,' Frank reassured Grant. 'We'll all get out – fast.'

261

'The faster, the better. Rupprecht was expecting replacements.'

'A tougher bunch, too,' Frank predicted. 'You were lucky.' His last shred of annoyance was dissipating rapidly. 'Rupprecht – Mandel's pet. Now that's something.' He looked down at Avril, who was trying again to sit up, and managed it this time with Grant's arm around her waist. 'How much did they find out?'

'They hadn't started to question—'

'Good.' Frank's smile was suddenly warm. 'Don't worry, Sweetheart. We'll treat Rupprecht and his men better than they treated you. But *we'll* question, and *we'll* get answers.'

The camper arrived, and two young men piled out. One Grant recognized: Joe from the garage; the other was a stranger. He raised Avril to her feet, drew the cape around the thin dress that clung to her just as the damp curls were pressed against her brow. 'Keep warm,' he told her. 'Can you walk?' He slipped an arm around her waist, and steadied her.

Frank said, 'You go with Renwick. That's his car pulling up. This—' he jerked a thumb at the camper, whose back was covered with travel-stickers – 'is the paddy wagon.'

Joe reported, 'We left the caretaker and his dog out in the woods.'

'Okay, okay. Now give Renwick a hand. Start carrying three men to the camper.' Frank noticed Avril's tense face. 'The caretaker shot first – too bad for him that he missed. A pity about the dog, but it was trained to attack. There's only one way to make sure it doesn't.' Then Frank's voice sharpened. 'Or would you prefer one of us dead and the other two savaged?' He signed to Renwick's two men to follow Joe and his friend.

Avril's eyes widened.

Grant said quickly, 'Without Frank we'd have been

nowhere.' He remembered the car keys and tossed them over. 'Not a scratch on your Porsche – good as new. Almost,' he added with a grin. 'And thanks. I—'

'One hell of a fine job, Grant,' Frank said as he turned to leave. 'You owe me for one grenade,' he called over his shoulder, and broke into a run.

21

The dispersal was efficient, and so rapid that it seemed to Grant he had barely got Avril settled in Renwick's car when the cortège of men, carrying and lifting other men, came out of the woods. The camper was already backed to the edge of trees. In a matter of seconds Rupprecht – jacket roughly tied round his wounded knee to prevent a trail of blood – was heaved inside. His two friends followed him; the big man was still groggy and stumbling but that didn't prevent his fast removal; the other's complaints had dribbled into an occasional moan of protest.

The camper left, with Joe at the wheel and Frank beside him, its chintz curtains swinging over tightly-closed windows. Inside, Frank's third agent kept guard with a shotgun. Walter was in charge of the jeep, and he too didn't waste one moment. He was already streaking across the meadow, by-passing *Waldheim* and heading for the line of trees on its south boundary.

'Let's go, let's go!' Renwick was yelling, pushing Grant into the back seat where Avril rested against one corner. 'Braun, you drive. Slevak – get in, get in!' The car started forward as Renwick's door was banging shut. He glanced back at the wood. Flames were no longer leaping high, only a spiralling cloud of smoke was visible. Thank God, he thought, this isn't California with its drought; these trees would have gone up like tinder. A patch of grass had caught fire, but Joe had yelled a warning in time and they beat it out. The little house had fallen in on itself, burned within the lower floor's solid foundation of stone walls. 'Even remembered to pick up Frank's binoculars,' he said, and laughed softly as he recalled the frantic movements, the terse commands, the incredible haste. In retrospect, it was exhilarating. He pulled on his jacket, tried to brush away the streaks of dust and smoke. 'How's Avril?' He leaned across Grant to touch her gently.

'I'll live,' she told him and tried to smile. She felt miserable. Nerves mostly, she thought, and this feeling of nausea which the drugs had caused, and the throbbing ache at her wrist which now seemed to be increasing.

'That's the girl.' Renwick pressed her hand, noticed its sudden flinch. His eyebrows rose.

'A cigarette burn,' Grant explained grimly. 'The big fellow was testing to see if she was feigning.' If I had known, I'd have broken his jaw when I landed that punch. 'Hey – I forgot to give Frank his knuckle-duster. And where's he going?' Like the jeep, the camper was bouncing at high speed across the grass to the side of *Waldheim*. Braun on the other hand, as soon as he had skirted the house, had taken the road to the highway. At the rate he is driving, thought Grant, we'll reach Neustrasse in five seconds. 'Leaving Frank behind?' It didn't make sense.

'He'll catch up. He's picking up Walter once he dumps the jeep beside Gruber and his dog. They are over there, behind the—' Renwick was silenced by a wild jolt as Braun applied the brakes to make a screeching left turn into Neustrasse and start up its hill. Grant caught Avril around her shoulders, held her firmly as he looked back for a last glimpse of *Waldheim* territory. In that split second, he saw Walter sprint out from a clump of bushes under a steep bank – no sign now of the jeep – to leap on to the camper as it swerved round to head for the road. From the lower reaches of Neustrasse came the distant blare of a horn. The volunteer fire department had begun its climb up the twisting highway. Grant said, 'Frank's cutting it pretty fine.'

'He'll make it. He thrives on emergencies.' Renwick sounded more confident than he felt. Like Grant, he was keeping his head turned to watch the highway behind them. 'There he is!' The camper was safely out, swerving precariously in its haste to follow Renwick's route. 'Ease up,' Renwick told Braun. They stopped just above the side road where Renwick and Grant had parked Frank's Porsche, watched the camper slow down to let Walter jump off. In another minute, the Porsche would be driven safely out to follow the camper uphill. Renwick gave a deep sigh of relief, then saying, 'Drive on!' slumped back into his corner.

'Just what was Frank staging back there?' Grant asked, still thinking of the jeep that had been abandoned.

'An accident seemingly. Gruber with neck broken after a heavy slip down a high bank, one shot fired as he fell, dog hit.'

'Who will believe that?'

'What else is there to believe? Gruber did drive out to that bank to see what was disturbing the dog. Okay, I agree. Not much of a scenario, but what d'you expect in the few minutes Frank had?'

Grant said nothing more. No doubt, Walter had used a silencer when he shot a dead dog to add a final touch to the 'explanation' of the accident. How had the dog been killed? A knife, a dart, hands at his neck? Suddenly, Grant felt sick; he could throw a grenade under a car to stop kidnappers from making an escape, but arranging a scenario – he concentrated on listening to the crescendo of klaxon, swelling into a hideous roar that seemed as if it were coming right up this hill, almost upon them, ready to devour everything before it. The blare dropped to a wail. The engine must have slowed for its turn into Mandel's property. He could hear cars behind it, too, horns wild with mounting excitement. Abruptly, all noise ceased. *Waldheim* must have come into their view, and there was nothing to see. Nothing but a placid house, empty and innocent. Nothing but a column of smoke hanging low in the still air over the trees behind a small meadow.

Grant glanced at his watch. 'Five thirty-two,' he said softly. And that, he told himself, is the last time I'm going to check on the passing minutes. I've had enough of it today to last me for ever. God, I'm exhausted . . . They were reaching Höhenstrasse, the road that climbed and twisted along the heights in this section of the Vienna woods. Here, there was a choice of routes; they took the right fork; behind them, followed closely by the Porsche, Frank's camper turned left. One short subdued bleep on its horn bade them goodbye and good luck.

The Höhenstrasse wove its way along the roll of wooded hills. Densely packed trees, thin trunks elbowing each other for growing space, would empty out, here and there, to show a down-stretching view towards the grey curves of the Danube. Below the road lay patches of deep green forests, sloping fields golden in the evening light, far-off clusters of red-roofed houses, and then – to the east, visible on its flat plain – Vienna. 'Take the first cut-off to the west,' Renwick instructed Braun, breaking his long silence. To Slevak, who had a map out and ready, 'We are aiming for Purkersdorf – two kilometres this side of the town. You'll see a sign: Rasthaus Winkelman.'

Braun nodded, squared his shoulders, tightened his grip on the wheel, and increased speed. A stolid capable type, thought Grant, not given to comment or suggestions. Slevak was even more impassive and imperturbable. Yet, Grant remembered, both had moved with unexpected speed and efficiency back on the meadow, even if they had come in totally unprepared for what they had found there. One moment of surprise from Braun, quickly mastered, and the two of them had piled in to help: not men to be underestimated, he reminded himself.

'Just ten minutes more,' Renwick was encouraging Avril. Her white face, dark eyes larger than ever, were as worrying to him as her complete silence. 'We'll get you to that rest-house where we can wash and brush up and get something to eat.' And, he thought, have that wrist attended to. What then? He added, 'We'll have to get you both as far away from Vienna as possible.'

Grant's head jerked round to face Renwick.

'Yes. You, too, Colin. Especially you. You've been a witness to just about everything.' The Bienvenue cheque, the Ruysdael substitution, the information about Gene Marck as an Intelligence agent in that last phone call from Lois Westerbrook . . . 'Just about everything,' he repeated. He didn't have to explain the details. Grant had got his message. So had Avril.

I might have known it, Grant realized; the danger isn't over, as I told Avril. Not for me at least. Once Gene Marck learns that the real Ruysdael is already in Basset's possession and out of Austria – he will learn, all right: too many people now know about Basset's quick visit to Vienna and they will talk, discreetly of course, but the talk will start leaking around, it always does – I'll be moved to the top of his priorities list. This morning, I suppose, he still thought I was fairly negligible – perhaps just the unsuspecting and blundering amateur he had hoped I'd be, someone (even if a bad choice on his part) to be tolerated until that Bienvenue cheque was signed and on its way to Geneva. But when I don't appear at the Majestic tonight – and why the hell did he arrange that time and place? Was it to be a last questioning and my last chance? Hadn't he already decided that I was expendable? Anyway, whatever the reason, I am now a prime target. No quarter for me from now on. 'Okay,' said Grant grimly, his face tense, 'I'll remember that.' He controlled his emotions, mustered a reassuring smile for Avril whose eyes – so large and dark and luminous – had opened in sudden fear for him.

'You'd better remember it,' Renwick advised him. Then lightening his voice, trying to make everything more normal, 'Once we've had an hour at the rest-house – it's safe, I know the people who run it – I'll have Braun drive Avril and you to a hotel just outside of Kitzbühl.' He tried not to think of all the urgent business he had dropped when the word had reached him about Avril's disappearance. 'Sorry I can't go with—'

Avril exclaimed, 'Hotel? Oh no!'

'It's safe. The owner's a friend. He'll take good care—'

'I haven't a passport or anything.' Not even a comb or a handkerchief, she thought, her misery deepening.

'It's safe.' Renwick was obdurate. 'And far enough from Vienna.'

Grant said, 'Too far for either of us tonight. Avril is—'

'I know, I know.' Renwick's impatience was growing.

'That would be at least a five-hour journey,' Grant persisted. He eased his voice: we're all exhausted, he thought, and too sharp-set. 'What about this rest-house? Isn't it safe enough for an overnight stay? We leave in the early morning and—'

'It's a short visit place. Not a hotel. You can get a shower, a cubicle with a cot, your clothes cleaned and pressed, something to eat. Good for brief stops and a quick rest.' His mouth tightened as he added, 'It's too near Vienna.' Even if Grant didn't realize what a dragnet Gene Marck and his willing helpers could throw around the city, Avril certainly did. There were more foreign agents and their hired spies packed into Vienna than even Geneva could claim nowadays: the price of neutrality, Renwick thought bitterly. He glanced at Avril to get her backing, but her face was unnaturally pale, her body drooping. Grant was right, he had to concede, and offered a compromise. 'There is another inn. Not quite as comfortable, but it isn't so far – just this side of Traunsee.'

Grant only shook his head. 'We would be bound to attract attention. Look at us, Bob! A couple of refugees from a disaster area. I haven't my passport either. We are foreigners, can't sign into a hotel without—'

'Where the hell's your passport?'

'In my suitcase with my American Express cheques.'

'That was a damned silly place—'

'And I was damned glad I wasn't trundling them around when I was clambering through these woods. Seems to me I was loaded down enough with Fra—'

'Sure, sure,' Renwick cut in quickly, made an effort to hold his temper in place. Temper? It was worry, deep and sharp, that was twisting his guts. 'This hotel at Traunsee is safe—'

'That's three hours from here. Still too far.'

'Well, have you a better idea?' demanded Renwick. Goddammit, he thought, this isn't my territory. How the hell do they think I can trot out a list of safe houses to let them pick and choose?

'Yes. If I can get to a telephone as soon as we reach the rest-house, I'll call—' Grant noticed the slight tilt of Braun's head. Listening? And watching me in the rear-view mirror, too. Grant's expression didn't change; his voice stayed neutral as he said, 'Oh, let's argue about this over dinner, Bob. I'm so damn tired and hungry that I can't think straight. Have we much further to go?'

'Almost there.' Renwick leaned forward, gave Slevak

270

and Braun some last directions. After that, he relaxed again and said to Grant, 'We can't spend too much time on discussion.'

'We won't.' Covertly, Grant kept a careful eye on Braun.

'I've got to leave for Vienna by seven at the latest.'

Grant nodded. Perhaps, he was thinking, Braun is just naturally inquisitive. The man might seem to be absorbed by the traffic which was now thickening on this highway, yet there was still that strained tilt to his head.

Renwick said, 'You needn't worry about heading for the Traunsee. With some expert driving, you will get there in less than three hours. I'll phone the hotel's owner – a good, reliable man – he will look after you. You didn't think I'd send you to some place I know nothing about?'

Grant shook his head. So Braun is inquisitive. And I'm suspicious. And Renwick is talking too much. Strange the after-effects of crisis on different men.

'Also,' Renwick's voice became strangely defensive, 'I'll arrange for Avril's clothes and passport and every damn thing to be packed up tonight. They'll be delivered – along with your luggage – first thing tomorrow morning.' If there was anything he hated, it was to explain the obvious. Did Grant really think he was the type to dump them in some benighted place and forget about them until his own business was over? His rancour vanished as he remembered the long grim day that lay behind them all. They ought to be celebrating, not fretting about details that were so damned small in comparison with what they had been through. 'There it is!' he told Braun and Slevak, pointing ahead to a large sign at the edge of the highway. Not too late, either, he thought with relief. It was barely six o'clock.

* * *

The rest-house, standing back from the busy main road, was two-storied, square shaped and simple, sparkling white, with one romantic touch in the red geraniums that spilled from a dark wood balcony. It stood, severely alone, in a large stretch of rough grass devoid – as yet – of trees and bushes. Everything spelled new. Neat and clean and businesslike. The gas pumps stood a safe distance to one side, a garage and repair shop to its rear. There was even a small booth attached to the filling station, Grant noticed, for the sale of candy and small items that a traveller might need. 'Pretty complete,' he observed as they clambered out of the car, 'except for customers.'

'It's the slow period of the day.' Renwick's normal good humour was returning. That's precisely why I chose this Rasthaus, he thought. They should see this place in the morning or early afternoon – everything from trucks and commercial travellers to Volkswagens loaded with tired children. 'Come in and meet the Winkelman family,' he said as he helped Grant to get Avril into the house by its back door. Braun and Slevak followed instructions to see to the car: gas, oil, and water. And the Winkelman family – a widow, three teenage girls, two older boys, an uncle who superintended their efforts – were rallying around. Grant relaxed as Frau Winkelman took charge of Avril and made his way into the front hall where he was told he'd find a telephone.

Then came the first snag. He had jotted down the Salzburg number that Helmut Fischer had given him, jammed the piece of paper into his tweed jacket pocket and it was still there. 'Dammit,' he told Renwick, 'Fischer's number is in my suitcase.'

'You've a mania for packing things away. Why call Fischer?'

'I'll explain later.' Grant thumbed through the Vienna

directory, found the number of Fischer's shop. Leni should still be there.

Renwick looked at him in alarm.

'Don't worry. I'll be careful. My neck's at stake, too, isn't it? See that Avril is okay.'

Who's in charge here? Renwick wondered. He didn't make an issue of the telephone call; this wasn't the time for squabbling. He left, telling himself that Grant was a stubborn bastard but not an idiot; he'd be careful. 'Keep it short!' he called back as he started up the staircase to the upper floor. 'Don't waste a minute!'

As if I didn't know that, Grant thought, and got through to the Singerstrasse shop. Leni was there. And recognized his voice. He cut short her sudden flow of words. 'Leni, please give me Herr Fischer's telephone number in Salzburg.'

'I'm sorry. That number is not to be given out to anyone.'

'I got it yesterday—'

'I'm sorry. Herr Fischer doesn't want phone calls—'

'Leni—' A movement behind him caught his attention. It was only one of the Winkelman girls entering the dining-room.

'I'm sorry,' Leni's precise voice was saying. 'His orders were strict. Why don't you have his number if he gave it to you?'

Better not mention that he had packed it away. 'Would you call Herr Fischer for me? This is important, Leni.'

'He may be leaving for the opera. It begins early in Salzburg and—'

'Then call at once. At once! Tell him I am taking him up on his offer, this week-end.'

'Is that all? You are taking him up on his offer, this week-end?'

'Yes. Call him, please.'

She said quickly before he cut her off, 'Herr Grant –

273

there was a man here this afternoon – just as soon as I opened the shop. He was asking for you.'

'For me? What man?'

'Your friend who bought the Ruysdael reproduction, Mr John Smith. You didn't tell us you knew him. He wondered if you had visited Herr Fischer earlier today just before we closed for lunch. I told him I hadn't seen you, and that Herr Fischer was out of town for the—'

'Leni! Call Herr Fischer right now!' Grant jammed down the receiver, raced for the staircase and a quick shower. Half-way up the stairs, he realized the full meaning behind Gene Marck's visit to Singerstrasse. Marck had half expected Grant, once he was out of the Klar warehouse, to head for Fischer's shop. There, he could have left the authentic Ruysdael for secure keeping in Fischer's safe. As I probably – no, certainly – would have done, Grant thought, if Renwick hadn't been there to help me escape with it. He wished he hadn't been so quick to end his call to Leni – God, how that girl liked to drag out explanations. Had she told Gene Marck that Fischer was out of town 'for the Salzburg Festival'? Or had she merely said 'for the week-end'? But this small puzzle was lost in the rush to get cleaned up, check on Avril, come back downstairs for food and final plans. By that time, when he thought over Leni's unfinished sentence, there seemed little importance to it. Leni was adamant about keeping Fischer's privacy intact. If she wouldn't give out his Salzburg telephone number, she certainly wasn't going to mention his address.

Grant had no way of knowing, nor had Leni, that the effusive Mr John Smith had managed – quite easily, when he had followed her into her office with a friendly afterthought – to slip a small recorder under the edge of her telephone table. It would not hear incoming talk, but everything outgoing (including her dialling) was registered on its miniature tape.

22

It was astonishing, thought Grant, how quickly a good shower and a hot meal could bring a man back to normal, especially when the one Scotch he had allowed as a pick-up (he would be driving and needed to keep all senses clear) was excellent, and his jacket was being cleaned and pressed.

Neither Renwick nor he had taken the time to stretch out in a neat cubicle with its spotless linen. There was too much to discuss and arrange. In shirt sleeves, they sat alone in the simple dining-room. Avril was asleep upstairs, her burned wrist nicely attended to, her dress washed and now being carefully ironed. She had, wisely, refused solid food, but had sipped broth from the excellent *Leberknödel* soup that the Winkelmans were having for supper. And then, wrapped in a rough bath towel, she had collapsed on a narrow cot. She was asleep before Grant had taken three steps away.

An additional comforting thought for Grant was the fact that Braun and Slevak had been steered by Renwick into the big kitchen to share the Winkelmans' evening meal. No objections had been raised. Slevak could have second or even third helpings of Frau Winkelman's excellent goulash. Like many thin men, he had an enormous appetite. As for Braun – he was having an amusing conversation with the prettiest daughter; he had, it seemed, a roving eye as well as an inquisitive ear. 'How long has Braun worked for you?' Grant asked suddenly.

Renwick, who had just been reporting on a successful

negotiation with Uncle Winkelman for the overnight rental of his Volkswagen, halted in some astonishment. 'Off and on for the last three years. Been with NATO six years, now – no, seven. Escaped from East Germany in 1970 with his boy who was killed at the frontier – the kid ran ahead and stepped on a mine.'

'No wife?'

'Wife couldn't leave – there was a sick baby. He's been trying to get them out. No go.'

'Looks as if he's beginning to forget her.'

Renwick nodded. 'That surprised me a little, but perhaps it is just as well. He was turning bitter.'

'Did he come to Vienna with you and Avril?'

Renwick, now studying the map spread out between them to verify the situation of Grünau – yes, it wasn't too far from here – looked up sharply. 'No. Braun arrived only three days ago, a replacement for Slevak's usual partner who was called back to Brussels.' His frown deepened as he waited for an explanation.

'Who arranged that replacement? The man who recalled Slevak's partner?'

'In God's name—' Renwick exploded.

'Okay, okay. Out of turn.' Grant waited for a few seconds, let Renwick regain his cool.

'How much do Braun and Slevak know about your mission here?'

'Nothing. They don't need to know.'

'They know nothing about the Ruysdael? Or why Avril was kidnapped?'

'They weren't even told she was working along with me. Their job is surveillance, when needed. Or to pitch in and help – as they did today.'

'Surely they must make a guess or two.'

'Don't we all?' Renwick asked cryptically. 'Mine, at this moment, are running wild. What the hell makes you ask about Braun? He's reliable; does his job, asks no questions. Now let's get on with our own business. Just why were you telephoning? What was so damned important?'

'I was trying to track down Fischer's address in Salzburg.'

'But you told me he had already offered you his house at Grünau for the weekend. So why waste—'

'A matter of protocol. He's a stickler for that. Also, it's just as well that I warn him I'm taking him up on his invitation. We don't want the neighbours putting in an alarm when they see lights in the Fischer house and smoke coming out of its chimney.'

Renwick pushed aside his coffee cup to make more room for the map. Grünau was at least a two-hour drive from Vienna, far enough – and certainly remote enough among its mountains – to be safe. Safety, that was his one worry. As for Helmut Fischer – he could be trusted, a thoroughly reliable type judging from the check that had been made on him. 'He comes well recommended.'

'Fischer?'

Renwick nodded.

'Glad you're satisfied.'

'Cut out the sarcasm, Colin. We had to be sure. Did you reach him on the phone?'

'I called his shop in Vienna and got his assistant, Leni. He's in Salzburg for the Festival. She'll relay my message there.'

'What?'

'Ease up, Bob. I disguised the message. But he'll get it.'

Renwick's alarm ended. Quietly he asked, 'What was the message?'

'She'll tell Fischer that I am delighted to accept his invitation.'

'No mention of Grünau?'

'Not a syllable.'

'She didn't overhear Fischer inviting you for the week-end?'

'No.' A worrying thought struck Grant: had Fischer told Leni, mentioned it in conversation? 'Dammit all,' he said, suddenly angry, 'surely we've got to trust some-one? We can't go around with suspicions of everyone.'

Now what touched him off? wondered Renwick. 'Of course not,' he said mildly. He looked at his watch and then at the map. 'I think you could make Grünau in just over an hour from here. So if you leave in the next ten minutes, you'll reach it around eight o'clock. That's when the long dusk starts to black out. You should be at the village just before night sets in.' That way you won't get lost on a dark country road, he thought. 'You can direct Braun to the house. When he gets back to Vienna, he'll report to me. Tomorrow, I'll get your luggage and Avril's clothes out to Grünau. Though I wouldn't be surprised,' Renwick added with a grin, 'if she'll find something wearable in Fischer's guest-room.'

'We don't need Braun. I'll drive. Your car, or the Volkswagen?'

'My car. It has the power you'll need. But you aren't driving.'

'Why not?'

'Man, you're dead on your feet! Think of the day you've just been through. Braun will—'

'No.'

'Why not?'

'I don't know why,' Grant said sharply. 'It's just a feeling. He was too damned interested in our talk about where Avril and I were going to stay.'

Too damned interested? Renwick's frown was back. If Braun had been over-curious, Renwick had missed notic-ing it. Part of his exhaustion? Come to think of it, Grant's suspicions could be laid to his own fatigue. And Renwick's earlier warning to Grant – be careful, watch

278

out, as our chief witness against Gene Marck and his crowd you're in real danger – yes, that hidden warning might have set him, tired as he was, to imagining threats in every small incident. Only, it wasn't like Grant to go off half-cocked. In the short but intense time that Renwick had known him, he had seemed to be competent and decisive, a man you could trust in a crisis. 'All right. Let's not waste time arguing,' Renwick said. 'Slevak can drive you to Grünau. Braun will go with me.'

'No,' Grant said, pouring himself another cup of black coffee. 'I'll drive.' The odd thing was, his exhaustion had been dissipated and replaced by cold determination. He was good for another two hours. After that, he could sleep the clock round. 'You square the bill and get Avril downstairs. I'll see you both at the car.' He glanced at his watch – hell, he thought, here I go again measuring the minutes – and began studying the map once more, memorizing each detail between here and Grünau.

Renwick raised an eyebrow. Just who is in command here? he wondered again. 'What's the location of Fischer's house?' he asked softly.

'At the end of the main street, there's a bridge; then a farmhouse. Keep on going uphill, curve round some trees. The house is on your right.'

'Stands alone?'

'Yes. But it isn't far from the farmhouse.'

Renwick nodded approvingly. 'I'll send your luggage tomorrow without fail.'

'Not with—' Grant didn't say Braun's name.

'Not with—' Renwick agreed. He half smiled, shook his head, went off to make sure of the final details. Slevak was still in the kitchen finishing his last plum dumpling. Braun? He was out in the backyard. Talking to himself? Renwick could have sworn he had heard a subdued voice. But as his footstep crunched on the gravel, Braun turned round to face him. It was a cigar

279

case he held in his hand, not a transmitter. He was
extracting a cigar, now, biting off the end as he slipped
the case back into his pocket and found a match.

'Nice evening,' Braun said. 'Thought I'd get some air.
Like a cigar, sir?'

'Thanks, don't use them,' Renwick said brusquely.
Dammit, he thought, Grant has got me distrusting my
own men. This won't do at all. 'Time to move. Just check
that the Volkswagen is tanked up.' Somehow he didn't
mention the change in plans. It was enough to tell Braun
he was driving to Vienna once Grant and Avril were
safely away. He met Slevak at the kitchen door, sent
him running to join Braun, and grew angrier with
himself by the minute.

Avril looked more normal. She was even feeling hungry
now that they were about to leave. Bad timing, she told
herself, and kept silent. She was puzzled, though. Just
Colin and herself in Bob's Citroën? And was Bob driving
to Vienna packed into that decrepit Volkswagen with
Braun and Slevak? Until now, she had paid little attention to what was going on around her. She had emerged
from a nightmare and entered a state of complete daze
that had lasted all through the journey to this house.
Then sleep, so deep and undisturbed that she couldn't
even guess how long – or brief – it had been. But she
had come out of it at the touch of a hand on her
shoulder, a gentle, friendly hand. She had said to the
smiling girl who was offering her the green dress that
no longer looked like a crumpled rag, 'Time to get up?'
Just as if this was an everyday morning. To get up for
what; or where was she going, or how? Here she was,
beginning to ask questions again. That was some kind
of proof, wasn't it, that her mind was alive once more?
I'm free of those drugs, she thought, free of those brain-
stealing drugs. Even her legs were steady now; as

280

–

Renwick led her down the narrow staircase she no longer felt she was walking over a waterbed. 'I'll be all right,' she told his watchful eyes.

He steered her towards the backyard, picked up a white plastic shopping bag he had left at the door. 'I'll check with you tomorrow—'

'Oh, yes – my report. It isn't much. They didn't learn—'

'I know that,' he said gently. 'Just one thing puzzles me. How did they get into your apartment?'

She hesitated for a moment. 'I opened the door.'

'You *what*? Without checking?' He was aghast.

'Well, I—' She paused again. 'It was almost one o'clock. I expected Colin. I—' Once more she halted.

'Avril, Avril,' he said, shaking his head. 'You can't have it both ways.'

'It's either – or?' She tried to smile. She was remembering Bob's early warning: no emotional entanglements while we're on a job; that can be deadly.

'Today proved that, didn't it?'

They reached the Citroën. Colin Grant was already at the wheel, welcoming her with a broad grin. 'Better take the back seat – you can catch more sleep there.'

'Better this one,' she told him, and stepped in beside him. 'My job now is to keep you talking *and* awake.' She glanced at Renwick for his approval. I haven't lost my wits altogether, she told herself. 'Where are we going, anyway?'

Grant gave a flicker of a glance at Braun's direction. Renwick said, 'Hey, Colin – you didn't pack away your driver's licence in that suitcase of yours?'

Grant shook his head. His licence was one item that never left his wallet. He hadn't the necessary Austrian permission to drive, though. Better not bring that up at this moment. Braun was looking longingly at the Citroën as if he wished he were behind the wheel. Of course,

Grant told himself, some men become addicted to certain cars, can't bear anyone else to handle them. He switched on the engine. It had a good sound.

'All set?' Renwick asked, and dropped the plastic shopping bag in Avril's lap. Quickly, he tucked the grey cape she abominated more closely around her shoulders. 'You're stuck with it,' he told her, and won a real smile. 'I'll send your mink tomorrow.' That made her laugh. Yes, she is recovering, he thought, and waved. And they were off.

He turned away to climb into the Volkswagen. Braun wasn't too happy about the car, neither was Slevak for that matter. Choosy blighters. 'I'll catnap,' he told them. 'You drive like hell.'

'To the Embassy?' Braun asked.

'Why not?' Where I go from there will be my own business, Renwick thought, curling himself in the rear seat's space.

'Quite a party we had today,' Braun said. 'Wasn't it?'

'That it was,' Renwick said, signalling a final goodbye to Uncle Winkelman. He closed his eyes, didn't have to answer Braun's next question. No post-mortems; no slipped information. Sleep was his best excuse.

23

The Citroën handled well. Grant skirted the town ahead, took the road for St Pölten. From there he had only to follow the highway that led away from the flat plains into the rising hills, aiming for Annaberg. Just beyond that village, he remembered, was the side road to Grünau with its encircling mountains. 'An hour's drive, and with luck we'll be at Fischer's house.'

'Helmut Fischer?' Her eyes were surprised. 'Does he know of our invasion?'

'I relayed a message to him.' Watching her automatic disquiet, he added with amusement, 'Don't worry. I was careful.' There was a strange tenseness in her face. 'Are you always so security-minded?' he teased, but the joke fell flat.

Barely audible, she said, 'No, I forgot it today.'

'Well, it all ended well. Except for your wrist. How is it?'

She brushed that question aside. 'And because I forgot, Bob had to be dragged away from Vienna. He ought to have been there this afternoon, in contact with Brussels and Geneva and—' She broke off, her voice strangling. 'After so much work, so many weeks—' She didn't finish.

'What's in that package he dumped on your lap?' At least the question had switched off her outbreak of emotion. She wasn't really back to normal, yet. He concentrated on the road as she opened the shopping bag and began pulling out its contents.

She found two wrapped sandwiches, miniature bottles

of Scotch and brandy, a thick slab of chocolate, cigarettes, an imitation-silk scarf with Lippizaner horses
prancing around its borders and Vienna's emblem complete with motto in its centre, a comb, a compact and
lipstick, a package of paper handkerchiefs, and – right
at the bottom of the bag, the heaviest item of all – a .22
calibre automatic with a silencer.

'Where did he scrounge all that?' Grant was grinning
broadly, but he wished he had thought of it. He hadn't.
Where had Renwick found the time? He glimpsed the
pistol. 'That's Frank's.'

A reminder of danger, she thought: all right, Bob, I'm
listening to you. She replaced it in the bag, and dropped
it out of sight. She combed her hair, twisted the present-
from-Vienna scarf around her head, looked in the compact's mirror. 'I'll have a yellow face,' she predicted: the
compact's powder was a deep tan, one to be avoided by
her fair complexion. The lipstick was scarlet – another
colour she never wore. She applied it lightly. 'It's supposed to make one feel better,' she said with a smile.
'Actually, I think I'll have a sandwich.' She offered the
other, but he refused. 'Scotch? Brandy?'

'After we've arrived.' This road was running through
easy countryside now; soon enough, he would need all
his reflexes for the winding climbs ahead.

That was wise. She decided to be wise, too. The effect
of the drugs had gone, but there might be some of them
still wandering around her bloodstream. She was about
to suggest a quick stop for a large cup of black coffee,
dropped the idea as she sensed it might only add to his
problems. She'd drink coffee by the gallon once they
had arrived at Fischer's house. No delays now. 'Where
is this house? Is it hard to reach?'

'It's at Grünau. In daylight, it's easy enough to find.
But when the dusk sets in – we could miss the turn-off

to the village. We won't though. We'll be there before night arrives.'

Thank heaven I resisted the idea of coffee, she thought, beginning to feel the urgency that lay behind his impassive face. There were certain types – Bob Renwick was another of them – who seemed to talk less when they had most to tell. 'Frank's pistol – how did Bob get hold of that?'

'Oh,' Grant said vaguely, 'he needed it.' Then more precisely, 'He had to use it, too. Three times, actually. Close range – it has to be close with that little pea-shooter. He was right up at the door, waiting for Rupprecht and his Luger.' In retrospect, it wasn't a comforting picture.

'I heard no shots. Just an explosion—'

'Rupprecht didn't even have a split second's time to pull a trigger. The .22 doesn't make much of a sound when it's fitted with a silencer.'

'And the explosion?'

'A grenade tossed under the car.'

Bob had been at the door of the house, she remembered. 'You threw the grenade?'

He nodded. Then he grinned. 'I didn't count on a fire. It makes me sweat, now, to think what I started. Damn fool. Still – it got results.'

'What about the third man? He left me and went downstairs.' Heavy footsteps, receding slowly, while all she could do was lie and listen and wait for them to return. As they would have.

'Knocked out for ten minutes or so.'

'Oh,' she said, her voice rising in aggravation, '*tell* me what happened. Stop being so cryptic. I feel as if I had lost *hours* of my life. A total blank. *Please*, Colin, tell me. Fill it in for me.'

So he did. 'Now, what's your story?' he asked as he ended.

'It isn't much. They took me – and you saw that. Then there was a house – somewhere in Vienna – but you know that. Next, a car. They had drugged me some more. I passed out – didn't know where I was when I half opened my eyes – again. Kept them closed. That's all.' There was a long pause. 'I don't remember very much that happened after you got me out into the meadow. It was you, wasn't it?' Another car ride, with now a feeling of safety, of unbelievable safety. With arguments too, about hotels and Traunsee. 'What were you and Bob fighting over? I thought you liked each other.'

'He's heavy competition.' Grant's eyes left the road and looked at her. Then he went back to driving. The flat dull landscape and its spread of houses had been left behind. The highway was now climbing through woods and rising hills.

Avril's stillness matched her silence.

'He's in love with you,' Grant said.

She shook her head. 'No. We wouldn't be working together if we were in love. Bob has strong opinions about that. It makes us too vulnerable. Today, for instance – oh, I don't have to explain. You saw it for yourself.'

'You're saying that today was an emergency where Renwick needed a cool, calm head and didn't go to pieces because you were his girl?' What nonsense, he thought, Renwick was as up-tight as I was about Avril's danger. We took chances, that was all; we didn't lose our heads.

She was embarrassed. 'Something like that,' she said briefly.

'Would you fall apart, be unable to think and act, if you were in love with him and *he* was the one who was in extreme danger?'

'Yes.'

'I don't buy that. You wouldn't panic.'

'I'd make mistakes.' I made two beauties today, she thought, all because I was worrying about you. I scarcely know you and yet your safety – getting a warning to you in time – no, panic wasn't my trouble; it was dumb stupidity. I relaxed when I should have kept taut, stayed alert.

'Small ones, surely,' he said to lighten her sudden depression.

'Yes,' she said bitterly, 'two small ones, lasting less than a minute each. One was outside Klar's Auction Rooms; the second in my own apartment. Because of them, I nearly ruined everything.'

'Not everything, surely,' he said. But she wouldn't be comforted. 'We have all got guilt,' he tried. 'You about your two small minutes. I, about drawing you into danger when you came to warn me this morning. Renwick, because he recruited you and brought you into this kind of life. Sure, he's got guilt about that. Must have.'

'This kind of life?' she quoted back to him. She was angry. 'What's so wrong with it? There's a job to be done, a necessary job. Someone has to do it, we can't all sit back and watch the totalitarians take over.' She eased her voice. 'And Bob didn't recruit me, not in the way you make it sound. I wanted to help. I had some skill in languages. So why not me? No one forced me into this job. It was my own free choice.'

'You enjoy it?'

'I believe in it. I know it has to be done. Or else we'll all end up as regimented nonentities, scared to death to step out of line or raise our voices. Everything and everyone in place according to the book of Marx. What kind of life is that?'

He agreed, yet he couldn't resist asking. 'The terrorists

you are trying to discourage – they don't fit into that scheme of everything and everyone in place, do they?'

'They prepare the way. What about human rights, then?'

Yes, first terrorism, disruption, anarchy; next, the totalitarian grab for power. That was the pattern. 'Some might say you had done enough.' He glanced at her wrist, bandaged loosely with white gauze. 'You've done your share, more than most of us. Your whole life can't be given up to this job. A girl as pretty and intelligent as you – there must have been a lot of men in love with you. How many wanted to marry you? A couple of hundred?'

She laughed, then. 'Only eight. I nearly married two of them.'

'Polygamist,' he said, keeping the light mood going.

'Not quite. There was a year between.'

'Why didn't you marry one of them?' Was it Renwick, he wondered, always there in the background, pulling her unconsciously to him? Grant couldn't get rid of that thought.

'I found I wasn't in love. Oh, they were attractive, bright, amusing – great fun to be with – I had some happy times. However—' She shrugged her shoulders. There was the soft smile of sweet memories lingering around her lips.

'However what?' he insisted. He had to know.

Her smile vanished. 'I couldn't make the choice.'

'Choice? Between your job and marriage?' He could feel his heart sink. Goddamned fool, he told himself. Did you ever imagine she'd fall for you?

'Which proved I really wasn't in love, didn't it?' You can't have it both ways, Bob had reminded her today. Only, that's what we all want when we're faced with a difficult choice: to have it both ways. Whatever made me even think, feel, imagine that Colin Grant was

288

attracted to me – in spite of himself? Just because I was attracted to him – in spite of myself? Abruptly, she changed the subject by reaching for the map on his knee. 'You need help with this. You can't drive and check our route and talk to me, all the same time. Where are we?' She bent her head over the map. The scarf had slipped; she removed it impatiently, stuck it back into the shopping bag, added the rest of her presents.

'Keep out a pack of cigarettes. I've run short,' Grant said.

'Want one now?'

He nodded, concentrating on the curves of the steadily ascending highway. There were some cars ahead, others behind him, all driving into the country for the weekend. Fortunately, their speed was brisk, no loitering, no delays. As the last of the small towns had given way to far-separated villages, the landscape had changed dramatically from gentle undulations to forested heights pressing closer and closer to the road. The sun had set, but the beginning of dusk had been scarcely perceptible, just a gentle and steady greying of blue skies. He switched on his headlights, and took the cigarette she had ready for him. She was studying the map once more, tracing the red lines they had been following from St Pölten. 'Where *are* we, Colin?' she asked again, annoyed with herself for having noticed so little about this journey.

'We passed some ski runs about five miles back. At Turnitz, I think.'

'I've got it.'

'Okay. Next village is Annaberg. Once we're through there, we'll take the first side road – uphill, to the left – it isn't on the map, we'll have to be on the alert for it. There should be a signpost marked Grünau.' We'd better not miss it, he warned himself: there might be no safe turning place beyond it, with cars pressing him from

289

behind – he'd have to drive up several hairpin bends to the next village before he could find space to point the Citroën back downhill.

She found Annaberg on the map. Still a little distance to go.

The light was fading, if slowly, certainly steadily, a gradual yet definite diminishing. 'We'll make it. The weather is on our side. No clouds, and the moon will be clear. There's a change predicted, though. Tomorrow night or Sunday. Rain.' Anything to keep the talk impersonal, less disturbing. 'The road is certainly good.'

'Fischer said it was a new highway. Actually, as far as I remember from seven years ago, it's still the same old road, but much upgraded.' It had been entirely re-surfaced, carefully cambered, and widened as much as the fall of hillside would allow.

'You know, you haven't told me what happened at Klar's today.'

'That will keep until we've got a fire going in Fischer's living-room. Too long a story to start now. How far to Annaberg?'

'About five minutes, I'd guess, at this speed. We've lost some of our company.' The two cars ahead had turned off into a side road; behind them, only one was now in sight.

'So I see.' Grant studied the Mercedes to his rear. Much too close, he thought. It can't be tailing us. It must be someone eager to get up to his cottage on the mountainside before night sets in. He slowed gradually. The Mercedes hesitated briefly, swept past him. He relaxed again, saw Avril's amused eyes watching him but she said nothing. He put on speed once more; in three minutes they were at Annaberg.

'Now!' he said. They kept their eyes on the darkening hillsides to their left. And there was the road to Grünau.

'It will be rough but short,' he told her. 'Uphill all the way on to a broad green valley.'

It was as he said. Except the colours were now lost as dusk ended and the valley was a darkling grey with distant mountain peaks serrated black against the sky. Just ahead, she saw a church spire, a cluster of houses, a swift-flowing stream that ran to meet them. Then – at the end of the little street – a low bridge with a solitary house on its far side. Nothing stirred, no one was to be seen; except for the perpetual rush of water and the Citroën's engine purring along at reduced speed, there was nothing but silence.

'Is this the Fischer place?' Avril asked as they came over the bridge. She looked doubtfully at the house they were approaching. It's too close to the village, she thought worriedly, too unprotected; a sprawl of buildings dumped down on an open field.

'No, that's a farm. Owned by a man called—' Dammit, he couldn't remember the name. 'He keeps an eye on Fischer's place – it's just a short way up this hill, can't see it until we pass the trees. A big family. It looks as if they are all in bed.'

'At five past eight?'

'If you rise at four in the morning, you—' Suddenly a dog barked savagely. Grant's grip stiffened on the wheel. Avril started. The door of the farmhouse was thrown wide, and a man stood there, silhouetted against the meagre light behind him. He stepped out to intercept them, silencing the dog that followed at his heels, and Grant brought the car to a quick halt. 'Goddammit,' he said under his breath. 'This is all we need: explanations, excuses—' Would the man recognize him again after all these years, believe he was a friend of Fischer's?

The man's stride brought him quickly to the car. He was a large and lumbering shape, purposeful. And what was his name? Grant switched on the interior light, lowered the windows. *'Grüss Gott,'* he tried. Thankfully, the name came to him as he looked at the rugged weathered face under its thatch of grizzled hair, Ernst? Yes, Ernst. But Ernst who?

'Grüss Gott.' Ernst, a rough jacket thrown over his shirt-sleeves, put two massive hands on the door, stared first at Avril, then studied Grant. His doubts gave way to a nod as he looked more closely. 'Herr Grant?'

'Ernst?' They shook hands across Avril. 'This is my friend, Miss Hoffman.' A smile from Avril, a brief bow from Ernst, and Grant could switch off the light.

'I sent the wife and Willi up to the house as soon as Herr Fischer telephoned. They have the fire lit and the bed ready.'

'He telephoned?'

'Aye.'

'Hope it didn't make him late for the opera.'

'He *was* in a bit of a hurry,' Ernst admitted, a small smile glimmering. It vanished. Pointedly, he added, 'Didn't say there would be anyone with you.' His face, like his voice, was now expressionless. 'The wife only prepared one bed. I'll send her back.'

'No need. It's late. I'm tired enough to sleep on the floor. Don't trouble your wife. Very kind of you. Much obliged.' With a parting wave, Grant rolled up the windows and started the car. 'Just around this curve, past the trees,' he told Avril, 'and we'll see the entrance of the driveway to our right.'

The driveway was short, narrow, and rough, ending in a clearing of grass dominated by Fischer's chalet. There, he drew up on the far side of the clearing. It was best to leave the car as hidden as possible, out of sight from the trail: too obvious to have it standing in front of the house. Had he forgotten anything else? He might have asked Ernst to keep their arrival secret; only that would have aroused curiosity, even suspicion. As for the villagers – they couldn't all have been in bed, but no one had bothered to glance out; windows had remained tightly curtained. It was possible the sound of a car driving through on a Friday night meant only one thing: Herr Fischer arriving for his usual week-end. He hoped so. The less attention drawn to his visit, the better.

Avril had stepped out of the car; then stopped. She drew the cape close to her shoulders, feeling the cold bite of the night air, and stood motionless, her eyes searching the deep shadows. The house was a solid black shape, two storeys high, with a wide spread of roof, everything lifeless except for one small light at the door.

'Come on, Avril,' Grant urged her forward. 'It's warmer inside.'

She gave one last look at the silent hillside rising behind the house, at the dark patches of forest that encircled her. It seemed innocent enough, still, peaceful; and yet – in the sudden fall of night – there was a feeling of terrifying loneliness. It's safe, she told herself, safe. No strangers thrusting their way into my room, seizing me. For a moment, she could feel the rough grip, the hand over her mouth, the violent threat. She shivered.

'Carry your luggage, ma'am?' Grant asked, holding out his hand for the plastic bag. He steadied her over the rough grass to the path that led up to a heavy door. With its shuttered windows, the house looked deserted except for the light at the entrance. Bless Frau Ernst, he thought: without the light, they'd have been stumbling around. He searched for the key – in the usual place, Fischer had told him – and found nothing; in dismay, he tried the door. It had been left open for him. Ernst's wife had even turned on a table lamp to lead them safely into the main room. 'No thieves around here,' he said with a short laugh to cover his embarrassment. 'Just try leaving your door unlocked in New York.' Gently, he urged her across the threshold. She was still trembling. What had frightened her out there? Should he go on making inane remarks or let her come out of this alone? He found the master switch, sending beams of warm light over the vast room to blot out its deep shadows, then turned the key that had been tactfully left in its lock. 'All secure,' he said.

Avril nodded, half smiled. She was still shaking as she moved to the middle of the room where the fireplace lay, its young flames leaping in welcome from the huge circular hearth that lay under a central chimney. She dropped the cape, sat on the broad stone curb that edged the hearth, felt the warmth from the crackling logs seep over her spine.

'Old-style chalet,' Grant said as he followed her. 'Historically correct.' He paused. Why the hell was he so nervous? 'With all modern comforts, of course. I think you'd better move over to this couch and face the fire. Else you'll end up a toasted marshmallow.'

'With curvature of the spine,' Avril said.

'What?'

'That's what my mother used to say: sit with your back close to the fire and you'll get curvature of the spine.' She began to laugh.

It didn't sound real. He looked at her worriedly, and took her hands to help her rise. Her grasp tightened on his. 'Darling, what's wrong?' The word had escaped him.

'With you, nothing.' She tried to smile. Her eyes – those wonderful large beautiful eyes – widened still more. 'A nightmare – a moment's nightmare, out there in the dark. Those men – the one that seized me—'

'No more. You're safe, Avril. Safe.'

'I know. And yet that memory, it was so real, as if it were happening all over again. His hand—'

'Don't,' he said, and put his arms round her to stop

294

the sudden trembling. She didn't draw away. The trembling ceased. She stood within his arms, slender waist encircled, dark hair against his shoulder. He felt the softness of her body, saw the curve of smooth cheek.

'If you hadn't arrived—' She raised her head, her eyes on his.

'But I did.' An unfair moment, he thought. I could take her with a kiss. And suddenly, he didn't give a damn whether it was fair or unfair. I'm in love with this girl. I've been in love with her from the day I first saw her. 'Avril—' he said, his voice filled with emotion. Abruptly, he let her go. For a moment, they stood looking at each other. Then just as abruptly, they came together again, her lips meeting his.

24

Gene Marck had rented a small attic room on this dingy street as far back as 1975. It was furnished only with essentials: a bed, a table and chair, a small stock of tinned food, a wardrobe for any necessary change of clothes. Most important, he had installed some equipment, nothing conspicuous but sufficient enough for necessary communications. The absentee landlord was content with regular payments (cash, delivered by messenger) and a tenant, Siegmund Baum by name, who made no complaints. The neighbours, forever changing, paid little attention to anything except their own problems. This wasn't a friendly building. The major asset, however, of this quiet room was its possible use as a hideaway if some emergency cropped up. If he had to drop out of sight for a few days until the situation was stabilized and the crisis contained, this place offered security. And today, he needed it. Today, the emergency had broken.

Not this morning. Everything had been under control at Klar's Auction Rooms.

Not at midday. He had gone straight to the Sacher, quietly picked up his more valuable property (Lois Westerbrook had talked about it in her last phone call), and left everything innocent if anyone were to examine his room.

Not this early afternoon. No one had followed him to Fischer's shop. The horse-faced woman was a nonentity. So sure of herself, she'd be the last to believe that all her outgoing telephone calls were now being recorded. One of his men had been detailed to visit Fischer's place before twelve tomorrow, when all shops closed on Saturday. The excuse? A workman checking on a defective telephone. While she argued, the man would retrieve the bug. By one o'clock tomorrow, it would be left in a safe drop – at a little café only a block away where he could be sure of a hot meal on his visits here. By two o'clock at the latest, he would listen to the miniature tape recording. He might learn something, he might learn nothing. Certainly, the shop had been a meeting place yesterday for the Hoffman girl and Colin Grant. They had talked briefly, but closely. Yet, this morning at Klar's, they had met as complete strangers. Interesting. Enough to have her picked up at her apartment.

There had been no alarm when she had been taken at one o'clock today. All had gone well. And considering the haste of their plan (and his use of Mandel's men until his own two replacements could arrive to take charge), the girl's abduction had been without incident. At three forty-five, Rupprecht's message to Mandel had been one of confident success. Mandel's cottage had been reached; Gruber on guard at the main house; the girl unconscious and safely installed. One hour later, a second report from Rupprecht: all quiet, the girl still unconscious.

Then something went wrong. What? How? The time was easy to place: within that brief period between Rupprecht's last message and the arrival of his two replacements. They had found a fire-truck on *Waldheim's* meadow, several cars, and smoking embers. The girl had vanished. So had Rupprecht and the two men with him. So had Gruber. Dog and jeep were gone, too; the big house empty, no forced entry, no disorder or struggle evident.

How? Marck asked again. He had made no mistakes;

in fact, he had shown foresight. He had come here, once he left Fischer's shop, to receive reports and send out any additional directions. He had been on top of that operation all the way, even if by remote control. If he had been at *Waldheim* himself, would it have made any difference? He couldn't be blamed for staying in the background. He knew of no crisis, no impending disaster that had to be averted by personal intervention. There had been a sense of danger in these last few days, but he was accustomed to living with that; and once the Hoffman girl had been thoroughly questioned, he would have known where to take action, nullify the threat. Why had she been drugged too heavily? Mandel's men, bloody fools, were inept or careless. The fault lay with Mandel. I took care of Lois Westerbrook all right, he reminded himself. Couldn't Mandel have been equally capable? Too busy fussing about that gift he was sending for his American brother-in-law – even neglected Mittendorf's advice and changed methods.

Mittendorf – that was the emergency that really had struck fear. Why hadn't he been sent word of Mittendorf's arrest as soon as it occurred? He could have transmitted the alarm to Rupprecht, told him to clear out, take the girl with him. Instead, his informant had only been able to send the message by five forty-five this evening: Mittendorf visited by police at four o'clock, taken into custody. Added to that, the second shock: Kurt and Gudrun Klar arrested. The charges? Mittendorf, for misuse of company funds; the Klars for attempted theft of a Ruysdael.

He had almost panicked, had thought of walking out – with one of his available passports and a change in his appearance – and heading for Czechoslovakia. Then reason reasserted itself. He began assessing the situation. When he was questioned, he must have replies ready.

For instance, he had no idea of what Mittendorf was involved in – he had trusted the man as Victor Basset had trusted him – Mittendorf's position in Allied Electronics was above question. He had never examined any cheques that Mittendorf had signed; they were handed over to Gudrun Klar. She dealt with all business matters for her firm and their clients. As for the Klars themselves – he was shocked, appalled. Couldn't believe they'd try anything so despicable, not with their firm's reputation at stake. All he knew about them was that they auctioned excellent paintings from time to time: the reason he had dealt with them, in order to add to Mr Basset's valuable collection.

Yes, he might just manage to make these stories stick. One thing was encouraging: the charges were limited. There was no mention of conspiracy or collusion in murder; no interest in *how* the Ruysdael had arrived in Vienna, no awareness of Ferenc Ady's death. The Klars, in any case, hadn't exact knowledge of these details. If they had any private thoughts, they'd bury them deep, or else they'd talk themselves into a life sentence.

As for Mittendorf – how could the super-clever Jacques ever have been uncovered? Well, he'd keep his mouth shut. The police had no idea of his politics, his covert activities. No knowledge either of Henri Bienvenue's account in Geneva or of its purpose. Mittendorf was just an embezzler, juggling his accounts. He'd take his sentence for that, in silence, lips tight: no explanations or self-justifications. There would be no slip of the tongue to rouse further suspicions or deeper investigation.

An emergency, yes. Devastating. Yet, not a total catastrophe. He could pull a lot out of the wreckage. But how had it happened?

That brought him back to Fischer and Grant and Avril Hoffman.

Fischer? A quick check had been made on Fischer before Marck had first approached the shop in Singerstrasse. Nothing much in that dossier: no political activities, no government connections; interests were art, beautiful women, music, in that order; busy social life; week-ends spent out of Vienna visiting friends or having them visit him; once an expert skier and mountain climber; small establishment, excellent collection of reproductions, framing shop adjacent, pleasant in business dealings, discreet. The brief file on Fischer had seemed adequate enough a few days ago for Marck's purpose; the shop was safe to visit. Now, he needed more. Damn that dossier – incomplete. But not my fault: it's Mandel's. Again.

As for Grant – I've checked and double-checked him. He isn't connected with the CIA – our informant there had access to their list of recently recruited agents. (The old ones, we knew about, and handed their names to Fidel. One of his American protégés did the rest; a book giving names and addresses. Very skilful, that: a lesson in how to launder information.) Grant hasn't the training for Intelligence work nor the stomach. He has brains, but he is lost in his art world. A dreamer and an introvert. In any case, we can soon stop worrying about him.

Avril Hoffman – translator employed part time by the American Embassy – job not important – part of a secretarial pool. Our informant there said she worked irregular hours, seemed to have no close association with any member of the staff. Then last week our informant reported she had been translating for Prescott Taylor, who handles defectors. And they have one defector right now, Gyorgy Korda, the Hungarian. That's what triggered our interest. Mittendorf put her under closer scrutiny, mostly to size her up – could she be approached? Was she in need of money, friendship, sex, or was she open to blackmail? She could, with proper handling, become a new source of information. Anyone who had been in close contact with Gyorgy Korda would be invaluable. Somehow, the girl had been difficult to follow, too elusive. Mittendorf's interest in her turned to suspicion; two days ago, he had put his best agent on the job of tailing her. Yesterday, in Fischer's shop, Mittendorf's suspicions had paid off.

Except, thought Marck as he rose to make himself a glass of tea and open a tin of beans, except you were too late, Mittendorf. For once, you were too late. I agree, there was a lot of involved planning in those last weeks; you had more to worry about than a little part-time translator. Not my fault: I'm clear on that.

So what now? He'd stay here, gather what information he could – his communications set-up for Vienna was excellent – and in a day or two he'd be able to gauge the situation. He might have to take a new identity to keep the Geneva account going, work from Paris or West Berlin, give up his life in America. Too bad. He had been nicely installed in Arizona – freedom to travel, generous salary and expenses. Victor Basset was an indulgent employer. As for Lois Westerbrook – what had made her turn traitor?

He returned to the table, drank the tea slowly. But he wasn't hungry. Cold beans were a nauseating mess. Once more, he thought of the comforts of Basset's house. Perhaps he might be able to hang on to that job if he could play the innocent well enough. Basset trusted him, and that was most of the battle won. If his story was plausible to the Austrian police, if no further revelations confronted him in Vienna, he might face no upheaval. His mission could go on without much change. His contacts in America were good. Too bad if they were to be disrupted after so many years of careful work.

* * *

A knock at the door jolted him out of the story he was concocting. It was after eleven o'clock. A neighbour? Surely not. None had ever come here. Quickly, he rose and found his revolver, jammed it into his belt. The gentle knock was repeated, a light staccato of sound forming a pattern he suddenly remembered. Vladimir Solovyev? Impossible. Solovyev was a man who stayed far back in the shadows. No contact was his rule. Nothing to link him with Mittendorf or any of their covert activities. He knew about their projects of course. As a member of the Soviet Embassy's Trade Department, he had his own ring of agents. He was in full control, but he kept it as remote as possible. If Gene Marck hadn't trained with him in Moscow, he wouldn't even have known Solovyev's name.

Impossible, thought Marck again. He opened the door as far as its tight chain would allow. 'Yes?'

'Leo,' a man said, and cleared his throat.

The old signal, the old name. Marck withdrew his hand from his pistol, unloosened the chain. Solovyev stepped quickly inside from the dark landing.

He took charge immediately, ignoring Marck's surprise and effusive welcome. Removing a shabby raincoat and heavy glasses – he had excellent sight and was known as a sharp dresser – he shook hands briskly, appropriated the only chair.

Marck refused to be impressed. Leo had been a close comrade, a one-time friend in Moscow, their rank equal until his promotion to the Vienna Embassy. 'So you know where to find me.' Marck was amused. Even Mittendorf hadn't been given that information.

'That is obvious.' The tone was cool. Not unfriendly, just coldly factual.

'I am flattered, Leo.' Marck studied him. He had put on weight, his hair was thinner, his face pallid. Once he had been a handsome young man, much the same type

302

as Marck himself; now he looked older than his forty-eight years. Exactly my age, thought Marck. 'You look well. But this visit is an honour I scarcely—'

'This visit was necessary. I have important information to give you. I did not think you would want to be seen wandering through the streets of Vienna to meet me, not at this critical time.'

Marck agreed with that. So Leo knew about the arrests. 'I thought I'd wait here until we see what develops. I was going to send you a coded message tomorrow as soon as I have gathered more facts. They are scarce.' He sat down on the bed, tried to look relaxed.

'They are disastrous. And I prefer to gather them in my own way. Do not contact me.'

A sharp reminder that Leo was following the apparently hands-off policy that allowed Moscow to disclaim any knowledge of any covert action. 'Not completely disastrous,' Marck protested. 'We can salvage—'

'Your Geneva project is finished.'

'Wait, wait! It gathered seven million dollars in three years. Since January we paid out one and a half to—' he remembered Leo's aversion to such details – 'to various groups. The account is too useful, too important. We can't let it—'

'Have it transferred elsewhere.'

'I'd have to go to Geneva. I opened that account myself, made discreet arrangements about any taxes.'

'Only you can draw on the money?' Leo was shocked.

'No, but I deal with the tax collector. The other two men who can draw cheques on the Bienvenue account know nothing about the tax angle.'

'Dependable men?'

'Yes. I selected them. I instruct them when and how much to withdraw.'

'No particulars necessary,' Leo interrupted sharply.

303

He probably knows all about them, Marck decided. How the hell did he find out about this room? He must have been watching me closely. It was a depressing thought. 'Let's drop this charade, Leo. We're old comrades. Nothing you say will ever be repeated by me. You know as much about our activities here as I do.' Possibly even more, but Marck let that ride. 'You may be sure that I search this room at each visit to make certain there are no bugs.'

'I am sure.' Leo almost smiled. Or else he would not have come here in the first place. 'I repeat, no details are necessary. If I want information, I shall ask you for it. Now, here are your instructions: transfer the Geneva money and be satisfied with what you have retrieved. End the entire project. Vienna was a test. It has failed. Drop your plans for the refugee trade in West Berlin. No more auctions. No more bank accounts opened, either in London or Paris. Nothing.'

'Leo, it's been too successful an operation. Vienna – yes, we can drop that market. But the plans for West Berlin—'

'Nothing!' Leo repeated. 'Until a year has safely passed. Then perhaps you can start your scheme again – with a varied approach, changes in the pattern. You'll need a new identity, too.'

'I don't agree. No need to change my name and history – the legend can stay as it is. I have been thinking about it for the last three hours, and I've come up with a fairly substantial story.' Quickly, he poured out his ideas on how to deal with either the Austrian police or Victor Basset.

Leo sat impassive. At the end he said quietly. 'How do you deal with NATO Intelligence? They'll watch every move that Gene Marck makes.'

'NATO?' So not Prescott Taylor. He wasn't connected with NATO. Nor was Avril Hoffman, according to her dossier. She had worked with a business firm in Paris – unless we've been fed false information. 'Someone at the American Embassy? The only recent addition there has been a military attaché on temporary assignment. He has been gathering any scraps of information available about Warsaw Pact defences. No doubt that's for NATO's use in the next disarmament talks.'

'That's what it seems. Renwick's own agents think his chief interest is in defence matters.'

'And why didn't you warn me?' Marck burst out.

'I *am* warning you,' Leo said quietly. 'Tonight I received a report. From an informant I have been successful in placing at the American Embassy. A double agent, to be precise. He's employed by NATO.'

Impatiently, Marck asked, 'He fingered Robert Renwick? Well, if he isn't in defence, then what?' NATO didn't go around chasing art thieves. That was Interpol's business.

'My informant doesn't know. He isn't trained to analyse the facts he gathers. But I find them important.'

Leo's playing with me, Marck thought angrily. There he is, slowly lighting a cigarette, enjoying my humiliation. We were in the same class and I graduated higher on the list than he did. We held the same rank for fifteen years, and now he is showing me how justified his appointment to Vienna was. He's a pure Russian, born and bred. My father was an American, my mother from Lithuania. Moscow never forgets that when it comes to promotions, never quite trusts anyone who isn't of their blood.

Marck's silence irritated Leo. His voice cracked like a whip. 'Are you not interested in how the Hoffman girl was taken from *Waldheim*? Or what happened to Rupprecht and his men? Or to Gruber?'

Marck stopped lounging on the bed. He sat up, spine straightened, face tensed.

'My informant—' Leo's voice had returned to normal, smooth yet businesslike, precise, calm – 'did not take part in the attack on the cottage. He arrived later, when the clean-up was in progress. No explanation was given him of what had happened. It was obviously a quick and decisive operation, well planned, boldly executed. By Robert Renwick and Colin Grant.'

'Grant?' Disbelief, dismay, shock. Marck got control of himself. 'And who else?'

'Only Renwick and Grant. Four other men dealt with Gruber, and then arrived at the meadow in a white camper – flowered curtains, many travel stickers on its sides, plate W232-259. They assisted Renwick, along with his own two agents, to remove all traces of the attack, Rupprecht and Marco had been wounded, the other man knocked out. They were driven away in the camper, destination unknown, captors unknown. But these were experts, worked in silence, knew exactly what to do. A team, obviously.'

'Grant—' began Marck impatiently.

'He left with Renwick, his two agents, and the woman.'

'Still drugged?'

'No. It seems she came out of her unconscious state with remarkable speed. There was only brief conversation in Renwick's car – a four-door 1977 black Citroën, W533-216 – talk of a hotel near the Traunsee, name not mentioned, where Grant and the woman could be hidden safely. Then they reached the outskirts of Purkersdorf, stopped at the Rasthaus Winkelman, stayed for an hour.'

'Why didn't your informant send in a quick report right away?' Marck asked sharply, blue eyes hard and narrowed.

'He tried. He was interrupted,' Leo said irritably. The fool ought to have made another effort, not left it until his return to Vienna. Too cautious. Or afraid? We'll stiffen his spine a little. 'My informant was unable to hear anything that Grant discussed with Renwick at the Rasthaus. Whatever it was, the decision was quickly made. By seven o'clock, Grant and the woman drove west in the Citroën. Renwick returned to Vienna.'

Marck's brow knitted in a frown, his mouth tightened, and he cursed.

Offhand in manner, bland in tone, Leo said, 'It appears that Grant won't be in Vienna tonight. I heard you had plans for dealing with him. Useless, now.'

'Unless he has the cold-blooded nerve to return by midnight. Once he deposited the woman safely, he might drive back.' Austria was a small country, traversed in a matters of hours.

'Hardly likely.'

'Why not? He'd go on playing his part, hope to trap me in his room at the Majestic.' The police might not be looking for Marck, but Renwick certainly was.

Leo shook his head. 'Cancel your arrangements.'

'At this hour?'

'They were much too dramatic anyway. Your idea?'

Marck ignored the jibe. 'Mandel is in charge of it.' He glanced at his watch. Eleven forty-five. 'Impossible to retrieve—'

'Wasn't remote control to be used?'

'That was Mittendorf's suggestion. Mandel changed it to something simpler. Distrusts remote control since that last failure.'

'A pity.' Leo paused delicately, added, 'A pity, too, about Grant. He is your greatest danger now. He can testify—'

'I know,' Marck cut in sharply.

'Do you also know that he delivered the Ruysdael to the American Embassy? He must have. Victor Basset received it there, I hear. It's on its way to New York – quite out of our hands. Yes, Grant is a cool operator.'

307

'Grant—' Marck's anger broke. 'I'll deal with him. I'll find him.' He mastered his rage, dropped his voice. 'Near Traunsee, you said?'

'Perhaps, perhaps not. Grant objected to it – too long a drive. Also, he refused the hotel idea. He had some place of his own in mind. He didn't name it. He only said he would make a telephone call as soon as they arrived at the Rasthaus. My informant couldn't listen to that call – he was sent out to the garage. However, one of the waitresses, young, talkative, overheard Grant telephoning his girl in Vienna. A girl called Leni.' A slight pause. 'Does that name mean anything to you?'

'Yes.'

'Is Leni his girl?'

'No.'

Leo frowned over one last detail. 'Do you know of any agent whose name, real or cover, could begin with Fra—?'

'Fratelli?'

'He's in Mexico City.' Leo rose, pulled on the soiled raincoat to conceal his expensive shirt and tie. A brimmed hat, well pulled down, to hide the shape of his head, the colour of his hair, the height of his brow. Glasses completed the change. Enough for the two dark streets he'd walk before he reached his parked car. He noticed Marck's preoccupation. 'Any questions?' He was impatient to leave.

'How far can this informant be trusted?' A double agent played a two-faced game. He could be Renwick's puppet, passing on calculated misinformation. Grant might never have been near that Rasthaus. Just a nicely planted lie to confuse the real trail.

'As far as he wants to see his wife and child again.'

In that case, thought Marck, the man may be dependable. Anyway, I can check his story tomorrow. By one o'clock, two at the latest, I'll learn if Leni did have a telephone call from Grant. If so, it was Fischer he was trying to reach.

Leo had the door open. He listened intently, then stepped out to look down the stairwell with its dimly lit landings. He nodded and began descending the worn stone steps, quickly but lightly, merging into the quiet shadows. His departure was as silent as his arrival.

No hand-clasp this time, noted Marck as he locked and chained the door. For a moment he stood quite motionless. Then, as he returned to the table and cleared it of uneaten food, he forced his mind away from Leo to the information he had been given. He'd concentrate on Fischer: the man could be a link in this chain of events. Important? Or as unimportant as his small dossier? Marck's memory went back over the facts: *once an expert skier and mountain climber – week-ends spent out of Vienna, visiting friends or having them visit him . . . Having them visit him . . .* Which meant he owned a place in the country. Where? If I know anything about old skiers and climbers, thought Marck as he placed his transceiver on the table, they'll choose a view of mountains when they buy a house in the country.

He set to work. There was no response to his first call. Damn Bernie – on a night of crisis like this, he ought to have someone listening. With Rupprecht and those two blunderers gone, was there no one he could trust? He should have stayed with his transceiver himself.

Three more unsuccessful tries. Had Bernard Mandel left, taken a quick jaunt abroad? Marck restrained his temper, made himself some tea. A fifth attempt. This time, successful. And almost an hour lost.

Mandel had an explanation, of course. He had been out, meeting a friend, only got back ten minutes ago. 'Did you hear the news? Rupprecht—'

'Yes. He's alive.' Unfortunately, thought Marck. 'He

will be difficult to deal with. The other two will talk, of course, but he isn't that type.'

'We do not know, do we?' Mandel said. He sounded morose. 'I must sign off. I have a lot of business to attend to.'

Packing? Ready to run? Marck said quickly, 'One moment – that item you sent me on Monday – it's incomplete. Refer back to your files and give me more details.'

'You have everything we have.'

'Insufficient. A slovenly job. No address of country residence.'

'Why should there be? You were interested in two things: the man himself; his place of business. I am not to blame if you—'

'Get his country address.'

'You will find that in any reference library.'

'Do you think I'm an idiot? I checked his entry in *Who's Who* before I got you to fill in the details. Residence given is in Vienna. Find where he spends the weekends.'

'If it isn't listed in—'

'Find it.'

'That may take time. You just do not walk up to one of his friends—'

'Try the girl in charge of the shop.' That meant tomorrow morning. Delay, delay. Marck's cold voice sharpened in anger. 'Send me word as soon as you know.'

'I may have to leave early tomorrow – my brother is sick – we are very close.'

Reference to Mittendorf? 'Your brother will be sicker if I don't get that address,' Marck said bitingly.

Mandel kept silent.

He's running scared, Marck thought, afraid that his association with Mittendorf could be traced. 'All right, all right. I'll find someone else for this job.' He ended contact.

Now, if only he could advance the schedule for retrieving that bug in Fischer's office. There was no way to reach the man who was to recover the recording device – he had already left for Graz, returning tomorrow in time to perform his telephone repairman act. Just before Saturday noon, Marck had instructed him. Then, Leni would be busy with closing up the shop, eager to get the workman out; also, she might have been – during the morning hours – in contact with Fischer. I was too damn clever, Marck thought, but how was I to foresee a telephone call from a Rasthaus? How the hell could I know what Grant was mixed up in? Grant . . . Two-faced bastard, double-dealing son of a bitch . . . Cursing Grant, he paced around the room until his rage ended and his mind was functioning again, calm enough to deal with the alarm signal that must be sent to Geneva.

That would have to be done by relay through Innsbruck. His equipment here didn't let him reach Switzerland direct. Leo could have had the alert sounded and saved this delay. Only, Leo must be kept uninvolved, must seem to have no connection with the Bienvenue operation. But behind his instructions and information tonight, in the secrecy of this room, there had been a warning. If Grant testified, the disaster was irretrievable. The blame would be fixed on Marck: his fault entirely. Recall, disciplinary action; thrust into outer darkness. End of a career. End of a life.

25

The morning was idyllic: blue cloudless sky, warm sun,
a faint breeze to send the tree tops gently stirring. A
perfect ending for a perfect night, thought Grant, and
the beginning of a new day . . . With one last look at the
rising, falling line of mountains guarding the far side of
the valley, crag upon crag, cliff and precipice high above
forested slopes, he closed the door to the balcony and
stepped into the bedroom. A new day and a new life.

Quietly, he drew the curtains together so that the
invading light would not wake Avril. He moved over to
the bed, stood watching her. It was a sleep so perfect
that he couldn't bring himself to disturb it. He touched
the rumpled dark head, felt a strange mixture of emotion
suddenly grip him, sheer exaltation of joy and happiness, of relief and thankfulness. Gently, his lips touched
the smooth curve of cheek, the firmness of her neck, the
rounded shoulder. She stirred, half smiled, long eye-
lashes trying to open, closing again. Once more she was
deeply, peacefully asleep. He tucked one outflung arm
back into the warmth of the white eiderdown, covered
the bare shoulder.

He'd shower downstairs in Fischer's own suite, keep
the sound of running water away from this room. Thank
heaven the outside noises were smothered by woods
and hills – the village was long awake and stirring. There
had been church bells for early mass, bringing him
briefly awake. Then a drift into sweet sleep again, her
body against his, warm, trusting, reassuring. It had been
no dream.

Lightly, he ran downstairs into the darkened living-room, smiling as he turned on one small light and saw the disorder. Not so funny, though, if Frau Ernst arrived. As she possibly might – it was well past ten o'clock, he noticed with surprise. He moved to pick up his clothes, Avril's green dress, her flimsy underthings, her high-heeled sandals. One thing he wouldn't be doing today, and that was taking her for a scramble up the hill to show her the view, not in those shoes. Everything she had worn was much too thin for this climate. So they'd stay house-bound today, and he wasn't averse to the idea. In haste now, he found her tights and the discarded cape she hated so much. Cold as she'd be, and he himself was beginning to freeze in this unheated room, she'd refuse to wear the cape. I'm beginning to know her, he thought, and that was a pleasing idea, too. With the clothes bundled roughly in his arms, he made for Fischer's bedroom.

In the dressing-room, he had to drop the clothes in a chair and reach for Fischer's bathrobe and slippers: there was a definite knocking on the back door, distant but audible in the total silence around him. He made a dash back through the vast room into the kitchen. It was Ernst's wife, a basket over her arm, her usually amiable face frowning at him. 'Good morning,' she said. 'The door was locked.'

'Sorry. Just woke up. Was about to have a shower.'

'The front door was locked, too.' She shook her head and stepped inside, moving lightly for such a solidly compact woman. 'No one will come bothering you here. Now, I'll just put these away.' She laid the basket on the table, began unpacking eggs and rolls, ham, milk, oranges. 'There's plenty of food in the larder, but I thought you'd need something fresh. Where is the young lady? I'll tell her about this stove.'

'Better tell me. Miss Hoffman is still asleep.'

At this hour? the upraised eyebrows asked.

Grant remembered the old advice, *Never explain, never apologize*. Whoever had coined that dictum never had to cope with Frau What's-her-name. Her bright blue eyes were noting Fischer's bathrobe. They lingered for a moment on the slippers, too small, backs pressed down.

'I know,' he said with a smile. 'I am not doing them one bit of good. Our luggage will arrive later today.' And a damned good thing he had covered his feet; bare toes, coldly scrutinized, wouldn't add to a man's self-confidence. Hair unkempt, beard unshaven, he didn't look much like one of Fischer's friends at this moment.

No luggage? Her question – grey head inclined, brow furrowed – was obvious.

'I'll have that shower,' he said, escaping into the main room. 'And thank you. Very kind of you.' This was only a courtesy visit; she had her own household to attend to.

'Did you let the fire go out?' she said as she followed him and caught sight of the hearth.

We watched it go out, he corrected her silently – at least down to the last glowing embers. 'It seemed safer.'

'I'll stay another ten minutes, and start it going. The lady will freeze to death in this big room.' She picked up a cushion he had overlooked, put it back in its proper place on the couch.

He thought of her return to the village. 'Oh, Frau—' he cleared his throat, embarrassed by the lack of a name.

'Yes?'

'Would you be so good as to – to keep our visit quiet? Outside of your own family, that is.'

She looked at him for a long moment. 'We don't gossip,' she told him, and turned away to draw back the curtains and open the shutters. He headed for the shower, damning his lack of *finesse*. Yet how did you keep people from talking, spreading the word? Eugene

314

Marck wasn't sitting in a Viennese café enjoying a leisurely cup of coffee with whipped cream on top while he watched the pretty girls stroll by.

He showered and shaved, drew on his clothes and was ready to face Frau Ernst's critical eye. Judging by the smell of coffee drifting through the house, her ten minutes had stretched to twenty. As he was about to step into the main room, he heard her voice, low and troubled. Who was with her? He entered; she was on the telephone. His tension sharpened. Who was calling? 'Yes, I'll warn Ernst,' she was saying. 'I'll be taking his lunch up to him in the high meadow in the next hour. Willi's there, too. Hans and Young Ernst, also. They are raking up the long grass and clover before the rain sets in—' She broke off, noticing Grant, raised her voice to normal as she caught sight of him and ended, 'He's here now.' She held out the receiver to him. 'It rang when you were in the shower, Herr Grant. It's Herr Fischer – phoning from Salzburg.' She looked at him, her soft round face creased with friendly anxiety. 'Must leave. I'll be back later,' she called to him as she hurried off at remarkable speed for a fifty-year-old who must tip the scales at a hundred and sixty pounds. Just what's going on? Grant wondered.

'Hello, hello there?' Fischer's voice was saying impatiently.

'I'm here. All's well. I brought a friend with me, by the way. I hope you don't—'

'Yes, Frau Lackner told me. Of course I don't mind, my dear fellow. Miss Hoffman, isn't it? A charming girl.'

Ernst had quick ears and a memory for names, Grant thought. Fischer was rushing on. 'Sorry to break in on you like this, but I simply had to find out if you were all right.'

'Everything is. We're most comfortable. Can't thank you enough. There's only one problem—' Grant tried to

315

sound amused, completely nonchalant '—our luggage is arriving later but heaven knows when.' He even managed a small laugh as he added, 'Avril has nothing to wear. Almost literally. Three-inch heels and a wisp of a dress. She'll be a pneumonia case—'

'Colin—' Fischer's impatience was growing—, 'I'm worried. I've been worried ever since an aquaintance of mine – one of the top men in the Art Fraud Section of State Security – telephoned me from Vienna an hour ago. Then I sat down to breakfast and turned on my radio. Haven't you heard?'

'No. Haven't been listening.' Grant was suddenly alert. Had *Waldheim* broken into the news?

'There was an explosion last night at the Majestic. In a room occupied by a Mr Colin Grant, an American, who was fortunately absent at the time. A fragmentation bomb of some kind that shattered every object in the room.'

Grant took a deep long breath. 'When did it happen? Midnight?'

'Actually, yes. How did you know?' Fischer's voice quickened. 'I am coming up to Grünau and we'll discuss—'

'No need, Helmut. Don't you get involved—'

'But I am. The inspector who called me—'

'Because I'm a friend of yours?'

'No. Because of a Ruysdael reproduction that I sold last week to a man called John Smith.'

Grant remained silent.

'Do you know his real name?'

'Yes.' One of them, anyway, Grant thought bitterly.

'I have an appointment here at one o'clock. The inspector is flying up to interview me and get particulars. Shall I mention the fact that you know the man's real name?'

316

Grant tried to think clearly. He said slowly, 'No, I think not. Not at this moment, Helmut.'

'It could be a safeguard – get you police protection.'

'It might lose us the man altogether.'

'Expect me – oh, I should say around five o'clock.'

'I said, keep out of it. This house is safe – we're all right here.'

'I'll make sure it's safe. I've already sent a message to Ernst Lackner to stay alert.'

'What did you say to his wife?' Grant asked quickly.

'My dear boy, I'm an old hand at mystification. The knack is to warn without disclosing too much. I may be worried about you, but I'm not indiscreet. Oh – tell Miss Hoffman to look in the second guest-room's wardrobe. She'll find some country clothes. They belong to my sister – the one who is in Washington – saves her a lot of packing when she comes to visit Grünau.' Fischer's voice changed. There was a slight note of sadness as he asked, 'Was it wise?'

'Wise?'

'To involve Miss Hoffman in something like this?'

Grant swallowed hard. 'I'll explain when I see you.' Another piece of mystification? The knack is to talk, without telling too much?

'Good,' Fischer said with obvious relief, and the call was over.

Grant reheated the coffee on an electric ring and avoided any crisis with a recalcitrant stove. He drank it slowly; he was still under slight shock. His room at the Majestic . . . It could have been one fragmented art dealer. Dealer? No, he was just an adviser: didn't sell pictures or buy them – except at one auction. That last thought sent him into a fit of sudden uncontrollable laughter. What the hell was he laughing about? The attack ended as abruptly as it had begun.

He poured another cup of coffee. Strangely, though, he could now take a cold look at the murder attempt. How had it been done – a package left in his room? Something so innocent in appearance that no one had questioned it. It should have been kept downstairs at the porter's desk, though. But if the delivery man already knew Grant's room number, had a key, and slipped inside when the corridor was quiet? Yes, that was feasible. How to make sure he would catch the full blast when the device went off? Eugene Marck hadn't planned on a wounded man, twenty feet away in that oversized bedroom, or on one lying stunned in the bathroom or dressing-room.

Grant had his third cup of coffee, pushed aside the roll and honey, lit a cigarette. The problem fascinated him in a horrible way; it dealt with his own death, didn't it? Okay, try this on for size, he told himself: a delivery man follows Marck's instructions, places the pretty package behind the telephone so I won't notice it when I first come into the room shortly before that midnight appointment – Marck expected me to be out on the town, didn't he? A minute or two before twelve, he rings to tell me he'll be ten minutes late. I just have time to hear his first sentence, if that, and whammo! – they'd be scraping me off the walls. Nice guy, Marck. Clever. Too clever by far.

One big question: why, if I *had* noticed the package when I got into my room, wouldn't I have opened it? Of course, it must have looked innocent enough inside its wrapping paper in case it was examined. But why wouldn't I have opened it? Because it wasn't for me. Addressed to someone else. A package that was marked as a gift – from good old Bernie Mandel to his dear brother-in-law. By God, I wonder if he even had the value for Customs declaration marked on the outside?

318

Grant stared at the remains of his breakfast. By God, he thought again, I could be right.

Abruptly he rose, left the kitchen, entered the main room, felt an urge to get out into the warm sun, have a walk over the fields. Better not, though: Avril was asleep upstairs, alone in a strange place, and Frau Lackner was taking Ernst's mid-day meal up to the high meadow. So he stayed, now feeling the emptiness of the house, its great isolation. Was he over-reacting? Probably. Marck couldn't have any idea where he was, far less that Avril was with him. He compromised. He searched for field-glasses and found them in the logical place, on a table near the gun rack in one corner of the room which Fischer kept for his own special interests. An excellent collection of art books caught Grant's eye – later, he thought, later. With binoculars in his hand, he left by the front door and began a tour around the house, keeping close to the outside wall and well under the protection of the overhanging balconies.

The house faced north. In front was the stretch of grass edged by the trees where he had parked the Citroën. They descended a steep slope, with one broad swathe of cleared timber to give a glimpse of village roofs and church spire. Beyond them, forested hills and a background of mountains.

To the west, where the terrace lay – tables and chairs, a large sun umbrella waiting for someone to sit down with a drink and admire the view – the wide spread of valley stretched before him. Not completely naked. Blobs of trees were strung, like so many green beads, along the stream that ran towards Annaberg. The road, perhaps to avoid spring floods, kept its distance from the rush of water and cut across the open meadows. Several small cars, Grünau-bound. A slow-moving reaper. And on either side of the valley – forested hills, of course, and higher peaks behind them.

At the back of the house, to the south (and in this part of Austria, the bad weather came from there: mountains, the really big fellows these ones, all snow-topped even now, gathered the rain clouds and wild winds and sent them hurtling northwards), there were green fields rising towards the hills. More forests high above those ski-slope meadows; and the signs of wood cutting. Giant firs, brought to earth, stripped of branches, bare trunks weathering, lay (precariously it seemed, from this distance) like so many scattered matches. He looked for Ernst and his sons working on the high meadow, and found them. Four figures grouped in a Brueghel scene near one of the neat small wooden huts which must store the fodder for the livestock. There were several of these huts, well-spaced around the meadows: the farmers didn't trust open haystacks in this land of storm and rain. Of sunshine, too, Grant thought: the weather had been glorious in the last two days. There wasn't a sign of any break. Blue sky, white puffs of soft clouds now. Everything looked settled and fine, with plenty of sun ahead. Yet Ernst and his boys seemed to be working at high speed. They must have had their midday meal. No leisurely *Déjeuner sur l'Herbe* in Manet style for them. He could see Frau Lackner making a quick descent by one of the zigzag paths that would bring her down towards village level. That route was too close to this house: she might appear here at any moment. Out of curiosity? What did Fisher actually tell her about me? Grant decided to waste no more time and moved round to the east side of the house.

Here, the back door lay. Side door, rather. Slightly lost its bearings, he thought, but no doubt it was avoiding the winter winds. Woods were thick, but one large space had been cleared in front of the kitchen: flowers, and a vegetable garden.

Once more to the front of the house, surveying its last

320

corner where the driveway emerged from the trees on to the rough lawn. Beyond it, the road that came up from the village and Lackner's farm was blotted out as it climbed on uphill, hidden by the woods opposite the kitchen. He studied the Citroën, Not too noticeable, and certainly not visible from the road.

Reassured, he went back into the house. As he replaced the field-glasses, he even felt slightly foolish. Suspicious idiot, he told himself: this house is safe – a quiet village, good people, what more do you want? It was Fischer, so unexpectedly worried, who had set him off. What really troubled Helmut anyway? Perhaps it was the thought that his house – a gem, no doubt about that, created over the years with tender loving care – might go up in a bang like Room 307 at the Majestic. If so, I wouldn't blame him; I'd blame myself for having drawn it into danger. But no one knows we are here, except Fischer and Renwick. And the Lackner family, he added to that. Ernst and Fischer are long-time friends. Dimly, he remembered some stories told him on his last visit here about the Nazi invasion and Ernst's help in Fischer's escape. Still more reassured, Grant picked up Kenneth Clark's *Landscape into Art* and settled in an armchair. He'd waken Avril in another half hour or so.

She was already awake; up and showered and in search of her clothes. There was complete silence downstairs, an enticing smell of coffee drifting faintly through the house and – as seen from the top of the stairs – an empty room, with windows spaced along two walls. Views of green trees. Not much sun though; the balconies were broad and cut off the outdoor light. And warmth. Thank heaven the fire had been relit. She tightened the bath sheet around her breast, tucked it securely to leave her hands free as she started down the stairs, lifting the

321

towel's heavy folds away from her ankles. Midway, she leaned over the banister. 'Colin?' she tried.

'Here,' he called back, coming out from an alcove of bookshelves.

The most marvellous sound, she thought. For a long moment, they looked at each other. She laughed and said, 'Good morning, darling.'

'A good morning it is.' He relaxed, could only stand there watching her, a smile spreading over his face. His last worry vanished: she shared his incredible happiness, made it real; no dream. There were no doubts, no regrets, in these beautiful eyes.

'My dress—'

'Forget it.'

'Do I wander around in my Roman toga?' It was slipping. She pulled it together with another laugh.

Beautiful eyes, beautiful face, beautiful everything. He held out his arms as he ran up to meet her. She met him half-way, a step above him, lips level with his.

A door opened and closed. Footsteps in the kitchen. His lips left Avril's, his head turned towards the sounds. He relaxed as he identified them. 'Ernst's wife. There goes our morning.'

'What was left of it.' Avril said, freeing herself from his arms, snatching up the bath sheet, draping it around her again as she ran back upstairs.

'You'll find some clothes in the next-door bedroom,' he called after her.

'I know. I didn't like to—'

'Take what you need. Fischer says okay.'

She paused in her flight. 'Fischer?'

'He telephoned.'

'Oh?' She disappeared into the second guest-room as Frau Lackner came looking for Grant.

Slowly, cursing under his breath, he came down into the big room. 'You're having a busy day, Frau Lackner.'

'Just brought some salad for lunch. Some cold cuts, too. Anna, my second oldest, will come up to cook dinner tonight.'

'That's far too much trouble. We can manage.'

'Herr Fischer always has Anna or Brigitte – that's my daughter-in-law, married Young Ernst, you remember him? – well, anyhow, one or the other always cooks dinner when he's here. Both of them, when there are guests.'

Daughter-in-law . . . 'Many of your children married?'

'Children!' That amused her. 'You should see them, Herr Grant. Young Ernst married last spring, the others are getting married this year. Except Minna, of course, and Willi – he's sixteen.'

'A couple of years to go?'

'That's about it.'

In-laws, he was thinking, and sweethearts with families – the news of Avril's arrival with me is bound to spread.

'I see the young lady is up and around. Did she have breakfast?'

'Not yet.'

'Then I'll get her tray ready. Orange juice? All Herr Fischer's guests like orange juice. I'll make some fresh coffee.'

'No, please don't bother. She will possibly combine breakfast with lunch.' He steered Frau Lackner, gently, into the kitchen.

'Is she a journalist, too?' Frau Lackner was awed.

For a moment, he stared at her.

'Oh, I'm sorry,' she rushed to apologize, her pink cheeks reddening. 'I didn't mean to—'

'It's all right. What did Herr Fischer tell you?' He kept a smile in place, his voice friendly. 'That I am a journalist, and I'm here to—?' He left the sentence for her to complete. She did that with a question of her own.

323

'It's these men who are after you – the ones you are writing a story about? But they won't be able to follow you here, will they?'

'Of course not,' he reassured her. So I'm an investigative reporter, who revealed too much. In a way that was a milder version of what had actually happened.

'Real criminals?' Her eyes were round and innocent.

'You could call them that.'

'American?'

'Some are.'

'Gangsters – that's what Ernst said. But don't worry, we'll keep our eyes open. Saturday is a bad day, though. Saturday and Sunday. There's a lot of traffic on the road, a lot of people coming out here for the afternoon, taking pictures – nothing much else to do.'

'The road didn't look too busy this morning.'

'You wait,' she told him. 'By two o'clock, the streets will be filled with cars.'

'Streets? I thought Grünau had one main street.'

'And the side street with the new gift shops. But the government makes them close at noon on Saturdays – what good is that for tourists? So they sit around the café, clutter up the pavement, park in front of people's gardens.'

A café, too. 'Any hotels now?'

'Oh, yes. There's another being planned, too. With tennis courts and a swimming pool.'

'Changed days.' They worried him. Grünau was scarcely the hideaway on which he had planned.

'Seven years are a long time,' she reminded him. 'It's the cars that have done it. Next year we are having a highway instead of a road down to Annaberg.'

'Talking of road, where does that one lead?' He gestured in the direction of the trees outside the kitchen window.

'The one that goes past here? Over the hill, up towards Josefsberg, where it joins the main highway.'

That worried him, too: a small country road linking Grünau with one of the major routes; more access to this place than he had bargained for.

Frau Lackner studied his face. 'Don't let that road bother you, Herr Grant. It's hardly ever used by the tourists – too rough for all their shiny motorcars.' She had given up hope of seeing Avril, except as a vanishing bath sheet on the upper gallery at the top of the staircase. 'Well, I'll get back to my own kitchen. A lot of baking to be done.' Her voice dropped appropriately. 'It's my cousin's funeral, tomorrow.' She paused at the door to say, 'Now don't you start worrying, Herr Grant. Ernst will keep a lookout for any strangers wandering up this way. By Monday, they'll all be gone, every one of them. We'll have Grünau back to ourselves again.'

I might be in a New England village, he thought: the same words, the same tone of relief when the summer tourists had departed, God rest their emptied wallets. Monday in Grünau won't come quickly enough for me.

'I am starved,' Avril said behind him. He turned from the window to see a slender girl in a dark green costume, red facings at the collar and cuffs, a white shirt and a red tie.

'How's your hand?' She had left off the bandage, he noticed.

'Healing. What about me?'

'Terrific. A trifle businesslike though.'

'Ladylike is the Austrian word. Colourful but restrained. It was this or a choice of long-skirted dirndls, heavenly things, silk and velvet, and brocaded aprons. Probably been in the family for a hundred years. Who owns my borrowed clothes?'

'Fischer's sister.'

'Slightly larger than I am, but not a bad fit. I'd rather

be loose than bulging like a sausage casing.' She looked down at the suit, decided she'd buy one when she got back to Vienna. She tapped her feet lightly, broke into a brief dance step.

He noticed the sandals, tights, too. 'So you found them.'

'Of course I did. I'm a detecativ, aren't I? Sort of, at least.' She laughed as she repeated the word. 'Detecativ – my six-year-old niece's word. I rather like it.' She was over at the table inspecting the cold cuts and the salad, considering the rolls and butter, hesitating with the eggs. 'I'll have everything,' she decided. 'But first, some coffee and orange juice.' She saw him watching her with a smile. 'That's better. You were much too serious, looking out of that window. Was Frau Whosis difficult?'

'Lackner.'

'Frau Lackner, then?'

'She's okay.'

'Sorry I left you to do the talking. I was rather scared to face her, actually.'

'Why?'

'How do I explain why I'm here? I hate lying to old ladies.'

'Old? She's middle-aged, no more than fifty.'

'With all those marrying children?'

'Country folk know how to live.' Grant found a bowl, searched for an egg-beater. 'I'll cook the omelette. Or what about scrambled?'

'You're the chef.' She leaned up and kissed him. 'Oh, Colin, my heart is bursting with joy.'

'And your stomach's hollow. You've had one cup of soup and half a sandwich since yesterday's breakfast.'

As if we've been doing this for ever and ever, Avril thought happily as they got their meal together. It didn't take long to cook or eat. By one o'clock, they were sitting across the kitchen table from one another, drinking a final cup of coffee.

'Why,' Avril asked, 'were you so worried, Colin? Over there.' She nodded to the window where he had been watching Frau Lackner take a short-cut down through the woods. So many trails, he had thought: they criss-crossed the fields, they vanished among trees. 'Colin – now you're plunged in gloom again. Bad news?'

'No. Fischer is coming up here.'

'Why?'

He grinned. 'Just to see whether we are tearing the place apart.'

'Come on, now.'

'He feels responsible for our safety, I think.'

'How much does he know?' Her face was as serious as his.

'He's been tapped to give evidence about the sale of a Ruysdael reproduction. Also, he heard a radio report about a bombing at the Majestic. Room 307.'

'When?' Her eyes widened in alarm.

'Midnight.'

'Oh, Colin!'

'I have to thank you for getting kidnapped,' he said lightly, 'and making sure I'd be in your arms a hundred miles away.'

'Not so funny. Who made sure of whose arms, anyway?' She took his hand. 'The bomb – was that Gene Marck's idea?'

'He made the midnight appointment with me to be in my room. But Mandel, Bernard Mandel of the Two Crowns, Frank's special target – yes, I think he co-operated fully.'

'How—'

'Don't know the details as yet. I hope Bob Renwick sends up a newspaper along with our luggage.' We have to expect its arrival, too, as well as Fischer's. And the

Lackner clan dotting in and out with food and encouraging words. 'You know what? I think our afternoon is shot to hell.' Nothing ever went as you hoped. Except Avril. He tightened his grip on her hand. 'Like some fresh air? There's a terrace on the other side of the house. We can wait for the expected invasions there.'

'And talk. There are still some things I don't know about yesterday. For instance, you mentioned an appointment with Marck, and I was bewildered. You didn't tell me about that. When did he make it?'

'After the auction. I didn't think it was important.'

Everything about you is important to me, she thought. She rose and began clearing the table. 'I left the upstairs presentable – bed made, everything back in place. We'll keep Frau Lackner happy by leaving no dish unwashed. Perhaps she'll accept me if she thinks I'm housebroken. Don't laugh, Colin. That's important. Keeps the peace between women. Has she found a reason why we should be here?' Avril handed him a washed plate and a dishcloth with a smile. 'And that's something else about women: they always need a reason.'

'Fischer gave her a lulu. I'm a reporter in some danger of reprisals. She has taken that one stage further, thinks you are my girl Friday.'

'You know, that's true in a way,' Avril said in surprise. 'Comic, isn't it?'

'It won't be so funny when I start trying to explain to Fischer why I brought you here.'

'Of course,' she said softly, 'he would want to know. He's one of those sweet men, the protective type.' She looked up. 'You too, darling. That's one of the reasons I love you.' As he stood watching her, she went on, 'Let me count the ways . . .' She didn't finish the quotation. He had taken her in his arms again.

They heard a clatter of footsteps on the brick wall outside the back entrance, a girl's voice calling excitedly.

They drew apart. Grant opened the door and the girl – a younger, much thinner version of Frau Lackner – with cheeks flaming and breath panting, halted her wild run as she burst into the kitchen. Grant stood helpless: the girl's words were coming out at such a speed that it was impossible to understand her. But Avril's German was excellent. Of course, he thought, a translator at the Embassy: that was no feeble cover story. 'I think,' Avril was saying as the girl ended her quick recital, 'she's telling us that her brother Peter is stationed down at the bridge and has stopped two cars. The men in them say they are our friends. One of them calls himself Bush. Sends his greetings to Sweetheart. Peter wants to know if they are okay.'

'Bush is Bob Renwick?'

'Himself, no less. Bright-eyed and bushy-tailed. That's how he got this name.' In the long-ago years, she thought, something to do with his college days and track record. She had never quite understood the phrase.

Grant was saying, 'Anna, tell Peter they are our friends.'

'Minna,' said the girl. 'I'm Minna.' Avril fascinated her. She had studied every detail, from hair style to high-heeled sandals, as Avril translated.

'Tell Peter,' Grant repeated urgently. 'Many thanks, Minna.'

Minna stepped out of doors, put her hands to cup her lips and gave a long clear call. From below the woods came a piercing whistle.

'Message received?' Avril asked with a smile. Minna nodded, stood just outside the threshold, still lost in study of the stranger. '*Auf Wiedersehen. Und vielen Dank.*' Minna took the hint regretfully, began walking to the short-cut that had brought her up here in four minutes flat.

'What did I tell you?' Grant said. 'Our afternoon is shot to hell.'

329

26

The first car was dark blue and impressive with two
quietly dressed men in the rear seat and its chauffeur –
navy jacket, hard-brimmed cap, large anti-glare glasses
– intent on parking neatly beside the Citroën. On its tail
came a svelte black Thunderbird with one occupant;
scanty fair hair, glasses and – when he stepped out of
the car – thin and tall. He was in tweeds and carried a
briefcase.

Avril said, 'That's Prescott Taylor! From the Embassy.'

'The one whose speciality is defectors?' Grant was
amused. The formal briefcase was hardly the correct
accessory for the country-style suit.

'Other things, too – such as handling Victor Basset.'

'Where's Bob Renwick?'

'That's his Thunderbird definitely.' She was per-
plexed. Then, nudging Grant gently, she began to smile
as the chauffeur, a newspaper tucked under an arm,
followed the others towards the house. The smaller of
the two strangers, their dark suits beginning to look like
a restrained uniform, was in charge of a black case,
handling it with care. His companion, matching Prescott
Taylor's height, had a leather envelope in his hand.

'An official visit?' Grant had time to suggest. Important too. Renwick wouldn't have driven from Vienna
disguised as a chauffeur for his own amusement.

'Could be.' Avril retreated into the room and Grant,
after a moment of surprise, joined her. So we meet our
visitors indoors and away from curious eyes, he
thought, even from friendly eyes. Avril hurried into the

kitchen to lock its door. She was back beside him before Taylor made the introductions. They were brief, discreet: Assistant Director Schwartz from the State Prosecutor's office, who placed the small black case on a table before he bowed and shook hands; Commissioner Seydlitz, State Security, Criminal Division, and looking – at close hand – more like a benevolent Herr Professor of Criminal Law about to examine a doctoral candidate. Then the two Austrians and Taylor, professing an interest in this astounding room, drew close to the central hearth. By prearrangement, thought Grant as Renwick was left alone with him and Avril.

'Got your hair cut, too,' Grant observed. 'What you fellows won't sacrifice for the sake of your art.'

Renwick wasn't in a joking mood. 'Avril, go and join the nice gentlemen. How's your wrist?'

'Merely a reminder not to make any more foolish mistakes.'

She had been watching Renwick nervously, wondering what reason had brought him here. Was their mission over, successfully? Was it a failure, and through her fault? Or, she thought, could he be sending me away, dismissing me for good? She turned on her heel, made her way towards the fireplace.

Grant was startled. *Any more foolish mistakes?* Surely she had made her choice – last night she had made the choice, hadn't she? This assignment was her last, and it was over as far as she was concerned. Or had she assumed too much?

For a brief second, Renwick studied Grant's face. He said, 'I'm leaving immediately. Just came to make sure this place was safe for another night.'

Grant looked at him sharply. Renwick didn't explain, went on, 'How did you get the local talent organized? Simple idea, but good.' He smiled, remembering the roadblock down at the bridge, the tractor stuck in the

331

middle of the narrow trail up to Fischer's house, and a husky young farmer with his sister beside him acting dumb until Renwick had got out of the car and talked with him. At a nod from her brother, the girl had taken off like a bullet, disappeared into a wood at the back of the farmhouse. Five minutes later, her call had ended all obstructions. Young farmer friendly, four city slickers regaining their cool.

'Not my idea. Fischer's.'

'When did he get into the act?'

'This morning. Put one and one together: my interest in the sale of a Ruysdael reproduction, plus the blast at the Majestic last night.'

'Ah – you know about that.'

'Bare details only.

Renwick indicated the newspaper lying beside his jacket. 'There's not much else known. Seydlitz—' he glanced towards the tall Viennese – 'is interested in the fact that Marck had made an appointment with you for midnight. I didn't tell him more than that, left the rest for you to explain. Any further thoughts on the matter?'

'The bomb could have been disguised as a present from Mandel to Max Seldov, his brother-in-law.'

'Mandel,' Renwick said thoughtfully. 'Careful how you deal with him. And for God's sake, don't mention *Waldheim*. In your deposition, keep strictly to the Ruysdael events – from Victor Basset and Lois Westerbrook to Marck, Mittendorf and the Klar couple. Nothing, but not one word, about Avril's kidnapping. Not one mention of Frank or of Israeli Intelligence. Or about our stopover at the Rasthaus. Got that?'

Grant nodded and looked pointedly at the black case, 'Deposition? That sounds as if you all expected a sudden end for your chief witness.'

'A matter of your convenience,' Renwick said quickly. 'Can't keep you hanging around Austria for the various trials to come up. We had a conference on that this morning, and decided you could leave if the prosecutor had your sworn statement. That's why I had to bust your security here, lead them to you.'

'Avril – how did you explain her?'

'I told them she's my contact – keeping an eye on your safety.'

No more she is, thought Grant, that day is over. 'You blew her cover?' Suits me, too; makes her separation from Renwick more likely.

'Well, there isn't much more for us to do in Vienna. That's the way it goes: you work like hell, produce results, and then the whole investigation is no longer yours. Vienna and Geneva and Brussels take over, and you find yourself in a back seat. An empty feeling. The only consolation is that there are plenty of other jobs to be done. There's no dearth of terrorists. Prepare yourself for some more murders and hijackings; newspapers won't offer pretty reading in the next few months.'

'At least you did end one source of money. No more subsidies from Henri Bienvenue's account.'

'A million and a half dollars have already been paid out,' Renwick said grimly. 'But we'll follow up on the payees, track them right to the end of the line.'

Grant's dismay was evident. 'Then there's little left in—'

'Enough. The Swiss tell us there's still five and a half million, give or take a couple of thousand.'

'Good God!'

'Yes,' said Renwick sombrely. 'Gene Marck is quite an accountant.'

'No sign of him?'

'Not so far. The police found Lois Westerbrook, however. In a sleazy little hotel over in the Prater district.'

'Dead?'

'Overdose of heroin.'

'She didn't use—'

'I know. And you know it. But most people will believe it.'

'No clues who took her there?'

'To that joint? Pay as you enter, stay out of sight, do your own thing? The slob who runs the place couldn't care less.' Renwick became businesslike again. 'Your luggage is in the Mercedes: Avril's belongings are packed and ready to go in the Thunderbird.'

Ready to go? Grant didn't like the sound of that phrase.

'Well – that's about all,' Renwick said, 'Except for a check on those people at the farmhouse. How much do they know?'

'Only enough to be wary of strangers who come asking for Herr Fischer's house.'

'They did that all right. One at the tractor blocking the road, another big fellow coming out of the barn – with a pitchfork. And the girl, of course. Any more of them?'

'Four men working on the high meadow – that's up the hill behind the house. They're the Lackner family: mostly about to be married, so they'll have some future in-laws, too, if needed.' He thought over that, then said, 'If needed? What the hell am I talking about? Marck has never heard of Grünau.'

Renwick's silence was marked.

'Sending me a warning?' So that's the chief reason that brought him here, Grant thought. 'Okay, spell it out.'

Renwick's hesitation ended. 'I don't think Marck knows where you actually are. He does know by this time that Avril is with you. Also about the Rasthaus Winkelman, and the road you took in a black Citroën. Also its plates. That's why I'll drive off in it, leave the Thunderbird for you. I hope to God he spends his

334

energies trying to track you down at the Traunsee. Yes, you were right about Braun.'

'Braun?'

From across the room Taylor's voice called urgently. 'Watch the time, Bob. You'll be late.'

Renwick said softly, 'Which means, watch their time. They're getting impatient, I think.'

'Braun?' repeated Grant. And last night I was sorry I ever mentioned the man's name, blamed it all on too much tension.

'On the way to Vienna, he asked a question he shouldn't have. Some party we must have had at *Waldheim* – what was it all about?' When we got to the Embassy, I kept him and Slevak hanging around for an hour before I gave them the evening off the chain. To play it safe, I had Braun followed, He telephoned from a public phone. After that, he went to a nice dark park, and met a nice quiet man, and had a nice long talk. When the stranger left, my agent decided he was the more important and switched to following him. Successfully to the Russian Embassy.'

'Are they in this?'

Renwick's laugh was brief and coarse. 'Oh dear me, no. How could anyone think such a thing!' He turned serious. 'They've no obvious connections with Marck or Mandel or Mittendorf – but they know what's going on. They drop useful tips or necessary information when there's a crisis situation. Marck's in one right now, up to his goddamned neck.'

Avril appeared at Renwick's elbow. 'Bob – it's quarter past two. You've a meeting, Prescott says, at half past four.'

Renwick reached for the chauffeur's coat and cap, added the tie and glasses with a grin. 'Give him these. Borrow his jacket.'

'He won't like it', she warned Renwick, but she left with the clothes bundled in her arms.

'Whatever Braun reported to his Soviet contact was passed on to Marck,' Grant said slowly. Suddenly his anger broke. 'Why the hell was Braun working with you? Wasn't he checked and double-checked?'

'He was a good agent, reliable and honest.' There was a note of real regret, of sadness in Renwick's voice. 'What turned him? Not money. Not ordinary blackmail – he had no sexual quirks, didn't use drugs.'

'Then how? His wife and baby?'

'Now a girl of seven. Yes, I think that's it. Two hostages to fortune. First comes a dangled promise: future release, safe arrival in the West. Later, to get full co-operation out of him, there will be threats. A bad deal.'

Avril was back, the blue Harris tweed safely in hand. 'He didn't like it. But who could refuse you?'

Renwick drew on Taylor's jacket, too long in the sleeves and skirt. 'I promise him I won't wear it into the Embassy. I only need it for the next ten minutes anyway. Well – goodbye, Colin. Take care of my car, will you? Hey, what about the Citroën's keys? Thank you.' Renwick slipped them into his pocket, his eyes on Avril. 'And *you* take care of yourself, Sweetheart. See you in Paris. Taylor will give you all the details – they're in his briefcase.' With a wave across the room to the others and a cheerful '*Auf Wiedersehen*,' Renwick left.

Grant faced her. 'Avril, why didn't you tell—'

'Darling, I've promised to make sandwiches and coffee.'

'Why didn't you tell him you won't be in Paris?'

'He didn't give me time, did he?' She was on her way to the kitchen. Taylor and the two Austrians had everything ready for the deposition. Grant gave up, went over

336

to the recording machine, sat down, and collected his thoughts.

'It's really quite simple,' Taylor was saying. 'Your name, address, place of business. Then you can begin your statement of facts about your first encounter with Gene Marck in New York.'

'With Lois Westerbrook. She approached me first about this visit to Vienna.'

'Good. With Lois Westerbrook. I think we can start now. Okay?'

With Lois Westerbrook – Grant's thoughts switched from a sleazy hotel, a contorted body left lying in some filthy room, to an elegant blonde, fastidious and beautiful, full of charm and grace. And of guile. Strangely, as if he were standing apart from the little group around the coffee table, he listened to his cool voice giving his name and address, his place of business; he even added his position there, and a quick summary of his qualifications. He paused, making sure of the sequence of events, cleared his throat and began. 'On 9th July, 1977, I was at the Schofeld Galleries, attending a Dali exhibition, when Lois Westerbrook . . .'

'Excellent!' Prescott Taylor said as Grant ended his statement. And then, trying to disguise his incredible relief, he reverted to the diplomat. 'Don't you think?' he asked Schwartz and Seydlitz.

'Succinct,' Schwartz agreed. 'Of course, there are one or two questions that should be added. Would you be so good as to answer them, Herr Grant?' The lawyer's eyes were friendly, wide and innocent. He was young, no more than forty, but obviously competent under his shield of politeness.

'Ask them,' said Grant. As he had guessed, the first question dealt with Renwick.

'You mentioned that Herr Renwick had warned you to be on your guard? When and how?'

'As soon as I arrived in Vienna. He sent Miss Hoffman to talk with me.'

'Was that when you started being suspicious of Westerbrook and Marck?'

'Not exactly. I was beginning to have some doubts of my own. Renwick's warning reinforced them, and they turned into suspicion. The events at the Klar Auction Rooms confirmed them.' He paused and added, 'Without that warning, you wouldn't have had a witness here today.' He pointed to the machine, still registering every word. 'No witness, no testimony.'

'Do you think the explosion in your room at the Majestic was an attempt to eliminate you as a witness?'

'Yes. Marck told me to meet him there at midnight.'

'Were you expecting a gift from anyone? The chambermaid coming in to remove the bed cover, noticed a small package.'

'Beside the telephone?' Grant was smiling. 'And I was to answer it at midnight? Marck's an ingenious fellow.'

Schwartz and Seydlitz exchanged a quick glance. Seydlitz nodded his assent, and Schwartz continued. 'The chambermaid says there was a piece of paper slipped under the ribbon on the package. She admits she looked at it. She saw some English words followed by $30. Have you any idea of what that could mean?'

'A description of contents, value thirty dollars. For Customs examination in New York.' Grant shook his head: good old Bernie had a black sense of humour. How he had enjoyed writing the innocent inscription – or getting some stooge to write it. (Safety first: the note could be intercepted.)

'Could you explain that?'

'Certainly.' He gave a brief account of his visit to Bernard Mandel. Too bad that I'm butting into Frank's investigation, he thought as he ended, but what else was to be done? You don't start concealing evidence to let Mandel off the hook.

'So you believe Mandel is connected with Marck?'

They've got me, he thought now. I was too damned clever. He said evenly. 'All I know is that Marck arranged a meeting in my room. All I know is that Mandel wanted me to take a gift for his brother-in-law through New York Customs. I agreed, if he'd mark contents and value on the package.'

'What makes you so sure that the package in your room was Mandel's gift?'

'No one else was sending me gifts.' That sounded weak, and it was. He countered with a wry smile. 'Too bad the chambermaid doesn't read English. She might be able to bear me out.' He suddenly remembered that chambermaid, like most of the employees at the Majestic, could at least speak some English. 'Doesn't she?' he asked, an eyebrow raised.

Schwartz, the lawyer, only looked at him quizzically. Schwartz, the man, broke into a smile. 'She does.'

Seydlitz was much amused. In his genial way, he added one more question. 'Have you heard of the death of the woman, Westerbrook?'

'Yes, I heard about that.' Now take care, Grant warned himself: no more bright suggestions.

'Did she use drugs?'

'Not that I know of.'

'Her arm showed many punctures. Did you never notice them?'

'No.'

'She always wore dresses with sleeves?'

'Except in Arizona. That was three years ago, of course.'

'Did her manner suggest drugs to you?'

'No. She was extremely capable and competent. Didn't drink, except for a glass of white wine.'

'When did she last talk with you?'

'On Thursday night. Late. She telephoned. She was – well, I thought hysterical. Almost incoherent. With anger. She had broken with Gene Marck. She wanted me to put her in touch with my friends. She was convinced, I think, that I was an American agent.'

'Have you ever been connected with American Intelligence?'

'Never.'

'Thank you, Herr Grant.'

But Schwartz had his own line of questioning to follow. 'Why did she want to get in touch with American Intelligence?'

'To tell them about Marck, I gathered. She talked of talcum tins and hairbrushes and lighters that could come apart. Tricks of the trade, I think she said. Something like that. It made little sense to me.'

At the mention of talcum tins and hairbrushes, Schwartz and Seydlitz again exchanged glances. No nods, this time. An investigation in progress? Grant wondered. Schwartz quickly changed the subject. 'Why did you come to Grünau, Herr Grant?'

'It seemed the safest thing to do. Once the Ruysdael was delivered to Victor Basset, I thought I'd better drop out of sight for a few days – until Commissioner Seydlitz has Marck safe in custody.'

'And Fraülein Hoffman? Why is she here? Was her safety threatened?'

'It could have been. She was seen with me at Klar's Auction Rooms. She had come to give me a last warning. About Mittendorf. A very necessary one. I had no suspicions about him at all. He was just an honest, dependable, but basically stupid man – so I thought. An easy mark, like me.'

'Not so easy, Herr Grant,' Schwartz said very quietly. 'Do you swear that this testimony, along with the answers you've given to our questions, is true? Please state the place and time of this interview. And the date.'

Grant did so. The recording machine was switched off, firmly closed.

'You'll receive transcriptions, of course,' Schwartz said. 'Sign them and return them to us. From New York, I suppose? If there is any change in your address, you will let us know immediately.'

'I'll do that.' There was a general handshaking, a feeling of something accomplished, a slow and friendly progress towards the door.

Suddenly, Prescott Taylor halted. 'The luggage!' he said with a laugh. 'If you don't mind waiting another two minutes,' he suggested to the Austrians, 'Grant and I can get the suitcases moved. I think it's wiser if you both stay out of sight as much as possible, don't you? It's really much more comfortable by the fire.' He beckoned to Grant and Avril, too, and hurried them towards the cars. His briefcase was firmly in his hand.

Once they were free of the house, Taylor said, 'Okay. You did fine, Grant. Several patches of thin ice but you skated over the top. Now for Renwick's instructions. He wants you out of Grünau by tomorrow morning. *Early* tomorrow morning. You'll drive to a small town near Salzburg where Slevak will be waiting for you. Route and name of town are all in here.' The briefcase was swung on to the top of the Mercedes' boot, quickly opened. 'All in here,' he repeated, bringing out an envelope and presenting it to Avril. 'Map's inside. Distances worked out. Time schedules, also.' He drew out two smaller envelopes. 'Avril, this one has your passport, et cetera, as well as your train ticket from Salzburg to Paris. Slevak will see you safely on board. Grant – you'll drive on to the Salzburg airport once you've dropped Avril at the designated place. This is your envelope: Austrian Airlines from Salzburg to

Zürich to New York by TWA; everything booked. First class space, courtesy of Victor Basset. Also his cheque for extra expenses – old Basset was firm about that. And a note in his own handwriting, believe it or not. He was as mad as hell at not having a talk with you.' Taylor closed his briefcase, heaved it inside the Mercedes, unlocked the boot. 'Let's get a move on, shall we? Avril, here are the Thunderbird keys – open it up. Start hauling.'

The Mercedes left, with Taylor now at the wheel. Perhaps it was the success of the visit, or his relief that all his forebodings had proved imaginary, but his mood was a smiling one even under the chauffeur's cap. The jacket fitted him better than it had Renwick. Dutifully, he wore the narrow black tie and donned the heavy dark glasses. 'What drives in, must drive out,' he said philosophically. In a month or two, this would all make an amusing story over a double martini.

Grant watched the Mercedes move gently out of sight. Then he turned on his heel, strode into the room, halted abruptly before Avril. His anger exploded. He drew out the envelope with his tickets, glared at it. 'Renwick says jump and we all jump. Is that it?'

Avril was seated on the high curb around the hearth. She didn't look up, kept studying the contents of the larger envelope that Taylor had given her. All the details of tomorrow's journey were here. 'We'll have to leave at six in the morning. No later.'

'You're taking his marching orders?'

She raised her head, eyes widening. 'There must be a good reason for them.'

Grant's anger ebbed. Yes, he had to admit there was a very good reason for Renwick's orders: its name was Braun. He jammed the plane tickets in his pocket, quieted his voice. 'Everything's arranged and decided.

342

Just like that? He might have discussed it with us – broken the news gently. Slipping away, letting diplomat Taylor take over. Come to think of it, Taylor wasn't so damned diplomatic either.'

She covered her astonishment with a smile that widened slowly and then broke into laughter. 'Considering he had about three minutes to deliver and explain and get our luggage out of the boot, I think Prescott is a darned good diplomat. His right hand scarcely knew what his left was doing. Certainly neither Schwartz nor Seydlitz knew. Quite amiable, weren't they?'

'They scared me stiff.'

'It didn't show. You were wonderful, darling.' She reached for his hand and coaxed him down beside her.

A damned uncomfortable seat for a man. 'Let's move over to the couch.'

'Just a minute—' She was gathering together the map and two small pages of closely typed instructions. 'We'll memorize these and then destruct.'

Abruptly he rose, saying, 'Do you have to use that jargon?'

'What's wrong with it? It's quicker than saying we'll burn Bob's instructions in this big beautiful fire.' Not so big now, she suddenly noticed. 'Do we put on another log?' Colin wasn't even listening.

'Why didn't you tell him? Tell him you are out?'

She stared at him.

'Resigning. As of last night.'

'Colin—'

'And what was all that about seeing you in Paris? You could have told him, right at that moment—'

'I had sandwiches to make.' Her voice was cold. 'An assistant prosecutor and a commissioner of police were waiting, growing impatient, possibly sharpening their questions. They were hungry and thirsty. Don't you

343

realize, Colin, how they had disrupted their day for your convenience?'

'Or to make sure they got my testimony. Better a live deposition than a dead witness.' He was sorry for his flippancy the moment after he had spoken. 'Forget that, Avril. Sure I know the idea behind the visit was to let me leave Austria as quickly as possible. It's just that—' He paused, weighed his words more carefully as the real reason for his anger surged out. 'Renwick has even booked you to Paris. You're going along with it?'

'Where else do I go? I live in Paris. I work there.'

'You work there?'

'When I'm not travelling around.'

'You are giving up that life. Last night—'

'I remember,' she said. She came over to where he stood near the couch. 'Let's sit and go over these instructions together.'

'Avril—' His worst fears were rising, swamping him. 'You can't have it both ways.'

Slowly, she sat down on the couch. 'I know.' She laid the map and sheets of paper carefully at her side, kept her hand on them as if to make sure they wouldn't slip away.

'Security?' he asked. His smile had little humour.

She ignored that. She repeated. 'I know. This time, I have made the choice. Last night wasn't just an affair, or a little romance between assignments. It was real, Colin. I love you.'

'And I love you.'

The words sounded strangely, spoken with a distance between them, no touch of hand, no movement towards each other. 'Two people who love and know so little about each other,' she said. 'Isn't that the difficulty now?'

'We'd learn about each other. We have years ahead of us to learn and keep on learning. But not if you are still

344

sharing your love, dividing it between me and—' He pointed to the instructions lying under her hand. 'It's me or Renwick,' he said, his mouth set. He turned and walked back to the fireplace.

'I'm not in love with him. I told you—'

'You're still in love with your job. He's part of it.'

'Colin – will you listen?' she asked, her voice sharpening.

'It didn't take us long to learn how to quarrel, did it?'

'It didn't take *you* long.' She drew a deep breath, calmed herself. 'Please, Colin – listen!' she pleaded. 'Look at it from my angle. Please. You don't just up and leave a job like mine. Believe it or not, people have spent a lot of their valuable time in training me. I have collected a lot in here—' she tapped her head – 'which I can't switch off, forget, pack away so that it's no good to anyone. The very least I can do when I'm bowing out is to pass on what I know to the agent who is replacing me. He or she won't find it in the files: just small details which I have gathered and stored in my own brain. Not of highest importance, I agree, but details that could be useful – at least a small help to others. As I was helped in the beginning.' At least, Colin was facing her now and listening honestly. No side thoughts of his own to distract his attention. 'Of course,' she went on, 'there are other ways to leave the service. You can get kicked out, which means you are untrustworthy – not a pleasant memory to live with. You can be given a leave of absence if you crack up or fall ill, an extended leave when necessary to let you down gently and prepare you for final separation. You can be moved into a less important area if you've made a forgivable mistake – a quiet demotion which can be remedied in time if you don't make any more mistakes. But you just don't up and out when one of your investigations is still in progress. It isn't over yet. It isn't, Colin.'

He said quietly, 'When does it end? Not with the Geneva account. Not with tracking down the people to whom cheques were paid out from that account. Not with tracing the money they passed on to others, perhaps to others beyond that. Until at last you reach the terrorist gangs, identify them, find their international link-up. It's a year's work. More than that. Even endless. For there will always be unexpected evidence cropping up, another defector with incredible information, always a new excitement.' He paused on that word. 'Yes, excitement. It makes life interesting, it makes you feel there is an urgency, an importance—' He broke off completely. Then he said, 'Avril, if you keep on with your job for even two months more, you'll be hooked permanently.'

'Nonsense, Colin.' Her voice had faltered. She tried to laugh. 'Darling, how can you believe that?'

'Because I'd be hooked.' He walked out of the room.

She didn't try to follow him. He's wrong, he's wrong, she kept repeating. Two months and I'll join him in New York. She replaced the map and papers in their envelope to take them upstairs and memorize while she changed out of borrowed clothes into her own. Memorize carefully. She'd have that little task all to herself. In his present mood, he would be likely to throw their schedule into the fire. Tomorrow morning, when they left at six, she could brief him on the route to take. Oh God, she thought in sudden anguish, I just pray he is wrong about all this. We'll be together. Two months, even three, we'll come together. And stay. For ever. And ever . . .

She rose and went over to her suitcase left lying with Colin's baggage near the front door. That was all her luggage except for the bag that contained cosmetics, toilet articles, and the little jewellery she owned. The rest of her belongings would be locked in a trunk and forwarded to Paris. Bob Renwick would make sure nothing was left behind. Whoever had packed the suitcase – probably one of the girls from the Embassy – had made a neat job of it, even tying the key securely to the handle. Avril's wool suit and blouse to match were right on top, along with her raincoat and flat-heeled shoes. All tactfully ready for her journey. She picked them out, along with a nightdress and some underthings. The suitcase could stay where it was. Bag in hand, clothes over an arm, the envelope of map and detailed instructions secure under the other (her passport, driver's licence, traveller's cheques, ready cash, train ticket were safe in the green jacket's pocket), she made her way across the room to the staircase. For a moment, she halted on the step where this morning Colin had met her, his arms outstretched. She began to weep.

At least, I didn't use tears as a weapon, she thought, as she brushed them away. Just words. And they were all true. Did he believe them? She dropped the bag and clothes and envelope beside the bed, threw herself on the white eiderdown cover, burying her face in its soft cloud to smother her anguish.

27

Once out of the front door, Grant came to an abrupt halt. He stood there, taking long deep breaths to steady himself. Then, as if on patrol, he walked around the house in order to calm his raw temper. There was nothing out here to worry over. Woods and fields were bathed in bright sunshine; no one in sight except Ernst and his boys still at work, raking off the last segment of meadow almost at the foot of the hill. They were within hailing distance, their faces now clearly discernible. One of them had seen him and spoken, for the four heads came up together, swivelling in his direction. They were alert all right. Grant gave a wave, Ernst responded, and four shoulders were bent once more over long wooden rakes.

Nothing out here to worry over, he repeated as he walked past the front door and stopped, this time on the terrace. Perhaps if I had brought Avril out here, approached the subject of Renwick and her job by stages, let this Bierstadt view give us some perspective – if, if, if . . . Damn me for a bloody fool, curse me for a blundering idiot. Yet, there was truth in what I said – the truth as I see it. What was there in Avril's words?

He sat down on the nearest chair, searched for his cigarettes, found he had left them on the table where Schwartz's recording angel had registered every syllable. He didn't rise and go indoors to find them. First, he'd make sure he was under control – too much tension had built up in the Schwartz-Seydlitz visit, perhaps. That was his excuse, a poor one, just admit he was all the more jealous of Renwick because he saw so much to like in the guy. Jealous of Renwick? Or was it of Avril's devotion to Renwick's job? She believes in what he is doing. It's important, it's necessary. What about my kind of work? Sure, I think it's important and necessary, although I can admit too – if I push myself hard enough – that art may soothe the soul and stimulate the mind but it doesn't save one life from terrorists' bombs or bullets.

For ten minutes or more, he watched the valley stretch out below him to the west, noted that the road was now alive with cars scudding along towards Grünau on their afternoon outings. He let his eyes range up over the hills to rest on the far mountain peaks. I should have brought Avril out here, he thought. Then it would have been easier to tell her that I was wrong. Wrong in my whole approach. My God, what would I have said if she had told me I must give up my job? What if she had been the kind of girl who'd never set foot in a museum unless she was dragged there? Was colour-blind or had no conception of line and composition? Some people were like that, just as others were tone-deaf and found music a pain in their ear. She might have hated New York and Washington, never wanted to live there. Change is good, why remain stuck with your paintings and your statues, how far have they got you? she would have asked – if she were that kind of girl. What would have been my reaction? Shock complete. And I'd have damned well put up an argument.

Okay, chauvinist, get inside and tell her you were wrong. Meet her half-way. He rose and started back towards the door.

From the trees in front of the house, a girl in a trim dirndl emerged, loaded down with two baskets. She was obviously one of the Lackner brood, an older version of Minna, younger one of her mother. *'Grüss Gott!'*

'Grüss Gott! You are Anna?' He took the heavy baskets of foodstuff in spite of her protests. Chauvinist? This was one aspect of male chauvinism he'd defend to the last.

'Ada. Anna is busy. Brigitte will be here, too. Herr Fischer is coming for dinner.'

And arriving soon, he realized as he glanced at his watch. It was about four o'clock. Quickly, he steered Ada through the front entrance, explaining that the kitchen door was probably still locked – had seemed safer when no one was in that wing of the house – and, by the way, was the path she had used the quickest route down to the farm? Only four minutes if you weren't carrying baskets? Why, he had taken just about four minutes to get up that hill by car last night. Much laughter from Ada, and a shriek of thanks following him after he dumped the baskets on the kitchen table and hurried back to the big room. Avril had been there, over at the desk, telephoning.

His heart rose again as he saw she was still there. She turned to face him with a smile. 'Darling,' he said, I'm sorry. Forgive—'

'For you, Colin.' She put the receiver in his hand. 'From Helmut Fischer. It's urgent.'

'Something wrong?' he asked softly.

'Didn't tell me much. You find out what it is.'

Fischer was definitely disturbed. He was still in Salzburg, delayed by a very long interview over a luncheon table with his friend from the Prosecutor's office. He would be late in arriving, perhaps wouldn't reach Grünau until seven o'clock. He had explained this to Fräulein Hoffman – what a charming girl she was, wholly delightful.

'Yes, she's all that,' Grant said, watching Avril as she

walked over to the couch. She had changed into her own clothes. Her hair gleamed with brushing, her complexion perfect, her figure remarkable: jacket just short enough to show the wool skirt smooth over slender hips. She was wearing flat-heeled shoes, neat and small – were they meant to be sensible? – letting her move with sureness and grace. 'Yes?' he had to ask Fischer. 'Sorry – I didn't quite hear you.'

Fischer was spending the night with them.

'No need. Everything is under control,' Grant told him. 'Besides, you have a concert to attend.'

But Fischer was firm about spending the night. Also, totally decided about sending Miss Hoffman down to the Lackner farm. He had already telephoned Frau Lackner and she would find a bed for Miss Hoffman once dinner was over. He would explain his reasons when he saw Grant.

'Better explain them now,' Grant said, suddenly brusque.

'Too long.'

'Please,' urgent Grant. 'Or do you want an ulcer case on your hands?'

'My dear fellow—' Fischer sighed, then plunged into his story. 'Valid, don't you think?' he asked as he ended it.

'Yes,' Grant said. 'Valid.'

'I'm just about to leave, so expect me around seven. We'll dine at once. *Auf Wiedersehen!*'

Slowly, Grant replaced the receiver.

'What is it, Colin?' Avril was beside him, her dark eyes wide with questions. The length of Fischer's call had been ominous.

'He will be here around seven. We have dinner immediately.'

That wasn't all, she saw by his face. She reached up

351

to kiss him, tried a small joke to stop him looking so grimly serious.

'It looks as if you were right: now our evening is shot to hell.'

'The night, too.' He put his arms around her, held her close, saying, 'I was wrong, darling. A foul-tempered oaf – I'm sorry. One thing I've decided: I'm not being shipped out to New York. I'm taking the train with you – I'll see you safe all the way to Paris.'

She stared at him.

'I won't break security,' he said, almost smiling. 'We'll have time to talk; we'll work things out.'

Mischief gleamed in her eyes. 'Your way or mine?'

'A little of both. Fifty-fifty decision. Agreed?'

'Agreed.' She kissed him again. 'We could even start working things out tonight. It needn't be lost just because Fischer is here.'

'You are sleeping down at the Lackner farm. It's all arranged.'

'What?' She recovered quickly. 'Isn't he fussing too much?'

'He thinks there are valid reasons.'

Valid – that word again. 'All right, tell me—'

With his arm around her waist, they started pacing slowly around the room. Fischer's story began with a call from Leni that had reached him on his return from lunch. It was the third she had made since one o'clock. She was overwhelmed with anxiety. A strange incident that morning; she now felt something was wrong. Perhaps thieves planning a robbery? Seemingly, in the shop, just before noon, a pleasant middle-aged woman, Elsa Kramer she called herself, had made a timid visit. She was sorry not to see Herr Fischer, but perhaps his assistant could help her? She was a cook who had worked temporarily for Herr Fischer's friends the Berensons, and she had heard from Frau Berenson – who

352

would give her an excellent reference – that Herr Fischer needed a cook-housekeeper for his place in the country. She didn't like the city, she came from Linz originally. She had a married daughter in Vienna and three grand-children, and wanted to be able to visit them twice a month if possible. Was Herr Fischer's place too far off for that? Her voice was soft and apologetic, her manner so correct that Leni felt sorry for her.

It might be, Leni had said, unless she had a small car of her own. There were no trains or buses running from Grünau. She had often advised Herr Fischer to have a permanent cook instead of relying on local help, some-one to live in. The woman had interrupted her, but sadly, saying she had no car of her own, it was too bad; Herr Fischer, when he came to dinner last week at the Berensons', had enjoyed her cooking. She left, just as a repair man arrived. Something about Leni's telephone not working properly. Leni was so frustrated – it was noon, and she still had to close up shop – that she almost forgot about Elsa Kramer until she reached home. She began to worry; she couldn't recall if Herr Fischer had actually visited the Berensons last week. So she had telephoned the Berenson villa and found they had been out of town all July. The caretaker-in-charge had said there never had been any temporary cook employed by Frau Berenson. No one called Kramer, in fact, for the last thirty years. He could vouch for that.

'So there it is,' Grant ended. 'Grünau uncovered.'

There was a long silence.

'How much does Fischer actually know?' Avril asked.

'About you? Nothing. He must have learned more today about the Ruysdael and the Klars and me – he was lunching with a friend from the Prosecutor's office.' Being interviewed, Fischer had said; if Grant knew anything about Fischer, he'd do a lot of interviewing himself in his own ingenious way.

'Then why, if he knows nothing about me, is he sending me down to—' Avril cut herself off. 'How stupid can I get? He expects trouble. He doesn't want any women around.' She managed a smile. 'Most gallant. I rather like that.' How very old-fashioned and darling, she thought. 'Well, I'll tell the girls in the kitchen to have dinner ready for seven o'clock, and warn them they'll have to serve it quickly. I expect Helmut wants all of us females out of the house by dark.' She looked at Grant. 'Is that when you expect something to happen?'

Her calm voice reassured him. The memories of yesterday must have begun to fade, thank God. 'Night is always good for an assault. If one is being planned,' he added, keeping his own voice casual. 'I still think Marck will wait for us at Annaberg.'

'Oh, Colin – take care.' Her control slipped. There was fear in her eyes. 'You'd better carry that automatic – the one Bob gave me.'

'No. You keep it. I'll borrow something from Fischer. Frankly, I don't think it will come to that. Too many Lackners patrolling around when night sets in. Have you seen them? They're a lusty crew, not one under six foot and shoulders like a barn door.'

She looked reassured. 'I haven't seen much around here,' she reminded him.

'Deal with Ada and Brigitte, and I'll clear our luggage out of the way. Then we'll take a tour of inspection – as far as the terrace. Only the Lackners know we are here. Better not show ourselves to the rest of the village.' Only the Lackners know, he thought as he started carrying cases and bags upstairs; and Gene Marck.

It took him two journeys to the guest-room, with Gene Marck on his mind every step of the way, before he had cleared all luggage from blocking the front entrance. By that time Avril was waiting for him at the door. She had opened it wide, breathed in the pure fresh air, said delightedly, 'What a wonderful smell from those firs! Come on, Colin. Show me the sights.' A few steps outside, she halted and looked at the trees where Colin had parked the Citroën last night. By daylight, so innocent and peaceful. She shook her head in disbelief over that strange attack of fright – or nerves, or hysteria? – that had almost paralysed her in the darkness.

'Yes,' Colin said, as if he had heard her thoughts, 'it all looks very different on a sunny afternoon.'

'No, it's the same. I am different.' And she laughed, taking his hand as they strolled towards the western terrace. 'Let's get business over,' she said, 'before we start thinking about us.' We get so easily sidetracked, she thought.

'Have you got Renwick's instructions with you?' He was both surprised and dismayed. 'They aren't necessary now. I'll get you to Paris—'

'Do you know the best route from here to Salzburg?'

'I can read a map.'

'But everything is worked out for us. Tomorrow is crowded on the highways.'

Yes, Sunday was a bad day for travel. 'All right, let's see his suggestions.'

'I've burned them.'

'What?' That delighted him.

'After some memorizing,' she said with a smile.

His own smile faded. 'Okay, okay. Let's sit down and hear them.'

'Only the main points, now. We leave here no later than six in the morning. From Annaberg we travel south—'

'North, surely! That will get us on the Autobahn and a quick—'

'We avoid the big motorways. We'll keep to less

travelled roads once we continue on the Annaberg highway north to Mariazell. From there we branch off to the west by the Gesäuse – a long, wild and lovely glen. It has no villages, little traffic – tourists hardly know it – plenty of scenery to keep us awake. Then Admont, Liezen and Bad Ischl. That's where Slevak will be waiting for me. Got all that, Colin? I'd like your memory in on this, too.'

He nodded. 'Got it. Except you don't leave with Slevak. You'll tell him to clear out. You'll stay with me.'

'No, really, it's *much* safer if we divide at Bad Ischl before we reach Salzburg. Not be seen together. Gene Marck could have alerted a watch at all airports and major railway stations, and Salzburg has—'

'Those were Renwick's thoughts yesterday,' Grant objected. 'It's a different set-up today. He doesn't know Marck has found Grünau. My bet is that Marck will either appear here tonight under cover of darkness, or wait for us at Annaberg. That's our one exit from here.'

'I'd better phone Bob.'

'It *isn't!*' Grant exclaimed, suddenly smiling.

'Isn't what?'

'Our only exit.' Quickly, he rose and pulled her on to her feet, urged her around the corner of the house, and pointed in the direction of the road, hidden by trees, that had brought them from the Lackner farm last night. 'It goes on, uphill and over; then down to join the main highway at Josefsberg. It's miles away from Annaberg.'

'Are you sure?' She laughed. 'You've really been doing your homework.'

'Oh, just a few questions here and there.' But he was delighted with the effect he had produced. How's that, Renwick?

'All the same, I'll phone Bob. He has to be told about Marck.'

'Okay,' he said, mustering some good grace. Then he grinned. 'How will you talk – in voice code?'

That sent her smiling into the house.

He went back to sit on the terrace, and as he waited he pulled out the envelope that Prescott Taylor had given him. Air space to New York via Zürich, all neat and nicely connected. The hell with them. He wasn't under orders to Renwick. Paris was where he was headed. For how long? The cheque he found in the envelope answered that nicely; for a couple of weeks and plane tickets for two. The amount was generous, more than generous. Victor Basset had really come through. Five thousand dollars. 'For additional expenses and personal losses,' someone had written on a slip of paper attached to the cheque. A one-liner was added in a different script: 'This should cover the cost of a necktie. B.R.' Renwick – and Grant had to smile. Dammit, I *like* that guy, he thought. Finally he opened the small sealed envelope that had also been enclosed. 'In Basset's own handwriting,' Taylor had said, amazement mixed with a touch of awe.

Indeed, the letter was handwritten without the benefit of secretary. A gesture? Yes, Grant conceded. He responded by reading it instead of jamming it back in his pocket. First came thanks, many thanks. Then disappointment at not having been able to talk with Grant himself. Next, his deepest regrets for having endangered Grant and immersed him in a 'perilous mission about which I knew so little. Please accept my sincere apologies.'

Apologies from Victor Basset? Grant raised an eyebrow and went on to the last paragraph of the letter. 'I would like to see the Basset Hill Museum controlled by a man of taste, judgment and decision. Recent events have convinced me that you are the best candidate for that job.'

Oh no, that's too much, thought Grant. Taste, judgment, decision? Embarrassed, yet pleased, he read on. 'I have heard of your objections to three of the paintings that will be exhibited. I agree with you, now that I have learned about the methods employed in bringing them to auction. The original owners have disappeared. My old friend, Ferenc Ady, is reported dead. I shall try to trace any legitimate heirs, residing outside the Communist bloc, to whom the pictures can be returned. In the meantime – for the search may be long or non-productive – I shall have a plaque placed under the Ruysdael stating *On Loan from Ferenc Ady*. The same procedures will be taken with the Monet and the Degas. In conclusion, I would like to have the pleasure of meeting you to talk over my proposals. I shall be in Washington for the next three weeks, completing the final arrangements for Basset Hill. After that, I bow out, and leave it to the new Director to make it the best museum of its kind in our country. Please call me at your convenience. Sincerely, Victor Basset.'

Well, thought Grant, well . . . Victor Basset, who prided himself on never exhibiting a picture *On Loan*. Never a borrower or a lender be. That was Basset.

Avril said, 'You look as if someone had just struck a neat karate chop right there.' She touched the side of his neck.

'Sorry,' he said rising in haste. 'I didn't even hear you come up behind me. You walk lightly, my love.'

'Or you were lost in daydreams.' She noted the smile on his face as he carefully placed a small envelope back in his pocket. 'Pleasant ones?'

'Surprising ones. I'm still a little dazed.' He showed her the cheque, heard her exclaim, said, 'That solves a lot of problems, doesn't it?'

'Not all of them. I couldn't reach Bob. He had just left

the Embassy. Prescott Taylor hasn't arrived yet – must be still on the road.'

'Of course he is. Don't worry, love. Nothing's going to happen to him when he's driving a Police Commissioner to Vienna.' Grant glanced at his watch. 'Almost five. Give Taylor another hour.'

'I'll try around six thirty. He's bound to be there by that time.'

'Is it so necessary—'

'Yes,' she said, 'it is. He can tell me where Bob is.'

'It's funny—' He paused, stared at the valley. The cars coming towards Grünau were now few and far spaced. The traffic flow was beginning to ebb back to Annaberg.

'What is?'

'I've been offered a job.'

'That isn't funny. That's wonderful! Or isn't it what you want?'

'It's what I've always wanted, I guess.'

'Then what is so strange—'

'If I take it, then I have Bob Renwick to thank for it.'

She couldn't follow his meaning. 'Is that so bad?' she teased.

He was thinking of Basset's letter. *I have heard of your objections to three of the paintings which will be exhibited* . . . Only Bob Renwick could have told Basset about that. Grant wondered just what language Renwick had used – direct quotes? Suddenly, he laughed. 'No,' he answered, 'not bad at all.'

She relaxed. Peace was breaking out, and it felt wonderful.

'Can you clear your desk in Paris in three weeks? I have to be in Washington by then. At the latest. If I want this Basset Hill job, that is.'

'Three weeks? Oh, no, darling. Impossible. I said two months and it may be even three. Why don't you go to Washington? I'll join you by October.'

'Or November, or December?'

'Well, even so – we'll be together before Christmas.'

Even so – He saw the anxiety in those beautiful, dark eyes, and took her in his arms. 'Even so, you're worth waiting for,' he said gently, and kissed her to drive away her fears. But what about his?

She sensed them. 'I *will* come to you, darling. Please – trust me. Please!'

He silenced her pleading with a long kiss, his arms tightening around her as if they would hold her for ever.

'Herr Grant! Herr Grant! Telephone!' It was Ada calling from the front door.

'There's a conspiracy going on to keep us apart,' he said as he released her. To Ada, he shouted, *'Komm' gleich!'* and left the terrace at a smart jog.

Avril followed him back to the house. Ada met her with a dramatic whisper. 'It's Herr Fischer calling from Salzburg.'

'Delayed?'

'Yes. What about dinner?' Ada wanted to know.

Avril allowed a possible three hours from Salzburg to Grünau. Even if he left now, Fischer wouldn't arrive here until after nightfall. 'Just cook for Herr Fischer and Herr Grant, and leave their food on the stove. I'll have a sandwich at seven o'clock before we go down to the farm.'

'A sandwich?' Ada looked horrified. A toss of blonde curls said, 'We'll see about that,' as she hurried away.

'I hear Helmut has been delayed,' Avril said when Grant at last left the telephone. 'What on earth was all that argument about?'

'Did you understand any of it?'

'Not much. I try not to listen, believe it or not.'

So Grant repeated most of Fischer's call. 'His silver Audi has been stolen. Left it parked in the street at the side of his hotel when he got back from lunch. Went in to phone us and got Leni's long call. When he went to collect the car, it was gone. No one noticed. Huge Saturday crowds, Festival and all that. He's had half of the hotel staff, or almost, out searching for it. Been in touch with the police of course. Now they want him to go and identify a light grey Audi that is reported caught in a giant traffic block near the German border – that's only ten or twelve miles from Salzburg. I talked him out of coming here. He could be delayed for hours. It's possibly not his car at the border, you know. If it is, he'll be tied up by red tape and regulations at a police station.'

'Did you tell him we're leaving by six tomorrow?'

'Didn't get round to that. He was too busy persuading me to spend the night down at the Lackner farm with you. I was to close up the house, put out all the lights, leave it obviously deserted. As if that would turn Marck away.' Grant had to smile, remembering Fischer's sweet ignorance of Marck's methods. 'I said you would go as arranged. With Ada and Brigitte. But I'd stay here with a couple of the Lackner boys for company, and keep an eye on his house. See that it wasn't fire-bombed.'

'That would startle him.'

'Not too much. He knows what happened to my room at the Majestic. I guess that's why he is so worried about his house. And so am I. It's my fault that it could be in danger. Oh, well—' Grant repressed a sigh, took a long deep breath. 'You'd better have something to eat—'

'All arranged for seven o'clock.'

'Eat right now. By six, anyway. And then get down to the farm.'

'That's too early. I don't need to leave—'

'How the hell is it,' he asked in complete exasperation, 'that you do as you're told when Renwick gives the orders? And all I get is one big argument?'

That silenced her. She smiled, blew him a kiss, and

361

ran upstairs to get night-things packed into the plastic shopping bag. It wasn't empty – the .22 automatic and its clips and silencer were still lying under Bob's fantastic imitation-silk scarf. She left them there until she could slip them to Colin. That wasn't necessary, however: when she came downstairs, she found him standing in front of Fischer's gun rack.

'Why can't they make up their minds?' Ada wanted to know when Avril had left the kitchen, the new time-table established. Her grumble was half-hearted. Fräulein Hoffman had shown some politeness and good sense in not suggesting she'd eat down at the farm. What with all that cooking and baking for tomorrow's funeral, and the boys coming in for their big evening meal, her mother and Anna had more than enough to do.

Brigitte had no complaints about the change in plans. She only hoped her Ernst would be given the first patrol with Willi; three and a half hours of keeping watch, he should be in his own bed by midnight. Father Lackner and Hans would take over the eleven thirty to three o'clock shift. Dawn would be coming up after then, so Peter and August could manage easily even if the American had fallen asleep by that time. 'Too bad Herr Fischer was delayed. When will he get here?'

Ada shrugged her shoulders. She laughed and said, 'Have you ever known him to be on time?' She began beating the eggs for a large omelette.

'Is there really some danger, d'you think?'

'No. Now get on with that salad and arrange a cheese plate.'

'Then why all this fuss and bother?'

Ada tested the pan, found it hot enough. 'Herr Fischer gets nervous with all these strangers coming into the village at week-ends. He worries about this house. Did you hear what happened last week-end at Oberdorf? The Brenner place was filled with a bunch of hippies – just moved in when the Brenners were in Italy, left with the silver and the paintings. It's those motorcars, they make everything so easy.'

'Next thing we'll all have to start locking our doors,' Brigitte predicted. 'Didn't Herr and Frau Brenner have someone to watch over their house when they're away?'

'Too mean.' Not like Herr Fischer, who never counted the schillings. 'And noses too high in the air.' Again, not like Herr Fischer: a pleasure to work for him. 'Now, how does this look?' Ada slid the golden omelette on to a warm plate. 'Ready?' Together, trays borne proudly, they marched into the big room.

'You were going to tell me about this job,' Avril said, as she halved the omelette. More eggs, she thought in dismay; I'll have eaten enough of them today to last me for the next three weeks.

'Was I?' Grant's smile was broad.

'Weren't you?' she asked, all innocence. 'Here, darling – you take some of this. Far too much for me. It's gargantuan. If we don't finish the omelette completely, they'll think I didn't like it.' He was scarcely listening, lost in thoughts far away from the food that was offered him.

'All right,' he began, pouring from the flask of white wine – two glasses had been tactfully brought – 'here's what Basset offered me.' He talked for the next fifteen minutes.

'You've got to take that offer, Colin.'

'Why?'

'Because you'd make a success of it.' Also, she thought, I saw the excitement in your eyes. Your voice was controlled, almost diffident; but your eyes, my darling, gave you away.

'I wonder.' But it was a challenge. And he needed that.

'Now you're being too modest. Please, Colin, don't talk yourself out of it. It's just right for you.'

'What about you?'

'Me?' She tried to sound off-hand, concentrated on helping him to cheese and salad.

'Yes. We'd live near the Museum. It's pure country out there.' Not Paris, or London, or Vienna. 'You're a city girl.'

'Mostly,' she conceded. 'It isn't far from Washington, though. We could live there.' No we couldn't, she thought, suddenly remembering his wife who had been murdered in a quiet Washington street. She bit her lip, tried to hide her distress.

He was silent. At last, he said slowly. 'Washington isn't all a bad memory. I had a lot of friends there, quite apart from the ones I shared with Jennifer.' The name was out, calmly spoken. 'Sometimes, in those last few months, I thought I was too quick to leave it. Running away is never any good, I suppose. The job at Schofeld's was only marking time. No future in it – not the kind I wanted, anyway. As for New York – well, the old Greenwich Village crowd had scattered. And new friends? – Perhaps we're all rushing about too much in New York, too, too many things to do, too little time to spend on the people you really want to know. The truth is, I was damned lonely. Kept thinking about the past because I didn't see much future.' He shook his head. 'Vienna certainly broke up that syndrome. I'm alive again.'

'Promise me,' she said quickly, 'promise me you'll stay that way. Whatever happens, now or later, you'll put it behind you. Not keep brooding about it. Promise me?'

'Yes.' His voice tightened. 'Whatever happens? Look, you are leaving your job by Christmas. No postponements, Avril. Don't let Renwick persuade you—'

'He won't. I'll postpone nothing. What's over is over.'

Grant thought he heard a touch of regret. Why not? he reminded himself. She had a career. He was asking her to break it off, leave it for ever. 'What's over is over,' he said. 'We'll both stick to that.' He looked round in annoyance as Ada's solid step entered the room.

Ada said, 'I'll just clear away the trays. It's almost time to leave. A quarter before seven, you said.' With no more changes of mind, she hoped. She looked at the plates, all nicely emptied, and smiled wholeheartedly. 'Brigitte and I are ready when you are, *gnädiges Fräulein.*'

Ten to seven. Grant stood watching the three women as they took the shortest short-cut down to the Lackner farm. Ada and Brigitte were ahead, Avril following them. She turned to smile and wave, and then vanished with the others behind the trees.

'Only eleven hours,' she had said as they parted. 'I'll be ready and waiting for you. Oh, heavens! I forgot to call Bob. Will you?'

'I'll do that.' He kissed her, silencing any other afterthoughts.

'Take care.'

'I'll do that, too.'

'The Embassy's number is 34–66–11,' she reminded him.

'Okay, okay. Now stop worrying.'

'But you're alone here. Must you guard this house?'

'I must. And you know it.' He kissed her again, felt her warm body tremble against his. 'I'll have some good company. Ada says the first pair of Lackners will be up here by eight. We'll probably spend the night playing skat and drinking beer. Now, pick up your feet and get the hell out, will you, darling?' With a hasty last kiss, he had sent her away laughing, running to catch up with her two guides, swinging the makeshift overnight bag as if she hadn't a care in this world.

He turned and walked slowly back to the house. At the door, he looked over his shoulder. Nothing but silence, now, and the golden light of late evening, casting the trees into relief, deepening their shadows. He entered, feeling the sudden loneliness of the room. All right, he told himself: set to work. He had plenty to do.

First, he'd secure all doors and windows, close the shutters and drapes. He's scatter the fire's last embers, let it die out: no smoke from the chimney. Turn on no lights except one small lamp – Fischer's idea of a house apparently in total darkness might be an advantage. Get a rifle from Fischer's gun rack. There was one he had handled and felt comfortable with its balance – a pity he couldn't fire a trial shot, find how true its aim was. When the first Lackners arrived, he'd be at the door to meet them. He knew where he'd like them posted: one watching that little road that came over the hill from Josefsberg; the other stationed at the trees on the southeast corner of the house, while he himself would take position at the north-west corner. That way, they'd have a clear view of all sides of the house. It would be a long, cool night. He'd borrow Fischer's loden cape to see him through it. Rest? Well, thank God Avril was an expert driver: she could take the first part of tomorrow's journey, let him catch up on his sleep for a couple of hours, spell him at later intervals. Yes, she could handle a car. He remembered the way she had driven him from the Capucin Church on the day they had first met.

On the day they had first met . . . How short a time ago, yet so packed with shared experiences that it seemed as if he had known her for weeks, months. Known her? he wondered. It would take a lifetime to know a woman like Avril; perhaps never. Would she follow him to America, or would old ties be stronger than anything he could offer? He couldn't even be sure of that. All he could do was trust.

Enough of this, he told himself, let's get moving. And then he remembered he was supposed to call Renwick. He cursed the delay, but kept his promise.

Renwick was not there.

He tried Prescott Taylor and found him. Where the hell was Renwick? In Zürich by this time, en route to Geneva. Wouldn't be back until Monday. Not a pleasure trip.

'Can you send him a message?' Grant asked. 'Tell him that Grünau is blown. Marck learned about it around noon today. I've sent Avril down to the farmhouse. I'm staying here, with a couple of the Lackner boys.'

'At noon?' The imperturbable Taylor had lost his easy-going calm. 'Better clear out.'

'Can't. I'm responsible for this house. Fischer can't get here – his car was stolen.'

'Good God.' Regaining his cool, Taylor said, 'I'll be up as quickly as we can get there.'

'No need.'

'No need, hell,' said the diplomat. 'Just don't take a pot shot at us when we arrive.' He hung up. Quickly, he telephoned Commissioner Seydlitz to ask for assistance in reaching Grünau – no extra manpower necessary, he was taking two Embassy guards along, but he'd be breaking the speed limit, didn't want to be stopped and delayed. Seydlitz caught the urgency in Taylor's voice, or perhaps the mention of Grünau was enough for that wise old dog. He said with his soft rumbling laugh, 'Only the police can break the law.' Quietly he added, 'You'll have an escort within ten minutes. Soon enough?'

I hope so, thought Taylor as he began arranging for the guards and the car. Renwick might object to calling on Seydlitz for help, but how else did you make sure of reaching Grünau in one and a half hours? He'd be there by half-past eight. Renwick himself could have done no better. All the same, it was one hell of a way to spend Saturday night.

Grant was echoing that phrase as he began checking windows upstairs and down. The balconies around the top floor of the house were no longer a pleasant decoration but an infernal headache. Am I beginning to over-react? he wondered, as he left the shutter nearest the front entrance slightly ajar – just enough space to let him identify the Lackners when they came up to join him.

Now the house was secure. He scattered the last of the fire's glowing embers, and went back to Fischer's gun rack. The rifle, or that heavy shotgun?

28

'Arrived and waiting,' they had radioed back to him, ten minutes ago. 'Three kilometres before you reach Annaberg.' And Marck, keeping his rented Volvo to the steady, unremarkable speed which had brought him unnoticed all the way from Vienna, could congratulate himself.

This morning, he had nothing definite to move on. Then, at noon, the name of Grünau. By one o'clock, he had picked up the tape retrieved from Fischer's office at the café he used as a drop. Within half an hour he was listening to Grant's phone call to Leni, followed by the girl's immediate call to Fischer – in Salzburg, at the Schwarzer Adler Hotel. How was that for a bonus? Yes, the risk he had taken in bugging Leni's telephone had paid off handsomely. Equally brilliant was his decision to send Vera, still enjoying her Elsa Kramer success as cook-housekeeper in search of a job, on a small scouting expedition. Now the schoolteacher on holiday, she had arrived at Grünau by ten past four with her little Volkswagen and her versatile camera. She had left at six thirty, trailing along with the last of the departing tourists, drawing no attention, arousing no curiosity. On a lonely stretch of the Grünau road, she had stopped her car for a few last photographs and spoken quietly into her camera. Her report reached him as he drove towards Annaberg.

In Vera's usual quiet way, she had given him the details he needed: length of time at regular speed limit to reach Grünau from Annaberg; size and location of

369

village; bridge at end of main street leading to rough narrow road past farm. Large chalet on wooded hill behind farm, identified by café owner as Fischer's place; road not much used, continuing over hill to meet highway near Josefsberg. Unable to approach house: tractor blocking road in front of farm; two farmhands watching. Photographed bridge and returned to café at corner of main street – owner talkative (recent incomer, no friend of the farmer named Lackner). Fischer's house reported unoccupied, but two cars also reported arriving together early afternoon; one large, dark blue; the second, small and black. Two men and chauffeur in big car; one man driving the other. Both cars allowed through roadblock. Café owner's wife saw them depart – same blue tweed jacket in black car, leaving first; much later, the dark blue car – same two men with chauffeur. Café owner's wife definite about this. Fischer's chalet not clearly visible from village; must lie near narrow road to Josefsberg. Chimney smoke observed briefly when strong breeze dropped. As last seen, tractor still blocking road, two farmhands working around barn. Otherwise, no activity. Grünau quiet.

Yes, Marck could certainly congratulate himself on his choice of Vera. That report might seem simple to the uninitiated, but they didn't know how much subtle questioning and delicate probing, all under the guise of chit-chat and harmless questions, had produced these bare details. (The best of his guidebooks had given Grünau three lines: charming village in Alpine setting; elevation 2,900 metres; population 409; Hotel Anny, inexpensive, 12 beds, 3 baths. Woodcarving. 18th-century church, undistinguished.) Nor did the café owner and his officious wife guess how skilfully they had been encouraged to talk by her enthusiasm for this delightful village. So there she was on her way back to Vienna, her camera now silent. She had passed him five minutes ago, one of a series of cars driving homeward.

Six forty-five, and just ahead of him – three kilometres from Annaberg – he saw the Ferret standing at the edge of the wood that lined the highway. Simultaneously, the Ferret identified the car: dark green Volvo; high make, right colour. Quickly he moved back into the shelter of the trees.

Slowing down, drawing the Volvo off the road's surface, Marck came to a halt. He left the two rifles, covered by a travelling-rug, on the back seat. Also the map, on which he had circled Josefsberg and marked the little third-class road with a pointing arrow as he listened to Vera's quiet voice. Carrying his cap and radio transmitter – the Ferret and Turk had their own transceiver – he entered the broad trail into the woods, hurrying to overtake the sharp-faced Austrian. Barely ten paces from the highway, he caught his first glimpse of the silver Audi.

The Ferret halted, swung round to block the path. There's a knife concealed in his hand, thought Marck, and produced a bright green handkerchief folded into a triangle, initials B.L clearly stitched in black. The Ferret nodded, slipped the knife back into his cuff, smiled thinly, and began removing the Graz plate that had covered the Audi's Vienna number. Turk, short and massive, had already stripped most of the thin line of red adhesive tape that had trimmed the car's sides. So that's how they had done it. 'Any difficulties?' Marck asked.

Turk said nothing, just eased off the last of the tape from the door panel. The Ferret said, 'None. Avoided the towns and police stations. Kept to side roads and villages. Took us an hour longer though.'

'It was well-timed.' Briskly, Marck gave them their next instructions. The Ferret pursed his lips, exchanged a look with Turk; if they had hoped they would be driving home to Salzburg, they made no other comment and listened intently. 'Now get to it!' ordered Marck. 'Half past seven. Map is in the car. Keys are in place.'

'Guns?' the Ferret asked. 'We couldn't risk carrying them – might have been stopped and searched by the police.'

'Rifles on back seat. Grenades in boot. Hurry! Be there at seven thirty. And wait for my signal!'

'We'll be there. We'll wait,' the Ferret said.

'Check your time: six fifty-four.'

The Ferret synchronized his watch as he moved, his step light and sure, back towards the highway. Turk crushed the cards of narrow tape into a large untidy ball, and as he lumbered after the Austrian, he threw it behind the nearest bush. Just like Turk, Marck thought; his room will be a pigsty but he can drive a car full speed over the roughest road and handle a rifle with deadly precision.

The Volvo left, a smooth performance, with Turk at the wheel. The Ferret would be studying the map, cursing the hairpin bends they'd have to ascend before they neared Josefsberg. Between them, they'd make the rendezvous on time. They had better, Marck thought grimly. He himself had at least fifteen minutes to spare. It was now six fifty-six. Slowly, he smoked two cigarettes. Then, straightening his cheap navy jacket, adjusting the black tie to sit more smoothly under the ill-cut collar of his white cotton shirt, he got into the Audi and switched on its engine. Carefully he backed on to the highway. Luck was holding: no car in sight. He took a last look at himself in the rear-view mirror as he cocked his chauffeur's cap in place, and was satisfied. His hair, combed straight back, was a credible deep brown, almost black, and the matching moustache looked natural. So did his darkened eyebrows and lashes. All part of the morning's preparations, an hour well-spent; not even the Ferret's sharp eyes would recognize him once he returned to normal.

At a steady speed, easy, unhurried, he drove towards Annaberg. As soon as he was on the Grünau road, he would accelerate to the legal limit of 100 kilometres an hour, making a perfectly natural and unremarkable approach to the village at the head of the valley.

29

In the Lackners' kitchen, the evening meal was over. The men, except for Willi and Hans who had been sent grumbling out to the barn, still sat around the table. Avril, banished politely to a window seat at the other end of the crowded room, her offers to help Frau Lackner and her bustling team of girls smilingly refused, could only try to make herself as unobtrusive as possible. Her welcome had been kindly though brief. I am, in fact, a perfect nuisance, she told herself. Just as Fischer's request had been even more of an imposition. Saturday night and the men couldn't drop down to the village, have their usual talk over a flask of wine at the local *Weinstüberl* or take their girls for a stroll through the woods. But the Lackner family, whatever their own private disappointments, were scrupulously correct, trying not to look too much in her direction, disguising their appraisal of her face and clothes, pretending to ignore her. And none of them, except Ernst Lackner himself, were taking this upset in their usual routine very seriously.

He was now pairing them off, giving them the times for their patrols. Good naturedly, they accepted his instructions, although their rough jokes had a slight edge of sarcasm. Perhaps, thought Avril, they are right. Fischer over-reacted. The warmth of the kitchen, the lingering smell of good food, the talk increasing in volume as bellies were filled and tired muscles relaxed, all added to the feeling of security. It was easier to be tense and worried when there were only two of you in an enormous room in an empty house – and what was Colin feeling, quite alone up there? Down here, with this cluster of shirt-sleeved men crammed shoulder to shoulder around a table, with Frau Lackner and her girls scurrying between kitchen and parlour where the baked feast for tomorrow's funeral was now being laid out, danger seemed remote, unbelievable. Even the golden evening, last lingering touch of a flaming sun as it sank behind western mountains, breathed peace.

The laughter was loud and increasing. They were joking now about the way their father had made them work today. He was having none of it. 'There'll be rain by tonight. I can smell it. The wind's from the south and the clouds are thickening. High winds and heavy rain. The fields will be flattened – take three weeks to dry out. By Tuesday, floods. Everywhere. Not just here. You mark my words.'

Avril thought of tomorrow's journey through the Gesäuse, and looked out of the window. Half an hour ago, even less, the clouds had been white fluffs tinged with pink, reflecting the approach of sunset. Now she saw that they had indeed thickened, grouping more closely together, joining into a heavy mass. Their apricot glow had faded, was streaked with grey, their outlines shaded black. Even on a bright clear day, the Gesäuse – well-named – was a place where the winds were never at rest: a narrow valley, but deep through towering stone peaks, with scarcely space for a road beside its swift running river. In a violent rainstorm – if Herr Lackner's sense of smell was to be trusted – it would be a difficult route. A tree uprooted, a rock fall, visibility only six feet ahead: more than difficult. Dangerous. Bob Renwick's timetable could be bogged up to its armpits in a mud-slide. If Herr Lackner was right. He probably was – you didn't live among mountains for fifty years without getting some weather sense. She had better be ready for six tomorrow morning with an alternative route to Bad Ischl. Was there one? All right, she told herself, start studying Bob's map once more. It was in the plastic shopping bag that she had kept beside her, unwilling to let good-natured Anna or young Minna unpack it helpfully – she was sharing their room tonight. So she rose now, the bag safe in her hand – how would all those merry blue eyes look if they knew a little automatic was packed under her nightdress and toothbrush? – and began bidding them good night.

'Time for everyone to get to bed,' Frau Lackner said. 'Off with you, every one of you. Except Willi and Hans who'll go up to the big house. Right, Father?' Some small protests and a frown from Brigitte in her husband's direction, but there was a general movement away from the table. *'Gute Nacht, angenehme Ruhe,'* Frau Lackner called after Avril, who was already mounting the steep narrow stairs, praying that she could have ten minutes to herself before whirlwind Minna came bursting into the little room. As she entered and closed the door, she heard the sound of a car. She paid little attention, absorbed as she was in spreading the map over her narrow cot, until she heard a loud sharp whistle from the barn and a clatter of feet downstairs. Curiosity drew her to the window. A silver Audi had pulled up, right in front of the tractor.

Blank astonishment gave way to a smile. So Helmut Fischer had found his car, and taken off like a hummingbird. He had made good time, too – surprisingly good; but, of course, he was bound to know the quickest route from Salzburg. It was a handsome car, jaunty and streamlined. No wonder he had been in such a flap when he thought he had lost it. She couldn't see him – he was at the wheel, talking with Hans who had reached the Audi, while Willi stood by the tractor. How slow they are, she thought, as Willi made no effort to climb into its driver's seat. Nor was Minna dashing up through the wood to let Colin know of the unexpected arrival. Instead, she was following her father who, still in shirt-sleeves, was striding down the road with his dog at his heels and a shotgun under his arm. Was all this to impress Herr Fischer? she wondered. The smile left her face. There was too much talk down there. Look, Mr Fischer, you don't have to recount *all* of your adventures today, they'll keep for tomorrow; get up to your house, Helmut! Start telling your amusing stories to Colin, will you? He needs a few laughs.

She wasn't the only one puzzled by the long roadside chat. From underneath her window, a buzz of questions and guesses came drifting up from the front door. From the babble of sound came a voice (Peter's) asking, 'Well, who is he?' Complete silence as if no one had any answer. Peter stepped out a few paces, calling to his father, 'Need some help?'

Who is he? Not Fischer? Who? Avril's spine tightened. Then, as Ernst Lackner waved his son back, replied to some comment from the man in the car and raised a loud laugh, Avril relaxed. All must be well, for Lackner was signalling to Willi to start moving the tractor, and Minna was sent racing towards the house.

'Father's coat, father's coat,' Minna called out. Reaching the family group, she explained in a rush of words, 'Father's taking him up to the big house, showing him the way.'

'What was so funny about that?' demanded Frau Lackner as she unhooked a heavy jacket from the back of the door and lifted Ernst's battered green hat from its peg.

'He just likes a good laugh.' Minna took the coat and hat, and turned to leave.

Peter caught her arm. 'Who *is* this joker?'

'The Berensons' man – Werner. Herr Fischer sent him

ahead because Herr Fischer is driving up with the Berensons,' Minna announced.

Her mother was appalled. 'They're coming here? And where will Frau Berenson stay? Packed into your room with the English miss? Herr Fischer is crazy. Why, the Berensons needed two whole bedrooms for themselves when they came up here last September.'

Berenson? Berenson? Avril caught her breath as she remembered the name. Colin had spoken it, heard it from Fischer, who had passed it on from Leni: a cook-housekeeper, false claims, and the Berensons on holiday. Avril was about to call out a warning, then smothered it abruptly. The Berensons might be out of Vienna for the summer, but that didn't mean they weren't in Salzburg for the Festival. And they were definitely Fischer's friends. That much was certain. Worriedly, she watched the tractor backing towards a section of the narrow road where the deep ditches decreased enough to allow it to jolt on to a stretch of grass. Yet the car's engine wasn't switched on, ready to leave. The driver seemed to have time to spare; no sign of impatience, no haste. Another joke, another laugh. It sounded easy and natural. Avril relaxed once more, thinking now that she would have cut a very comic figure with these solid characters if she had let out a scream of alarm.

She had lost the thread of Frau Lackner's next question – there were several, actually, locked together as one, but she heard Minna's clear reply. 'They'll soon be here. Just behind him, Werner said. Unless the champagne keeps on popping.'

'Minna!' Frau Lackner was shocked.

Indignantly, Minna said, 'That was *his* joke.' She raced away to deliver the coat and hat. She returned more slowly, her brows down, still smarting from the open rebuke. 'I wasn't saying Herr Fischer drinks too much.' An open guffaw from one of her brothers made her angrier. 'Well,' she said turning on him, 'there *is* plenty of champagne at big parties. And this was a *very* big reception. Opera stars and conductors and everyone who—'

'Stop the car! Avril cried out. 'Stop it!' But the Audi was already rounding the curve to climb the tree-lined road. Below her window, faces looked up, astounded, uncomprehending. She reached the cot, grabbed the plastic bag and sent its contents spilling. She seized the automatic and ran. As she pelted down the wooden stairs and jumped the last three, the group crowding the front door turned to stare in silent wonder. The back entrance, she decided, the quickest way, and she kept on running through the kitchen.

'Something wrong?' Peter yelled after her.

'Yes,' she shouted back, and startled Young Ernst and Brigitte, who were having a quiet nuzzle in the kitchen's darkest corner. Young Ernst drew apart with a curse, froze as he saw the gun in her hand. Abruptly she halted, remembering the telephone. 'Call the big house. Warn Grant. Quick – call him!'

'But why?' and 'What's wrong?' came the questions.

'Fischer wasn't at any reception!' With that, she was out into the back porch and through its door. Will they telephone? Or argue about it? Think I'm crazy? I ought to have explained more, but there was no time. How long did it take me to get the automatic and come downstairs? Too long perhaps. The evening chill struck at her shoulders, and she shivered.

In the kitchen, Young Ernst and Peter exchanged a long look. Then they moved. 'Telephone!' Peter told his mother as they pulled on their jackets, jammed on their hats, picked up their shotguns, pocketed a handful of shells.

Anna made the call. 'Engaged,' she said, as the busy signal bleeped in her ear. 'What do we do? Keep trying?'

'Of all things—' her mother broke out, anger disguising her anxiety. 'What's the American thinking of?' (At that moment, he was waiting patiently by Fischer's desk. 'Just one moment,' the voice from the American Embassy had said. 'Mr Taylor left an important message for you. His secretary will give it to you. Please hold.' So he held. Always the way, he thought: you dash to answer the telephone and some bright voice asks you to wait. And wait. And wait.)

Half across the field, Young Ernst and Peter raced to catch up. The English girl was ahead of them, running like a deer, taking the short-cut through the wood up to Fischer's house.

Marck drove the Audi past the tractor, gave a friendly wave to the farmer's lout, and hid his anger. Everything had been going well, he thought. Sure I arrived early, ahead of schedule, but better to have time to spare than risk being late. No appearance of hurry, no sign of urgency. Yes, everything had been going well until this peasant said he'd show me the way. Out of suspicion? That may just be his nature. In any case, he won't be difficult to deal with. In fact, he could be an advantage if I use him properly. I don't like that shotgun, though. The farmer's quick eyes had noticed his glance. He tried to joke it away. 'First time I've ever had an armed escort.'

Lackner only said as they rounded the curve and started climbing, 'Straight up.'

'This road looks simple enough. I'm giving you a lot of trouble.'

'I'm used to it.'

'Herr Fischer mentioned he had guests staying at the house – young couple.'

'Just one of them there, now.'

'Why? Something wrong?'

'No. We've got the girl with us.'

So they had been expecting trouble. Marck forced another small laugh. 'You're her chaperone?' That got no response. 'Any servants in the house?' Lackner shook his head. 'What do I do? Just wait around until the Berensons and Fischer get here? I tell you I'm hungry, could use a good meal.'

'You'll find food in the kitchen.'

Carefully, Marck eyed his watch. Seven twenty-nine. He had timed it neatly. So had the Ferret and Turk: a green Volvo had just come into sight at the crest of the hill. He tried to draw Lackner's attention to the dashboard. 'Did you ever see such a collection of gadgets?'

Lackner said, 'There's a car up there. Standing.' And he didn't like it. The heavy furrows on his brown face deepened, the bright blue eyes narrowed.

'Probably getting its bearings. These small roads are difficult for tourists. Not enough signposts. Where's this house?'

'Turn right at that big birch.' Lackner pointed ahead to a silvered tree trunk, kept watching the car at the top of the hill.

Marck slowed down as he reached the birch and blinked his lights. Brief and gentle as that had been, Lackner had noticed. 'No need to switch on, now. You've got a good half-hour before that,' he told Marck. 'And don't drive straight to the house. There's a garage – a barn – among the trees on your left. What's wrong?'

'Almost stalled, there. Just taking it a bit easy.' Easy for the Ferret and Turk to follow. Marck swung off the road to enter Fischer's driveway, and passed the barn.

'You missed it!' Lackner shouted, and swore.

'Didn't see it in time. I'll turn round at the house.'

'Herr Fischer doesn't like his car standing out. Too much sap from the trees, gums it—'

'I'll get it under cover.' Did this peasant think I was

going to block Turk's entry, while I struggled with a barn door? Here was the house itself, and a clearing of grass pretending to be a lawn. A car was parked well to one side – a black Thunderbird, he noted, as he swept the Audi round to face back towards the driveway, and came to a halt directly in front of the house entrance. What, no black Citroën? Naughty tricks these boys played, but not quite clever enough. As a signal to Turk, who must have slid downhill in neutral by this time, he let the Audi's engine roar for a moment before he switched it off. It should fetch Grant, too; he'd probably recognize Fischer's car and come hurrying out to welcome him. If he didn't? Then, thought Marck, I send the farmer to get the front door open. And that's where I want Grant, right on top of that mound, looking down at Berenson's man. No way he could recognize me, not even at this short distance. Marck slipped his hand inside his jacket, and quietly unsnapped his holster. 'Better get out,' he told Lackner. Else I'll have to shoot through you. 'Are you sure someone is inside?' he asked blandly. 'The place looks empty.' Hurry, he told Lackner, hurry goddamn you.

'He's here.' Lackner stepped out of the car, surveyed the house, nodded approvingly at the tightly closed shutters, just one – nearest the front door – left ajar. No fool after all, that American, Lackner reached back for his shotgun.

'You need that?' Marck asked with a grin. 'I don't see any rabbits around.'

'Two-legged rabbits. I'll have a look at that green car on the hill.' Lackner raised his voice to shout, 'Herr Grant!' There was no movement at the slightly opened shutter, no opening of a door. 'He'll be upstairs. Maybe at the back of the house. Better sound your horn.'

Marck hesitated. He thought he heard the Volvo beginning its gentle approach from the road. Turk might stop if the horn blasted off, take it as an alarm.

'Herr Grant!' Lackner was calling. 'Herr Fischer sent his car ahead. He will be here soon.' Then irritably to Marck, 'Get out! Let the man see you.' And I'll know, thought Lackner, if this Werner is as good as his word. Too many smiles and grins for my taste, though his story seems true. If the American recognizes him, he's bad news. 'What's that?' he asked sharply as he heard a car coming quietly up the driveway.

Marck, noticing that forbidding frown on Lackner's face, had already withdrawn his hand from his revolver and stepped out of the Audi. 'Someone has lost his way.'

Lackner was staring at the green car that had come into sight. It pulled up as it reached the open stretch of grass. The devil take him. What in—'

'Better set them straight.' Marck's eyes were on the window near the front door: a slight movement, there, pushing the barely opened shutters further apart. Have a good look, he told Grant. He raised his voice, thickening his German – Grant couldn't recognize the accent, either – and said jovially, 'I'll wait here. Just point them in the right direction for the village.'

'I'll do that,' Lackner said grimly, and strode off.

Marck thumbed his cap on to the back of his head, showing a quiff of black hair, while his right hand reached gently for his revolver. Only his head could be seen from the house: from the shoulders down, the Audi blotted out any clear view of him. Firm in his grip, the pistol was lowered close to his thigh. Unconcerned and slightly bored, he sauntered a few paces towards the front of the car, halting half-way, the lower part of his body sheltered by the hood. Casually, his left hand extracted a cigarette from the pack in his breast pocket. He seemed to be admiring the fretted design of the front balcony as he flicked his lighter and inhaled deeply. Nothing suspicious here, Grant – see? But his right hand, down by his side, was ready to come up as he'd drop to a crouch behind the hood. Soon now . . . From the side of the clearing where the Volvo stood, he could hear a mumble of voices: the Ferret was keeping it low-keyed, polite. A sudden scuffle; complete silence. The farmer didn't even have time to let out the beginning of a yell. Marck repressed a smile, kept his eyes on the house. Grant could have heard nothing, couldn't have any view of the Volvo either, not until he stepped out. Come on, come on, Marck urged him, as a heavy bolt was loosened and the door swung partly open. Incongruously, a telephone began to ring. Bloody hell, don't answer, don't go back to pick it up: come out, Grant, come well out!

A shot sounded. From the trees behind him. Instinctively he wheeled round, saw the girl and fired. And swung back to face the door and fire again. He was a fraction too late. His bullet struck the balcony as Grant's shotgun caught him full blast in the chest. The noise reverberated over the hillside and the telephone stopped ringing.

'Avril!' Grant was shouting, dropping his gun, racing down over the mound. 'Avril!' She was lying quite still. Two of the Lackner boys now reaching her.

For a split second, Peter looked down at her, then at Grant racing past the silver Audi, then at the strange green car where a man was prone on the ground, his rifle sighting carefully. 'Look out!' Peter yelled as the rifle cracked, its sharp sound overlaid by a heavy burst from Ernst's shotgun. 'Got him,' Young Ernst said quietly. He had spoiled the man's aim too: the American's jacket might have been grazed across the back of his shoulders, nothing more than that. He was still on his feet. But he had halted his wild run as he turned to stare at the Volvo.

In that brief moment, the second rifle was fired. Its bullet caught Grant on his left side, sent him staggering.

The Ferret didn't risk another shot. He crouched low behind the protection of the car as two shotguns blasted its windshield. He began running, dropping the rifle to add to his speed, cursing as blood dripped from his cheek and hand where fragments of splintered glass had cut deep.

Peter reached Grant who had struggled back on his feet again. 'Bad?' Peter asked.

Grant shook his head. Holding his side, he moved slowly towards Avril.

He's the lucky one, thought Peter, and followed his brother towards the Volvo. Father, he was thinking now, what happened to my father? They found him stretched out on his face. But he was alive and groaning. 'Hit on the back of the head,' Young Ernst said as they turned him over. 'He'll be harvesting on Monday.'

'If it isn't raining,' Peter added, and they stood there grinning with relief. They raised him to his feet. Lackner tried to speak, grimaced at the stab of pain at the back of his skull.

'Take it easy, take it easy,' Young Ernst said.

Two men—'

'We shot one of them. The other took to the hills. When night comes, he'll be helpless up here. We'll find him.'

'Get help – police at Mariazell,' Lackner told Peter.

'And the doctor. The American was hit. Left side, not too bad. He made a difficult target – ran fast, jerked to a halt. That sharpshooter must have been cussing mad. We made sure he didn't get a second shot.' Yes, we did some good tonight, thought Peter as he raced towards the house and the telephone.

'I can walk,' Lackner told Young Ernst, but he didn't shrug off his son's strong arm around him. As they

385

made their way slowly across the grass, he saw Grant kneeling beside the girl. Ernst Lackner halted, stood still. 'What was she doing here?'

'She came running up with us chasing after her. She fired a warning shot. For Grant. For you.' That was all it had been: a warning. 'That bastard Werner caught her with his first bullet.' And Young Ernst felt his father's weight heavier on his arm. Hans and Willi were now coming out of the wood, stopping abruptly to stare down at the girl. They spoke to the American. He neither heard nor saw them.

'Get her indoors,' Lackner said. 'Grant, too. Soon the whole village will be here.'

'What about these?' Young Ernst jerked his head towards the two dead men.

'Leave them as they lie,' Lackner said, his voice suddenly harsh. It was beginning to rain, the first drops falling softly, darkened sky above promising a torrential downpour. He didn't even notice.

30

The rest of the night was a blur of memories. Too many faces, some known, others strange, around him. Shock, they said, when he had suddenly collapsed once the old doctor had cleaned his wound and bound his side. Too many voices, too many faces, and Avril not among them. After he became conscious again, one short hour later, perhaps even less, they told him she had gone. The tall fair-haired American from the Embassy had arrived and taken her away. At once. Before the heavy rains started, blocking the roads, they said. Nothing they could do for her here, so the American had put her in the ambulance that had followed the policemen from Mariazell and driven off. Where? They did not know. Perhaps to Mariazell. Perhaps to Vienna. She was still alive? God willing, they said, evading an answer, and moved back into the shadows.

Against his will, he had fallen asleep. The old doctor had seen to that. When he awoke, it was morning with thick dark couds blotting out the hills. He struggled to rise, found he was weaker than he thought, lay back on Fischer's giant bed and listened to the battering of rain against windows. It was six o'clock. We should have been starting out on our journey, he thought. In that rain and wind? No, he told himself, we'll never start on any journeys – not today, not tomorrow, not ever. He did not need to ask about Avril. He knew. He knew she was dead.

* * *

Two days of violent storm. Two days of fever. And then they said he was normal again. Normal? In some ways, yes. He got out of bed, tried walking around Fischer's room, went gladly back to bed. But they were giving him messages, now, as well as Frau Lackner's soups and jellies. She had had her share of nursing men who had been wounded in hunting accidents, or whose leg had been hacked by a slipping axe. Blood transfusions? Nonsense, she said: the right food and rest, and a healthy man repairs himself.

The first message was from Fischer. He was on his way as soon as the storm abated and made road travel possible.

The second message was from Prescott Taylor. Avril's brother had flown out from London and was taking her home.

'How long before I leave?' Grant asked on the day the rains ended.

The old doctor, six feet, spare and strong, eighty-three years old, white hair above firm suntanned cheeks, noted the impatience in the young man's eyes and remembered Frau Lackner's words. Too many memories for him here, Frau Lackner had said: that's why he stays inside Herr Fischer's room, doesn't even try walking outside. 'It won't be comfortable travelling. To New York?'

'To Washington.'

'Another ten days,' the doctor suggested.

'Five days,' said Grant.

'Make it a week.'

'Five days. I'm fit enough now.'

Not as fit as he thinks. But never argue with a man whose mind is made up. Besides, he is in good physical condition, recovery should be quick. Emotionally? Much improved. 'Five days,' the doctor agreed, 'provided you start walking and sitting outside. The minute your wound starts hurting, find a seat in the sun. Don't step over the threshold of pain.'

What about a different kind of pain? Grant looked long at the light blue eyes that were studying him intently. I'd get the same advice for that, he thought. And the old man could be right: don't wallow in suffering. 'I won't,' Grant said.

'I'll come up to see you tomorrow and the next day. The day after that I expect you down at my consulting room.'

'I'll be there.'

Now he could make arrangements for travel. He telephoned the Embassy in Vienna.

'Sure you're fit enough?' Prescott Taylor asked.

'Sure.'

'You could stay as long as you like at Grünau – Fischer would like you to be his guest.'

'I know. We talked about that when he was up here yesterday. So we compromised. He's coming back this week-end and will drive me to Salzburg airport on Sunday.'

Taylor laughed. 'Do you always get your own way when you compromise? Okay, Sunday – leaving Salzburg. For Zürich and New York?'

'For Zürich, Paris and Washington.'

'We'll arrange it. We'll send some people up to Grünau on Saturday with your plane tickets. They'll collect Renwick's Thunderbird, too. Get it out of your way. Well – good luck, Grant. When you get back to Vienna, give me a call.'

'I'll remember. Where's Renwick?'

'Returning here tomorrow to clear out his desk.'

'Moving on?'

'Yes.'

'Where could I reach him?'

There was a moment's pause. 'I'll tell him you'd like to see him. He will be in touch.'

'Good.'

They left it at that.

In the evening, two quiet police officers paid an unexpected visit. A matter for their final report, they said: it had been difficult to question him last Saturday. Frau Lackner gave an indignant toss of her head. 'Difficult?' she asked, 'it was impossible, and you know it.' She retreated obediently to the kitchen door, stood within its threshold ready to return if Herr Grant needed her help, and called back the last word. 'Don't go making him ill again!'

'I'm all right,' Grant told them. 'What questions do you want to ask?'

Not many, he was assured. The Lackner family had filled in most of the details. (Frau Lackner, listening intently, nodded her agreement.) It seemed as if he had fired in self-defence. Why did he have a shotgun beside the door? It was usually in its rack, wasn't it?

'Herr Fischer had been worried about his house.'

Yes. Herr Fischer and Ernst Lackner had already stated that. Had he intended to use the shotgun? Or was it just to warn off any thieves who might appear?

'I'd have shot over their heads and the Lackner men would have heard it and come running.'

'But the man Werner shot at you?'

'He shot at – at Miss Hoffman, first. I was still inside the house, the door half-opened.'

'Why the delay?'

'No delay – except that the telephone rang and I hesitated for a moment, wondered if it was an important call. I heard a shot. I picked up the gun and stepped outside and saw Miss Hoffman fall and the man turning back to fire again. He did, I think. He – he was aiming at me, certainly.'

'He did fire at you. We found that bullet. On the balcony. Peter Lackner noticed the splintering wood.'

Then what is all the questioning about? wondered Grant.

'Did you know the man who shot at you?'

Grant shook his head.

'You didn't have time to see him?'

'Yes – when I was still indoors. I looked out of the window after Lackner had called to me and then went off somewhere, I thought towards the driveway, but I hadn't any clear view of that.'

'You didn't recognize the man?'

'No.'

'Did you see his revolver?'

'No. I only saw him light a cigarette.'

'Using both hands?'

'Only his left hand,' Grant stared at the two policemen. 'He pushed back his cap with his left hand, too.' Grant's jaws clamped tight to steady his lips. Avril never had a chance, the man had been waiting and ready. For him. At last he could trust his voice enough to say, Who was he?'

'No identification on him except for his driver's licence – Werner Kranz – and it was a fake. But Commissioner Seydlitz had his men working on that.'

'Seydlitz? Is he interested in this man?'

'Interested in his fingerprints.'

'Then Kranz must have a police record?'

The two police officers were saying no more. With noncommittal politeness, they thanked him and took their leave.

Frau Lackner had her own comments. 'Herr Fischer told them, we told them – what did they expect to hear from you? Nonsense, I call it.'

'No, not nonsense. I killed a man.'

'Or he would have killed you. They know that.'

Yes, he thought. But they also wonder why Werner Kranz was waiting and ready: no ordinary burglar, that one. He was sent by Gene Marck, of course. I'll leave that piece of information for Commissioner Seydlitz to deal with, in his own way and his own good time.

Frau Lackner added some more of her last words. 'A bad lot, these three men. Herr Fischer had every reason to be afraid for his house. You know what?' She dropped her voice. 'In the boot of that green car, the police found grenades. Peter was there, saw them. And a can of petrol. Can you believe it?' Blue eyes were round with horror at the evil in men's minds. 'Ernst says you were in real danger, Herr Grant. These men weren't just robbers as the newspapers tell it. Terrorists, that's what Ernst thinks. Perhaps you wrote something about them – something they didn't like? Oh, don't worry, we aren't talking. Less said, the safer we'll all be. Isn't that right?'

Grant nodded.

'The man who ran off – there's no sign of him. He hasn't been seen in any village. The police are searching the hills, now. That was a wild storm – he may be dead,' she added hopefully, waiting for Grant's agreement.

'Could be,' he said to reassure her. But such men didn't die so easily.

She returned to normal, hurried off to make Herr Grant a fresh cup of coffee.

On Saturday, Fischer arrived, apologizing for being a day late. It seemed that business had been excessively brisk at his shop. 'My dear Colin, everyone is coming to visit me there. Incredible how a piece of sensational news draws the crowds. I never knew I had so many friends. Or such curious ones, either.'

'I hope they are looking at your pictures, too.'

'Yes. I can't complain.' With that, he dropped the entire subject of last Saturday's happenings, and branched on to a description of some new acquisitions he had just made. As if, thought Grant, he is trying to edge me back into my own world again. Fischer managed it, too, until – they heard a car approaching from the road.

'Expecting someone?' Fischer was rising to his feet, suddenly alert.

So his nerves weren't altogether under the control they had appeared to be, Grant thought as the two of them walked side by side towards the front of the house. 'Possibly my plane tickets being delivered. They were promised for today,' he said easily, hiding his own tension. Another surprise package from Gene Marck?

A grey Fiat was drawing up beside the Audi; the two men stepped out. Bob Renwick. And Slevak. Grant relaxed.

'You know them?' Fischer asked.

'Yes. It's all right.'

'Want me to stay?'

'Not necessary.'

'Good. I have a lot of things to attend to.' Fischer, with a friendly wave to the strangers, went indoors.

Slevak's visit was limited to a nod and a wide grin as he walked around the Fiat's hood to take the driver's seat. Within a minute, he was on his way back to Vienna.

Renwick reached Grant. In silence, they shook hands. Then Grant led the way to the terrace.

It was an awkward beginning, both of them thinking of Avril and never mentioning her name. 'Handsome,' Renwick said, taking a comfortable chair and looking at the view. 'Reminds me of that painter chap, the one who worked in the Far West, never can remember his name – connected with something to drink—'

393

'Bürstadt. Yes, he would have painted this.' And they both looked out at the distant mountains. 'So you're moving on. What's next? Or is that classified information?'

'More or less. But I imagine you can make a pretty good guess what I'm after.'

'No shortage of terrorists,' Grant observed grimly. They came in all dimensions: groups of political fanatics with blind obedience and perverted social conscience; the trained assassins tracking down their victim in a peaceful Austrian village; a boy in a quiet Washington street killing on vicious impulse. All of them, however different they seemed, bent on destruction. All of them, however motivated, with total contempt for human life.

'No shortage,' Renwick agreed, equally grim. 'Not for several years to come.' He drew out an envelope from his pocket and placed it on the table between them. 'Your tickets. You'll be in Washington by Monday. Okay? I thought you were rushing things, but you look better than I expected. How's the wound?'

'It's healing.'

Renwick added a small bottle to the envelope. 'These pills are pure magic. One every three hours when your side starts to give you hell – but cut out the booze.'

'Yes, doctor,' Grant said with a sudden smile.

Renwick's answering grin was wide. He relaxed and lit a cigarette. 'One thing, anyway: you don't have to keep looking over your shoulder for Gene Marck.'

'No? I don't think he'll give up so easily.'

'He's dead, man. You got him. Werner Kranz – wasn't that what he was calling himself?'

Grant shook his head in disbelief. 'It couldn't have been Marck.'

'Why not? Don't tell me you've never heard of dyed hair and a false moustache?'

'Kranz was an expert with a gun. The way he moved – quick and sure. He was a trained killer.'

'He was. Trained by the KGB. Eugene Marck.'

Grant stared at Renwick. But Renwick meant what he said. 'Fingerprints?' That's what the police had mentioned: Commissioner Seydlitz was interested in the man's fingerprints.

'Not a bad guess.'

'Not mine. The police tipped me off.'

'You've had them buzzing around you?'

'Briefly. And politely. No sweat.'

'Seydlitz passed the word they were to leave you alone.'

'But my friend Seydlitz is in Vienna, and they are local.'

'Independent types?' Renwick asked with a laugh.

'With a report to complete.'

'Yes, there's always that – in triplicate.'

Grant was back to Seydlitz. 'Were Marck's fingerprints on file?'

'No. But they were on the luggage, harmless stuff, that he left at the Sacher. Seydlitz had his men round there on Friday, checking. They left Marck's suitcase in his room, just as they had found it – after picking up some good prints. It will be interesting to see who will collect that suitcase.'

'Efficient Seydlitz. Clairvoyant, too? How do you start connecting a chauffeur called Kranz with Gene Marck?'

'The dye on his hair was a tint – that's the right word, my secretary tells me. It washes off easily. Old Lackner left him lying outside, the rain started, and when the local police arrived – just about ten minutes later before Taylor and Seydlitz got here – one of them saw a black streak in front of Kranz's ear. He touched the man's hair and his hand came away smudged. So they rubbed some more of the gunk off his hair and peeled away the moustache – the rain had loosened that, too. When Taylor and Seydlitz saw him—'

'Seydlitz? He made a second trip here, that day?'

'Yes. In his dinner jacket, believe it or not. Taylor called him as soon as you telephoned, asking for help in breaking all speed limits to get here in time.'

Except, thought Grant, his smile fading, they didn't get here in time.

Renwick sensed the change. Shouldn't have said that, he told himself angrily. Grant had seemed so normal, so much in control. 'Can't stay too long,' he said, rising. 'I'll be leaving Vienna on Tuesday. Just when you're about to have that interview with old Basset. It's in the bag, Colin. You've got the job.'

'I don't know about that.'

'That's a lot of bull. He's determined to have you at Basset Hill.'

'Not when he hears what I'm going to say. I thought of writing him a letter – tore up three attempts, in fact. Then I decided I owed him a face-to-face explanation.'

So that's why he is rushing home, thought Renwick. 'About what? I thought it was all settled. You want the job. He wants you for it. What the hell's got into you?'

There was a long silence. Grant said, 'Need any volunteers?'

Renwick looked at him intently: he was serious, deadly serious. Renwick regained his breath. 'Yes', he said at last, 'we can always use volunteers. Of the right calibre.' And you'd be good, you would be damned good, he thought.

Grant said. 'But you wouldn't recruit me now – or, at least, start the process, whatever it is?'

'No. Not at this moment.'

'Because you think I am—' Grant searched for the right word – 'unreliable?'

'No. Never that.'

'Vindictive, perhaps,' Grant suggested bitterly.

'Not that either.'

'You feel I'm too personally involved?'

'Yes,' Renwick said quietly. 'That's about it.'

'And that's dangerous?'

'It leads to wild chances, mistakes.' Renwick thought of Gene Marck, the cool professional who had let his hatred for Grant grow into a personal vendetta. 'It could get you killed.' He lightened his voice. 'Or even someone like me. I'd object to that, Colin. I really would.'

How can he stay so detached? Grant wondered. He has had some bad moments about Avril: that I can see from his face, thinner, and his eyes strained. Yet he is right: a lust for revenge can blind you, make you vulnerable. 'I get your point,' Grant said. He rose, pocketing the tickets and the bottle of pills. 'Thanks for these. They'll be useful.'

Renwick was silent as they walked slowly to his car, and Grant had his own thoughts for company. As they reached it, Renwick asked, 'What are you going to say to Victor Basset?'

'I think I'll tell him exactly how I feel.'

'He's in a mood to be sympathetic. I had a little talk with him on the phone yesterday. About Gene Marck. And Lois Westerbrook. I gave it to him straight.' A small smile. 'Without breaking security, of course. I explained that Marck was trying to eliminate you as chief witness against him, and in the process, he over-reached himself. How's that for the diplomatic approach?'

'To Basset or to me?' Grant asked. 'Okay, Bob – I won't add any details to your account. Marck over-reached himself. That's all I know.' He added thoughtfully, 'Of course, Marck's death doesn't end this business. There are others who'd like to eliminate a chief witness. Perhaps Basset may think I'd be a very short-term director for his museum. Even shorter than I had planned.'

'What do you mean?'

'I decided five minutes ago that I'd ask him – if he was agreeable – for a year's appointment. By that time, I'd have the right staff chosen, get the museum started in the direction I'd like to see it take, delegate authority – and if I were to leave then, Basset would have lost nothing. By that time, too, you might find me less of a liability.'

'In a year's time—' Renwick began. He shook his head. 'You will change your mind once you're back in your own line of work.'

'Perhaps. Perhaps not. Keep in touch with me, will you?'

There was a brief silence, a firm hand-clasp. Then Renwick nodded, got into his car, switched on the ignition, seemed to be listening to the engine. Better tell him, Renwick thought, even if I was supposed to keep my mouth shut. 'You can drop that idea of being a short-term museum director. No interest in you now from Marck's friends. Commissioner Seydlitz had the news of your deposition leaked in the right places. It's the best insurance policy you ever took out, Colin.' With one of his old warm smiles, and a brisk goodbye, he turned the Thunderbird – splotched with rain and leaves and resin streaks – to face the driveway. As he drove past the gap in the trees with its short-cut to the Lackner farm, he averted his eyes. The smile had vanished. His mouth was set and grim. And I wasn't there to help her, he thought. I wasn't there.

Grant watched Renwick's car until the heavy foliage blotted it out of sight. For a long minute he listened to its steady hum drawing further and further away until all sound ceased. The silence around him stirred memories. This is where he had stood, watching Avril run down that path between the trees towards the farm. She had been laughing at something he had said as she hurried to catch up with the Lackner girls, swinging the makeshift overnight bag as if she hadn't a care in this world. He could see her now, the smooth dark hair gleaming in a stray beam of sunlight, her head turned for a last smile. That was how he would remember her. The good memories were for keeping.

He began walking, found himself on the terrace. He sat there for almost an hour, watching the play of light and shadow over the stretches of crags and forests. This morning, mists had blotted out all shapes and colours; the mountains had vanished, didn't exist. Now, in sunlight, their peaks were clear and bold against the sky. Another world, it seemed. Yet the same. Enduring.

He rose and went indoors to pack. Tomorrow was an early start. And just keep going, he told himself. That's all you can do. That's all any of us can do.